The Way To Go Home

by Catharine Leggett

UFP Fiction Series
Three Fires Confederacy
Waawiiyaatanong ✦ Windsor, ON

First Edition. September 2019

Library and Archives Canada Cataloguing in Publication

The Way to Go Home / by Catharine Leggett.

Leggett, Catharine, author.

Identifiers: Canadiana 2019008040X

ISBN 978-1-98821-427-6 (softcover)
978-1-988214-35-1 (ebook)

LCC PS8623.E466725 W39 2019 DDC C813/.6—dc23

Book cover design: D.A. Lockhart
Book cover image: Jordan Cameron "_MG_2849"
Book layout: D.A. Lockhart
Book Editor: Maeve Keating
Author Photo: Anita Watkins

The UFP Fiction Series is a line of books that showcases established and emerging voices from across North America. The books in this series represent what the editors at UFP believe to be some of the strongest voices in both American and Canadian fiction writing.

Published in the United States of America and Canada by

Urban Farmhouse Press
www.urbanfarmhousepress.com

Printed in Abode Garamond Pro

To the memory of my father,
James Frederick Leggett (Fred)

Book One

Southern Ontario — June 1973

Under the Tree

Buddy's eyes opened to the sway of foliage, black lace shifting over blue. High above the treetops a murder of crows crossed in silent passage. Somewhere, he thought, something must have died. How long had he been lying here under the maple, its roots gouging into his back? How long had he been out? He could have been killed. What a story that would make. Crazy old bugger checks out because of a horseback riding accident. After all the bragging he'd done about his expert riding. A ridiculous ending. Catastrophic. Maybe the one he deserved. A slight chuckle aroused a searing pain deep in his groin and grabbed his breath. He winced and waited for the pain to subside. What had he done? Something had broken, that was certain. It happened so fast, so unexpectedly. One minute he was riding along listening to the wind in the trees, the sound of the birds chirping, enjoying a sense of calm, and the next...

What made the horse behave like that?

He remembered. A long garter snake wriggled across the trail. Spirit reared back, front legs swimming through the air, and Buddy slid out of the saddle and onto the ground, his right foot snagged in the stirrup. His back burned as he was dragged over rough ground, his shoulders smashing against rocks. A crack rammed through his bones and exploded in his ears. Overhead the canopy flickered on and off, on and off. Then nothing.

His shoulder rippled with pain as he brought his hand to his temple. Blood coated the end of his fingertips. Hot patches burned across his back where the skin was scraped, but his broken body wouldn't shift to change the pressure points.

Helpless. Splayed over the ground like a crushed bug. He would do an inventory of his moving parts, but so far it didn't look promising.

His right leg wouldn't move and felt as if it wasn't attached to his body. Every particle of his being seemed connected through pain, a throbbing circuitry alive inside him. His left toes wiggled, his left leg shifted, but only slightly. Not without causing excruciating discomfort.

He would wait until the acute stage of pain passed. His body would be adjusting to shock. He'd work up to sitting, then standing.

Carolyn would come looking. It could take a while. For one thing, she'd no idea of the direction he'd gone; neither did he. He craned his neck to see what lay to the right. A hill, steep and dense with tree coverage. The horse had dragged him all the way to the bottom of the ravine where the canopy was even thicker. He'd intended to go back for Carolyn—the thought had just crossed his mind when the snake appeared. She would come looking for him as soon as she could, as soon as she figured out he was missing. But how long would that take? She was so green at riding he wouldn't even call her a beginner, nor would he call her a hesitant rider. A resistant rider—she was definitely that. She was mightily pissed off at him for dragging her along, which wasn't even fair because when he told her his plan to go riding she said it sounded like fun. Until she got on the horse.

Even to a man in serious pain, the sight of Carolyn riding atop Smokey—maybe riding wasn't exactly the right word—was nothing short of comical. When they first headed out Buddy kept twisting in his saddle to look back to see how she was doing. Smokey fell behind every chance he could and there was Carolyn, her legs sticking out stiff as sticks, pitching from side to side as the dapple grey ambled along, a steady stream of chatter pouring out of her like water from a tap. Her legs were too short. Her bum hurt. "I hate this horse, it's too big! This is a stupid idea. Why did I ever let you talk me into this?"

Such a stink. She couldn't make it any plainer how much she wasn't enjoying herself. But it was important to him they share this outing. She was only here for a few days and would soon be going back to her apartment in Toronto to be with Lenny. She and Lenny were making plans to move farther away. His only daughter, the last of his brood of four to go—he wanted to give her a good memory of home. Something she could take with her. So much for good intentions.

On the drive he couldn't help staring at her and noticing, as if for the first time, how quickly she'd grown up. Where had time gone? Her golden hair whipped around in the wind blowing through the open windows. She looked so much like his mother, and of course her own mother, Meg.

He could have been a better father.

"Dad, can I bum a smoke?"

"You shouldn't be smoking, Kitten. Especially when you see what it's done to me." Meg wouldn't hear of her smoking, never mind do it in front of her.

"Carolyn," she corrected him. "Do you think that works, Dad? Do as I say, not as I do?"

They lit their cigarettes and rode in silence past farmland and woodlots, and headed south towards Lake Erie. The smell of warm earth filled the car.

"Dad?" Carolyn's elbow rested on the open window while her right hand clutched the steering wheel, the cigarette burning between two fingers. "You know how Donnie is saving money to go out west? Well, Lenny and I are going west too. We've already saved the money. We're going to B.C. on the train."

Carolyn and Lenny had been a couple for a long time; he shouldn't be surprised. Out on the highway kids stood in bunches with their thumbs stuck out to hitch rides, wandering somewhere, looking for something—a whole generation overcome by restlessness. Sometimes he wished he could join them.

"When are you thinking about going?"

"In a couple of months or so."

"Have you told your mother?" She shook her head. "When are you telling her?"

Carolyn shrugged her shoulders. "Don't know. Soon I guess."

Meg wouldn't like it. Not one bit. She didn't go in for all this shacking up business; she didn't know Carolyn and Lenny were living together.

As for Carolyn going west, Meg would ask if it was any wonder after all the stories Buddy had spoon-fed the kids since they were old enough to listen. He put ideas in their heads before they could form their own. That's what Meg said.

What did he want for her, his little Kitten? He wanted her to be happy. Simple enough. To have all the happiness he'd never had. She had to have her own adventures and go far enough away to figure things out on her own. Get away from Buddy and Meg. None of their problems were her doing. Away from his bad habits too—they were killing him.

A gust of wind heaved the massive tree crown in a slow lumbering motion. What kind of a tree was it? He could barely make out the leaves. Chestnut? No, he didn't think so. Oak then. No, too big for oak. Maple. Yes it was a maple. The largest tree in the ravine. Would Carolyn be able to see him from the top of the hill? Would she ride Smokey down here? He knew the answer.

But the sight of her on Smokey. He chuckled, and pain ripped through his body like a bullet.

"What if I fall off?" she'd shouted.

"What if you do, Kitten?"

Of course her muscles hurt, unaccustomed as they were to wrapping around the girth of such a beast—not a natural act, not for her anyway. "Loosen up," he told her. "Move with the horse, don't fight it." Buddy knew enough about horses, especially stable horses, to know that Smokey would exploit the novice rider first chance he got. Old horses like Smokey had it all figured out and wouldn't make one extra step if he didn't have to. Carolyn would enjoy the experience a whole lot more if she complained a little less, but there was no settling her down, no convincing her riding a horse could actually be fun.

A pain ripped through his pelvis, snaring his breath. Then, just as quickly it passed, leaving his skin clammy with perspiration. Control his breathing, keeping it even and regular would control panic. He could not become panicked; it would only make his situation worse.

What was it Father used to say about riding a horse, said it with a chuckle, too. Wait, it was coming. Riding a horse was a good way to prepare the muscles of the inner thigh for the most pleasurable business of an adult's life. Buddy remembered the day he told him that out in the barn, and Buddy, no more than eight or nine, had no idea what he was talking about—not at first. And somehow, into the manly chitchat he slipped in his praise, praise Buddy had held dear his entire life. "You're a gifted horseman, Buddy. But even gifted riders need to be careful at all times. Always stay alert. Never let down your guard."

Exactly what he hadn't done. Exactly the reason he was lying here right now all busted up. "Good advice, Father," Buddy said, startled by the scratchiness of his voice thin with pain. "Wish I'd remembered a little earlier."

Where had Spirit gone? If ever a horse deserved its name, that one sure as hell did. He knew Spirit hadn't been ridden for a while, the way his muscles shimmered and trembled when Buddy first mounted him. Such a shame, and not an old horse either. Criminal to keep him penned up like that. Same kind of horse as Breeze, back home in Wyoming, high-spirited, restless, wanted to be pushed. A willful horse, wild at heart. Same as Whitey's horse, Peat.

He saw fire in Spirit's eyes the moment the stable owner led him out of the barn. Father said devilishness could be spotted in a horse's eyes and warned him that kind of horse waited to catch a rider off-guard. He said it was in their nature, the same as it was for some people. Buddy should have paid attention, stayed alert, and avoided this whole predicament. He had only himself to blame.

For this, and a whole lot of other things.

Shafts of dust-filled sunlight slanted down through the trees. Angel shafts delivering angels to Earth, his mother used to say. Buddy raised his head to look for Spirit but he saw nothing in the shadowy forest. Maybe the horse had taken off. He lowered his head back down to the ground as the pain was rekindled and too sharp to bear. At least he wasn't completely paralyzed; he should be grateful.

A slight adjustment of the left leg told him just how bad the break was—hip, back, upper thigh, all of them? Broken pelvis? Whatever had snapped, he was nailed to this patch of dirt beneath this massive maple and wouldn't be getting up. He wasn't going anywhere. No point fooling himself. Usually, he was pretty good at that.

Above him a squirrel scratched along a limb. Leaves rustled, then *whoosh*, it leapt and left a bobbing branch in its wake. Birds twittered in the background, ground sparrows, house finches, and every so often the shriek of a jay. The birds sounded like they were talking about him, while the jay's piercing screech, laughter. *There lies a stupid ass*. A fitting epitaph for his grave marker. If it came to that. He tried to chuckle but a heaviness lay on his chest as if a boulder rested there. He'd probably broken a couple of ribs. At least. Well, why not? No point doing something half-assed.

A thud carried through the ground. Carolyn coming, bringing with her the owner of the Home on the Range Riding Stables. The hard-nosed character with the red flannel shirt, rubber boots, blue jeans, and scarecrow hair. How carefully she reviewed her pay structure with Buddy. If they came in off the trails early before their time was up that was their business, she didn't care one way or another, but they still had to pay the full hour because a person needs to make a living. A great deal of the living she made went into buying cigarettes judging from the nicotine stains on her fingers, though he shouldn't talk in that regard. What if she saw him now, sprawled here on the ground unable to move? *I'm not liable, in case you've got any notion of suing. You asked for a horse with spunk, remember?* Suing her? Why not try to teach a turnip to talk?

Didn't her eyes light up when he bought two hours of riding time for each of them, though he knew Carolyn wouldn't last the whole time. It was humorous how she thought Smokey was going to take off running since she could barely get him moving. "Jab the horse's haunches with your heels. Hard. Harder!" he shouted at her when they started out. She answered in her whiny little-girl voice, the one she could turn on with the flick of a switch, telling him how she didn't want to hurt it, or that it might start to stampede—her word (most unlikely)—and she'd fall off and break something.

They had turned down the path behind the barn, Carolyn gripping the saddle horn, hanging on for dear life, and looking so brittle she might snap in two. Smokey already preparing for his first full stop once Buddy and Spirit were far enough ahead.

Spirit. A horse of another colour. Buddy hadn't ridden in over thirty years—maybe longer—but he knew this one wanted a certain kind of ride. And he was the man to give it to him on this very day. A day when he rose early, went outside to his garden, looked at the sky, and was overcome with restlessness and energy and something else. What was it? A sense of possibility? A need to recapture something. But how to go about it? Have an adventure. Prove to himself he could still do some things.

He steered Spirit towards a large open meadow, pulled back on the reins, and stopped to take in the sky. A flock of birds flew in a dense cluster, scattered in all directions, and came back together again. To the south the sky was darkening over Lake Erie, but if there was a storm coming it wouldn't be for a while. He breathed in deeply, Spirit's tail trailing in the breeze, and took in the gloriousness of the day overcome by a sense of calm, something he hadn't felt for a long time.

Across the meadow on the side closest to the barn, Carolyn was screaming. Smokey had stopped and she appeared to be rocking in the saddle to get the horse to move, her long blond hair sweeping across her face in the wind. A pretty picture, if you could plug your ears. The only way to keep Smokey moving was to lead with Spirit a few feet ahead; he knew this kind of horse. He could go and ask the stable owner for another horse, but if he did Carolyn would say she'd had enough of riding and insist on going home. He wanted to give her an experience to remember. He rode back and got Smokey going again, led them to the forest's edge, and stopped.

Spirit raised his head, shook it, muscles twisting and tightening down his neck and shoulders. Buddy knew what he had to do. He told Carolyn to wait there—unnecessary as old Smokey had already demonstrated his preference for standing stationary—and rode back to the open meadow, the wind-swept grass rippling all around them. He patted Spirit's neck, ran his hand through the horse's mane, wiry to the touch, and bent down low to take in his scent. It'd been a while since Spirit had been properly groomed. "I'll give you a day to remember," he whispered. And he would give his daughter a little riding demonstration.

One sharp jab into Spirit's sides and they were off. Wind streaked past his ears, the air stuffed with the sweetness of hay, the freshness of a distant Lake Erie, and the smell of an approaching storm. He found the rhythm in Spirit's strides, a motion still echoing through him from long ago, and melded his body's movement with the horse. Hooves pounded a repetitive rhythm long unheard—a racing heartbeat, a pounding drum, the thunder of being fully alive, lost in motion—free. He pushed Spirit harder, his legs tightening around him as they gained speed. He sank lower into the saddle and leaned deeper into the movement, allowing it to flow through him, as if Buddy were an appendage. Air pummelled his face forcing his eyes to squint and water. His spine crunched with the thrust of up and down, rattling him from the inside out; the horse's snorts of exertion a sign he put everything into it. "Go Spirit, go. That's it, run it out." Spirit pushed harder with each jab of the heel.

A boy again, racing Breeze across the plains, pushing the horse as hard as he dared despite Father and Mother's warning against doing something so foolish on Breeze. Racing Peat across Whitey's fields, pushing the horse as hard as he could. Until something in Peat burned away. The years of not being ridden worked out of its muscles. The same for Spirit. His muscles ignited, shot them headlong into a frenzy of motion and energy and rage until the horse's body began to give. Buddy felt completely alive; it would be the same for the horse.

They rode the meadow's perimeter so many times Buddy lost count, rode until he knew the horse was spent and the fire that burned through his muscles reduced to a smoulder. He slowed to a canter and rode back to Carolyn.

What was it she'd said? She didn't know he could ride like that. After all his *In the West* stories she didn't know? Hadn't she been listening? What could she understand about him if she didn't know he rode? Kids. Who knew what they took in? She did seem impressed though. He told her the horse needed it and he had too. They both had something to work out of their systems.

He promised her the rest of the ride would be an easy ramble and took the narrow trail that meandered through the woods, skirting along the top of the ravine. A pleasant trail; cool and soothing in the woods, surrounded by the constant lull of leaves and bird chatter. Spirit's coat gleamed with sweat. Buddy knew from the way Spirit rode something had been partly extinguished, some of his restlessness worked out of him. Smokey fell farther and farther behind and took Carolyn's blather of protest along with him. He'd check on her soon or Smokey would be up to his usual trick of stopping—he might even charge to the stable—but he wanted to give Carolyn the opportunity to keep old Smokey going and enjoy the sense of accomplishment that would come with it, so he rode on.

And then the snake. And Buddy dragged off to who-knew-where, far away from the path, where he now lay broken.

He angled his head to see if he could spot the trail, hoping to see Carolyn's face, hoping to see the expression she always wore when she got worked up. The one he saw when he and Meg fought—*Mom, Dad, stop it! Stop your fighting!*—worry, fear, maybe hatred.

Wind agitated the trees. The squawk of seagulls far in the distance. He spotted them high in the sky, wings extended to catch the updraught and sweep them in circles. A fist of pain tightened in his chest.

Another thump.

Spirit stood forty feet away partly concealed by shadows: motionless, reins slack, eyes gleaming through the darkness and set on him. He backed in close to low shrubs as if he might be cowering.

"See what you've done? How could you? Even after I gave you the ride of your life. You've got the devil in you. Father would agree with that."

The horse didn't move.

"It's what you wanted to do, isn't it? You had something to prove. I guess I did too. I'm a damned old fool. I already knew that." His voice barely above a whisper.

The pressure in his chest increased, cut short his breathing, and gathered the pain around his shattered bones. A rock gouged his neck as he rested his head and drew in shallow breaths. He had to get back to steady breathing and keep it under control; it helped ease his discomfort and took his mind off pain.

Someone should be coming soon. He'd been lying here long enough, hadn't he?

If Spirit wandered back to the stable without a rider the owner would know something had happened. Perhaps Smokey made a beeline—might already be in his stall with Carolyn still clinging to the saddle. Wouldn't do him much good if she was afraid to get off the horse. How would the stable owner know there'd been an accident? If Smokey took Carolyn back to the barn, her screaming would eventually attract the owner and they'd come looking for him. It was only a matter of time—a matter of waiting. Or Smokey might be standing in the woods or in the pasture unwilling to budge, Carolyn stuck on his back jabbing his sides with her timid little kicks and screaming blue blazes. Eventually the stable owner would figure out something had happened and come looking. Wouldn't she?

Buddy opened his hand and dragged it over the dirt feeling for a stone—not many to choose from with his limited range. He found one, a reasonable size, not as big he'd hoped, and rolled it in his fingers. The horse's skittish nature might work in his favour. The snake startled the horse, hadn't it? Maybe. Anyway, his plan was worth a try. If he could startle the horse by throwing something at it, get it to move, it might go back to the stable. His aim had to be accurate, as good as the time he scooped the ball and got it to first—*out*—then second—*out*—and second to home—*out.* Triple play! Remember that—*His Best Baseball Game* story, when he played for the Detroit City Police Team? Bugs swarmed around the night lights. Crickets chirping on warm summer nights. Those were the days back in Detroit. Doug, David, and Donnie loved that story. *Tell us the Best Baseball Game story, Dad.* Every time he told it he was a hero.

He raised his right arm slowly and pain ripped down his left side. Ignore it. Focus on the pitch. Aim for accuracy. No more stones within reach. He heaved the stone towards the horse. It landed just a few feet away from his foot and tumbled along with as much force as a butterfly zigzagging through the air. The exertion of tossing increased the pressure in his chest and stole his breath. His dry lips caught on his teeth. Water. What he wouldn't do for a drink right now.

Thirst. God's punishment. Odd, he hadn't wanted a drink today—the other kind of drink. Hadn't even thought about it until now.

Spirit stood still, eyes locked on him, mocking him, amused by the attempt to get him moving. *Nice try, Buddy. But it won't work.* The horse had done what it wanted to do—topple its rider. Buddy had no doubt.

Served him right. Hadn't he let the reins go slack, his body limp and relaxed after the hard ride? He'd let down his guard—hadn't stayed alert.

"I'm a bloody old fool, I know it," he told Spirit. "Sixty-three and carrying on like an eighteen-year-old. You might have won round one, but I am not down for the count." The horse, still in the shadows, shifted slightly. Because the thing of it was, Spirit would have seen many snakes and the fear he reared back from had nothing to do with the reptile. It was about going back to the stable. It was about being trapped in a stall day after day.

Maybe Buddy was trying to escape something, too. All the botched living he'd done, the sorry moments, and the pain he'd caused his family. Regrets—plenty of those. Wasn't he trying to relive something? Opening up the horse the way he'd done brought him back a sliver of a life he once lived. He could easily imagine what Meg would say. *If reliving your youth was what you wanted to do, then why didn't you go to your chair in the basement, and have a few drinks and a good old reminisce like you usually do? Tell yourself your old stories. Stay stuck in time.*

Couldn't she see how the stories reminded him of who he was, rooted him in a life he understood? Who was he without his stories? More than once they'd saved him and they would save him again. He would remember and they would keep him afloat until Carolyn came. Meg was wrong; his stories didn't keep him stuck in the past, they helped him navigate the present.

A wisp of air cooled Buddy's damp forehead. "Don't you worry, Spirit. I've got myself out of worse predicaments than this." Carolyn would be back with someone eventually. It was only a matter of time, of waiting. That he could do. What choice did he have?

He'd waited out far worse situations, hadn't he? *The Terrible Storm*—one of Carolyn's favourite stories. He couldn't remember a longer night of waiting. Waiting for his older brother Ray to return. He'd never forget it. Worst storm in memory. So much sadness, so much sadness.

Chapter 1

The Terrible Storm

Late March — 1923 —Wyoming

Buddy sat with Sammy on the floor making corrals with wood blocks and placing Father's hand-carved horses inside them. When the horses wanted exercise, he romped them through the gate and out onto the floor.

"Giddy up horsey," Sammy giggled.

Pearl, Maudy, Hazel, and Chuck were close by, drawn together by the fire's warmth. Orwin was still in the bedroom helping Mother with Father. Buddy was doing his best to keep the children quiet and let Father rest undisturbed.

Father had stumbled in from the barn two days ago and said he was on his way to lie down since a spell had come over him. Later, when he tried to get up for chores, he made it as far as the table; his legs went as bendy as the reeds in Tangle Creek during spring flow. And Mother, no more than five feet and these days as wide as she was tall on account of the baby coming, snagged him under the arm and around the waist to help him back to bed.

"You're on fire," she said, leading him to the bedroom.

By nightfall he sounded like the roaming preacher that came by sometimes. Shouting about the devil and his work; about things burning up and rats and snakes and lizards. He scared the little ones. Buddy too if he admitted it, which he didn't, especially not to his older brother, Ray.

Orwin helped Mother, hauling in buckets of snow to rub over Father's burning skin. Buddy watched him carry pails, broad shoulders and muscular arms. A born boxer, Father always said of him. Sometimes he'd get them all throwing a few punches out in the yard and tease the older two about how Orwin could give them a licking even though he was younger. He was the right one for the carrying job. Ray and Buddy had chores too. This morning they fed and watered the horses, and Mother, worry settling heavy on her face, told Ray he'd better ride the eight miles to get the doctor and bring him back. "You're the oldest, Ray. You're the best for the job."

Mother shuffled out of the bedroom, waddling like a goose, her hands spread over her big bump. Her eyes, always darkly circled, appeared more deeply sunk in her head and her hair a mass of tumbles like water pouring over rocks. Usually she wore it caught back and fastened at the nape of her neck with a ribbon, but she'd no time for such frills now.

"Ray not back yet?" she asked Buddy.

He looked up past the mound of baby swell. "No, and the last time I looked out, the sky was as purple as a bruise off in the distance."

"Oh, Buddy," she shook her head and smiled, her teeth catching at her lower lip. He thought for a minute she might cry. "There goes that imagination of yours." She went to the window and peered out, speaking aloud but as if to herself. "He should've been back long ago. The storm's coming in fast and it's not long till nightfall. He might be lost, might even be lost with Doc. Ray knows the way, but if Old Doc takes a notion he's right and Ray is wrong, there's no telling where they'll end up. Doc's a good man, but he can be awful stubborn." She turned away from the window, crossed her arms, her shoulders hunched, and took in all the children sitting quietly watching her.

"I need you to look for Ray, Buddy. But mind you keep an eye on the sky. Do you hear?"

"Yes."

"Don't be going off in your story world and getting distracted. You pay attention to the sky, let it inform your brain and not your imagination. Even if you don't find Ray, you come home before the storm hits. Do you hear?"

She usually encouraged his storytelling. "Tell me a story," she'd say as she kneaded bread at the table or sat with a basket of mending in her lap. One night after he told everyone the *Falling*

Through the Ice When I was Five Years Old story, she said, "You're a budding storyteller. And it seems to me," she fixed him with a look implying she knew something he didn't, "every time I hear that story, the ice gets thinner and thinner and the water gets colder and colder." From then on he was Buddy, his given name fell away, unused.

"You watch that sky and give yourself plenty of time to get back home," she said, in case he didn't hear her the first time.

"You already said."

She stopped at the bedroom door and told him to take Misty. "She'll bring you back in a storm. Your father'd tell you the same if he could."

Buddy took his coat and hat from the pegs by the door, slipped on his boots and mitts, and looked at the children. Pearl paced with Sammy hoisted on her hip to try to settle him.

"Bubby, Bubby, no go, no go," he screamed, and Pearl told him to hush. Hazel scooped up Chuck, sobbing now, too. Sometimes all it took was just one to get the rest of them stirred up. Maudy played with her sock doll and took no notice of what was going on around her.

He crossed the ranch yard, head down into the wind, collar up, and snow crunching underfoot. He pulled the barn door back against a snowdrift and entered into the dank warmth, the horses fidgeting in their stalls.

"Whoa now. It's just me." He began to sing, "Show me the way to go home, I'm tired and I want to go to bed," soothing them with a low soft voice the way Father would. The horses sensed a storm well ahead of its breaking and it made them uneasy.

He went from stall to stall—Breeze, Soldier, Daisy, Buck, Moss, Sly—stopping at Misty to rub her between the eyes. "Ready to go out, old girl?" He pressed his cheek against her nose and whispered, "First, I've got something to do."

A wooden barrel stood in the far corner of the barn. He slid off the lid, reached down and grabbed a fork, its tines twisted from being jabbed into the partly frozen cabbage. The taste of sour cabbage pierced his mouth and sent a ripple up his nose. He took a few more bites, but not enough for Mother to notice anything missing, and forced himself to stop. He'd learned his lesson about being a pig by stuffing himself so full he spent the better part of an afternoon in the outhouse, his stomach aching like there was no tomorrow while his back end explained who was boss. He stabbed the fork into the pickling cabbage and slid the lid back on. Sometimes he hid in the hay behind the barrel to avoid chores and no one ever thought to look for him there. Mother would come out to the barn and stop to turn the cabbage in the brine, making mention of how the contents appeared to be shrinking. "I think we've got barn rats. Sophisticated barn rats accustomed to using food utensils."

Buddy bridled and saddled Misty and led her out of the barn, securing the door latch behind him in case the wind blew up and flung the door open. Up in the saddle, he pulled his hat down over his eyebrows, raised his shoulders high, and headed towards Old Doc's place about seven miles away.

Misty struck up her usual pace and plodded along faithfully. He peeked out from under his woollen hat scanning the plains for Ray and Bishop or for Doc and his wagon, hoping to see all of them, and saw nothing but the skittish twists of snow devils. Behind him the dark sky tumbled closer.

Around the halfway point, Misty stopped. "What's the matter? You tired already?" She was slow and steady, but she never just stopped, always finishing the job she set out to do. He dug his heels into her, got her going again, then she came to a standstill.

Buddy slid down from the saddle and grabbed her bridle, lowering her head to look in her brown eyes. "What's got into you?"

He walked, pulling her along by the reins and noticed her back left leg raise. He examined the hoof but saw nothing. A damaged tendon or a strained muscle; Father would know and he'd know what to do.

The search for Ray had to stop. If he rode back home he could beat the storm, but now that he had to walk he didn't stand a chance of getting back to the house before it broke. Ray and Doc could be out there wandering right now. Bishop was a good horse, had speed on his side, but he was no Misty and couldn't get you home in a blizzard. Misty brought Father home many times during blizzards—delivered him right up to the barn door, Father's eyes clogged with snow and ice, so tightly sealed he might as well have been blind.

Buddy pushed through the wind coming hard at his face. He stumbled as his boots broke through surface crust. Snow drove down harder. He pulled Misty along behind, careful not to go too fast to allow for her lameness. He searched for his tracks but they were all but covered and fast disappearing. By nightfall he wouldn't be able to see anything.

From ranch to ranch stories spread about people dying in storms. One spring Father found Ned Burrell out on the plains—he had been there since the middle of winter when he went missing. Buddy had to keep his wits, do what Mother always said and let common sense prevail; keep his thoughts clear of what might happen.

He pushed on, the fist of the storm banging onto the top of his head. He sank up to his knees, toppling head first, the sky so dark with the storm and nightfall he couldn't see anything. He didn't know where he was going but knew he must keep on moving.

He thought he heard something but imagined it was the wind moaning and groaning all around him. The voices of ghosts Father would say, those who had perished under similar circumstances. There it was again—a rattling sound. Maybe he was near a barn or a house but if he was, he'd gone way off course since there was nothing between the ranch and Doc's place in the village and the Rankin's place was clear in the other direction.

A shape emerged out of the curtain of snow—a horse pulling a sled, the bells on its bridle jingling. A small hunched figure brought the sled up beside him. A face shrouded in a black shawl leaned over to get a closer look at him.

"You lost?" a rough voice asked. He couldn't determine if this was a man or a woman, only that it was an old person.

"Yes," he said trying hard not to cry.

"Your horse lame?"

"Yes."

"Tether it to the sled and climb up here. You're one of the Scott boys, aren't you?"

"Yes." He didn't think he'd ever set eyes on this person before and he knew just about everyone around these parts.

"I'll take you home. We'll take her slow for your lame horse, but I'll get you there. I know your ranch, know it well." The voice sounded rough and spiky, more like a woman's than a man's. But it seemed unlikely an old woman would be out roaming around the countryside on her own on such a night.

He fastened Misty to the sled and climbed up into the seat, sliding in under the buffalo robe she raised for him, its warmth hugging his numb limbs. She drew the hide up higher around his shoulders and face. "You look about near frozen to death." Then she clucked and shook the reins over the horse's rump and they started back, Buddy's teeth smashing so hard together it made his jaw ache.

They rode on through the darkness, the world raging, tossing white sheets around them, blinding them, and he thought how they would be lost though they would be protected by the buffalo hide. For a time.

"Gee," she shouted, pulling the reins, and the horse changed direction. She might have gone faster but she seemed mindful of Misty and her lameness. After a while Buddy thought he spotted a light in the distance.

"There, look, a house." He pointed at it when he was certain his eyes weren't playing tricks on him.

She turned to him and smiled, and he saw a face so ugly he could hardly stand to look at her. She laughed a hideous cackle, her mouth opening like a black hole. "I know," she said. "It's yours."

She pulled up by the barn and he climbed down from the wagon. A snowdrift arched across the yard and made Buddy think of a whale.

"You'd better come in and take shelter," he told her. It was the way of these parts to take in complete strangers, offer a place to stay and some food, but he hated the idea of her showing her hideous face to the children.

"No," her voice clipped short. "I know where I'm going. I've been out in worse and even if I didn't make it, I'm old. Some would say ancient. You take the horse to the barn and rub the leg with liniment. Wrap it too, if you can, then get yourself right quick inside. This is going to blow up worse."

He watched her slide off into the night and wondered if he'd even seen her; she seemed like something out of a dream.

After he rubbed Misty with liniment that stung his hands,

wrapped her leg in cotton strips, and put her in her stall, he ran across the ranch yard as fast as he could go. Maybe Ray had come back.

The children erupted when Buddy came through the door and stomped snow from his boots. Sammy rushed across the room, threw his arms around Buddy's legs, and squeezed. "You fweezing," he said.

Mother came from the bedroom, her eyes anxious and weary.

"Oh Buddy, I was so…" her voice cracked like she might cry but she reeled her emotions in quickly and regained her composure; it wouldn't do to upset the little ones. She touched his cheek then brushed his wet hair aside and took his hand in hers. "You're as cold as ice. Sit by the fire." She paused and he knew what she was about to ask.

"No." He shook his head before she said anything.

"Well maybe he's at Doc's. Maybe they knew they couldn't get back before the storm." She pushed her hair back off her face and her gaze went to the window. "Why were you gone so long?"

He told her about Misty going lame and walking with her and getting lost in the storm.

"And then you know what happened?" he asked, hoping to see her eyes brighten; a sign he'd distracted her from her worry if only for a minute.

"No, what?"

"I met an old hag out on the plain, after I got lost."

"I don't like you calling someone an old hag, Buddy. It's not nice. You've not been raised to be a name caller. Who was this old woman?"

"At first I thought she was a witch," Buddy whispered.

"Make the story short Buddy; I've got to get back to your father."

"She was scary looking, with a long nose and a wart on the end, her skin withered up like an old potato, and the worst teeth you've ever seen; the inside of her mouth was as black as shoe polish. She made a hideous noise when she laughed, like the squawk of a crow."

"My word! You certainly make her sound awful." For a moment Mother looked entertained by the description, then her face went back to the way it had been, settling into worry.

The other children listened with rapt attention—their mouths open, their eyes wide. "But I don't think she was. You know what I think she was?"

"What?"

"An angel."

"Really? Well I suppose angels don't have to be pretty."

"Yes. She brought me home. If she didn't find me, I don't know what would have happened."

"Well then Buddy, you are very lucky. Let's hope she watches over anyone who is out there tonight." He knew who she meant, but she couldn't bring herself to say it. "If we believe in God, then we must believe in angels, agents of God. I'd feel a whole lot better if I had angels watching over all of us," Mother said. She retreated back into the bedroom and closed the door.

Throughout the long night Buddy went to the window and spread his hand wide over the frozen window pane to melt a patch of ice the size of a leaf. Snow came down as dense as milk in a bucket, tracing diagonal lines towards the ground. The wind rose and dropped, sent white ripples through the air. The ghosts of settlers who died taking on the land—that's what Father always said. Lost souls wandering. All Buddy could think was that Ray was going to be one of them.

Later, Mother came from the bedroom to look outside but the wailing wind and the world blanked out by white made her shake her head and sigh. She stopped at the empty hearth on her way back to the bedroom and reminded him to replenish the wood and for the woodstove too. "I'd send Orwin to help you but he's too busy helping me, and the girls need to take care of the children."

Buddy should have done it earlier instead of waiting in the hopes the storm would end. With so much sickness—Sammy and Chuck with runny noses, Pearl's cough rattling in her chest like a stone in a tin can, Father with his fever, and Mother with the baby coming any day—the house had to be kept warm.

He dressed in his soggy clothes and warned the children playing at the hearth to ready themselves for the blast. The three older girls gathered the younger ones into a huddle in the far corner of the room, looped their arms around them, and told them to keep their heads down.

Wind bashed inside, shivered snow through the house, danced the clothes on the line across the hearth, and made the children howl.

Buddy used force to pull the door shut against the wind.

Outside, snow had driven in beneath the thin lip of porch and painted the front of the house white. He stepped down into the yard searching for the corral fence, the shed, the chicken coop and the barn, but couldn't see anything. He started across the whirling frenzy, the wild ruckus of storm surrounding him, and feared being sucked away, tossed about as easily as tumbleweed in the wind.

He stood in snow up to his knees, cupping his face in his hands, staring ahead, not knowing which way to turn, and thought about going back inside. But he'd already messed up badly today by not finding Ray, so he ploughed on then stopped to glance back; the house had vanished. What if the wind had blown it apart? Father always said, every time he drove a nail into rotting wood or made repairs, that one day he'd build something fine that would hold up. Not the home he claimed when he came to Wyoming, a home someone else gave up on, a structure flimsy on its foundations.

He stood somewhere between the house and barn, neither of which he could see, and wondered how Mother could do something so foolish as sending Ray out for Doc when she knew there was a storm on the way. She knew how unpredictable they could be. It was her fault Ray was lost out there somewhere, maybe dead, and only fifteen years old.

Something rolled out of Buddy from deep inside. A howl of despair, the sound of an injured animal snatched away, lifted out into the night, beaten down and weakened by the storm. If Ray didn't come back it was Buddy's fault. If he'd left earlier, didn't waste time calming the horses, not bothered to wait and eat sauerkraut, he would have had time to come back for another horse after Misty went lame.

His gut spasmed; he wrapped both arms around his middle and doubled over losing the contents of his stomach out on to the snow. Sauerkraut burned up his throat, a reminder of his dawdling, of the forkfuls he shoved into his gob savouring every bite. Like a silent monster the storm approached, sliding down from the foothills, creeping over the plains, and purpling the sky with banks of clouds.

Mother should have known. She could read the sky too. She could see how fast it was coming. How could she do something so stupid?

He knew how. For two days, all day long and all night long she tended to Father, settling the children in between times whenever she could. Two days with no sleep. Shame on him for blaming her.

If the angel hadn't found him out there on the plains leading Misty he'd still be out there wandering. He would die, his bones picked clean in the spring by coyotes, wolves, and buzzards.

He flexed his hands, his fingers stiff and paining, scooped some snow and bit into it to rid his mouth of the taste of vomit.

Should he turn back toward the house or keep going for the wood?

He couldn't turn back, not twice in one day. What kind of story would that make? Twice disgraced; twice remembered for weakness. He could almost hear Ray's ridicule, the teasing that would go on out in the barn where Mother couldn't hear. *Sissy. Sissy.* If Ray was alive.

If he died hauling wood people would talk about how he was a hero, a brave boy, gathering wood to prevent his family from freezing to death. But they would die too. They would be found in their beds strung together like Mother's knitting, blue with cold, and still.

He raised his legs high, tromped down hard into the snow, and headed towards a vague outline while the wind angled him off to the side. He came up from behind the barn, something he'd never expected, his senses scrambled upside down and inside out—twisted every which way. He put his hands against the wood, slid around to the front door, and thought to go in to calm the horses. But the door, wobbly on its hinges, might rip from his hands and be tossed into the night. He pressed along the side of the barn until he came to the woodpile.

Arms laden, he began the trek back, his hands as wooden as the load and mitts frozen stiff. Cold set deep into his bones, reminded him to keep moving or freeze to death. He had to keep pushing forward with every ounce of energy he possessed.

His high steps threw his balance and he fell face first, the wood spilling from his arms into the deep snow. He groped for it, snow coating his lashes so thick he couldn't see, his hands so numb they barely felt the nudge of hardness when he found a piece. He recovered a few sticks and struggled to his feet, crossing the barnyard with his paltry pile while the storm pushed hard into his back.

He'd end up like Ray Booth, found during one spring

melt down on his knees, jaw open, eyes open, a few scrawny birch logs still in his arms, staring straight at his house no more than twenty feet away. Or Willis Forton, riding around out on the plains sitting up in his buckboard, the reins in his hands, the horse still moving. Willis frozen solid as a monument. Caught in a storm that pounced out of nowhere and claimed him. For once Buddy wished he could forget Father's stories.

Buddy came to the stairs, stumbled up, and dumped the load by the door. He thought to go inside to warm his hands, but to do so meant losing his footprints and one load wouldn't last long. He followed the irregularity sketching his route back to the pile and made three more trips until he knew he had enough to last until daylight. With luck the storm would be over by then.

Buddy sank into a chair, his cheeks, hands, and feet tingling and burning as feeling came back into them. He leaned back and closed his eyes. Ray would never make it. Only fifteen years old and he was going to die. Or he already had.

Pearl declared she was at her wits end as the children squabbled and cried. Buddy sang some of Father's cute little ditties when he rode—*tum, deedle deedle dee, deedle die*—and it quieted them down. He told them a story about the storm fairies who came from caves deep in the mountains to ranch houses on nights such as this to make sure everyone was safe and warm; and they would protect all of them, Ray too. The children smiled with the notion of it. His story, as strong as a tonic, made them sleepy.

Hazel prepared the beds with a warmer and, one by one, she and Pearl carried the little ones away, coming back once they were settled to join him by the fire. They unfastened each other's braids and brushed each other's hair—a nightly ritual that always included Mother—their arms sweeping over the honey-golden hair. Hazel pulled long strands of Pearl's hair from the brush, tossed them into the flames, watched the crackle and hiss and smelled the putrid odour. "A sign of the devil," Mother always said. "The devil's noise and the devil's stench."

Tonight the devil was everywhere.

Before the girls went to bed Buddy told them he would wait up. Worry would not let him sleep. He'd stay by the fire and keep it going.

Outside, something knocked about in the blizzard. The corral gate sprung loose or something pried off the barn, left to rattle. When the storm broke he'd check the horses and assess the damage to the barn and report to Father. If he hadn't taken ill Father would be here pacing from one window to another, and Mother, mending by the fire, would tell him to sit down or he'd wear a hole in the floor.

Buddy ached with tiredness as he watched the flames tilt and leap. A couple of times his head dropped, startling him awake. As much as he wanted to wait up for Ray, sleep pushed against his eyelids and weariness overtook him.

Chapter 2

Father and Ray

Mother sat at the table, her eyes steady on him, heavy lidded and grey circled. She appeared calm, almost peaceful. Her mussy hair netted the pale morning light coming through the window behind her, a shawl draped over her shoulders. Buddy seated himself opposite her and waited for her to speak. Her silence and look of tranquility made him think Ray must have come back during the night and Father's fever had broken. Good. Life could return to the way it was before.

She looked beyond him to the window.

"Ray came back, didn't he?" Buddy finally asked.

She stared at him as if he'd spoken in a foreign language. He'd never seen her so weary, but now it was over and he felt an aching tenderness towards her and all she'd been through. "Is Ray sleeping?"

"No." Her chin buckled and a cascade of tears dribbled down her face. She pressed her hand over her mouth to dam up the crying and he knew she was trying to be quiet and not to disturb the sleeping children. "He's gone, Buddy."

"What do you mean? Did someone send word of Ray?"

She shook her head and clamped her hand once again over her mouth.

"He'll come back. He's tough like Father." He felt he could reason this into the truth if only he insisted.

"No, your Father, Buddy. He died. In the night." She struggled to make her voice clear. "Around when the storm broke, as if it took him with it."

She was not in her right mind having gone without sleep for so long. Surely he could not trust what she was saying.

"He's died of the fever. I did everything I could, but it took him just as surely as it has taken so many around here."

Typhoid came in the water, invisible and deadly, and made a person buckle with pain, gave them cramps and diarrhea, until the body weakened and gave up. Typhoid stalked the ranchers like a mountain lion prowling in the night: silent, invisible, ready to pounce. It came in waves and swept through the ranches. But it happened to others—not to his family, not to Father. He'd never been sick a day Buddy could remember. He'd survived a mountain lion attack, bears, rattlesnake bites, got tossed off more horses than a person could count, reset his own broken arm, and got lost in storms out on the prairie but always came back.

"You've made a mistake."

"No mistake." She reached across the table and placed her hand over his. "It breaks my heart to say. Do you want to know what I'm thinking?" She faced the front windows where sunlight announced a beautiful day and seemed to mock yesterday. "The best that could happen to this house is that we only lose one."

"I'll go look for Ray."

"I want you to sit here with me. We'll pray for your father, and his soul, and ask he be granted eternal peace, and for Ray to be brought back safely to us."

"Do you want me to wake up Pearl and Hazel?"

"Let them sleep. Nothing can change what's happened. Don't bring them from their dreams; it's about all they have left of their childhood." She sounded distant, as if she too would like to be asleep or removed somehow from the terrible sadness of this morning.

"Is Orwin still in the bedroom with him?"

"No, I sent him to bed when I knew nothing more could be done and that whatever happened from then on was out of our hands." Orwin had great physical strength, but he could not have witnessed anything as terrible as Father dying. "I want to see Father."

"No. It's unwise."

"I want to."

Her sorrowful eyes examined him and he wondered if she even saw him—she seemed to look straight through him—then she glanced at the bedroom door as if she expected Father to appear.

"You're the man of the house now, I suppose. For the time being, until we know about Ray. Do you want me to go with you?"

"No." He wanted to be alone with Father so he could say his goodbyes in private.

At the bedroom door he turned back to Mother hoping to find something in her eyes, something that said none of this was true, the whole thing was a nightmare and she was sleepwalking and confused. She was looking down at her hands and twisting them in her shawl.

In the bedroom, a curtain over the window threw soft amber light. The air, musky from being closed up, smelled of sweat and piss and shit and dirty clothes. And death—though he had no real knowledge of what it might smell like. Father's shape lay long and thin and motionless, drawn out like a ploughed furrow under the blanket. The floor creaked as he inched towards the window and pulled the curtain aside.

He turned to the bed but couldn't move towards it. I am the man of the house now, he thought, a flicker of pride and importance quickly extinguishing. He didn't want to be the man of the house, not at age thirteen, not when it meant taking over from his father and Ray. And if Ray made it through the night, being the man of the house would be something he and Ray would share. He thought of his mother, her overburdened shape hunched at the table, and felt an aching wish for time to reverse itself.

It was no use; he couldn't hold back his tears. At the end of the bed, he wiped his face with his sleeve and sniffed back his blubbering hoping Mother wouldn't hear him. He stepped to the head of the bed and slowly lifted the blanket back.

Father lay with two long socks tied together and wrapped around his head. It struck Buddy as odd and made him think this might be a joke. But no, not the kind of joke Mother would make. Apart from the socks he looked asleep. She might have made a mistake. He reached for his father's hand and went to raise it, but it was stiff, the fingers, the wrist, the arm, fused together into one—his skin waxy, blue, and cold. Even in death he looked handsome: a tall lean man with a thick lustrous honey-brown moustache he groomed up into handlebars, an angular face like it was chiselled out of stone—Mother's description for it—and deep-set eyes. His body didn't look like a place where illness could take hold. Cold, as cold as the frozen ground outside, flowed from his flesh everywhere Buddy touched.

He could imagine what his father would say to him, standing there bawling by the bedside. "No sense crying over spilt milk."

Buddy whispered to him. He knew he was up in Heaven, knew he could hear him even if he couldn't say anything back. He couldn't think of what else to say so he talked to him the way he always did. "Ray and I did the chores yesterday. I'm going out to look around, see what damage the storm did. Ray hasn't come back yet, but he'll be here soon. Mother's got no cause for alarm. A mare's comin' into colt soon. I know it. Her belly's swelled bigger than a pot-belly stove and she's got that look in her eyes says she'd tear off your head if you got in a stall with her. I don't expect trouble, so don't you worry. Me and Ray will take care of her."

After he said his goodbyes to Father, he passed Mother in the big room and stepped outside for air. He looked out on the same thing he looked out on to everyday but now it seemed like a place he no longer knew. The cloudless blue sky fit like a lid over the vast sheet of snow stretching across the plains and to the hills beyond. Deep cold spread stillness, not so much as a tremor in the corn stalks, still enough for Buddy to hear the ache of a bird's wings passing overhead, its dark shadow sliding over the snow. Strong sunlight fell on him and his skin stung with cold. He stepped back inside.

Seated in the rocking chair with the children pressed around her, Mother explained to them what had happened.

"The angels came and took him," she said, her hand gliding over Maudy's head.

"We didn't hear them." Maudy clutched her rag doll tightly in her arms and pushed deeper into the folds of Mother's dress.

Chuck and Sammy, too little to know about death, unable to understand Father was on a trip from which he'd never return, liked the idea he'd gone off with angels. "They come for us? Take us way up in the sky?" Chuck asked, his round face lifted to the ceiling.

"No, not for you."

He lost? He lost, can't find his house? He pick berries?" Sammy asked. Last summer Mother and Sammy got lost in the bush while picking berries.

"No, Sammy, he's not lost. He didn't want to go, but he had to. God made him."

"Tell God no!" Sammy stomped his foot and crossed his arms, chubby as sausage links, lips cast in a downward pout. Mother stroked his head and kissed the top of it, his hair growing in thicker now, blond and fine.

Buddy built a fire and Hazel made porridge. After the children ate, they sat on the rug in front of the fire and played with their wooden toys.

Mother spoke to them from her rocking chair, her voice filling the room, but somehow remaining soft and consoling.

"Children, all of you, I want you to listen to me. Something terrible has happened in this house. Death has taken your father, but we must stay strong. We must be strong for Ray, too. Let us pray to God he comes home safely."

The children watched, their mouths open and their eyes wide, her solemn words strange to them—something new.

"We'll go about doing what we always do. We must. Your father's soul has gone to Heaven but his body remains in our care. And right now it is poison to us. It will have to be taken away so no one else becomes ill." Mother's voice wobbled with emotion; she swiped her cheek with the back of her hand, drew in a deep breath, and examined each one of them. "We've got to be brave. Can you do that?" She forced a smile and they sniffled and mumbled, yes, they could.

"We pwo-miss." Sammy rose, went to her, and lay his head on her lap.

"We've got to keep on going," Mother said, "though sadness resides deep in our hearts. Your father would want us to take care of each other and to be strong. There'll be plenty of time for grieving. Right now, we have to get on with it." She ran her finger over Sammy's cheek. "Buddy, saddle up Breeze, ride over to the Rankins' and get Gus and his boy Will, bring them back. Tell them what's happened to your father. They'll know what to do. People around here have seen it plenty of times. No one needs instructions about what's to be done."

Mother spoke to the two oldest girls. "Pearl and Hazel, you're coming to the barn with me. We'll feed the horses and milk the cow. Maudy you'll stay here and take care of the little ones. Can you do that?"

Maudy said yes, she'd make them behave. "You don't have to do that, Maudy. Just watch them, don't let them near the fire."

Buddy bundled up for the long ride over to the Rankins' across miles of grazing land, then he'd head up over the ridge, and drop down to their ranch.

Mother wrapped a couple of biscuits in an old cloth for him to tuck in the saddle bag and reminded him to eat them before they froze. "They'll be hard as rocks, of no use then if they won't provide you with an ounce of energy."

In the barn he saddled up Breeze, stroked his neck, put his face in his mane and whispered, "You're going for a ride. You need to work up some speed." He rubbed around his ears and his upper lip pulled back exposing large yellow teeth. Breeze wasn't all that reliable, but he was fast and Buddy loved riding him.

Buddy waved goodbye to the others clustered at the door to see him off, rode out of the barnyard and onto the plains heading west to the Rankins'.

The crusty snow sparkled with pink and blue gems—the air so cold and crisp it choked him and pained his lungs. Around him dead weeds rattled in a slight wind. He pulled a scarf around his mouth for protection against the cold and to snag the warmth of his own breath. He rode on, scanning the distance, eyes on a constant lookout for Ray. After he'd been riding for a long time he brought Breeze to a standstill and examined the distant range—the direction he was headed.

He could ask the question here, far from the house, away from his mother, where she wouldn't see his fear or his sadness. What would become of all them without Father?

He and Ray would have to fill their father's shoes. They would have to run the ranch and take care of the others. If Ray came back. But what if he didn't?

Once Buddy had been impatient to go out on hunting trips by himself, bring the horses back from grazing alone, or go on cattle round-ups. Now he wanted life as before with Father making the decisions: telling him and Ray what to do, explaining things to them, shouldering the responsibility, telling him no. The time would come when he could go off on his own but he had to wait; all things came in their own good time.

He swung Breeze towards the notch in the range. A trick Father taught him to gauge the way to the Rankins' ranch.

Was there something in the distance? With the sun so strong and reflecting off the snow he couldn't trust his eyes, teary and blurred by wind and sun. He shielded his eyes with his hand and scrolled across the plains. A horse, was it? What else could it be? Storms often forced open barn doors and animals escaped, usually out of fear. Now he was certain it was a horse, and as it came closer he made out something on its back, low and hunkered down. He rode to meet it and once he got closer he knew it was Ray on Bishop.

The reins dangled free. Ray's face and hands were sunk deep into the horse's mane and the fringe of hair around his cap matted with the horse's, spun together with snow and ice.

Buddy slid off Breeze and grabbed Bishop's bridle.

"Ray!" Ray didn't move. Buddy grabbed Ray's foot, lifted it out of the stirrup, and shook it. It felt stiff and inflexible. "Ray! Ray!" He clutched the reins to steady Bishop. Here it was then, his family's worst fears coming true; Ray frozen to death on the back of the horse.

He shouted louder, shook Ray's leg harder, a fear rising up inside him like he'd never known. He moved around to the other side of Bishop to try to see Ray's face, but it was no use, as buried on that side as it was on the other.

He thought he saw movement. As he shook his leg and arm Ray lifted his head and slowly turned to Buddy, his face a mix-up of pink, blue, and purple and swollen, as if he'd taken the worst kind of beating. His lips, puffed up twice their size, cracked with fissures of frozen blood. His eyes were no larger than thin slits; his brows and lashes crusted with snow and ice.

"Jesus, Ray. Say something." Buddy was about to tell him to get down off the horse but that would be foolish. He'd never get him back up. Ray tried to speak but could only manage an indecipherable slur through his thick lips.

Buddy tried to move in closer to Ray. "I can't figure you."

"I said I imagine I don't look my best," Ray managed to push out.

"If I weren't wide awake, I'd swear I was having one god-awful nightmare."

"What you doing? Looking for me?"

"I'm on my way to the Rankins'."

"Baby coming?"

"Never mind all that. You and Bishop get to home. Now hang on." Ray turned his face back into the horse's mane and Buddy struck Bishop's rump and watched the horse gallop towards home and disappear over the next rise in a bluster of snow. There was no telling just what kind of damage had been done to Ray.

Mrs. Rankin must have spotted Buddy coming and stood in her doorway as Buddy and Breeze crossed the barnyard. She wasn't a sight for his sad eyes. Whenever she came to the house to help with Mother's births, she bossed the whole family around, even Father, as soon as she set foot in the door. She assigned them all chores and told them to stay as far away as possible and to keep the racket down. "While I'm here doing my work, it's my house. I'm here to deliver a baby and there'll be no sass and nonsense." The children listened to her, strung out in a row like soldiers stone-faced and miserable, wishing she wasn't there even if it was to help out. She rolled up her sleeves in preparation for scrubbing everything down, as she put it, as if their house was some kind of pig-sty.

She greeted him and asked, "Baby?"

"No, it's my father. He died from the fever. We need Mr. Rankin and Will to come and take care of the body." It wasn't the kind of help a person should ever have to go asking for, especially not a son for his father. Without a father he'd be begging favours all the time.

He wished Will didn't have to put his filthy paws on Father on account of Will having a mouth on him like a pit toilet. Once, at school, Buddy cleaned his clock when he made a remark about Hazel being ripe for the picking as if she were no better than an animal. Buddy pounded him until his knuckles hurt, stuck his face in Will's, and hissed at him he wasn't fit to be in the same room with his sister—make that the whole goddamn state of Wyoming.

"Dear Lord," Mrs. Rankin said. "God rest his soul. Well, I'm sorry to hear it, boy."

She went back into the house and Mr. Rankin and Will appeared. They nodded at Buddy, acknowledging his awful news by mumbling something, and disappeared inside the barn to saddle up. "Better get this done fast," Mr. Rankin said.

There'd been enough typhoid fever they knew what had to be done, knew any lingering around the body could make more people sick. Buddy overheard folks one day after church, out in the yard, speaking in low tones about the number the fever took. The bodies had to be disposed of far away from humans and water. People said how it was hard to take an invisible killer seriously. They were used to looking down a gun barrel at something—a cougar, or a bear, or a wolf. Typhoid was deadlier, and you couldn't even see it, and that made it hard to figure.

Ray lay on the floor in front of the fire wrapped up like a cocoon, his whole body shaking and vibrating, his teeth knocking together so hard it sounded like a red squirrel's chatter. Hazel and Pearl sat on the floor and rubbed him through the blanket trying to bring circulation back into his limbs.

"Emma," Mr. Rankin said to Mother. "Sorry for your loss." Will didn't say anything and stood dumb as a cabbage, his mouth hanging open.

Mother had wrapped Father's body up in the blanket from their bed. It would have to be disposed of, the sheets boiled in a big pot on the stove. They couldn't afford to burn them or Mother would have to go without, and she'd already lost a blanket. Where could she get a new one now? And with what money and nothing to trade?

Mr. Rankin and Will carried the body from the bedroom out to the kitchen.

"Put him there." Mother pointed to the table. They stretched him out full across the plank, looked at Mother, and stepped away.

"Buddy, help me with Ray," Mother said.

They gripped Ray under the arms and brought him to his feet. Buddy could feel Ray's body shaking and trembling right through the blanket. Ray sagged heavily on Buddy as he limped to the table and sank down on a chair.

Mother asked everyone to gather round the table. "Bow your heads in prayer." Mother did her best to give Father a decent service but her voice broke several times as her emotions took charge. When she finished they all said, "Amen". The Rankins picked him up using the blanket and carried him out the door, forever out of his house and away from his family.

"I hate angels," Pearl said.

"Me too." Maudy slipped her arm around Pearl's shoulder.

"When I big," Chuck said, "I shoot them. I blast their heads off. I tell them, get the hell out of the way."

"That's not nice talk." Mother crossed the room, sat on her rocker, and put her head back. She looked so much older, so tired. "Pipe down, all of you. There's no changing the course of these events. We should be thankful for Ray's return."

That night, Buddy and Hazel did the barn chores and Pearl and Maudy prepared the stew. Pain took hold of Mother and sat her down. All of them, even the little ones, knew to be quiet. Ray's violent shaking stopped long enough for him to manage a few mouthfuls of food, then he limped around the room and rubbed his hands together as he worked to revive himself.

Chapter 3

New Baby

The day after Father died, Mother was slower, drowsy, and cranky. She seemed to drift to somewhere else as if she was caught up in a daydream. After the evening chores, when Buddy came back in from the barn, she lay on her bed moaning and writhing in pain. It was time to get Mrs. Rankin. Just as surely as a new day would dawn tomorrow the baby was on its way.

"Take the lamp," Ray told him as Buddy slipped on his winter coat.

Buddy didn't. On the way to the barn he saw the moon shining bright over the plains, and in the distance, the faint outline of hills. Tiredness hung in his arms as he saddled up Bishop. He hadn't slept well for nights, tossing and turning, overcome with worry by all the terrible and sudden changes. As he started out into the moonlit night, bitter cold struck his face.

For an hour all he heard was the sound of Bishop's hooves crunching through the snow and the slight whisper of wind. He longed to hear a human voice. Once he might have felt proud of the importance of his task, but not tonight. Father always went for Mrs. Rankin while Buddy stayed at home sharing in the excitement of a new brother or sister on the way. They played the "Name the Baby" game and came up with such gems as Alowishus, Rubybegonia, Stallion, and Magilicutty as they tried to outdo one another with their silliness.

This new life about to be born already had no father. What kind of a life would it have? Or the rest of them?

Mother had an answer for everything. He could almost hear her saying, *We'll be strong. We'll make do*. He trusted her words and as he rode along he spoke them aloud, "Be strong," the sound of his own voice bringing a small measure of comfort in the vast silence.

Ahead something moved in the blue moonlight. He couldn't make it out and decided he must be seeing things, tired as he was, suffering from a mind loaded up with impossible worry and little sleep. Still he kept his eyes peeled and recalled how Father always said to keep a sharp lookout.

Bishop whinnied. Buddy pulled on the reins and the horse stopped, shifted nervously. There was something out there.

Off in the distance, shapes slid low to the ground. Wolves. A pack of six, maybe seven. Enough to bring a horse down, especially now late in winter when they were lean as fence posts, half-starved, and would use all their strength for a kill. Buddy's heart thundered, gushing blood up into his ears. He swung Bishop in a full circle remembering how Father called them cagey hunters that would split and circle their prey, some coming up from behind and the rest of the pack closing in from the front.

A quick dig into Bishop's sides put him into a hard gallop as Buddy veered off to the left. The wolves charged from the right, running hard, chasing him. Mangy and scrawny, they pushed every ounce of their instinct to survive through their gaunt bodies. Their horrible, hungry panting and yowls, the scratch of their claws on the hardened snow, close by. All it would take would be for one wolf to latch onto Bishop's leg and bring the horse down. The entire pack would swarm them in seconds and ravage their flesh.

"Heigh-ya, heigh-ya!" he shouted, kicking Bishop as hard as he could.

He forced Bishop to run like wind itself, the cold air pounding at his face, risking the horse's hooves catching on crusty snow. There was no other choice but to ride hard and put his faith in the horse. Faster, faster, faster. They raced ahead, snow flying up around them, Buddy sneaking glimpses behind. The shapes still there—long, scrawny shapes streaking after him. "Heigh-ya, heigh ya!"

The chase went on for miles until one by one the wolves fell away and slinked into a thicket of shrubs. They'd gather there, try to flush out birds, rabbits, and mice.

When he reached a distance where he finally felt safe he slowed

Bishop to a walk, turned back, and saw the glaze of blue moonlight shimmering over the plains.

Adrift and lost in a sea of snow lit by the moon and millions of stars, he felt small and exposed. He couldn't see the row of hills; couldn't line himself up with the notch. Finally, after retracing Bishop's tracks, he came to the point where he once again found the ridge, his eyes tired from straining into the night on a constant watch for the liquid shapes of wolves.

He wouldn't tell Mrs. Rankin about the pack and chance her refusing to come back with him. The rest of the way to the Rankins' he kept a sharp lookout, but he'd outrun the wolves, and figured he'd brought them close to death.

Mother's moans were louder. "You help me carry her to the table," Mrs. Rankin said as she unbuttoned her coat then tied on an apron. "Let's get some water boiling."

Buddy knew what had to be done; they'd done this so many times before.

Ray sat beside Mother's bed, hunched over, worried. As they lifted her out of bed, they knew this birth would be different. A large patch of blood stained the feather tick.

"Let's just get her moved," Mrs. Rankin said, anticipating one of them to badger her with questions, but they knew not to say anything about the blood, most of all for Mother's sake.

Ray, Buddy, and Mrs. Rankin carried her to the table where all the babies had been born.

"What took you so long to get Mrs. Rankin?" Hazel asked Buddy as he stepped back from the table. "Were you dilly-dallying? Father could have been there and back five times in the time it took for you to go once."

"I'm not Father."

"You were daydreaming, weren't you? The way you do. And Mother in so much pain."

"That's enough out of the two of you," Mrs. Rankin said, her voice low. "There'll be no squabbling here tonight." Mother smiled weakly somewhere between asleep and awake. Her hands clutched the edges of the table and opened and closed with her spasms. Her long auburn hair spilled over the end of the table.

Mrs. Rankin pulled the sheets up over Mother's knees and motioned for Hazel to bring the basin and the kettle with hot water. Already with her sweater off and her sleeves rolled up, she dipped her hands into the water and pulled them back quickly.

"Better get some snow in there, Buddy." She motioned to the pail by the door. "Not too much mind; the water's got to stay hot."

Mrs. Rankin washed right up to her elbows. "Get me as many clean towels and sheets as you can," she told Hazel. "It's okay, Emma." She patted Mother on the knee. "You're doing fine. Just keep on like you are, stay nice and quiet, save up for when the contractions get harder. You'll need all of your strength."

Mother smiled faintly but it was impossible to know if she understood.

Mrs. Rankin had come so many times before, in all hours of the day and night, when the children got sick and for births. Buddy had never seen her look the way she did right now, so serious, as if she might be mulling something over.

"Is everything okay?" he whispered to her.

"Pearl will stay here with me. You and Ray take the others into the bedroom and you put them to bed. You keep them quiet, you hear me?"

"I hear you," Buddy said. Mother gave him a weak smile, her eyes still half-opened, and he knew she meant for him to follow Mrs. Rankin's orders.

Mother thought Mrs. Rankin had a bossy nature though she never said, not in so many words. "She gets the job done with little fuss," was how she put it. "She's the best midwife in the region. We're lucky to have her so close." He'd go along with her bossiness; he'd do it for Mother. The way Mother looked now, pale and waxy, he'd do anything she wanted if it would make the pain stop.

Buddy told the children the *Father and the Cougar* story, the time the cougar launched itself on Father from where it had been hiding in a tree. He choked up when he heard himself using the exact words Father had. "I always thought trees were for birds, itty-bitty things that balance on the end of a twig, and not for hundred-pound cats. I never thought to look up."

As he told the stories he knew he would make a habit of this, save Father's voice from silence. He'd never be gone—he would stay alive in Buddy.

By the end of the next story everyone had fallen asleep and did not stir through the screams coming from the next room.

Finally, all became silent and the cries of a newborn could be heard. A sound so comforting, so reassuring, that the fear of the night slipped away and exhausted, Buddy slept.

Buddy shifted Sammy's head away from his chest—a patch of drool darkened his long johns—eased Maudy aside, pushed the quilt away, and stepped out onto the cold floor. Morning threw enough light he knew he'd overslept, and still the animals to feed, their stalls cleaned, the cow milked, and a new brother or sister to meet.

Mrs. Rankin sat by the fire, a new baby wrapped in the blanket Mother knit before Chuck was born. Across from her, Pearl leaned forward in a straight-back chair, her arms hugging her middle as if she'd taken a chill and tried to warm herself, her face hidden behind strands of tumbling hair.

Thick heat rose from the fire and brought the quick comfort of knowing someone was up before him. He turned to the kitchen, half expecting to see Mother stoking the stove or stirring porridge.

Mother lay on the table.

Mrs. Rankin looked up from the baby and shook her head.

Pearl's shoulders heaved, and as her head rose and their eyes met, he saw that they were red-rimmed. She dabbed tears with the tip of her shawl.

Buddy edged his way to the table. Mother appeared to be in the deepest sleep. She looked younger than she had yesterday now that the baby had come and she wore the hint of a smile as she slept and dreamed.

Why would they leave her here on the table, the boards hard and unyielding under her paining hips? Why did the blanket lay folded at her feet? She must have told them before dropping off she was hot and to leave the blankets off her. He touched her hand, felt coldness.

His heart jolted with a terrible suddenness and his body weakened as if all the blood suddenly drained from it. He covered her forehead with his palm and again felt the cold, a familiar cold, the same kind that resided in his father only two days ago. A noise came out of him, a slow sorrowful moan from deep in his belly.

"Hush now or you'll wake the others. No need of them finding out what's in store for them any sooner than is necessary." Mrs. Rankin's face looked even more pinched and angular. "There's nothing to be done. Life's hard, boy, I grant you and I am sorry for it, and the sooner you learn that the better off you'll be. Take hold, you hear me?"

Pearl crossed the room and wrapped her arms around him, her sobs shuddering through him. He stroked her head.

The rocker runners wobbled over the uneven floor and through Mrs. Rankin's voice.

"She died as a result of childbirth." Her eyes fell to the bundle still and silent in her arms then she looked up at Buddy, her face set hard. "She lost too much blood. The baby came breach and tore her open wide as a smashed melon."

How dare she speak of Mother in such a way. The gentlest person he'd ever known, tough when she had to be, but without an ounce of meanness and undeserving of such an ugly description. *As tender as a lamb*. That was how Father described her.

"I told her after the last one she shouldn't have any more, warned her of the danger; she took no heed."

She should stop with her stupid useless opinions. What did it matter now?

Pearl's tears soaked through his clothes. The room, this house, seemed as open as the prairies, open to anything: marauding animals, whipping winds, the coldest temperatures, bad men, and disease. This place couldn't be trusted and Mrs. Rankin's presence felt different from before. He wanted to rush at her with his arms thrashing and punch her as hard as he could, but he heard his mother's voice. *We reason things out. We don't punch them out. We are more refined than that.* He hugged Pearl closer to him.

Mrs. Rankin stared at him, her silent hard eyes ridiculing him for his tears, his weakness. He guided Pearl back to a chair and mumbled in a choked voice he was going outside. He grabbed his coat and stepped out into a world he no longer understood, and unfamiliar to him. He ran across the yard to the barn, put his hand on the door latch, and bent over as nausea overtook him. He staggered to the corral fence, leaned against it, and retched several times until there was nothing left for his body to get rid of and he wished he'd die. He wished for the whole works of them to die—there was no reason to live. He dropped to his knees. Spasms flowed through him leaving him weak, a vessel so empty and dry he couldn't muster a mouthful of gob or cry another tear.

He had no idea how long he knelt in the snow with the wind lashing against his back and cold creeping through him; he'd lost all sense of time. He opened his hands wide and placed them on the snow's surface. They looked blue, almost black against the white, like a raven's claws.

He staggered inside the barn and felt the warmth of the animals. His eyes adjusted slowly to the muted light. Bishop, Breeze, Misty, Robin, Sailor, Daisy, Dew, and Soldier raised their heads to watch as he passed their stalls. The horses sensed something, perhaps his sorrow, as they waited for his movements to become familiar and bring them food, water, a clean stall, or turn them out into the corral.

The early light of morning broke through the dimness inside the barn. Ray closed the door and hobbled in, his head bowed to the floor.

"Hard to believe all this bad luck could come to one family in such a short time." He picked a piece of straw off the barn floor and fiddled with it, all the time looking down. Buddy knew Ray didn't want to let on he was crying, too. "Mrs. Rankin told me I have to go get the minister for Mother. The little ones are beside themselves. Pearl and Hazel are doing their best to comfort them," Ray said.

Buddy leaned against his pitchfork. "At least the girls know how to make Johnny cakes and stew. I don't suppose either of them could wring a chicken's neck."

"This is a damn poor time for you to be thinking about your belly," Ray sobbed.

"I'm not! I can't think straight, that's all. They just don't know much, that's all I'm getting at. And that just seems impossible right now." Ray had no business being a bully, not now, not with all this sorrow.

Ray grabbed a pitchfork and heaved straw and dung out of a stall. He stood only a little taller than Buddy but his muscular build put ease to his shovelling, despite his bandaged hands.

"I'll ride and tell the minister," Buddy said. "You're not ready yet. You're still hurting from the other night. Then I'll go and tell Grandpa Scott, Aunt Gabby, and Uncle Wes."

Grandpa might not understand. The little people visited him, the leprechauns he called them, and he claimed they lived in the sacks of potatoes in his kitchen. "Makes sense, I suppose," Buddy overheard him telling Father. "The Irish and potatoes. Where else would the little people go?"

He'd have to come up with an excuse so he wouldn't have to stay at Aunt Gabby and Uncle Wes's overnight. Aunt Gabby he could take any day of the week, but Uncle Wes was another matter.

Word of his father's death travelled quickly around the ranches and once people heard it was typhus, everyone, including the minister, knew to stay away. But with Mother it would be different.

"I'll leave once chores are done. You help the others," Buddy said.

"I know what to do," Ray said, acting like he'd already taken over the job of being in charge.

When they were almost finished cleaning stalls and feeding the animals, Mrs. Rankin came out to the barn, the new baby in her arms tucked away in a blanket.

"Mr. Rankin will be coming for me soon. My boy Will came up earlier to see when to fetch me. I told him to send his father back 'round nine this morning." She raised the baby up a little. "This poor little fellow will need a wet nurse. He's fine now, he's still tired from the business of being born into this wretched world, and he'll be tired for a couple more days. After that, he'll need to suckle. There's a woman over near Sage Ridge just had a baby. I'm certain she'll tend to him. I'll be taking him with me."

Buddy waited for Ray to tell her no, the baby would stay here with them where it belonged, with its family. Instead, Ray turned to the window.

What would they do with the baby here? What else could they

do but let him go? They didn't know how to take care of it. Still, it didn't seem right.

"Couldn't we give it cow's milk?" Buddy asked.

"No. That would make him sick and weak." Mrs. Rankin jostled the bundle in her arms. "He's already at a terrible disadvantage without his mother's milk. We'll do the best we can, but much will depend on the strength of the child."

Buddy watched Mrs. Rankin standing in the barn door holding his new brother. He wouldn't look at this child who'd been born into a world with no parents, whose very life meant the end of another's. It was nature's way—the child never asked to get born, but he couldn't look at something so much a part of him, of his whole family, who could disappear forever as soon as Mrs. Rankin walked out of the barn. Better to remember nothing but a faceless bundle in Mrs. Rankin's arms.

"You'll be fine. Your sisters seem pretty sure of themselves with the young ones and the cooking, for now anyway, so I'll be on my way. Better get this little fellow tended to." Mrs. Rankin pulled open the barn door and stepped out. "Did you have a name in mind for him?"

Ray and Buddy looked at each other. "No," Ray said. "Mother and Father never said."

She seemed to wait for them to say something more but they didn't.

"We're obliged for all you've done," Ray called after her and heaved a fork full of horse manure out into the centre of the barn.

When the barn chores were close to being done Buddy heard the rattle of horse bridles as Mr. Rankin pulled his cutter into the yard. Buddy thought to go to the door and watch them leave, but he couldn't move from where he stood at the back of the barn, couldn't bring himself to watch them ride away.

Chapter 4

The News Takes Hold

The minister appeared saddened by the news of Mother's passing but kept a strong reserve.

"I'm sorry for your losses and all your trouble." He asked about the others and said he'd be at the ranch first thing tomorrow. "God be with you."

Buddy left his front porch and climbed on Bishop as quick as he could, his emotions welling up inside him with the force of a spring creek. If God was with him or his family, he wouldn't be making this journey, he thought.

He banged on Grandpa Scott's door and heard a shrill call to come inside.

Grandpa sat in the kitchen in his favourite chair, twisted up with rheumatism like a diseased plum tree. He sat within reaching distance of a pot belly stove so he could shove sticks into the fire. His eyes burned as lively as embers as he craned his neck to look at Buddy.

"I'll be. Never thought I'd see the likes of you standing in my kitchen, looking at me." His shoulders so stooped they made his neck disappear. Long, stringy hair, tufted around his head, dry and dead as prairie sage.

The kitchen table held the clutter of his life, the signs of what he couldn't do for himself—plates of leftover food, hardened and moldy, a bowl of rotting apples, a pair of socks. Two oil lamps threw a sallow light, yellowing the room and its contents as if the whole works had been dipped in egg yolk. The air was thick with mingled scents.

"You going to tell me why you've come or are you going to stand there gawking at me like the cat's got your tongue? These other fellows do enough staring at me." He motioned around the room, but whatever he was indicating Buddy couldn't see.

"Sit down." Grandpa pointed to a kitchen chair. "Maybe your tongue will work better if you take a load off your feet." He landed a splat of tobacco juice in the spittoon.

Buddy pulled the chair over closer to him, squeezing into a small space between a sack of potatoes, a stack of wood, and his spittoon.

"I've got news, Grandpa." A lump in his throat threatened to choke him. Usually Father did the talking with Grandpa.

"I can't listen any better than I am right now."

Buddy studied the old man and it hit him then, how he was charged now with bringing the news of the family to the eldest, his father's father. "It's about my father and my mother," Buddy said. He paused, then blurted the news out as fast as he could so he wouldn't break down and stop himself from making any kind of sense at all.

"What's that you're saying?" The old man shifted in his chair to get a better look at him, connecting the news with the face of the person who brought it. "You've not come all this way to talk nonsense to me, have you? Now say it again and make it plain so I understand."

Emotions knotted in Buddy's throat but he caught his breath and forced the words out again as orderly as he could, stopping to breathe when choking threatened to overtake him.

"Lord God Almighty! Are you sure, boy?"

He didn't ride all this way to tell him some kind of made-up fairytale, did he? He nodded his head and stared hard at the small window of flame on the stove.

The old man stared into the pot belly stove and seemed to settle with the news. The fire sizzled and snapped with the sap of young wood.

"You sit still for a change and never mind all your hopping around." Grandpa waved his hand in the air as he spoke gruffly and stared at the bag of potatoes.

"Who you talking to, Grandpa?"

"The little people. They've gone inside the sacks. They're always flying around here, getting into this and that, making a terrible mess. They're an awful nuisance, I can tell you. A terrible distraction."

The old man's red, watery eyes met Buddy's. "What's to be

done?" It wasn't the kind of question that got answered—a flag without wind—he let it alone.

He waited for Grandpa to say more but the old man fidgeted with the wood stove door and seemed to have forgotten about him. Buddy had said what he came here to say. He wouldn't tell him about the baby. What good would it do? For all Grandpa knew the baby hadn't even been born.

Firelight flickered across Grandpa's face, his skin as wrinkled as cottonwood bark. It would be just as well as if he forgot the whole works of what Buddy told him and stayed in the world of the little people.

"I've got to get on out to Uncle Wes's and tell him, then I'm headed back to the ranch. Ray needs me there." Buddy rose and raised the collar of his coat.

Grandpa gazed hard at the stove's window, liquid with flames, and spoke slowly. "Go on then. Before you go, you remember one thing." He raised a crooked finger and jabbed at the air. Grandpa seemed to speak with every ounce of strength he possessed, a note of anger in his voice. "That should have been me who died, not your folks. If I could I'd change places with them, I'd do it in a minute, and I'd be right glad to do it, too. Just you remember that." His lower lip trembled as he pawed his stubbled chin with his misshapen hand.

Buddy took himself outside into the pale light of late afternoon not wanting to witness Grandpa Scott breaking down. Some things should remain private.

He steered Bishop out of town and across the plains heading in the opposite direction of the ranch, into the wind. It would be a long two-mile ride.

Taking the news to Uncle Wes and Aunt Gabby stuck like a thorn in his side. Mother wouldn't hear one nasty one word about Uncle Wes and scolded Father when he called him a mean son-of-a-bitch. "Now George, that isn't right. You take that kind of talk out to the barn, and you keep it away from the children. The world's harsh enough without nastiness settling under this roof."

He rehearsed how he'd deliver the news. He'd refuse to go inside, tell them he had to get back in a hurry, and ride off as fast as he could. If he went inside he'd have to sit through one of Wes's never-ending scripture readings. Like Father said, no one tolerated a steady diet of the Bible, especially the kind Wes was always shoving down their throats.

Once, Uncle Wes came to the ranch with a milking cow to give to Father while Buddy and Ray played in the barnyard. "Why do you want to go and have all them youngsters, anyway? You don't want to live like a bunch of roughians out here in this God-forsaken land, trying to scratch a living out of dust, do you? I'd hire you on as a hand if you'd move closer."

Father didn't waste a second coming up with an answer. "I'm certain you could keep me employed. You'd have me going night and day, pay me next to nothing, give me an overdose of your God-fearing rhetoric, and line your pockets with the proceeds made by the sweat off my back. I think I'll decline your generous offer."

Buddy rode down the long lane and spotted the light in the kitchen windows. Aunt Gabby would be fixing dinner; the girls would be setting the table or waiting in the parlour for Bible reading.

He tethered Bishop, stepped up on to the back porch, and gave a hard rap. Uncle Wes, tall, lean, and severe, came to the door and stared down his beak of a nose. "What brings you here, boy?" his voice boomed.

"I've got news," Buddy said, his voice low and somber.

"Take off your hat!" Wes shouted. "Don't you know it's bad manners for a boy your age to speak to an elder with his hat on? Or don't they teach you that out there where you live?"

Buddy slipped off the cap mother knit and clutched it in his hands; felt the cold upon his head.

"Now before you start up with whatever story has got you itching so bad you can't remember your manners, you'll step inside and sit down at the table and we'll proceed like civilized folk." Uncle Wes stepped back to make way for Buddy to come inside.

Buddy stood still. "I can't come in. I've got to get back to the ranch."

Uncle Wes gave a short laugh.

"I'm not taking any news from you standing there. You'll come inside or you'll be on your way, your load lessened not by one word by telling it to me. Whatever it is that's got you forgetting your manners will have to wait."

Buddy's legs and arms twitched with muscles fired to jump back up on Bishop and ride like hell out of there, away from this hawk of a man.

Inside, he took Buddy's coat and pointed to the table. "Before you get going on what's burning up your mind your Aunt Gabby will give us a cup of tea and biscuits and we'll get on with it."

Buddy's cousins, Ava and Nellie, slipped into the room and snickered behind Wes. Ava, the tallest and oldest, was Ray's age, and Nellie was Buddy's. They were a pair of lookers, a revelation Father often commented on. "How come such an ugly cuss as you, Wes, has two fine specimens of daughters?" That brought on Wes's lecture about how his daughters were agents of kindness and caring and servitude, and their real beauty lay beneath their skin, visible through their exemplary deeds.

Aunt Gabby stood in front of a shiny black stove and smiled when she saw Buddy. "What's brought you here at suppertime and on such a cold night?"

Wes told Aunt Gabby that Buddy came with news but first they'd have their tea and biscuits. All the time he talked Ava and Nellie stood behind him sticking out their tongues and crossing their eyes. Buddy avoided looking at them and instead stared at the pictures on the wall or out the window, dimming with the last light of day.

Wes might have suspected some kind of tomfoolery; he turned quickly to look at the girls, whose expressions flashed to stone-faced innocence in less than a second. "Help your mother with the tea," he said. As he waited at the table, Buddy's eyes roamed to a plaque on the wall. A needlepoint Aunt Gabby had made, the verse provided by Uncle Wes:

If all the world was just like me,
What a wonderful world this would be.

Father always said there was no need guessing about Wes's opinion of himself since it hung there, plain for all to see.

Aunt Gabby crossed the kitchen, placed her hand on Buddy's shoulder, and squeezed. "I've got biscuits one hour out of the oven, and cheese. That'll warm you up."

"While you're preparing tea, we'll have a little scripture reading." Uncle Wes reached to the sideboard behind him and took a Bible from where it sat in the centre of a doily. "I don't imagine you've heard any scripture today?" The thin pages of the Bible rattled like onion skins.

"You'd imagine right."

The God of Mercy Uncle Wes started reading about was cruel and being forced to sit and listen to his praise made Buddy feel sick. It was all he could do to keep a quiet tongue in his head. He'd give his news as soon as he could and take off like a shot.

Wes droned on and Aunt Gabby and the girls arranged the table. Every time Nellie or Ava set something down they poked Buddy in the back or gave his sides a quick tickle, making him squirm in his chair. Finally everyone was seated and Aunt Gabby poured the tea. Uncle Wes put the Bible away and gave the blessings. Nellie and Ava kicked Buddy under the table.

"Now then, what is this news that couldn't wait?" Uncle Wes smeared a chunk of butter over a warm biscuit.

Buddy told them straight out, resisting any kind of flourish, glad to have the information dispersed and gladder still that he could now leave this house and make the long ride back home. His biscuits sat untouched.

Aunt Gabby gasped with the news. Ava and Nellie sat poker straight and still. Wes said, "It is God's will. God has claimed them for his own and God's will must not be questioned."

Aunt Gabby's hand shook as she placed her tea cup on a saucer, raised her hand to her lips, and turned her sorrowful eyes to Buddy. "I'm so sorry. You've had a terrible heartbreak. Two parents in almost as many days. What about the new baby?" Her soft hazel eyes searched his face.

After he told her about Mrs. Rankin taking it off to the wet nurse, she asked about the others and how they were managing.

Uncle Wes stroked his chin as he listened. "You go back. We'll go ahead and do what we have to do in the village, make the arrangements for your mother. We'll take care of the details," he said. "Nine children all orphaned leaves a lot of loose ends. That's a lot of orphans." Orphans. The word struck with the harshness of Cyler Winthall's club hammer on the anvil as he shod horses, struck red hot and searing. Orphan meant no ties with anyone in the whole world. It meant alone.

He had all his brothers and sisters, all blood ties. How could you have nobody when you had all those brothers and sisters? Uncle Wes was wrong but he knew better than to argue with him.

Buddy stood, loosened the twine around his waist to prevent his pants from inching up and pinching him in the crotch, and lowered his pants down on his hips to cover his red, chafed ankles, sore from being exposed to the wind and snow. "I'd better get."

"He could stay here tonight, couldn't he Wes? Make the ride early in the morning?" Aunt Gabby asked.

"I've got to get back." He appreciated Aunt Gabby's offer but he knew where he wanted to be.

She went to the counter and turned biscuits out of a pan, cut off a chunk of cheese, and bundled it all in a cloth which she handed to Buddy. "Take this back to share with the others." She touched his face with her hand, warm and soft, and leaned in to kiss his forehead. "You've had an awful loss. Your mother and your father were good people. Never forget that."

Uncle Wes held the door open.

Out on the prairie, the sunset streaked the sky with shades of orange and pink, as if the whole universe had caught fire. There he stood, alone and tiny under the blazing cathedral roof, under the eye of God. A strong wind whipped and curled the snow. He dreaded the long ride back but looked forward to the fire's warmth. He heard his mother's voice plain as plain—*Peel off those cold things and get warm by the fire.* She'd said it so many times before. He let the reins drop. Bishop stopped. Out in the bare open world of wind and cold there was no one to see him cry. He didn't have to pretend to be brave or to be an adult; he could cry; he could still be a boy.

Chapter 5

Goodbye, Mother

The grave diggers shoveled steadily. Reverend Potter read from the Bible next to the hole in the ground, his black robe fluttering, sleet in the air. Sammy squirmed at the end of Buddy's hand and sniffed; he hoisted him up and the boy wrapped his arms around him and buried his face in his neck. Buddy turned from the hole and walked away.

Overhead, two crows attacked each other, squawked, and flew off in opposite directions.

Mourners stepped away from the graveside, speaking quietly as they made their way to the buggies and wagons.

A short caravan snaked across the open plain and headed back to the house where everyone would gather. The hint of sunshine that brought in the day was replaced by a bloated grey sky filled with spikes of sleet and a raw wind.

Sammy sat on Buddy's knee, Maudy tucked in by his side, as they rode with the minister at the end of the procession. Uncle Wes and Aunt Gabby were up ahead with the others.

At the house, Buddy moved among the crowd, the smell of mothballs and wood smoke coming off their clothes. Mother always said how folks in the area liked a funeral; a chance to visit and tell stories. Father never had such a send-off, but there was plenty of talk about him today.

The last few days Buddy only picked at food and today his interest in it was no better. He picked up scraps of conversations and watched over his brothers and sisters, all of them turned out in their Sunday clothes but lacking the polish of their mother's touch. Pearl ironed the boys' shirts—burned herself while heating the flat iron—tucked in shirt tails, helped the little ones with their buttons, and fixed the girls' tangled hair. They tidied up the house; swept and scrubbed with some help from the neighbour ladies who came early and worked during the burial.

Ray stood in the corner, hands shoved in his overall pockets, scowling at the people. Father always said you could read his face like an open book.

"You eat anything yet?" Buddy asked him.

Ray shook his head. "No appetite. You listening to what they're saying?"

"No."

"Well I have. They're talking about who we're getting farmed out to. They're not letting us stay here."

"They can't make us leave. This is our house."

"I've been listening to Rankin, Wilkins, and Hap Finster. They're saying how Father owed them and others, too. Trades and work and money. Now they say the land gets divided up to pay off the debts, and they got folks moving in here, some of the wranglers Father used to go on drives with."

"They can't do that."

"To hell they can't." Ray stared hard at the crowd. These people who came here with their food and sad faces, expressing their sorrow, and would now take their home away from them. "How can we stop them? Especially if they say Father owed them. I don't know anything about any debt."

"There can't be debt," Buddy said. Sometimes Father talked about how he owned all this as he stood looking out over his land, eyes squinting against the sun spilling down on the earth and withering the crops, the grasshoppers and locusts flying up from the dust. "This land was given to us by the United States President. Thank you, Mr. President," he said, and then he laughed.

"From what I'm hearing, Father owed money and feed and livestock," Ray said.

"It's just talk." Sometimes Ray seemed suspicious of everyone. He had a way of looking for trouble. "How they going to get us to leave? And anyway, we've got nowhere to go. This is where we live, right here."

Ray scowled at him, shook his head and walked over to the

table, picked up a slice of bread, and came back to where Buddy stood. "You know, you ought to use your head for more than growing hair."

Uncle Wes and Aunt Gabby stayed behind after the others left.

"We've got some things need our tending the next couple of days and we'll be back out," Uncle Wes said. "Mind you say your prayers. Now your folks are gone, we don't want you turning into a bunch of heathens."

"You don't need to hurry back," Ray said, a ring of snarl in his voice. "We know how busy you are. We'll make out just fine."

Uncle Wes's hawk's eyes were crowded over by nests of bushy black brows, his jaw set square, firm and hard, and looked as if he was about to say something until Aunt Gabby hastened them away. She wanted to get home before nightfall.

"Take care of each other." Aunt Gabby kissed all the children on the cheek.

Two ranch women offered to stay the night, but Ray said no, they'd manage just fine. It was plain to see he wanted an end to the outsiders in their home. The women left behind enough food they didn't need to worry about doing any cooking for a few days.

After barn chores and a meal of leftovers, they sat together in front of the fire and the younger children began to cry. Not hurt cries—not like what happened when they stubbed a toe on a rock, or fell off a fence—but sputters flaring up like flames out of ashes. "Where's Mama?" they sobbed. Buddy, close to tears himself, nagged along by a sensation in his gut. A worry that no matter how often he assured himself things would work out, that everything would be fine, he had no proof.

"Send a child to bed, happy," Mother always said. "Take away fear to invite sweet dreams. It is the best gift we can give to anyone." Her words a precious well from which he must now draw.

"Who wants a story?" The little ones looked up, sadness drawn away from them by this sudden possibility.

"Don't get them all jumpy before bed," Pearl cautioned, sounding so much like Mother, strange from someone so young.

Buddy watched Ray muck out Misty's stall. Each day Ray's hands improved but they were still bound in rags. He scattered straw for Misty and rationed out some feed to all the horses, the supply dwindling so low they began to fear how long it would last and how they'd get more. But with warmer weather coming soon they could turn the horses to pasture.

Hazel ran into the barn in her bare feet. The weather had changed quickly to spring, as it often did this time of year, the snow from the last storm almost gone.

"How many times do I have to tell you to put on your boots?" Buddy's memory was still fresh from the time he ran to the barn to scoop sauerkraut out of the pickling barrel and stepped on a rattler. The feel of the snake on the bottom of his bare foot burned an impression he'd never forget.

"There's a bunch of folks headed here. Come and see," Hazel shouted and ran back outside.

Buddy and Ray threw down their pitchforks and rushed out into the barnyard. A group of buggies swayed down the lane. As they drew closer Buddy recognized Doc, the Rankins, Miss Skinner, Uncle Wes and Aunt Gabby, Mr. and Mrs. Upfold from town, Hap Finster, Wilkins, Dirk Howlett from the Tangle Creek General Store, Buck and Mrs. Williams—ranchers from Copper Valley, and Reverend Potter. They must have met somewhere on the road in order to arrive all at once. They were dressed in their Sunday finest, though this was a Thursday morning.

Ray stood with his hands on his hips staring hard at the approaching group, a racket of rattling harnesses and squeaking wagon wheels. "Here comes trouble, sure as hell."

"You shouldn't swear. Mother wouldn't like that." Pearl stood next to them, drawn outside by the clatter of the approaching wagons. "We'll receive them the same way Mother would and extend our hospitality." Her lip quivered when she said it. She was putting on an act, pretending to be like their mother when anyone could see she'd much rather be herself. Pearl, their mother said, had a tendency towards fussing, called her high strung and warned the others to leave her alone when she got beside herself.

The buggies clattered into the yard and the people gathered

in front of the tiny porch where all the children now stood. Ray's face scrunched against an early afternoon sun, his upper lip raised like a snarling dog.

"Good day, Ray, Buddy." Reverend Potter stepped forward and nodded to both of them, his hands sunk into his woolen suit jacket. "Is everyone well? Holding up?"

"Fine," they said.

"Well good to hear." Reverend Potter looked at the others huddled at the door, open-mouthed and wide-eyed, watching. "No trouble at all?"

"Not a bit," Ray said in a voice without any hint of an invitation for them to go inside.

Reverend Potter pointed to the visitors standing behind him. "These folks and myself are concerned about you youngsters out here on the ranch on your own. We've come to talk and to offer some help. Could we come in?"

"That'd be fine," Ray said, "but bear in mind we're not set up today for receiving visitors."

Pearl piped up then, anxiousness surfacing in her voice. "The place is a terrible mess. I try to keep it tidy but I can't keep up with it." She wrung her hands and her eyes teared.

"Don't worry, dear, we didn't come to inspect your housekeeping," Mrs. Upfold said. "We'd like to come in and sit down and speak sensibly, if we could."

Before these people came Buddy didn't notice the mess inside the house. Now he rushed in ahead of them, pushed aside stacks of dirty dishes on the table, shoved wood heaped in the middle of the floor beside the hearth, and pushed chairs and a couple of benches up closer to the table. Mrs. Rankin gathered the little ones, Sammy, Maudy, and Chuck, and herded them into the bedroom.

Maybe they came with money, Buddy thought. Sometimes in church they passed the collection plate for needy families. That would put an end to their fears about running out of animal feed, or flour, oats, and cornmeal.

"Now then," Reverend Potter began once everyone seated themselves around the table, "as stated, we're very concerned about you youngsters being out here alone without any adults to supervise. It's not right and it is fitting for us, as concerned citizens, to step in and take control."

"I'm an adult," Ray said. "I take care of them and myself, too." The visitors' eyes strayed to the dirty dishes, the pails of peel and water slop, the clothes drying on a line across the fire—which their mother wouldn't have used now that the weather had turned fair.

"Fact is, son," Doc said, "you're not an adult. And the rest of them are even younger. And this situation here won't do, with all of you left alone the way you are. How are you going to get by?"

"Other aspects need thinking through," Mr. Rankin said. "Your father owed me some horses, a trade we had in place for feed."

"Your father owed me money," Dirk Howlett, the general store owner said. "This doesn't seem the right time to collect on a debt, and I wish to God there could be another way, for this is not what I intended, but my family needs to eat, too."

Buddy used to lay in bed listening to his parents talk, unable to make out the words but understanding the tone, knowing whatever had them whispering into the night was serious. Serious enough the children shouldn't hear.

"We've strayed from the point of our visit," Reverend Potter said. "We've not come to talk about debts owed."

Ray looked relieved and Buddy waited for the collection proceeds from church to come out and be plunked in the centre of the table.

"We're here to take you all from here. We've got places for almost everyone." Reverend Potter looked at his folded hands as he spoke.

"No," Ray said, not wasting any time between Reverend Potter's declaration and his own reaction. "We're staying put. This is our home. This is where we live."

How much he sounded like Father just then, Buddy thought.

"Well, the thing is son," Mr. Rankin seated next to Ray leaned in a little closer. "Here's what everyone's pussyfooting around and needs to be stated with outright clarity. Your folks owed so much this isn't really your home anymore. There, now I've said it, cleared the slate so we can all speak the same language." Rankin eyed the others like he was looking for their approval, but they all looked stricken. "Your folks owed a lot to ranchers around here, pretty near all they had, most of the livestock, even some of the land. And what's left over isn't enough to do anything with. Now, you listen here." He stared hard at Ray then his eyes shifted over to Buddy. Hazel and Pearl were crying. "We've got spots for everyone but one."

"Who's that?" Ray asked.

"Sammy. I'm not sure what we can do with him."

Buddy's heart jolted. No place for Sammy? How could that be? Sammy with his big blue eyes, his sweet, sweet smile, and happy disposition? The cutest little fellow to ever walk the face of the earth who'd taken to Buddy from the time he was big enough to utter a sound? How could he not have a place?

"No," Buddy said, "we're not going anywhere."

"I am afraid," said Reverend Potter, "that this matter is not up for debate. While it's true what Mr. Rankin says about the debt owed, our principal concern is for your safety, and without adult supervision out here your safety is not being met. Your Uncle Wes is your guardian, since he's the next of kin, so he is the one who decides for you."

Uncle Wes nodded. Aunt Gabby dabbed her cheeks with a hanky. So far Wes kept his mouth shut on account of the Reverend being here and taking over. The Reverend spoke from a higher authority being closer to God than Wes. Even Wes knew that.

Reverend Potter continued. "Your grandfather Scott is still alive, but you know as well I do he's barely able to take care of himself and the people in the village look in on him. We all know he's not going to last much longer, God bless him. We see the wisdom in this proposal even if you can't. It's not easy, we understand, we truly do, but you can't stay here." Reverend Potter drummed his fingers on the table then drew a piece of paper out of his pocket and began to read who would take the children, assigning each child to the name of a family.

"Where will Sammy go?" Buddy asked.

"There's an orphanage two towns over up by Stone Ridge. Word is they've got spots there," Reverend Potter said.

Buddy had heard terrible stories about orphanages. How they beat you with a whip and gave you grey slop to eat, and how people said you went to those places because nobody wanted you.

"I don't know the folks you said wanted me, but I'm not going to them. Sammy can have my spot or I'll tie myself to the corral fence and I won't go. I swear to God, I will. I'll die before I go."

Silence surrounded the table. Then Wes spoke. "I suppose Buddy can stay with me. I was going to take the older one, so I suppose it won't be too much to take the next oldest, too. Sammy can have Buddy's spot."

Aunt Gabby gave Buddy a weak smile she meant as encouragement but he couldn't think what kind of hope could possibly come out of this situation.

"When do we go?" Ray's eyes settled with steeliness on Reverend Potter, his voice cocky and brash. His tone would have Mother twist his ear and tell him no one talked to Reverend Potter, God's agent on earth, in such a manner.

The adults fidgeted, hands planted in their laps or folded on the table, their eyes fixed down or somewhere across the room unwilling to look at all the Scott children seated at the table. All but Uncle Wes, whose stare journeyed down one side of the table and up the other to take in their reaction. He seemed to have the hint of a smile. Ray met his glance and stared him down, his jaw set hard as he took in each visitor who came with this horrible task, hatred in his eyes for each one of them. Ray would be thinking along the same lines as Buddy, that this whole thing was concocted to give the ranch away to greedy shysters with little concern for the well-being of the Scott children.

Father always called Ray's temper peppery, and judging by the way he always said it, Buddy knew it made him proud. "No one's going to order him around and get away with it." Then he chuckled.

How could they keep the ranch and the children, a chore that would mostly fall to Ray, Buddy, and Pearl? Pearl already looked done in by trying to take care of this brood. Underneath the anger that bubbled up inside him, Buddy sensed something of the truth coming from the folks here today.

He studied the grim faces gathered around the table. The changes that would take the family apart would be temporary—until they got a little older and could take care of themselves. One day and not too long in the future, he and Ray would bring the family back together in a home they would provide, a better home. Things would be as they were but without fear of money and food. They would find New Baby and bring him back too.

"We'll be back in two days for everyone," Reverend Potter said in a voice as solemn as if he was ending a prayer. "It will be for the better. You'll see it's for your own good," a comment he cast out to the space in the room, now filled with shafts of light coming through the windows and illuminating swirls of dust.

Reverend Potter came back with Uncle Wes and all the Scott children were rounded up, loaded into the wagons, and taken the eight miles to the church where they would be dispersed. They carried their few worldly possessions except for the furniture which got left and which, when they closed the door on the ranch a final time, appeared to be very little. All the knickknacks: rodent skeletons, fossils found out on the prairies that lined the window sills, rattles cut from snakes, family pictures, a vase belonging to grandmother Scott, silverware from grandmother Cornell (who they met only once before she died back in Iowa) all the little mementoes got divided among them. The little ones clutched their clothing rolled up into bundles. Pearl got the only suitcase as she was the oldest girl. She insisted they dress in their Sunday clothes. Buddy felt proud of his family, how they journeyed this far with tragedy such a short distance behind them, and how their parents would be proud too if only they could see them now.

And they could. He believed with all his heart they watched from somewhere, his idea of Heaven being like a ring-side seat at the rodeo. They'd be watching and they'd be cheering. Maybe there wasn't a God but there had to be a Heaven.

Two wagonloads of Scott children pulled out of the ranch, the big wheels sinking into deep pits made by the frost's heave and the unevenness of spring weather, their bodies jostling with the motion of the carts. The wagons lurched down the long windy lane and out on to the road that crossed the open prairie. Spring winds touched with the chill from distant mountains, the prairie snow mostly gone now, carried the smell of slowly warming earth—the decay of plant and animal life, the promise of new life, new crops and new creatures—all still to be born out of the land.

Sammy squirmed in Buddy's lap. Buddy rested his chin on Sammy's head and breathed in deep the smell of him. He still smelled of baby.

The ranch shrank in the distance, the grey outlines of the barn and the house merging finally with the yellow-grey sky. In the west a storm brewed and would spill itself over the land, thunder down upon it.

Buddy blinked back tears and tried to control the quiver in his chin. All the horses— Misty, Bishop, Breeze, Robin, Daisy, Soldier, and Dew, the chickens and the cow they kept for milking and butchering, were dispersed to other farms as payment for debts. Buddy and Ray walked out on the prairie while the animals were given away, too heart-broken to say goodbye, especially to the horses. Mr. Rankin arranged for the disbursement of the animals and told Ray that the proceeds, if there were any, would be put aside for the children. "But don't get your hopes up," he cautioned.

Ray tried to convince Uncle Wes to take the horses to his farm, especially Bishop, Breeze, and Misty. He said he had no use for old sway backs that couldn't earn their keep.

"They're damn fine horses," Ray said stubbornly.

"There'll be no cussing at my house and there'll be no further arguments out of you. Your father would be here today if he'd listened to me a long time ago and raised cattle and a dairy herd closer to town. Horses only brought him trouble."

Ray muttered, "Son-of-a-bitch," under his breath and it was a good thing Uncle Wes didn't hear him. If he had Buddy didn't know what might happen, but guaranteed it'd be ugly.

Chapter 6

Spread Out

A terrible day the family was divided, sent to various ranches in the area, taken in according to the type of work they'd do—the girls for housework and child care, the boys for farm work. The whole wretched business made worse somehow taking place at the church the way it did. Sammy's cries, "Bubby, Bubby," from the church door, a stranger restraining him by clamping his hands on his small shoulders as Buddy and Ray rode off in Wes's wagon.

Buddy sat in the back with Ray and hugged his legs, his chin to his chest. By the time they got to Wes's farm the wind had blown up stronger, roughed through with ice pellets. Ray's lips were blue with cold and his teeth chattered. Buddy knew coldness; he'd known it over and over again, but this was something more than the weather. It had to do with thinness inside his heart. Weak and bloodless, it felt like it wanted to quit. His anchor, his father, at times stern and distant and always in control, at others full of fun and mischief–his life's teacher, gone. His beloved mother, soft with a heart full of kindness and caring, firm when she had to be; loving, fun, the heart of a lamb—also gone. And now all the rest of his family gone too, except Ray, who sat huddled beside him as miserable and angry as anyone could be. And the ranch with all the creatures, all the horses there all his life like his family, gone too. Nothing to replace any of them.

Uncle Wes's farm appeared out of the distance, a hazy collection of cubes crowded together under a grey sky. The farm seized the landscape as they approached, and the closer they got the more Buddy's stomach kicked up a rumpus.

At the barn, Wes climbed down off the buckboard and came around to the back of the wagon. "Well, what are you waiting for? Are you expecting a brass band?" His fur hat surrounded his face like a nest. Buddy thought of the poor raccoon that sacrificed its life to keep Wes's head warm.

"Down you get. We've got horses to unhitch, then prayers. You're lucky I brought in a couple of milkers from over on Jerrod's ranch, or you'd be doing that before a morsel of food passed your lips."

"Jesus," Ray mumbled and shook his head as his eyes fell to the ground.

They followed Wes and the horses into the barn, Ray's boots dragging along the ground as they went. Wes turned around quickly. "Pick up those feet and walk smart, boy. There'll be no foot dragging around this farm, I can tell you that." It wasn't Ray's fault he had to wear Father's old boots, several sizes too large.

They worked alongside Wes, their hands slow and thick from cold, as they fumbled with the harness buckles. They fed and watered the horses then went to the house.

"It's prayer time, then supper. Now that you're both here, I don't mind telling you, you'll earn your keep. I hadn't bargained on two more mouths to feed, but there didn't seem to be much of a choice and I can always put extra hands to work. I am a man of the Lord and taking you both in is doing the Lord's service," Wes told them on their way across the yard.

"Not a man of the Lord," Ray whispered. "Thinks he's God."

Uncle Wes turned around quickly. "Did I hear someone?"

"No sir," they both said.

"Let's set something straight right now. Around here you speak when you are spoken to. And not until."

The smell of cooking drifted from the kitchen. The Johnny cakes from this morning had long since worn off and all the cold and shivering increased Buddy's appetite by several degrees.

Aunt Gabby worked at the large black stove that threw a dense, luxurious heat clear across the room.

"Welcome." She wiped her hands on her apron and approached them, placed her hands on their shoulders, and gave them a squeeze. "It's been a hard day for the two of you. Let's see if we can work on making it a little better. I hope you brought your appetites. I've made a nice supper with two hungry boys in mind. I can't make up for all the losses you've suffered, but something hot and tasty might help to ease things up. It always does for me. You can take your things upstairs to the spare room. I'll get one of the girls to show you where it is."

"Slow up there now. That won't be necessary." Wes hung his coat and hat on hooks by the door. "Leave your things right here. You'll stay in the barn, in the hired hand's quarters. He's long gone. It's comfortable enough out there."

"It's too cold for them to stay out there now. I could see it if this was summer." Aunt Gabby gathered her apron skirt in her hands, her eyes clouding over with concern.

"They can use the pot belly. There's plenty of wood."

"I don't think it's a good place for..." Some of Aunt Gabby's hair had sprung from the loose bun gathered at the back and curled on her collar bone like a wisp of smoke.

"There'll be no further argument about it. We can't have them staying in the house with the girls."

Why not? Buddy wondered. There were lots of girls at his house. There wasn't much to it; about as regular as the sun rising and setting. Aunt Gabby went back to the stove and stirred something in a large pot, the pleasantness in her face replaced by a look of weariness.

Ava and Nellie appeared at the door, whispering, their hands over their mouths as they pressed their heads together and giggled.

"The works of you, into the parlour. Time for scriptures," Uncle Wes ordered.

The parlour was without the generous warmth of the kitchen. "Take your seats." He pointed to the furniture lining the walls around an open, bare floor. Buddy sat on a settee designed for paying attention. He saw his breath in the air. Aunt Gabby entered the room and sat with her apron folded on her lap, a shawl wrapped around her shoulders. Wes stood at the far end of the room beside a high table that held a thick, worn bible, and lit a lamp which filled the room with shadows. He picked up the Bible and began to read.

Deep into the scripture, Wes aimed his vision at them over the tops of his reading spectacles, scanning his tiny congregation for signs of inattentiveness. Buddy felt the descent of a drop travel very slowly down his nostril until finally it dangled off the end of his nose and grew larger. He dared not move or it would fall, splatter conspicuously on the wood floor. He couldn't swipe it with his hand or Wes's eyes would be fast on him.

Ray squirmed beside him and coaxed a spring's croak from deep inside the horsehair stuffing.

"Silence!" Wes boomed and Buddy took advantage of the brief commotion to dispense with the drip. "Let us pray."

The prayer lasted the eternity Wes spoke of. Buddy couldn't keep his eyes shut any longer. He sneaked a peek across the room at Ava, seated opposite. She was staring at him! She crossed her eyes and stuck out her tongue, a gesture so unexpected Buddy snorted with laughter. Wes's eyes snapped open and Buddy's clamped tight, but with Ava's playfulness, fraught with danger as it was, a tiny glimmer of light entered this most wretched of days.

The prayer ended and Wes started in on what sounded like a sermon. Buddy let his eyes shift to Nellie. She flashed him a quick grin. He looked at the hole worn through the knee-patch on his pants then back up at her. She grinned again, such a quick flinch of the lips it might have been a tic like Old Man Heller's, which sometimes made his face jump around like a frog.

Ava crossed her eyes and made another funny face. Buddy choked back a laugh, made it sound like a cough.

Wes stopped his scripture reading and glared at him. "God spare us from whatever kind of pestilence you've brought into this house."

Aunt Gabby excused herself to tend to the food, and finally, after what seemed like forever and Buddy's stomach rumbling with hunger—his body chilled right through from sitting in the cold parlour for so long—they filed into the kitchen. Plates of steaming beef stew topped with dumplings sat at each place, and in the centre of the table a high stack of homemade bread surrounded by preserves and pickles. A feast the likes of which he and Ray hadn't seen for weeks, not since after Mother's funeral, and them too heartsick to eat it.

Aunt Gabby pointed to their chairs and they grabbed their spoons ready to dig into the chunks of meat and vegetables swimming around in the thick brown gravy.

"You'll wait until we say our blessings." Uncle Wes caught Ray by the wrist.

"What the devil was all that business in the parlour?" Ray

blurted and Ava and Nellie buckled with laughter.

"Be quiet!" Wes snarled and the girls went silent. His fist smashed the table. "There'll be no supper for you." He shook his finger at Ray. "You don't speak to me like that. Maybe that's how you behaved out there living like a pack of wild animals, but here, closer to town, we don't act like that. We're civilized folks." His dark eyes shot to Aunt Gabby. "And you asked me why they have to stay in the barn."

"Give him a warning. If the problem persists that's another matter, but the boy has been through a lot today and a good meal will calm him down." She held her eyes steady on Wes with a rigidness in her chin and a thinness in her lips. She meant business.

Buddy wanted to hug this new strong Aunt Gabby as much as he wanted to hug the one he already knew, the gentle one. She set her jaw hard and faced down Wes, neither smiling or frowning, just giving a long, hard stare.

"As you say." Wes released his hand from around Ray's wrist. "But that's the last warning he gets."

Wes told Ava and Nellie there'd be no talking to the boys. They were to be treated the same way they treated the farm hands. As he said this, something bashed against Buddy's shin and he winced with the sudden pain. He snuck a sideways glance at Ray, but Ray seemed entirely absorbed by the meal before him. "Yes, Father," Ava said and Buddy felt another kick.

After dinner Wes took them out to the barn. With the warmth of the kitchen still in their clothes the barn felt cold and damp. The cows stirred. Clouds of moist air puffed from their nostrils and their massive bodies threw heat. Wes had a fine herd, much admired in these parts, but nobody liked the way he'd acquired most of it. By preying on the hardship of others: waiting until their farming situation got so bad he could go in at the last minute and offer peanuts for the cows, which the starving farmer had to accept. Father spoke of his brother's methods, called him a vulture picking away at the bones. Most of the other farmers pitched in to keep each other afloat, but not Wes. Father said Wes was too busy tending his own farm, taking care of his own, to go traipsing around offering free help to those too lazy or too stupid (in his estimation) to tend to their own matters. Father said that for a man of God Wes possessed not an ounce of charity, and how it was much easier preaching God's Word than practicing it.

At the back of the barn Wes unlocked a door. The room was so dark at first they could only make out the vague outline of things, but slowly more of the room revealed itself. Wes struck a match and lit a lamp. Horse tack draped the walls and smelled of sweat, a smell they knew well. Two narrow cots stretched along opposite walls. "That's where you'll sleep. There's plenty of blankets on the bed, more over there." A stack of blankets sat on a table beside the lamp. "Blow out the lamp before you go to sleep. Kerosene costs money. There's the stove and plenty of wood beside it. Matches there on the table. The water pump's out in the yard. You'll find the outhouse out back, about fifty feet from the barn door."

"Mind you say your prayers before going to sleep. I'll be out before dawn and that's when the work day starts. It stops when the sun goes down." With that he closed the door and they followed the sound of his footsteps back up the centre of the barn.

"Son-of-a-bitch," Ray said, dropped his bundle of clothes down on the bed, and collapsed down on top of it. "There goes one ugly man."

Buddy perched on the side of his cot eyeing the unlit stove. Tiredness weighed heavy on his limbs. It was a kind of weariness he'd never known before, the weariness of carrying so much sorrow. He rose, crossed to the window, and looked back at Ray lying with his head on his bundle. His legs dangled over the bed, his arms stretched out on either side, and snoring to beat the band.

He covered Ray with a couple of scratchy wool blankets and blew out the lamp. He lingered at the window and stared out across the prairie, covered in a new skiff of snow and shined over by paper-thin ice, in the direction of his home, a home someone else had taken over. His childhood back there, now to be viewed from the distance of memory, and the faces of his mother and father, brothers and sisters, forever fading.

In the morning Wes got them up before the sun met the horizon and the air, laced with night's chill, caught their breath in clouds.

"There's work to do," he shouted as he tore off their blankets.

"What about something to eat?" Ray scratched his head and it made his hair stand on end.

"Once the chores are done."

Mother always served breakfast before chores. "You come first. The animals can wait," she said.

"Milking first," Wes headed down the rows of cows and pointed out two milking stools for them to grab. "You boys know how to milk, don't you?" They nodded. They kept cows on the ranch for milking, and at one time had as many as six. He gave them buckets, told them to get to it, and left the barn. Buddy looked down the rows of cattle and estimated there to be at least thirty. They milked until their hands ached and Ray had to stop to shake out his fingers. "They're cramping," he told Buddy.

Wes came back into the barn just then and asked him what he was doing sitting idle. Ray told him his hands hurt. "More work will soon toughen them up," he said. He eyed the cans filled with milk and said the two of them together didn't give the results of one.

Chapter 7

Poetry — August 1924

Buddy lay on his cot in the barn with his eyes wide open, his body locked in rigid tension as he waited for wind to peel the roof off the barn, flatten the walls, send the shattered wood flying like so many splinters, and the cows spinning and tumbling off into the night. Tonight, like so many others this hot August, the air hung thick and sticky as the sky wrinkled with lightning veins. Distant hills trapped the after-voice of the thunder, reducing it to low growls. At any moment a funnel could twist out of the smoky clouds and skip across the plains.

"Won't matter a tinker's damn if we do get carried away and end up on the other side of the ocean," Ray said. He meant the one close by California. "There's no one to miss us."

Buddy wouldn't argue it. Sometimes on their trips to town they saw Pearl or Maudy but Uncle Wes barely gave them time to say hello. Maudy was rescued from the farm she was shipped to; she couldn't keep up with the chores or handle the kids, turning her into just another mouth to feed—someone who couldn't pull her weight. A well-to-do woman close to town took her in and set about to civilize and educate her. Now she was all decked out in a fancy dress and gloves, a satchel snagged at her elbow, and didn't resemble the girl they knew. The girl who, along with Hazel, climbed trees, waded across creeks and rode horses, got their pinafores so dirty Mother would say she didn't know what to do with them and their tomboy natures. Her swagger seemed even more comical in her new frilly dress. The family who adopted Sammy asked her not to speak to him even though they lived fairly close. They wanted to give him a new life that would have him forget the one he came from. Buddy knew Sammy would never forget him. They were too close for Sammy to ever forget. The woman who took

Maudy in was planning a move but she didn't know where yet, but as soon as she did she'd send word to Uncle Wes's.

A light tap sounded on the window.

"Must be the girls." Ray rose from his cot and looked out. "Wonder what they've got up their sleeves so late?" The secret barn visits the girls made in the night, or when Aunt Gabby and Uncle Wes went off to church meetings, added spice to their lives and the girls' lives too.

Ray let them in through the milking parlour door.

"The storm woke us up so we thought we'd pay you a visit," Nellie said. She looked so much like Maudy sometimes Buddy couldn't stop staring. Right down to the square set in her jaw, her upright posture, and square shoulders. Built like a brick shithouse, Father said of Maudy, but not around Mother. She wore her hair the same way too: cut straight above the eyes and blunt at the chin. Uncle Wes was always trying to bring out the girly side in her, Ava, too. "We wondered if you boys would like to have a smoke with us," Nellie snickered.

Ava reached into a sweater pocket and waved a hand-rolled cigarette.

"God will strike you dead," Ray said.

"Yes, and probably tonight." Ava pointed to the window, her eyes widening at the storm's clamour. "It's headed straight for us. I'd be damned surprised if there wasn't a twister in it. We might as well have some fun before we head to our graves."

Buddy liked his cousin-friends; Ray did too. They ate Sunday dinner with the family, at Aunt Gabby's insistence, and the scrimmage of kick-tag the girls started under the table bore no resemblance to the orderliness of fine china and display of good manners above the table. Wes had no idea the slight rise of a left brow meant the girls would be visiting the barn that night, or the wide-eyed response from the boys, both brows raised high meant, not tonight, they required sleep. Wes worked them to the point of exhaustion especially during crop planting.

"Our Father's one mean son-of-a-bitch." Ava lit a cigarette and passed it to Nellie.

"Amen to that," Nellie said. "He made us scrub the kitchen floor twice tonight before bed, since Ava spilled her cider at dinner and

I laughed my ass off."

Ava rolled her eyes at her sister. Tall and thin with long wispy blond hair falling half across her face, covering one blue eye completely. At first Buddy took her for shy until he observed how she chose to stay on the edges, taking it all in. "All I can think when he's teaching us scriptures, and that's morning, noon, and night, is how I'd like to pump his skinny backside full of buckshot," Ava said.

"Be a good waste of buckshot." Nellie took a long drag, choked, and handed the smoke to Ray.

Ray pulled on it and it sparked and spit. He coughed and passed it on. "Where did you come across the tobacco?"

"Promise you won't tell?" Ava said. "We stole it from Dirk Howlett's store."

"Your father would kill you if he found out" Buddy said.

They were showing off, but it helped let off steam about their father. Across the darkness between their cots, he and Ray spoke their plain feelings about Wes, and during the day they steered clear of his nasty disposition the same way their old dog Rock steered clear of a worked up rattler.

A sudden crack of lightning shook the barn. They listened, their eyes shifting about the room as if waiting for something to happen.

"Doomsday approaches," Nellie said.

After a while Ava said, "Tell us about your family." She leaned back against the wall, her black boots dangling over the side of Ray's cot. She resembled her father in stature but that's where the resemblance ended. Wes looked like a bird of prey; she was an elegant swan and possessed not a speck of his disposition.

Buddy and Ray took turns telling stories about the family right up to the birth of New Baby, the deaths of their parents, and the family break-up. "We had bad times," Ray summed it up; "plenty of good ones, too. But that was then, and this is now. No use thinking about it. Can't change anything." Ray concentrated on rolling another cigarette between two fingers and held it up to examine it. He took a pull off the smoke and handed it to Nellie.

"What are you going to do?" Nellie inhaled then exhaled slowly, her eyes fixed on the long plume of smoke her mouth produced. "You can't stay here forever."

She was right. Who'd want to hang around here with Wes?

They'd gone over it many times, how they could hardly wait to leave here. But by the end of every day they were so tired from work they lacked the energy to even plan an escape. And if they did manage to break free, then what? Nowhere to go; no money to get there with. Not exactly a promising start to a new future.

"For your own good, you'd better be thinking about heading out. The only reason we didn't run away a long time ago is because of our mother; we can't leave her. But someday we're going to. We've got some money hidden away. And we're going to take her, too. Damn right we are!" Nellie said.

"How'd you manage to get money?" Buddy slid to the edge of his cot and stared at his cousins, not quite believing what he was hearing.

"We steal it from him." Nellie grinned and swung her feet over the side of the cot. "I'd rather work in the worst whorehouse in the whole of the United States than stay here with him."

"Me too," Ava tucked a wisp of hair behind her ear. "We came out here tonight to give you boys something." She slipped a hand into her pocket and pulled out a wad of bills which she pressed into Ray's hand.

"We can't take this." Ray's eyes fell to the roll secured with twine.

"Why not? Isn't it good enough for you?" Nellie thrust out her chin and crossed her arms over her chest.

"What are you going to use?" Ray asked.

"Don't you worry about us," Ava said. "We've got plenty more."

"You do?" Buddy asked.

"One thing about all that preaching and praying our father does, it tires him out so he sleeps like a stone, leaving us free for night raids on his savings box he hides in the parlour. We don't take too much at a time, just a little over a long period. Then we don't get caught."

Ray turned the wad in his fingertips examining it as if he expected it to burst into flames. "Tell you what. We'll stick this away in case a rainy day comes along. If we don't need it, you get it back. Deal?"

"You'll need it, all right. I guarantee it. Just think of it as a gift between cousins." Ava tromped on the cigarette, picked up the butt, and stuck it in her pocket.

A snap of lightning broke directly over the barn.

"Mom knows we come out here." Nellie watched a black spider move like a drop along a harness hanging next to Buddy's bed.

"We could tell her we steal from Father and she wouldn't stop us. She might be glad of it. The other night she caught us sneaking into the house. I thought she was going to give us the dickens, but do you know what she said?" They shook their heads. "She said that the two of you were a fine pair of boys and that we are all from the same blood. That's all she said." Nellie raised her open hands as if she'd released the words. "I think she was saying it was okay our meeting up with you. Okay with her."

Nellie landed the spider on her open palm. "You know what I can't imagine?" she seemed to say to the spider. "Our parents doing it."

"They don't do it anymore," Ava said. "It's one of the reasons he's so taken with the Lord and Jesus Christ Almighty. He's frustrated as all get out. I heard her one night, a long time ago, fighting him off, like she was getting mauled by a cougar. Right after that she moved into her own bedroom."

"That's good because thinking about him doing it to her turns my stomach. Anyways, I've got an idea." Nellie crossed the room to the door, picked up a sack she left there when she first came in, and pulled something out of it. "Wait until you hear my plan." She pulled out the needlepoint plaque that hung in the kitchen and held it up:

If all the world was just like me,
What a wonderful world this would be.

"Looking at this every mealtime puts me off my food." Nellie set the plaque on a little table shoved up by the window and pulled two small cans of paint and two brushes out of the sack. "This is going to get us into a heap of trouble," she stirred the paint, "but it'll be worth it. Everyone understand?"

They all said yes, not clear what she had in mind, but they'd go along with whatever she had up her sleeve.

She dipped a brush into the red paint and said, "There will be repercussions. Just so long as you know."

Ray went to her side to watch as she drew the paintbrush over the plaque.

"What the Sam Hill are you doing?" Ray asked.

"I'm making a few corrections," Nellie said.

She blotted out me and most of the second line. They all shared another smoke and waited for the paint to dry. She began to paint again, adding new words in white paint over top of what she'd painted over. She instructed the others to sit down and wait until she finished. "I don't want to ruin the surprise." Finally, she stepped back from the table and with the plaque in her hands, held it up for them to see:

If all the world was just like Wes
This whole world would be in a hell of a mess.

The four of them laughed, stopping sometimes to recite the new version and to congratulate Nellie on her *stroke* of genius. "You mean strokes of genius," she said, laughing. Whatever fallout was headed their way, they all agreed it would be worth it. Buddy regretted they wouldn't be in the house when Wes discovered the alteration but the girls promised a faithful report.

Chapter 8

Predictable Fallout

The next morning Wes showed up at milking and gave his usual assessment of their work. He commented on their slowness, made them aware of their worthlessness and how he did them a favour by allowing them to milk his cows. He was more generous with his criticisms today. Buddy knew why.

After milking, he told them they'd go directly to weeding in the fields and skip breakfast.

"You'll work faster, more efficient on an empty stomach," he said, a glint in his hawkish eyes. A twitch at the corner of his mouth showed how much he enjoyed this. "When you're done, come back for the evening milking."

They worked all day in the fields, taking turns to keep watch for Wes while the other rested, then around dusk went back to the barn to milk the cows. Exhausted, they limped back into their room and found sacks of pickled pork sandwiches and spice cake hidden under their pillows, the handiwork of Aunt Gabby and the girls. Ray read aloud a note attached to his sack. "Uncle Wes isn't too happy today boys."

Wes came out later as they lay sprawled on their cots, exhausted from the day's work and full of Aunt Gabby's food. From the doorway he asked what they thought they had to say for themselves.

"I'm hungry," Buddy said, his stomach full to bursting.

"Me too," Ray piped up. "My stomach's rumbling so loud I went to the window to see when the storm might hit."

What a whopper that was, the sun streaming through the window even now as it prepared to set.

"I think you know why you've not been granted food today." Wes's glance skirted from one cot to the other. "I want both of you to follow me out into the barn, and there'll be no foot dragging, I can tell you." As they filed out behind Wes, Buddy exchanged glances with Ray. What kind of punishment did the evil bugger have in store for them now; dusting the barn rafters?

"Stand right there," he instructed and disappeared into the tack room.

The cows seemed somewhat curious and mildly bored as they chewed their hay.

Wes reappeared carrying a horsewhip. "Now I've got a surprise for you, since you boys seem to have an aptitude for surprises." He brought the whip down lightly across his open palm. "The devil's work has been going on around here and I won't have it. The girls have told me they did it, but I know they're covering up for the pair of you. That's the kind of girls I've raised—Christian and generous, willing to take the blame to save others from punishment. They're not capable of the kind of disrespect that got played out in my house, right under my nose." He wound the long whip around his right hand. "I'll not be made a fool by the likes of you, a pair of unChristian, ungrateful heathens. I'll start with the oldest. Wes stepped in front of Ray, eyes beating down under a nest of dark brows. "Take off your shirt."

Ray looked Wes hard in the eye but didn't move; not so much as a muscle twitch.

"You heard what I said, boy. Take off your shirt or I'll tear it off you."

Buddy's gut twisted with nervousness. Ray started to unbutton his shirt, his defiant eyes riveted on Wes, taking his own sweet time with each button.

"I don't have all day, boy," Wes said. "Take off your shirt and turn around with your back to me. Walk straight ahead to the wall and put your hands up on it."

Ray turned slowly and as he did he raised his eyebrows to Buddy in a way that said he'd outlast this mean son-of-a-bitch, just watch him.

Wes raised the whip and thrust his arm forward to let it unfurl over Ray's back. Ray winced but uttered not a peep. Buddy counted ten lashes then stopped, concentrating instead on controlling an urge to scream, an urge to charge Wes and grab the whip from his hands. Ray's silent defiance ignited Wes even more and seemed to shout *no matter how hard you try you can't break me*; it would take more of a man to do that. Finally the crack of the whip and Wes's grunts of exertion stopped. Ray dragged his hands slowly down the wall and lowered them to his sides.

"Put your shirt back on and go to your room," Wes ordered.

Ray stepped away from the wall and stood before Wes and looked him hard in the eye, his jaw set with anger. "It's too bad God's work is so messy. He must be an awful tough boss."

"You mocking me?"

"No, sir. I'm just making an assessment about your employer." Ray took his shirt from where it hung on a nail.

Buddy waited for him to crack the whip at Ray again, but he didn't. "Your turn," he said to Buddy. "Get the shirt off and get over there where your brother stood."

Buddy wanted to shout how even the devil wasn't as nasty as him and how he wasn't fit to be in the same room with them. Instead he held his tongue, removed his shirt, and put his hands up on the wall the same way Ray had. He'd be just as strong, just as tough as Ray. He'd do it for Father, too. Not a peep came out of Ray and not a peep would come out of him. He wouldn't give Wes the satisfaction of making him think he'd broken him.

The whip seared his back, laid down strips of heat one piled atop the other: the first ones burning embers beneath the last leaping flames. He bit his tongue hard, the way Doc had him do when he got treated once for a snake bite, so he wouldn't scream out. If he didn't cry for a snake he sure as hell wasn't going to cry over this serpent. He stared at a knot in the barn wood as hard as he'd ever stared at anything, going deep inside it, a black hole into which he buried his pain. If his father were alive he'd half kill Wes for laying a hand on one of his boys, never mind whipping them like a couple of animals.

That night as Buddy lay on his stomach, searing stings crossed his back with every breath and every muscle twitch. Across the room Ray lay on his cot. The dried blood in his wounds made his back look covered in stripes like a zebra's.

Ray found a note under his pillow. "It's from Ava," he said.

Dear Cousins:

This is how Wes the Mess looked when he saw the plaque. Take one large very ripe tomato. Place it in the sun on a 100 degree day. Watch it get redder and redder and redder. It will rot and ferment inside its skin and then it will explode! That's how Wes the Mess looked!

His face exploded! He stomped all around the kitchen, ranting and raving!

Mother and Nellie and I were a little frightened, but it was okay. He blamed you boys right away. Then Nellie stepped up and said she did it, and he refused to believe her. So I said I did it and he wouldn't believe me either. He said it was just like us, two good Christian girls, to try to take the blame for something we didn't do. And then Nellie said the most amazing thing. She said that was the biggest load of horse shit she'd ever heard and that he was nothing but a damn fool. Mother hustled us to our room straightaway. I think she was afraid he might hurt us, though I don't think he would have. He said you two must have taught Nellie to talk like that, since we were pure before you came. We sat at the top of the stairs and listened to him carry on so you'd think he had a bunch of bees shoved right up his arse, or that he'd fallen into a patch of stinging nettles bare naked. But I tell you, Nellie and I found a lot of fun in his performance. It was all we could do to control our laughter. We know you got an awful whipping, and we're real sorry for that. But if it makes you feel any better, he sure looked like a right idiot.

Signed: The night marauders N and A (partners in crime and paint and poetry)

After he read the letter, Ray lay quietly, the letter beside him. He seemed far away.

In a while Buddy asked, "Any idea what we're going to do?" He'd a notion the worst was still in store for them.

"Don't know." Ray stared straight up to the ceiling, then he slowly rose from his bed, careful not to reopen his wounds, and went to the window.

He wouldn't be seeing anything; he was too busy thinking something through and might as well be a million miles away from here. As far away as it was possible to get in his imagination and still be trapped here.

The next morning Wes ripped off their blankets earlier than usual and shouted for them to get up.

"You've obviously got too much idle time on your hands, and I know the cure." With his thumbs hooked around his suspender straps didn't he just look right pleased with himself? "I'm going to give you the opportunity to express your artistic side; I want the old paint scraped off the side of the barn before you start your regular chores. I want two hours of scraping, then you can go in for breakfast, and after that the milking."

Outside it was still pitch-black. How could they see to scrape off old paint?

Wes seemed to know what Buddy was thinking as he stared at the window. "Don't you worry; I'm happy to provide a lantern."

They scraped old paint until dawn pinked the sky then went inside for breakfast.

Aunt Gabby was at the stove, shoving in pieces of wood to keep the heat going for something she was baking.

"Your Uncle Wes is going into town late this afternoon. I want you boys to come see me then. I'll take a look at you, rub you down with ointment." She seemed sad, or maybe just tired, or both. "I know something your uncle doesn't—kids get up to mischief and it's not all bad. And I know something else too, that it wasn't all your doing. Girls get up to high jinks just as readily as boys do. I was young once. Uncle Wes is going to work you harder from here on. It's going to take a while for him to get over the plaque business." She studied them with her sad eyes and shook her head. "The two of you look as haggard as a pair of old-timers."

They tied into their porridge as if they might find buried treasure hidden at the bottom of the bowl, grabbed some bread, and slathered on a thick layer of freshly churned butter.

"Well, your wounds haven't dampened your appetites any, I can see that." Aunt Gabby stood by the table with two packets in her hands. Upstairs, they heard Uncle Wes stomping about.

"You boys mind yourselves."

Wes's footsteps pounded on the stairs.

"He's planning on working you through lunch." She handed each of them a packet. "Take this; stick them in your overalls. It's food for when you're out in the fields." She rushed back to the stove and appeared to have been there all along by the time Wes appeared in the kitchen.

"The girls are confined to their rooms again today," he said, "as punishment for trying to take the blame for what you two did. It's noble of them, but it's still dishonest, and dishonesty seeks punishment."

After breakfast Buddy and Ray got to work on their milking chores and were mostly done by the time Wes came out to the barn. He loomed behind Buddy's stool and looked down into his bucket. "You taking a holiday today, boy?"

In truth, Buddy worked harder and with better results this morning than usual, despite the hot pain across his back as he bent, reopening his wounds. Wes would find fault in everything they did; it didn't take a genius to figure it.

Wes went around to Ray. Ray never did get the hang of milking and didn't take to it like Buddy. Father said Ray didn't have the hands for it, but not to mind; those hands, short and slender would come in handy for something, just not milking. "Means he's got a little pecker," Buddy blurted and Father cuffed him. "It'll be all you can do to keep track of your own hands and pecker, Buddy my boy, never mind commenting on your brother's."

"You don't put any effort into it," Wes said, stalking Ray from behind. "You're practically asleep sitting there. Move your arms, get higher up on the teat." He watched as Ray stepped up his efforts to put more strength into his strokes.

"Faster, I said. You're lazy, that's your problem."

"I'm not lazy," Ray said. "And even if I was, I'd never get a chance to prove it around here!"

"Why you...you giving me back-talk, boy? Is that what I am hearing?" Wes shouted.

"No, I'm not giving you anything. I am paying for everything I'm doing for you and I'm telling the plain damn truth. And while I'm being honest, I'll tell you I'd like to see you do half of what I do around here in a day. So far, all I see is you criticizing and beyond that I don't see you do much of anything, except for praising the Lord."

If Ray didn't get him about as provoked as he could be up until then, this time he really managed it.

Wes froze, turned white, as if all the blood drained from his body, and Buddy thought of the story in the Bible where someone peeks when they're not supposed to and they turn to salt. Wes had turned to salt, then he kind of woke up and charged into action, taking long angry steps to the tack room and Buddy knew why.

Ray rose from his milk stool and stood beside the big cow which craned its neck to see what was going on behind it, its jaws sliding.

"You'll step over here right now," Uncle Wes pointed to where he stood. Wes never went too close to the cows. He seemed to be afraid of them.

"I'm not going anywhere. You want me, you come and get me." Ray said this so calmly he sounded like he rehearsed it all night.

Wes stepped forward and yanked Ray away from the cow and pulled him towards the centre of the barn.

"Let him go," Buddy shouted, his voice strong and forceful. "Get your goddamn ugly paws off my brother."

Wes glared at Buddy, his face burning like a prairie grass fire.

"I'll do him and then I'm coming after you," he pointed at Buddy, his hawk-eyes blazing.

"You think so?" Buddy asked him, not quite believing he managed to get the words out and so convincing, too, even though he shook on the inside and his knees were ready to buckle.

"I know so." Wes raised his arm, the whip clenched tight in his hand ready to bring it down on Ray, not even caring, by the looks of him, where he struck. So violent was his hatred for this person who dared to make fun of him.

No one raises a hand to my boys. Buddy grabbed the milk pail by the handle and rushed towards him before he had a chance to strike Ray. He heaved the contents at Wes, splashing him full in the face. For a moment all three froze in disbelief, then Buddy knew he had to act fast. Once Wes's temper took hold, Buddy would be buried alive in trouble. Buddy heaved the empty bucket across the barn and he and Ray high-tailed it out of there, ran across the yard, and down the drive towards the road at full tilt.

Buddy glanced back over his shoulder to see how close Wes was to them, see how much ground he gained on them, but Wes lagged far behind. Ava and Nellie stood in their bedroom windows, waving. In his pocket, the bundle of money slapped against his thigh. The rainy day Nellie and Ava predicted had come.

Book Two

Under the Tree — June 1973

What was that sound? A gunshot? No. He'd been dreaming; or had he? Memories pouring in thick as fog. The sound must be Carolyn coming for him. Finally.

He raised his head to try to see but pain stopped him. He wiggled his fingers on his left hand. They felt thick and swollen. He couldn't move his left leg, not a fraction of an inch. Now both legs no longer felt connected to his body.

The heaviness in his chest had increased and even the shallowest breaths pained.

He had to piss. Badly. He could hold it a little longer but eventually he would have to figure something out. It was too much to think about now.

He listened for her voice or the voices of others, the help she would bring. The wind whooshed through the trees, stirring them up into a dance, and retreating—like breathing. The sky was darker. Was this nightfall or was a storm coming? He heard it again. Thunder. Approaching from somewhere in the distance, probably out over the lake. He raised his head to look for Spirit; he might have gone back to the stable, but there he stood as before. Close to the bushes, shifting, but not moving, the white diamond between his eyes glowing like a marker in the fading light.

How much time had passed? Was this even the same day? He left his watch on the dresser; he never wore it. *It's a lovely watch, you should wear it. It represents something for you to be proud of.* That was Meg's take. If you called slaving for a company for over thirty years with nothing more than a watch at the end to show for it something to be proud of. Precisely why he didn't wear it. He didn't want to be reminded of the dairy, and in particular Jack Bodeli, his manager. Jack

Ass everyone called him because he was such an idiot; an arrogant green upstart full of himself. Even thinking about him made his heart rate increase, snatched his breath away, and sent stabs deep into his chest. The mention of the guy's name got him going every single time and sent him right back to that Friday afternoon after he'd punched out, when Jack called him into his tidy office for a consult—Jack's words—and told him to sit down. He hummed and hawed, whacked his pad of paper with the end of his pen, and asked Buddy how long he'd been with Greenfield Dairies. Then, without listening to his answer, told Buddy he was being pulled off the milk route and that he should look on the bright side: he wouldn't have to haul around milk crates all day, and everyone around the dairy noticed how much trouble he was having with his breathing, and he wasn't getting any younger. Buddy thought it was no one's business how he breathed. Being a route milkman was in his blood he'd been doing it for so long. For Christ sakes, when he started it was a horse and wagon—old Molly! Beautiful horse, as gentle as Misty. Buddy wanted to shout at him that he had more life experience in his little finger than Jack had, or would ever have, in his entire being. But instead he spun his route cap in his hands watching his name, written in gold letters above the shiny black visor, blur by.

Maybe it was a good thing he'd had a few drinks with Ernie, the last customer on his route, that day. Maybe that helped soften the blow. Stopped him from jumping up and trimming Bodeli's clock.

He told Jack he'd worked in a garage before. He was about to tell him a man by the name of Mr. Henry Ford owned that garage—had Jack heard of him?— when Jack got up from behind his desk and closed the Venetian blinds. He didn't show any interest, and Buddy thought to hell with him. He wasn't going to bother to tell him who he worked for. There were bigger fish than Jack Bodeli, that was for bloody sure.

Another round of thunder boomed much closer.

What was that girl's name Doug brought home from university? Why would he think of her now? Pain scrambled his thoughts, sent him off in one direction, then another. Now it was imperative he remember her name. It would drive him crazy if he couldn't. Alice? Nancy? Mabel. That was unlikely. But it was something short and familiar. Surprisingly so, since she was an exotic creature, in her own way.

Linda! That was it. Linda. He liked her from the moment they first met. She stepped down off the Greyhound Bus during a snowstorm, the night she and Doug rode in from Winnipeg when they came home for slack week. If you asked Buddy the whole university experience seemed pretty slack. Doug would be around twenty. Was he with Linda now? He can't remember. He hoped so; he'd ask Meg when he got home. She'd said something about Linda the other day but he wasn't paying attention, or he blocked out what she was saying. Meg didn't like Linda—too much of a hippie for Meg. But Buddy saw beyond that, saw her for who she really was.

She had one of those wide-open smiles, straight perfect teeth, and seemed to wear her heart on her sleeve. Very frank, very honest, very direct. He didn't mind she said fuck a lot, but he was glad she toned it down for Meg. She acted like nothing could faze her. A flower child for sure. She probably didn't shave her armpits, but he was only guessing since she never took off the plaid men's work shirt she wore the whole weekend.

Buddy lifted his head to speak to the horse. "We raised hell that night." Spirit's ears twitched with the strength of the wind. "I was feeling some kind of frisky; don't know what got into me." Well, actually he did. The joint of Jamaican Linda produced when they were down in the basement. It went well with the Crown Royal. Everyone else had gone to bed. David and Rhonda went off with the baby—she'd be up early and like good parents they modified their lives. Doug had checked out, said he had some studying to do. Said he'd heard the stories so many times before he thought he might have lived them himself—that was an exaggeration— and Carolyn was out with Lenny since they were tied at the hip. Meg was in bed, had given up listening to his stories a long time ago. Donnie, of course, was at the apartment he shared with buddies. So that left him and Linda. They went to the basement so as not to disturb the rest of the house. That was partly true. They did have the wacky tobacky to hide. Linda warned him it would *blow his fuckin' head off man* and it was much stronger than anything he'd tried before back in his Detroit days. And the Crown Royal went down as smooth as it always did.

Linda looked so pretty sitting on the floor. *Could I touch your hair?* Like silk, shiny and smooth and glowing chestnut red under the bare bulb dangling from the rafters.

Sure, man. Big smile.

He stroked it lightly. Long, parted down the middle; so beautiful to touch. He even thought about kissing her, an innocent kiss on her freckled cheek; how soft her skin would feel.

You're cool, Buddy. Linda sat on a mat on the basement floor, her skirt wrapped around her bare feet, arms encircling her knees. A ragged line of salt traced the skirt's hem from where it dragged in slush. He invited her to sit down in the chair beside his, but no, she liked the floor better. She was a hippie. They plunked themselves down anywhere; they didn't seem to need furniture.

Tell me another story. Her eyes partly closed and red from the weed.

The night before, while they were sitting by themselves in the living room, he told her *The Night of the Storm* and *Fetching Mr. Rankin*, and *Father Dying* stories. Meg said she had kitchen work to do, and anyway she could recite the stories chapter and verse.

Linda was such a good listener, though at one point she appeared to have fallen asleep. Didn't matter, he kept talking anyway; she could be listening with her eyes closed. Who knew? It was really good weed and nothing was going to stop him.

He told her about going for Mrs. Rankin for Mother and about what happened after. How one part of his life ended and another started with a terrible sadness that stayed locked in his heart forever. He told her about being farmed to Wes's, that miserable Bible-thumping mean excuse of a human being, and *The Bucket of Milk* story. And at the end of it she insisted he tell her more, sat up and rolled another joint, even though it was in the wee small hours of the morning. He shouldn't—he'd pay the price the next day—but the Crown Royal was going down smooth and he had an audience. The pot made his memories more vivid and after so many years of remembering on his own, he thought, what the hell.

Chapter 9

On the Run — August 1924

They ran until Uncle Wes shrank from a man chasing them to a stick figure waving a fist in the air against a vast blue sky, to a speck the size of an ant, until they couldn't see him at all. Still they kept running.

They ran for hours in the heat, the thick gummy air paining their lungs, until their feet burned and their legs could no longer hold out. They collapsed on the dusty grass of a sloping creek bed, blurting out pieces of the story between gasps and explosions of laughter.

"Did you see the look on his face?"

"He had milk in his eyebrows."

"He was covered in it."

"It dripped off the end of his nose."

"All I could see was two beady little hawk eyes."

"His face was so red it heated up the milk!"

"To boiling!"

"The look on his face turned the milk sour! Sour puss!"

"I bet he shit his pants!"

They laughed and panted, wiping the sweat off their foreheads with the backs of their hands. Their fear about what they'd done was erased by distance and the triumph of escape. They couldn't let the story go. They told it over and over, each time finding a new detail, an observation, their rehashing of the escape payment for the weeks of misery and hard labour. Every whip lash was worth it! It bought their freedom!

"He didn't know what the hell happened."

"I saw milk running out of his nose!"

"He had milk in his ears!"

Buddy could hardly believe what he'd done. "I wasn't going to stand by and watch that son-of-a-bitch whip you again. I heard Father speak. I heard him as plain as I am hearing you. I heard it like he was standing right beside me."

"You believe that? That he spoke to you?" Ray asked.

"Yes."

"You've been working too hard. You've gone batty like old Mrs. Carswell." Ray sat cross-legged and rolled a pebble in his hand, his face streaked with dust and sweat, his hair dripping and whipped like cream.

He had heard Father's voice—*No one raises a hand to my boys*—in the split second before he launched at his uncle with a full bucket of milk. He flew into action without a moment's thought as soon as Father spoke. Mrs. Carswell was one hundred years old and her dead husband Orvil's voice had been coming to her from out of the woodpile for years. The way she sat in her rocking chair jabbering at the logs, everyone knew she wasn't all there. Hearing Father's voice was something completely different. He spoke from Heaven to save their lives.

Ray chewed on the end of a long piece of grass, his head tipped back to the sky, his face no longer pinched with brooding anger—his constant expression of these last months. His chuckle started up again and turned into full-blown laughter. Buddy joined in.

"He wanted to cuss, I know he did. His special arrangement with God wouldn't permit it. Serves him right!" Ray slapped his knee and laughed.

What a terrible thrashing he'd give them if he could wrap his hands around their scrawny necks. "I hope we gave the bastard a heart attack. Beatin' up on kids. It would serve him right." Buddy faced the direction from which they came and tried to assess the distance. "How far do you think we got?"

"Ten miles, maybe more."

"We need to get moving," Ray said. "In case he comes looking for us. He can ride faster than we can run. A few more minutes and then we'll go. But first, I'm going into the water to cool myself down." He whipped off his clothes and waded into the creek.

The idea of Wes suddenly appearing, tracking them down, made Buddy think they'd better get, and quick. But where to? They planned their journey to the point of knowing they must leave and go somewhere far away in the opposite direction of where they came from but that's as far as they got.

Buddy stripped off his overalls, waded into the creek, and stretched back to let the water cool his head and take the sting out of the lashes on his back. Though the sun beat down hard and the water was warm, a shiver went through him at the thought of Aunt Gabby, Ava, and Nellie alone with Wes. They would meet again; he would see to it.

"This feels good now, but it won't if he finds us here," Ray said. "We better not stay too long." They dried off in the sun and dipped their shirts into the creek to bring some lasting relief.

As they trudged on Ray said, "I always wanted to go to New York City. Everybody's rich there." He pointed off in the distance. "That's where it is." He stared hard across the plains as if he might actually see the tall buildings of New York, though they'd only ever heard stories about them.

"How'd you know that's where it is?"

"It's in the east. Mother said that's where her people came from before they went to Iowa and then Wyoming."

"Yeah, but how do you know that's east?"

"That's where the sun comes up. The sun rises in the east, sets in the west. Jesus, Buddy. Didn't you pay any attention to Miss Skinner, the teacher?"

So what if he didn't? The sun would rise and set just the same whether he knew the direction or not. "How come we don't go west?"

"It's too close to Wes. If we get to the ocean there'll be nowhere to hide, we'll have painted ourselves into a corner."

That sounded about right. Ray had thought it all through and he knew a lot more about this country than Buddy, so he'd go along with it. What did it matter anyway? East, west, they had nowhere to go in either direction—all they could do was pick one. What about south or north?

Buddy put some run into his step to catch up with Ray so he could ask him.

"South's too hot. North's too cold, and nothing but wilderness filled with bears that will eat you," Ray said.

What choices did they have then? Too hot, too cold and wild, too close to Wes, or where everyone had money. No choice when he thought it through.

The sun burned down on his shoulders until he thought he could fry eggs on them.

"What's in New York City?" Buddy asked.

"Everything you can imagine. Fancy food, motor vehicles, houses, clothes, and candy. Everybody's got a job. There's so much money, it's like picking fruit off a tree."

Buddy's imagination lingered at the food part. Ever since his stomach started kicking up a rumpus and he had to concentrate on not thinking about his hunger or food.

They plodded along for miles repeating the story often to remind them of the danger of slowing down. Their thoughts formed around something solid, an event gone by safe in its history, and it kept them from thinking of the uncertain topic of where they might be headed. They were certain their mother would tell them how she was proud of them for standing up to the bully Wes; congratulate them for their bravery. They lingered there imagining her praise.

Their boots kicked up dust so fine Buddy tasted it and made him think of the times he had a fever.

Less often now they jumped back into the story and laughed all over again.

"The cows gave us more milk this morning because they knew what was coming. Here boys, those cows were thinking. Clobber him for us, while you're at it," Ray laughed.

When they couldn't find one more undiscovered detail, Ray said, "I'm proud of you Buddy."

A tingly sensation rippled through Buddy's body. He couldn't help smiling. "Someone had to do it." He sounded so brave.

Night fell and hunger and fatigue sapped their strength, their story no longer pumping them full of courage. Two lost boys roaming alone on the prairies beneath a darkening sky with little to eat and nowhere to go.

"We've got to stop for the night," Ray said. "My feet hurt so bad I feel like I'm walking on hot coals."

Nightfall would bring dew and the temperature would drop.

With nothing but the clothes they wore they had to find somewhere to shelter. Off in the distance Buddy spotted something, but in the faint light of a sinking sun he couldn't make it out.

"Maybe it's a barn," Ray said, "or some kind of outbuilding where no one will find us."

They headed towards it steering clear of rattlers shaking their warnings but as they got closer, and through the thickness of dusk, they saw it was a haystack. They scooped out hollows to make chairs in the stack and settled in, the warmth of the afternoon sun coming out of the hay and into their backs.

"This here's what I've been waiting for all day." Buddy pulled the packet of food Aunt Gabby gave them from inside his overalls and untied the twine from around the thick brown paper. In the faint light he saw splotches of grease, held the paper up to his nose and inhaled thoughts of Aunt Gabby, her warm kitchen, and her cooking.

"I'm saving some of mine," Ray said and took a bite of his thick pork sandwich. "We don't know what will happen tomorrow. We might not see food all day."

Buddy would ration his too though it tasted delicious. He could easily devour it and a whole lot more. He stretched out in the hay and chewed, gazed up into the sky, dimming into the night world.

Buddy broke off a chunk of cheese, warm and greasy from pressing into his chest all day, and savoured the taste as it melted on his tongue. Supper tasted of freedom: every bite swallowed in the open air, the expanse of sky, the soft blanket of a summer's night, the music of night hawks and crickets, and the graceful swoops of swallows around the haystack.

He wrapped up the remainder of his food. They hadn't seen a solitary soul this long day, not even in the distance. And tomorrow who knew where they would find food or drink, or even if they would. He was too done in to worry about it now. He rubbed his lips together spreading oil from the cheese over the cracks.

They lay back in the hay speaking infrequently in exhausted fragments and assessing the events of the day in voices weak with fatigue.

Light faded slowly out of the sky. Buddy couldn't remember when he felt so relaxed. And safe. Even though he had no home.

He could wake up without a nervous gut and wondering what Wes had in store for them. Good enough to do his slaving; not good enough to be near his family. Little better than trash.

Stars, hesitant specks, grew brighter as night deepened. Occasionally, one would let go and fly across the sky dragging a tail.

Beside him Ray breathed lightly, already asleep. Buddy looked up at the sky and thought about his family. He listed them in order of age to make them feel nearer and bring him comfort. Sometimes at night when he lay in bed, he thought about each one in an effort to hold on to their fading memories. His mother's soft, thick hair caught at the nape of her neck, fastened with a ribbon or loosely wound and pinned. Her smoky eyes and steady gaze as she listened to one of her children, a patient listener with the hint of a smile on her lips. The way she turned ragged clothing into something that looked like new and made you feel wonderful when you put it on— as if it had been store-bought. The magic of her fingers, the caress of her hand on his head, and her soft voice, "Buddy you're such a good boy. An excellent storyteller. I'm proud of you. Don't you ever forget." He put his arms around her waist and hugged her, took in her smell and her warmth.

And Father. Could fix anything, knew everything, and provided for them no matter how harsh the weather or how severe the drought or insects. The way he rode along on a horse humming or whistling, singing his ditties. He'd never again hear that voice coaching him—teaching him. All gone, his brothers and sisters too. Except Ray sleeping beside him now. All that was left.

The sky bloomed like a magical garden, filling with the glitter of stars. He saw a cluster, dense and bright, and decided that was his family. The strong ones near the centre, his parents, the dimmer ones surrounding them, his brothers and sisters. The Scott Constellation. And himself and Ray in it, too. All of them together dazzling and bright. Whenever he felt alone or lost he'd look up into the sky and find his family. That's what he would do. He made a promise to himself.

A trail of slime crossed Buddy's cheek. He opened his eyes into the sun, so strong it blackened a square object close to his face. He wiped moisture off his skin with the back of his hand and shielded his eyes. "What the Sam hell!"

A cow stared down on him, its nostrils, moist, pink, and flared: jaws sliding on a wad of straw. A coarse tongue slipped out and took another swipe at Buddy's face.

Wouldn't he be just like a cow lollypop with the salt from yesterday's sweat still on his skin? Ahead of him a forest of legs. Tails flicked and dispersed flies into the air like black water droplets.

Beyond the restless shifting and the huff and snort of cattle, someone shouted. A man rode up on a horse, stopped in front of them, and crossed both arms over the saddle horn.

"What have we got here?" He leaned forward and pushed his hat back off his forehead. "A couple of scare crows fallen from their perches?"

Ray stirred, groaned, then fell back to sleep. Buddy gave him a poke in the ribs. "Wake up!"

Buddy pulled himself out of the haystack and brushed off his overalls. Ray moaned louder as he opened his eyes.

"What are you boys up to?" the man on the horse asked.

"Having a nap," Buddy said.

"I imagine I can see that. Did you find the hay comfortable?"

"Yup."

"Where you headed?"

"East," Buddy said. He looked around at the spill of prairie and pointed in the direction they went in yesterday. Across the burnt yellow fields opposite from the direction of Wes's place. "There. That's where we're headed."

"Where's your folks?"

"We don't have any." Up until now he'd never had to be so blunt.

"Everyone's got parents. It's hard getting born without them." The cowboy had a wide smile with white teeth and skin that crinkled up around his eyes.

"They're dead." Ray sounded as flat as the prairies.

The man's horse reared its head back, jostled by the restless cattle surrounding it. "Sorry to hear." He touched the brim of his hat, a gesture adults made which was meant to show respect. "How'd it happen?"

"Disease."

If Ray could whittle his explanation down further he would. He stood up, shook himself off, ran his hands through his hair—which looked much like the stuff they'd slept in—and thrust his hands into his pockets.

A couple of ranch hands rode up beside the cowboy and looked at the boys but didn't say anything.

"Typhoid Fever?" the cowboy asked.

"Yup." Ray lobbed a huge gob off to the side. It was plain he wasn't offering any details. Father always said Ray never cottoned well to strangers and he was born with a suspicious nature, while Buddy would talk to just about anyone.

"We're on our way to New York City," Buddy said. "We're going to visit our relatives there. They're rich. They're waiting for us." Buddy felt better telling the stranger the story; he convinced himself it might be true.

"That so?" the cowboy asked.

"Our relatives own a factory," Ray said.

Buddy didn't expect Ray to add to the tale but he was glad he joined in. It made Buddy feel even stronger, more convincing.

"Well now, what kind of factory might that be?"

"They make..." Ray looked across the land as if searching for something to rise up out of the flatness and fill in the blank of the question.

"Barrels." Buddy jumped in with an answer before the cowboy could sniff a lie. "Great big barrels for shipping things in, especially sauerkraut. Pickles sometimes, too. Stuff like that."

"It's a wonder those rich folks didn't send you money for your trip." The cowboy screwed up his mouth as if he was mulling something over. His big rough hands showed he was no stranger to ranch work.

"They did. I'll show you, I've got a big wad of it here in my pocket, if you want proof." Ray rummaged in his pocket and pulled out the wad of bills Ava and Nellie gave them and which Buddy had passed on to him yesterday for safe keeping.

"Here's some advice, son. Don't go waving your money around in front of folks you don't know." The cowboy rubbed his chin. "Tell you what boys, why don't you hop on the horses," he motioned to the ranch hands, "and we'll take you up to the house for breakfast. I mean, if I'm running a hotel here," he motioned to the haystack, "providing overnight lodging, breakfast should come with it. Don't you think?"

"Sure," Buddy said, quick on the uptake with Ray accepting

right after.

On top of the horses, tucked in behind the cowhands, they glimpsed the biggest herd of cattle Buddy had ever seen. Everywhere a restless sea of brown. Buddy craned his neck. In the distance, probably a quarter mile away, a number of buildings hunched against the vast sky.

At the ranch house, the hands led the horses away and Buddy and Ray followed the cowboy up the wide front porch steps and entered into a world of gleaming wood floors, red carpets, shiny furniture, and gold lamps with electric bulbs. Across a broad vestibule, a staircase with a window at the turn rose up. Buddy breathed in the smell of linseed and lemons, the smell of scrubbing and polishing.

"Come with me." The rancher hooked his hat on a fancy hanger and led them through a dining room with the biggest table Buddy had ever seen. He counted twelve chairs around it. Above the centre of the table a light dangled like a huge shiny spider.

In the kitchen, a black woman studied them as if they were something the cat had dragged in. The cowboy drew her aside and spoke to her in a voice too low for them to hear. She smiled and kept up her stare as she nodded then wiped her hands on her apron.

"I know just what to do with these boys, Mr. Oliver."

Mr. Oliver stood with his hat in hand and wore a constant smile. "Oh I'm sure you do," he said.

"You boys go on over there and clean yourselves off." The black woman said and pointed across the room to a washbasin in a sink with taps. "I'll get some towels. You can eat first, then after we'll see you get a proper scrubbing down."

Another woman, pretty and young looking, came into the kitchen. She gave the boys the once-over, then the cowboy spoke to her so they couldn't hear. "Yes, yes," she said, all the time watching as they scrubbed all the way up to their elbows and gave their faces a good wash. As she walked over to them her peacock blue dress made a ruffling sound.

"Oliver tells me you boys are on your way to New York City. I hope you found our haystack comfortable." Two dimples drilled deep into her cheeks.

"Yes ma'am." Buddy ran a towel over his face then handed it to

Ray.

"Well how about we get you something to eat." She turned to speak to the black woman.

"After breakfast Coral, I think a bath might be in order. Looks like they could both do with a good scrubbing."

"I'd have to agree with that, Mrs. Lydia." Coral cracked eggs into a large bowl and beat them with such ferocity her whole backside jiggled.

"My husband's got some old clothes that look newer than yours. I think he'll agree to retire them to your young bodies, won't you Oliver?"

The cowboy chuckled, said it would be his pleasure. "You boys eat, get cleaned up, and put on your new duds, and I'll show you around the ranch." He was headed outside and would come back for them after they ate.

They tied into a breakfast big enough to satisfy the appetites of ten. Coral piled on more flapjacks, bacon, eggs, potatoes, and tomatoes until they told her to stop. They did something they never did at home; they left food. Coral stood by the table, hands on her hips, shaking her head and laughing.

Ray leaned back in his chair, patted his stomach, and told Coral her breakfast was delicious, the best he'd ever eaten. Coral said she might have guessed even if he hadn't mentioned it and laughed again. She led them to an indoor bathroom, much fancier than Uncle Wes's, (which they only got to look at and never use). Coral prepared a tub full of hot water, and on a low bureau sat a stack of towels, clean clothes, and boots.

"Now you boys take your things off and I'll come back for them. Throw them out the door and into the hall once you're out of them, and I'll take them to the fumigators. That all right with you boys?"

They didn't have a clue what she was talking about but so far everything that went on at the ranch seemed top drawer, so they'd go along with that too.

"Fine, Ma'am. Long as it's not too much trouble." Ray's manners seemed to come back with his full belly.

"Oh, no trouble at all." She closed the door and they heard her say, "It will be my pleasure to take care of them."

They sank into the tub and the warm water soothed their backs. The streaks across Ray's back were less red—Aunt Gaby's treatment had worked— and Buddy's own wounds from the whipping pained him less the farther from Wes they ran. They toweled dry, dressed, and slipped on the fancy boots with heels that made them two inches taller. Then Mrs. Lydia came to give them a tour.

"We're hoping you boys will stay a few nights. I hope your travel itinerary hasn't been too firmly established," she said after she led them around the house.

"No," Buddy said. He could stay here forever.

Ray elbowed him, gave him the evil eye and did something with his shoulders, wiggling them around as if he had some kind of rash as they followed her up the broad staircase.

After the house tour they drank lemonade on the front porch and watched Mr. Oliver lead three horses up from the corral. "Off you go," Lydia said. "Oliver will show you the ranch."

Buddy and Ray knew quality tack and good horsemanship when they saw it. How Father would have loved this—he would have hit it right off with Mr. Oliver. He would have admired these superior animals, and the aching squeak of the leather saddles. They rode out of the barnyard and onto the plains. The dry wind carried the sweet mingled scent of mellowed straw and heat, and swept tumbleweeds across Mr. Oliver's vast property.

"Are you rich, Mr. Oliver?" Buddy blurted despite an inkling it might not be the kind of question to ask. Mother always said not to snoop into folk's private business.

"You don't ask those kinds of questions," Ray snapped. "Don't mind my brother, Mr. Oliver. He says some pretty stupid things."

"I've got eyes," Buddy said. "I'm not stupid. Stop telling me what to say."

"That's enough boys. No harm done. Buddy's right. Some things are obvious. So obvious I don't feel a need to answer the question." He jabbed his horse and rode ahead and the two of them rallied to keep up.

At the end of his tour, which gave them an idea of some of his property, he said, "You boys could hire on here if you like. I've got a nice bunk house and a good crew for you to work with. You've got ranch experience. You're both excellent riders—I see that. What do you think?"

Ray spoke up. "I don't think so Mr. Oliver. We'd like to but our rich New York City relatives will wonder where we are."

"We could send them a telegram and tell them you've changed your minds, for a while anyway." He smiled when he said it and Buddy figured he knew why. "Tell you what, why don't you sleep on it. Give yourself a couple of days to think it over. It's a paying job."

"We've got money," Ray said.

That much was true. Sort of.

They slept in the biggest, highest bed they'd ever slept in. Buddy had to stretch his legs out to reach the floor. They slept in nightshirts, smooth and white and crisp, the smell of sage and sunshine in them. The events of the days and nights since Wes's beating overtook Buddy as soon as his head sank into the pillow.

"Buddy, Buddy, wake up."

"What?" Where was he? He looked about expecting to see the curved bodies of his brothers and sisters surrounding him. Moonlight glow came in through the big open window and a breeze fluttered the curtains.

"Buddy." A finger jabbed at his arm.

"What the hell is it?"

"I heard them talking. They're getting in touch with the sheriff first thing in the morning. They know we're runaways. They'll hitch us back up with Uncle Wes quick as Billy-be-damned. Come on. We've got to go."

Every muscle in Buddy's body said for him to stay right there in the big comfortable bed. "We'll sneak off in the morning. It can wait. I need to sleep."

"Do you want to go back to Wes's? We need to get a good start to outdistance their horses." Ray grabbed Buddy's arm and shook it hard. "Get up or I'm leaving without you."

Buddy slid out of bed and away from one of the deepest sleeps he ever remembered. But the mention of Wes got his heart beating faster and frightened him awake. He gathered up the new clothes and boots and followed Ray, stepping cautiously out into the airy hall, the floor cool beneath his feet. They heard snoring—must be Oliver—and stood stalk still when they heard the house creak.

Ahead of him, Ray picked his way across the gleaming floor as if inching over spring ice and headed for the top of the stairs, his long white nightgown falling to his ankles, illuminated by moonlight streaming in the window. They tiptoed downstairs silent as tumbling dust balls. If anyone saw them steal down the wide staircase, cross the open vestibule to the front door with the heavy brass handle, inch it open and squeeze out, closing the door after them without so much as stirring the air, they'd say they were certain they saw ghosts, their bodies glowing white in the dark.

Chapter 10

The Jungle

They ran behind the barn, peeled off their nightgowns, and pulled on Cowboy Oliver's new clothes. Buddy kept an eye on the ranch dog, Mighty, as he stirred out of his house, stretched, yawned, sniffed around their legs, and ambled back to his straw bed. Mighty must have figured them for folks who had settled in and not for strangers. Barking seemed about the last thing on the old dog's mind.

"I wish we didn't have to go." Buddy pulled on his pants and zipped up his fly. "They seemed nice to me."

"It's the nice ones you got to watch out for. They're cagey. Come on! Hurry up, before the dog changes his mind and starts barking."

When they reached the road Ray said they had to make a run for it, put some miles between themselves and the rancher.

Buddy's body ached for the wonderful sleep he was plucked from to run another marathon. Father always said he was built too close to the ground to be any good at running, his short, squat body better suited to throwing punches and wrestling. He always said he and Orwin were definitely cut from the same cloth in that regard. And now here he was again, and to make matters worse, hauling around a bundle of clothes to slow him down even more. Cowboy Oliver said, "I'm going to purge my closet," once he saw how well his hand-me-downs fit them. They got more clothes than all the Scott kids put together—exciting at the time—but right now it made running awkward.

On the run again, away from the mountains and the ocean, towards the open land and another ocean—towards New York City. They ran until their fancy new boots rubbed their feet raw. They stopped to take them off, their heels large patches of bleeding flesh.

"My whole body feels like it's made up of nothing but feet." Buddy poked a blister on his toe. They'd put several miles behind them and so far not a hint of light in the sky. They couldn't have slept more than an hour. "I don't know if I can keep going like this." He leaned up against a huge rock. For the first time in he couldn't remember when, tears welled up in his eyes. He blinked them back. He didn't want Ray to see.

"We'll grab some rest, then we run some more. Then we can ease up; there'll be enough distance between us and them." Ray gave a worried look back in the direction they came.

Buddy felt a trickle across the top of his foot. He raised it to drag it across his pant leg and something wiggled across his other foot.

"Holy shit!" Buddy jumped clear away from the rock. He felt a rustle at his ear and shoulder then saw a shape dive down to the base of the rock and fly off dangling something from its claws, a long dark dribble against the moonlit sky.

A night predator, an owl or an eagle had plucked a snake away. Buddy's foot itched with a squirming sensation. "Let's get the hell out of here." The idea of snakes swarming around them in the night worked his stomach up like a butter churn.

They ran, stopping only for quick rests, then ran again until shapes began to emerge out of early morning light.

The whole long, hot day, they only laid eyes on a horse and buggy off in the distance. They ran towards it and as soon as they got to within shouting distance the stooped figure on the buggy cracked the reins over the horse's back and rode off, disappearing into the distance. Buddy was so tired he wondered if he actually saw the carriage or if his brain conjured up something he wanted to be real.

They trudged on, tired, thirsty, and hungry. They exchanged few words and none of them complaints, because complaining would only make matters worse and each new step more painful than the last.

Late in the afternoon Ray told Buddy Mr. Oliver and lovely Mrs. Lydia hadn't made any plans to call the authorities about them. "I made it up. Had to. They would have turned us in. I feel certain. I had to protect us."

Buddy let go with a string of cussing strong enough to scald the feathers off a chicken. Who the hell did Ray think he was?

Ray argued for clearing these parts beyond a day's good run from Wes and the cowboy in order to escape danger. "It's for our own good."

Buddy was too tired to argue it. Maybe Ray was right.

As night fell, every ounce of strength got walked out of them. Buddy concentrated on placing one foot in front of the other, each plodding step harder than the last. They carried their hand-me-down boots with the fancy leather decorated with swirls and high heels which gave them height closer to a grown man's, and which ravaged their feet—rubbed them raw. Carrying the boots reminded them of who they were and who they were not. They limped along, mile after mile, down dusty roads and across fields.

Ray pointed to the trees in the distance. "That's where we're headed. The trees will give us shelter."

Buddy gazed at the flat featureless land surrounding them. Tired as he was, he didn't like the idea of curling up on the ground out here in this wide, open place. He'd just as soon keep on walking, which he imagined he could do in his sleep, his body so accustomed to one step following the other. Every time he thought about the rock and the snake he got the willies. When they slept under the sky with Father, if something went wrong he was there. But sleeping out in the open with nowhere else to go, with no one there to protect them, well that was another matter. Sometimes the great big sky made him feel naked and as if he could fly right off the face of the earth. He wanted to curl up into a ball tight as a caterpillar.

By the time they reached the trees night surrounded them thick as molasses, and a hint of cool relief came off a river they couldn't see from a distance, but which explained the presence of trees. They fell on their knees and scooped out palms full of water. They splashed over their faces and necks and down their arms. Buddy tasted salt from his skin.

They walked beneath the trees' canopy. With little in the way of underbrush, they ducked beneath the lowest limbs and made their way following the riverbank.

"This will be a great place to camp tonight," Ray said.

Ray was attempting to cheer him up; Buddy recognized his

tone and he wasn't convinced.

"Camp? Where's our tent? Where's our bedroll and our food and our campfire? I don't call it camping, I call it flopping because we're too tired and hungry to walk another damn step." Buddy remembered the ranch they'd just left; the delicious food, the hot bath, the soft bed, the smell of clean sheets. They'd given it all up because they might be in danger of being turned in?

"We'll follow along the river, then we'll go deeper into the trees." Ray's head bobbed along in front of him and Buddy stayed close.

Ray stopped suddenly and pressed his fingers to his lips motioning for Buddy to be quiet.

The sound of singing came from somewhere, and not just one voice, though the singing was too far away to know how many people there were. Ray picked his way ahead and looked back over his shoulder, his finger still to his lips. "Let's look," he whispered.

"I don't want to." Buddy's chest pinched with fear; his breath came short. "Let's get out of here."

"Let's see who it is. Maybe they've got food."

Mother used to warn about folks they didn't know, how they should be wary, especially of Gypsies. Gypsies stole children, carried them off to big cities across the ocean and made them perform for money or they got sold as slaves.

"No." Buddy raised his voice as much as he dared. "What if they're bad people? Murderers or kidnappers?"

"Don't be such a cry-baby." Ray inched ahead. "I just want to see who it is. Doesn't mean I want to meet them."

They picked through the trees following along beside the river. Twice Buddy pulled on Ray's shirt to hold him back. Ray had a damn curious nature and one day it would land them in a pile of trouble, but Buddy was determined tonight wouldn't be the night. If you're planning trouble, have a good night's sleep, tuck a good meal under your belt, then tackle it. But don't go after something feeling the way he felt right now; sick with fatigue, beyond the point of hunger and caring.

A faint glow lay ahead and blackened the trees in front of them. Wood smoke lingered in the air and closer in Buddy heard the crackle of a fire.

Through the trees they spied a group of men, twenty or so,

gathered around a huge bonfire. Flames tongued high in the air and spit out a column of sparks. A few men stood by the fire milling about. Every now and then one of them tossed a gob onto the flames, tobacco chawers probably. Most of the men sat around the fire singing, their voices soft and woozy in the night. *Show me the way to go home, I'm tired and I want to go to bed.* Voices rose up and joined the sound of the river's flow. Father loved to sing the same song.

"Come on," Ray whispered, "let's get closer."

"No." Buddy made a grab at Ray's shirt to hold him back but Ray jerked free and moved ahead.

No way Buddy was going to be left behind. "You're stupid to go closer. They might be bad men."

"You going to stay a sissy all your life?"

Ray knew he hated being called that name. Back at home, Buddy would have jumped him and dropped him to the ground but Ray took advantage of the situation. He knew this was no time to get into a ruckus.

They inched ahead to hide behind a larger tree to get a better view of the men sitting around the fire. Most had their backs to them, their stooped shapes curved like rocks against the fiery backdrop; faces glowed out of darkness on the other side of the fire and appeared bodiless. Ray crept in a little closer and left Buddy clinging to the tree trunk as if steeling himself against a sudden blast of wind.

Nearby, a dog barked and growled.

Buddy sank to the ground and cowered next to the tree, its trunk rough against his cheek. Ray dropped to his stomach and lay flat.

Men stopped singing and turned to the woods toward where Ray and Buddy hid.

The dog barked louder.

A few trees over, a mangy looking mutt strained on the end of a rope. It snarled and reared back on its two hind legs, pulling against a chain.

Buddy prayed the mutt would shut up. He dared not move an inch.

Something clamped around Buddy's neck and squeezed hard. "What have we got here?" a gruff voice said.

Buddy drew his shoulders up to ease the pressure around his

neck, but it didn't do much good. The hands pinched harder around his neck and made him squirm.

Another man had snared Ray by the arm and dragged him to his feet. "A couple of little girlsh, ishn't it?" The other man slurred as if he spoke through a mouthful of spittle. "Do you girlsh mind telling ush what you're doing shnoopin' 'round here."

"Yeah," the gruff voice behind Buddy said. "You better tell us what's going on or you're gonna get a private meeting with the lil' doggy over there."

"I can't talk with you squeezing my throat," Buddy whispered.

"Shesh got a point there, Duke," the other fellow said.

The fingers slipped away from Buddy's neck. He rubbed the soreness and looked up at a giant of a man, broad shouldered and with a very large head, staring down on him, his head crowned with a ragged crop of red hair.

The other fellow yanked Ray over by the scruff of his neck. "What you two girlsh doin? Hey?"

"First off, we're not girls," Ray snarled, his eyes squinty with anger. Ray thrust his chin up at the skinny guy whose hand clamped around his arm. The runt's narrow face shadowed with several days of whisker stubble and framed by his greasy hair hanging in strings to his shoulders.

"Oh? That so? You sure now? You checked, have ya?" The big fellow bent over and laughed in Buddy's face. His breath stank; Buddy turned away. "That look like a boy to you, Squire?"

"Can't tell, Duke."

Squire shoved his face up closer to Ray's and snorted.

Buddy made out a black cave of a mouth and a few stubby teeth.

"Well, maybe you're not a girl. The way you were tip-toeing around here, I'd have thought sho. Pransching around here like a pretty ballerina." He laughed heartily and slapped his knee. "What do you think Duke? A pair o' ballerinash?"

"I think so." Duke touched Buddy's hair and Buddy jerked his head away. "This here's a lively one."

"We're passing through, is all," Ray said. "We were walking along the river and we found you bunch."

"Walking along the river in the pitch black? Hiding behind the trees and lying flat on the ground is a funny way of walking, I'd say. What you think, Squire? Sound funny to you?"

"Can't shay I never heard nothin' like it before. Shoundsh fishy. Could be theshe boysh wash planning to rob ush. By the looksh of their clothesh they don't need to shteal from anyone. Maybe we should be shtealing from them, by the looksh of it. What you shay there, laddie? Got a little shomepin to greashe my palm?" Squire held out his open hand to Ray then rubbed his fingertips together.

Ray made a move to step away but Squire grabbed him by the arm and held him back. "Whoa, now. You shlow down, shonny boy."

"Oh, he's a live one, too. Seems like we caught ourselves a regular pair," Duke laughed, high-pitched and squealing.

The giant spoke to Buddy. "How about you just tell old Duke and the Squire here, what you boys was doing snoopin' around our camp. And here's something to consider before you commence on your tale. Better make it good, lest you want to go for a late-night swim."

Buddy's knees shook. Any minute he might sink to the ground. "We're hungry," Buddy said.

"We were coming to ask if you had anything to eat. That's all there is to it," Ray said.

"When's the last you ate?" Duke said.

"Last night," Ray stepped away from Squire and came closer to Duke. "We've been walking this whole day long."

Buddy looked up at Duke and waited for him to say something to Ray that would show he cared. It was no wonder Duke went out to check for intruders. The size of him would scare the living daylights out of anyone. The other guy, Squire, wouldn't threaten a kitten with his scrawny build, but his way of sneering and poking fun made him sly as a weasel.

"Now, how is it you boys would be wandering the woods at night, snooping on innocent folk like us, searching for a scrap of bread? You mind telling me that?" Duke must have figured Ray for the oldest since he put the question to him.

"Eshpecialy in thosh fancy getupsh. Boysh dresshed the way you is, looksh like they've never misshed a meal in their livesh." Squire nodded and scratched at his face.

"We're runaways," Ray said. "These clothes were given to us."

Ray launched into the truth like he'd jumped into the river without stopping to wet his toes first, reciting the whole story, chapter and verse, from start to now.

Duke's eyebrows pinched closer and planted a corduroy road over his nose. He stroked his chin and seemed to be engaged in careful thought.

"What a shad, shad, shad shtory," Squire said. "What you make of it Duke?"

Duke's mouth puckered as he mulled it over. "So sad it might not be true."

"It is too, every goddamn word of it." Ray stood with his hands on his hips, his chin thrust up defiantly. "Believe it or not, I don't care. It doesn't make any difference to us. Won't change anything, since it's already happened."

"Oh my, my. Someone's got a temper. Maybe he ought to go for a swim and cool down," Duke said.

"Look," Ray said, why don't you just let us go? We'll be on our way and won't bother anyone."

"Without something to eat?" Duke asked.

"Yeah," Ray said. "We don't want your food."

"Well now then see, there you go," Duke said, stepping closer to Ray. "If you were really hungry you'd be begging me for something to eat, wouldn't you now? And since you're not, what's to stop me from thinking you're some smart-ass rich kid who's going to tell their daddy about us being camped down here and send the law along after us?"

Duke turned meaner and Buddy was having thoughts of running like hell out of there. He'd rip through the trees as fast as his legs would carry him—which wouldn't be fast enough— held back as he was by his bloody, blistered heels and awkward bundle of belongings.

Ray's eyes narrowed in a menacing way. Any moment now Buddy expected him to make a run for it. But he didn't. He seized up and just stood glaring at them, stiff and still, eyes blazing, chin tipped up, going from Duke to Squire and back again. "You going to kill us?"

Buddy grabbed a tree, overcome by a sudden wave of weakness. It took all his effort and full concentration for his knees to hold him upright.

Duke started laughing, then Squire joined in, and for the life of him Buddy had no idea what to make of their laughing fit except it might be caused by some terrible meanness.

Ray shrugged at Buddy—he had no idea either—and kept close watch over Duke and Squire.

"No, we're not going to kill you. We may not be civilized in the conventional sense but we're not barbarians neither. Unless you're thinking of trying to kill us first. Killing's just not the right way to settle disputes. It has a certain depressing finality about it and it's been known to ruin a perfectly good evening. Squire here will tell you so."

"'Tis a fact. Can ruin the besht of eveningsh. Come on ladsh, follow ush."

Buddy shot Ray a questioning look,—would they be risking their lives by going along with the two of them?—but Ray followed Squire towards the bonfire and the other men gathered there. The dog on the rope, quiet now, lay down beside the tree to which it was tethered.

They came out of the woods and into a clearing close to the river, and the gathering of men. They stood in plain sight for all to see.

"Gentlemen," Duke said. "We've got company. Let's show them our hospitality. This here's a pair of runaways looking for a meal." The men gathered around the fire in various stages of lounging and relaxing, eyed the pair with slow eyes as if they'd been asleep, or drunk, or they didn't much care.

They hadn't been looking for a meal handout (not much of one anyway), but now the possibility of a meal was raised, it was all Buddy could think about. From a large pot over hot embers, came a smell so delicious he could almost taste it. Buddy couldn't keep his eyes off the big pot.

A stack of tin bowls sat on the ground. Duke grabbed a couple, and with a mug, scooped something into dishes and handed one to Ray, then Buddy. He pulled a loaf of bread from a knapsack, tore off a couple of fair-sized chunks, and handed it to them. "There you go boys. Eat up."

It tasted as good as anything Buddy ever ate. Thick gravy, loaded with potatoes, carrots, and some kind of meat. Squire fixed his eyes on them, all the time smiling so they could see into his mouth and the gaps between his sporadic teeth.

"Guessh the boysh wash telling the truth about being hungry." Squire got them each another bowlful once they'd run their fingers around the inside and licked away traces of gravy.

As they ate, the other men spoke in slow, gentle rhythms, so low they couldn't make out the words. Some of them poked sticks in the fire and stirred up sparks, and every so often someone broke into a song and a few others joined in. They sang so soft and solemn it put Buddy in mind of church, as if this rag-tag lot might be singing to God.

Duke and the Squire wanted to know where they were going. Ray told them about New York City but didn't tell about the rich relatives; they had noses for lies and would easily sniff him out.

"You boys have got a ways to go, gauging from my sense of where things are." Duke sat on the ground, his feet stuck out front, his toes coming out of the crack between the sole and the boot uppers. "Some time, the Squire and me will show you something that will ease up your travel plans considerable. It's something the boys around here," he waved to take in the men around the circle, "know a lot about, something us hobos figured out a long time ago. But you have to be patient. We'll tell you when we're ready."

Ray started to say something but Duke stopped him. "It can wait, boy. You've had enough for one day. You and your brother." He gave Buddy a thorough up and down. "You're kind of a quiet one aren't you? Looks like you'd all but jump out of your skin if I said boo."

"Don't you worry, is what I'm saying. Out there in the woods," Duke motioned towards the darkness, "we had to shake you up a little, to properly assess who was out there snooping on us. You understand?"

"Yes," they both said.

"Well now we know. You are what you say you are, so you've got nothing to fear from us." Duke pointed to a couple of blankets laid out on the ground. "You two go on over there and lie down. Tomorrow can wait. It always does. There ain't nothing can't wait until tomorrow."

"You boysh ushe your bundlesh there for a pillow. Shome of the boysh get to shleep walking, ish what I'm shaying. Fingersh git itchin and goesh where they don't belong."

"You both look a sorry sight. I don't think I could bear to look at you all day tomorrow if you're going to look the way you do right now. There ain't a darn thing pretty about you." Duke stretched out flat on his back, his head resting in his open palms, and closed his eyes.

Nothing could be truer—weariness had kicked their bodies limp. They crawled off to the blankets, cushioned underneath by a thatch of twigs and grass, and stretched out full, their eyes following sparks up into night.

Someone began to sing, then the others joined in. Somehow they all seemed to know when to let some voices overpower another, as if this was all rehearsed. Like when Father sang in the church choir, and Buddy, Ray, and Mother and the others would be in their pew listening and Sammy would say out loud, "There's Father," and together they all whispered, shshsh.

The sweetest night of sleep he'd ever had in his life. Right there under the stars, surrounded by strangers. A night of camping.

Chapter 11

The One Big Thing

They didn't wake up until late morning, the bonfire a pile of smoldering embers. Squire and Duke brought them bowls of porridge.

"What do you fellows do?" Ray examined the men milling about, wiped the sleep from his eyes, and squinted against the sun.

Duke thought it over and squatted beside Ray, his eyes on him as he scooped porridge into his mouth. "We don't actually do anything. Least not the kind of activity most folks recognize as doing. We make a study of getting by in the most unconventional of ways. We practice the art of survival and subsistence. Wouldn't you say, Squire?

Squire nodded. "Shounds 'bout right, Duke. A near enough approxshimashon of the truth."

Squire was what Father would call simple, his face so pinched around his eyes it made them look crossed or like it might have been slammed in a door. Didn't leave a lot of room for a brain. It seemed odd that in the light of morning he looked scarier than last night.

"For a long time we tried to earn what some call an honest living, but there's nothing out there for us. We looked and looked, and finally accepted our lot in life. So we don't do anything. And, if I'm not mistaken, we do it pretty well."

Squire agreed. "He'sh right. One thing you boysh need to know. Doin' nothin' ish not as eashy ash it looksh."

"Just say," Duke elaborated, "we don't tie ourselves down the way other folks do. No home, no wife, no kids, no cares. We enjoy a nomadic existence, which is to say, we enjoy travel. We give particular attention to cultivating the life of freedom and we work hard at it."

Buddy got the gist of it. Ray scowled a little, probably put off by Duke's fancy talk.

"You boys tidy up your bed-rolls and we'll commence your education on the ways of the hobo. You need to learn and listen and if you turn out to be ace students we'll show you *The One Big Thing*. But you've got to earn it," Duke said.

"What is *The One Big Thing*?" Ray always wanted to know things straight out—had a tendency towards impatience. Mother said so too.

"Didn't you just hear me, boy?" Duke wagged a finger at Ray. "No, sir. You never ever get to ask about *The One Big Thing*. You got it now?"

"Yeah, I guess so."

"We'll tell you when we think you're ready. If you're ready. And you'll never be told if you ask us again. I hope the two of you've got *Lesson Number One* through your noggins?" Duke looked back and forth between Buddy and Ray. They both nodded.

"It could be we've got a pair of shlow learnersh, Duke." Squire sneered.

Every day they followed Duke and Squire. At night, lying on their beds, they whispered to each other about *The One Big Thing*. Sometimes doubting its existence: thought it might be a trick or a joke. But if they wanted to eat they had to go along with it.

The foursome roamed the countryside seeking ranch chores and handouts. Ray and Buddy stood back with Squire while Duke went to the door, usually with a dog yapping and nipping at his ankles. He introduced himself as Buddy and Ray's father, Squire as his brother, though anyone could see there was no way they were a family. But Duke had a way about him; could easily turn on and off the charm to suit his purposes, and he won people over. They hired on for chores, often shovelling manure and cleaning stalls, a job Squire complained about bitterly. Buddy and Ray felt right at home at the end of a pitchfork. Or they stacked bales of hay into the mow. They traded their labour for food, coming away with bread and preserves, sometimes a hunk of meat. Most vegetables they plucked straight out of the garden patches they came upon—usually without asking permission.

"We're doing some thinning for folks, free of charge," Duke said. He wiped a carrot across his pant leg to remove the dirt and chomped on the end of it.

They walked miles to avoid going to the same ranch too many times. "I don't like to make myself familiar. My middle name is Passing Through," Duke said.

Every day ended with songs around the campfire, songs Buddy and Ray learned—shy at first, until they relaxed enough to join in. Buddy knew just sitting there singing with the other men made him feel about as good as he had in a long time, and he could see Ray felt the same. Father used to speak about the power of song and how it could arouse the spirit. *Show me the way to go home, I'm tired and I want to go to bed.*

They learned to snare rabbits, make mattresses from weeds, twigs and grass, wash their clothes in the river, sharpen a knife on a rock, test its sharpness on a blade of grass, use kerosene to get rid of head lice, make camp stew, and catch fish. They learned who to watch out for in camp, how to sleep with one eye open, and the philosophy of never trusting anyone.

"You shee, when you're camped with a bunch of guysh who think the shame way, you've alwaysh got to be on the alert. Don't you now?" Squire cocked his right eyebrow up. "You never let down your guard."

One night over a bowl of rabbit stew and parsnips, Duke said it was time Buddy and Ray learned about *The One Big Thing*. So many times Buddy wanted to ask, remembered Duke's rule, and bit his tongue.

The next morning, the mist still in the trees and the rest of the camp asleep, Duke shook them awake. Ray went to say something and Duke whispered for the two of them to keep quiet. They dressed in silence and sneaked out of camp.

They walked for miles down roads and cut across open fields until they came to another camp of men in a cluster of trees, a smaller camp than the one they left. A few of the men gave them the once-over; they looked mean.

"You headed out?" A fat bald man, chewing on a stick asked

Duke and Squire. He didn't wait for either of them to answer. "If you are, you got a wait ahead of you. There's no bumping up in line, unless you want to pay. Then that's another matter altogether."

"I know the ropes," Duke said. Unlike the other camp, Duke didn't seem to be a boss here. Duke must have noticed the bald man eyeing Buddy and Ray. "These here are a couple of the uninitiated. We're staying the night while Squire and I show them what's what. How this here is the hobo's main ally, his number one resource."

The fat man laughed. "You'll get no dispute out of me."

All this laughing and funny talk made Buddy suspicious. Why couldn't they just speak clear—straight-forward? Maybe he and Ray had been suckered by Duke and the Squire, and now this little fat man, too. He heard about snakes lying in the grass; knew enough about the devil from church and Uncle Wes's parlour rants to know the devil was everywhere. Squire moved along to talk to someone and Buddy snagged Ray by the arm.

"We can't trust them."

"We can't trust anybody and we never could, but we've been with these two for a while and it's been okay. We'll go along with it; it's all we've got to go on." Ray pointed to his trouser pocket and showed Buddy a corner of a bill. The money Ava and Nellie gave them. "This here's what we've got to worry about."

Buddy tried to talk Ray into digging a hole in the woods and stashing the money but he'd have none of it. "The safest place is right here by my nuts. Anyone try to get anything out of my pocket has to dig around the jewels."

They ate dinner at the camp. Buddy and Ray stayed silent and listened to the stories of the hobos. Everyone seemed restless, as if they were waiting for something, or the law to show up unannounced. After night fell, sitting around a bonfire, the bald fat man—who seemed preoccupied with the timepiece he kept pulling from his pocket—said it was time to roll.

Half a dozen men gathered up their bundles and started through the trees. The bald man turned to Buddy, Ray, Squire, and Duke and said, "Don't forget: you're spectators. You're along to watch, not participate. You got that?"

They walked a long way to a road, a column of men, ten

altogether. Their feet made a grumbled chorus on the gravel, their heads and shoulders bobbing in the moonlight. On and on the ragged group walked with Buddy and Ray sometimes running to catch up. For the life of him Buddy couldn't figure how the men, some big and burly, moved through those night fields without making so much as a sound, stealthy as cats.

Someone motioned for everyone to lie down. They flattened down in a ditch behind a steep embankment. Somewhere out of the hip-high grass, drenched in night's dew, a whisper came for everyone to shut up.

Not a breath could be heard, only the sound of the crickets around them. Something sounded in the distance. A low rumble like a threshing machine. But that couldn't be—not in the pitch dark. The chugging grew louder and up through the ground came a steady wave of vibrations.

"It's a train," Buddy whispered to Ray. A light shone in the distance, dim as a distant star, then it grew larger and brighter as the sound of the engine drew near. "You boysh watch and pay attenshion," Squire said.

The locomotive seemed to be losing speed, a great black monster wearing a plume of steam like a feather in a lady's hat. A massive white cloud that hung in the air, then it passed in front of them inching along at a thunderous crawl and came to a squealing, screeching, shuddering stop, not far from where they lay hidden in the weeds.

"It sits here a while, until another train goes by," Duke whispered.

The black engine sat at some distance and gave off gasps of steam like a worked-up bull. Directly in front of them sat a boxcar followed along by many others as far down the line as they could see. A couple of men in coveralls and hats climbed down out of the engine.

"Keep your trapsh shut," Squire whispered. "Headsh down and not a word or Duke will knock your blocksh off."

The two trainmen passed close, the gravel crunching beneath their boots as they spoke in low tones. They moved down the line, bending to inspect the great crushing wheels of the train and to test a few boxcar doors, then worked their way back again to the engine. They circled the front, bent to look at something, then moved up the track.

They climbed back up into the engine.

The men in the ditch waited a while longer then one got up, crawled out of the ditch, and up the embankment. The hobo tapped lightly on the door of the boxcar directly in front of them. The door slid open and a head came out. The two men exchanged a few words then the hobo came back to the ditch and said, "We're clear for the first one." A hunched figure rose out of the tall grass, climbed the embankment, and disappeared inside the boxcar. The first fellow went right on down the line, coming back each time with the numbers—one, then two—and the men followed him back until all the men hiding in the grass had gone.

"When are they coming back?" Buddy whispered to Duke.

"Oh, you never know. The hobo brethren have a way of turning up. You don't know where, you don't know when. That there's the beauty of it. And don't try to ask them neither. We come and go as we please. Don't abide by clock or calendar. That's hobo law."

Now it was only the four of them. In the distance another train approached fast, its steam banking high. The engine appeared, big, black, carved out of the night, and chugged by the other train. It blasted its long shrill whistle and almost launched Buddy and Ray clear out of their fancy boots, which made Squire and Duke laugh.

After the second train passed, the two trainmen went back to the track ahead of them to pull on something. They climbed back up into the engine and it started a slow crawl away from them. They waited until nothing could be seen or heard of it, not even a distant rumbling, and patches of trampled grass was all that remained of the men who had lain there with them.

As they rose to start the trek back to the hobo jungle, Duke said, "In four days you'll be on the train bound for New York City. I made you a reservation."

Buddy stared into the fire and waited for one of the fellows seated around it to start up another song. The one they just finished, about the sun and the moon and the stars, brought a sense of calm and wonder; the way he felt when he listened to his father's stories. He looked up at

Duke seated beside him, at the square jaw and thick neck supporting the box-shaped head and the crop of red hair it sprouted.

"Couldn't we stay here? With you two? We could work for you. We could swipe food out of gardens and bring it to you and you wouldn't have to do anything. We could earn money and give it to you." Buddy spoke quietly so Ray wouldn't hear. Ray was all for high-tailing out of here for the city—start living high off the hog.

Duke turned his head slowly and looked down on Buddy. "Oh my, you are a slow learner, boy. What have I been telling you all along?"

Buddy shrugged. "A bunch of stuff, I guess."

"You been listening to any of it? You got corn growing in your ears?"

"I've been listening. There's no corn." Buddy stuck a finger in one ear then the other. Nothing there but some wax. Bath night Mother always said to scrub behind the ears, poke his baby finger inside his ear and give it wiggle.

"Well let's just go over a few of the ground rules again. The hobo never stays put. You want to be a hobo?"

"I guess so." The way Duke and Squire talked it sounded pretty good. But thinking about drifting from place to place with Ray made Buddy's stomach go jumpy.

"Let me repeat, just in case you didn't get it. The hobo never stays put—just passing through is our middle name. Remember? You want to settle somewhere, then me and Squire will march you straight off to the orphanage right now. That what you want?"

"Jesus, no!" Buddy would keep his trap shut for the next four days. And something else for certain: he'd be on the train. No orphanage for him.

Duke put his big mitt of a hand on Buddy's head, roughed up his hair, and gave his head a push. "I'm a born teacher!" he said. Duke liked him, Buddy had known it ever since that first night he found him in the woods.

"Look here, you two," Duke's weary eyes went from one to the other, "you've got to remember one thing. The Squire and I won't be here much longer either. You can count on that. We've been contemplating Mexico."

"Thatsh right," Squire squealed. "We wantsh to shee them

lovely sheenyoureenashs."

"We'll be headed out right after the two of you, but we're headed somewhere else."

The idea of riding on that big black mountain of iron thrilled Buddy; he'd always wanted to ride a train. But it would take him somewhere he'd never been, somewhere far. He and Ray would be on their own again. Why couldn't they go to Mexico, too?

"Something you need to bear in mind while you're waiting to take your leave," Duke pulled his jackknife out of his pocket and slid it along a twig he'd been whittling, shaping the tip into a fine point, the strips of wood alighting on his pant legs. "You're still students of the vagabond's life. As long as you're here, you'll continue to learn and toe the line. Learn as much as you can; soon you'll be on your own again. If I've taught you one thing," Duke shook a finger at them, "it better be this: Don't let yourself get so comfortable that you let your guard down. Never, ever, do that."

Duke eyed them as if he might be checking to see if they understood what he meant. "Out in the world," he glanced at the trees surrounding the camp, "there's a lot of rats waiting to do rat business. Isn't that so, Squire?"

Squire sat cross-legged in the dirt and whisked flies away from his face, their buzz exaggerating the afternoon's heat. No wonder the flies found him attractive; Buddy got whiffs of him clear over here. "Thatsh the truth like it washn't shpoken before. Oh, indeedy, plenty of ratsh."

The fourth day came. Ray and Buddy packed up their gear, along with a few of the other men. "Once we get to New York," Ray said, shoving his clothes together into a pile, "there'll be no more scrounging. No more being dependent on someone else."

Ray was crankier than usual this morning and Buddy figured he wasn't looking forward to the drifter's life again either.

"We'll get jobs, make a lot of money and buy a house. We'll send for our brothers and sisters and we'll be together again." Ray tightened his bundle with a belt, gave it a couple of shakes, tossed the whole contraption over his shoulder, and took a few steps to test it.

Buddy thought about the whole Scott family together again. Back at the ranch in Wyoming, everyone the same as before when they were together, everyone but Ray. He looked as he did now; taller, even without his fancy boots, the roundness gone from his face, leaner now, more like a man's and covered in a two or three-day growth. But the others, all the same. And that couldn't be true, could it? If Ray had changed the rest of them would too. What would they look like now? Would he even recognize any of them if he saw them? Sammy, just a little guy of two; he would be a little boy. And New Baby—he'd be the age of Chuck when he last set eyes on him. Pearl? Maudy? How would it be possible to round them all up and take them to a house clear across the country? How would they know where to find them?

Buddy surveyed the camp: the smoke lazily drifting out of the fire pit, the sun streaking in through the treetops, throwing a pattern of dark and light over boulders, the riverbank, water, dirt, and grass. Some of the men stretched out on blankets napping. Others swam in the river. This could be home. But in hobo law a home did not exist. Or it was everywhere.

Duke must have seen a look come over him. "We'll meet again, if that's what's got you troubled. Ours is a big yard, and we have a habit of popping up here and there, like gophers out of the hole." He squeezed Buddy's shoulder so hard it made him wince. "We're all hobos on this earth. After all, aren't we all just passing through?"

That night the train rolled into sight, a shuddering black beast creeping through darkness.

The engineer and fireman dropped down from the engine and strolled up the track swinging their lanterns and came back. They talked as they inspected the engine and advanced down the boxcars. They returned to the engine, swung themselves back up and into the front, and waited.

Buddy and Ray lay in the ditch along with several other rail riders. "Okay," one of them said. "Come with me. Stay low, don't make no noise."

Buddy turned to Duke and Squire, went to say something but Duke spoke first. "The hobo never says goodbye. Get along."

They followed the man alongside the train, staying in snug with it and crouching low until they reached a boxcar close to the end, the only sound the crunch of stone beneath their feet. The man rapped four times on a boxcar door. Four knocks came from the other side.

"They've got room for two in there."

The door opened slowly. "Git." The next thing Buddy knew he was hoisted up and into the opening. Several hands grabbed at him and pulled him inside into darkness.

"Get out of the way," someone snarled. "Another one's coming in." They hoisted Ray up and closed the door. Inside the darkness became more consuming.

"Here's what happens now," someone whispered, his breath hot and stinky in Buddy's face. "You shut up until this thing moves. Then we'll have a chit chat, complete with introductions and pleasantries. You got that?"

"Yes," they whispered.

"Find yourselves a bare patch."

A hand on Buddy's arms pushed him forward. "Go," someone whispered. He groped through the darkness until he found space on the floor covered in straw. "Get down," a voice came out of the blackness. "Settle down, enjoy the ride, go to sleep, and shut up."

Buddy felt someone beside him. "Is that you Ray?"

"It's me."

"Shut up," someone hissed.

The straw rustled as Ray inched closer.

"Lay the fuck still. If we get caught and kicked out I'll skin you alive."

Buddy lay as still as still for what seemed like an eternity, trying not to move so much as a muscle. A tickle settled into his throat and brought tears to his eyes, worsened by the gummy air of straw dust and hot breath. He swallowed his own spit. So black inside he couldn't make out his hand in front of his face, like being in a pit a mile down in the earth. His heart pounding so hard it filled his ears. His breath came in short shallow spurts like a panting dog's.

He had to slow down—make himself calm. Heat beaded sweat across his brow at the hairline; a drop trickled down his face and settled inside his ear. If he'd known it would be like this—like the inside of a coffin—he wouldn't have agreed to riding the train. He thought of Mother and what she would have said to him. *Think sweet thoughts.* He recited the line over and over to contain his fear: the feeling of being trapped. *Let calm reason prevail over a frightened mind.*

His shoes connected with something. Someone pushed his foot away. He closed his eyes and listened to the rhythms of breathing around him. Someone snored.

"Shsh," a voice snarled. Probably the person who'd told them to shut up.

"Someone wake up whoever it is or we'll get caught," a voice came out of the dark.

Silence again for a long time. Outside the boxcar the crunch of footsteps came up along the train and stopped in front of their door. Keys rattled.

"I checked this one at the last siding. Empty," a voice outside said.

"We'll leave it go, then," another voice said.

The footsteps continued down the line, fading to nothing, then once again approached and passed going back the way they came. When they had gone again Buddy let out a deep breath.

"Shut up!"

Fear and discomfort changed the passing of time, stretched seconds out to what might have been hours for all he could tell. And having to piss didn't help. Something must have happened to the other train; it was taking much longer than it had before when they came to watch. Finally its sound could be heard off in the distance. The whole boxcar shook as it passed and in time, they heard the squeal of the train's wheels on the rails and the sway of motion. They were underway.

Buddy didn't know how long he'd been sleeping but something wakened him. He was about to say something out loud but saw the blackness surrounding him and remembered. He shifted. Something had touched his inner thigh. He reached down...

He lay awake waiting for the morning light, searching for its appearance in the cracks, wanting it to come in so he could get a look at the rat's nest he was trapped in. There must have been at least thirty men—more than he'd imagined. A group gathered in a circle sitting in the straw, others lay curled up, fast asleep. Men leaned against the boxcar walls, steadying themselves against the back and forth toss of the train. Every so often one of them spit out a chunk of tobacco and wiped the juice off their chins with blackened sleeves. A mangy bunch and no wonder, holed up inside a little box like a bunch of cattle. Buddy avoided eye contact with any of them for fear of looking evil in the eye. *Never let down your guard. Rats waiting to do rat business.*

It felt like a hundred degrees inside the car. Last night this was the black pit of a deep, deep hole, and now it was an oven.

Ray rolled over closer to Buddy to talk. "The Duke said we take this down four stops and then we wait for another one, headed north. It's got to stop soon. We've been going a long time. At this rate we'll run out of country."

"We're getting off first stop."

"What the hell you talking about?"

"I heard the Duke, and now you hear me. I'm getting off first stop and you can go on if you want." Buddy lowered his voice, head down to the floor so no one would hear him.

"You boys got something to share with us?" A man with a pinched face, eyes encircled with dark rings started towards them. "Making a little conspiracy, are you? Figuring on robbing us?"

"No." Ray didn't sound convincing.

"I'd hate to tell you what happened to the last fella who tried that. 'Bout your age, too."

The man circled them slowly, his upper lip lifting over yellow teeth. Buddy and Ray stood stock-still, let him finish with his threatening look, then he went back to where he'd been leaning up against the wall and spit on the floor. They didn't say another word until the train stopped and they slipped off and down into a ditch.

They lay flat and looked up and down the train, watching as dozens of men jumped off and disappeared, blending into the tall grass like grasshoppers.

Buddy wouldn't budge until he saw the train had gone and the terrible thing that happened in the night, gone with it.

They walked all day without seeing another soul and settled down by some bushes for the night.

"Where the dickens are we?" Ray asked.

The subject of where they were was not occupying Buddy's thoughts. Hours back they ate the provisions Duke and Squire helped put together back at the camp, and just now they finished sucking the flavour out of the paper it came wrapped in. He was more worried about when and where the next meal would come from.

"I think we're pretty close to New York City." Ray stretched out on the ground, hands clasped behind his head and resting in his open palms.

"What makes you say so?"

"The hills. It's hilly around New York."

"How do you know?"

"I just know it."

A mosquito stung the back of Buddy's neck. He swiped at it and examined the blood smeared across his fingers.

"Something happened," Ray said suddenly.

What? Had the same disgusting thing that crawled out of the darkness in the boxcar visited Ray too? The thing that Buddy vowed he'd never tell a soul about so long as he lived?

"What do you mean?"

"I mean something's happened that's going to change our travel plans."

"What?"

Ray got up and walked over to stand in front of Buddy. "Watch this." He slipped both hands into his pant pockets and pulled the pockets out, so that the inside hung on the outside.

"See."

"Yeah, so? What of it?"

"Well, what I mean is, my pockets got picked clean."

"Son-of-a-bitch!" Buddy leapt up and planted his face directly in front of Ray's. "I swear to God if this is your idea of a joke I'll clean your clock."

Ray didn't look like he was joking. He just stood there, all solemn and serious without the hint of a smile on his face—more like a scowl. "Punch me if you want. It won't bring back the money."

"Who? Who did it?"

"One of the fellows back at the river camp. Could have been Duke or Squire; I don't know. I checked my pockets the morning we were packing to leave and that's when I found it gone." Ray glanced down at his cowboy boots, busted up and dirty, the left one tipping way over to the side.

Buddy remembered how sour Ray was in the morning as they packed up to leave camp. They told us not to trust anyone and by the Christ they sure as hell meant it! That's one expensive lesson they taught us." The way Buddy saw it, one way or another, they'd both been robbed. If he had a choice to make, having the money stolen from him was better than what happened to him in the boxcar. It all added up to a pile of bad luck.

"Now what?" He searched Ray's face for an answer and saw, in the shade of the descending night, a striking resemblance to their mother. Then, in an instant the sense of her presence vanished like dust. He knew the answer to his own question. They'd keep on going until they found something. Calm reason would prevail.

They stared into night's deepening shadows and lapsed into silence.

Mother made her presence clear to him in Ray's face for a reason. She always made them say their prayers but Buddy stopped praying a long time ago. Prayer represents hope, she said, and hope was the future. There can't be life without a future. And then she'd say how they were such humble creatures. He didn't need convincing. She used to say they must pray for God's guidance and for humility.

Buddy sensed what this humility thing might be. It meant never desiring anything. But he desired and wanted badly. Wanted a soft bed and a good night's sleep, food, proper shoes that didn't hurt every time he took a step, and clothes that fit and not the baggy duds of an adult. He wanted away from the company of thieves. He wanted a mother and father, sisters, and brothers. He wanted a home. He wanted the home he once had back again. Oh how he wanted. His chin quivered, his mouth pinched as he fought back tears, and a sensation that started in his belly tried to push its way up through his throat. All this wanting all at his own peril, for surely his lack of this thing called humility and all his wanting brought them a terrible load of bad luck.

Now, more than ever he longed to hear his mother's voice and keep it alive—employ her words.

"Don't worry," he told Ray with as much reassurance as he

could muster. "We'll get there."

"Where? Where will we get to? We don't even know which direction we're headed."

"Well that makes it easier then, doesn't it? If you don't know where you're going then for certain you'll get there. In fact, we're there right now." Buddy liked riddles the same way Father did.

"Shut up and quit talking foolish nonsense."

Foolish nonsense, Buddy thought, was a damn sight better than no nonsense at all. At least he had the pleasure of it. "Why don't we go north?" He had no more desire to go south to Mexico where a spider's bite was bad enough to kill you. He wanted to escape the sun beating down on them all day.

"I already told you that's Canada. It's filled with snow and ice and bears and trees and lakes as far as the eye can see. And Eskimos who live in igloos, houses made of ice. No one but them lives there, it's so cold."

Buddy thought of a vast, pure and perfect whiteness; creatures wandering forests of cool tall pines, lakes and rivers teaming with fish. "Let's go there," he said. He wanted to feel cold again; he wanted to go where there were no people. "It sounds safe." The crowded streets of New York didn't seem inviting anymore.

"We're going to New York City to find jobs. There are no jobs in Canada and we don't know enough about trapping. We should be trying to find a rabbit right now."

"I'm too tired to eat. I'm going to sleep." Stretched out on his back, he watched the stars flicker to life in the sky. He'd stay awake to look for the Scott Constellation. Tonight he was glad of the sky's vastness and openness. He felt safe under it, under the watchful gaze of his family, glad not be shut away inside a black box with a bunch of lowlifes.

Chapter 12

Sandy's Travelling Mercantile

Ray's words pulled Buddy up out of somewhere as if he was swimming to a surface and never quite getting there. "Buddy, wake up."

"What?" He sat bolt upright, fear pounding in his ears. Was there an animal out there in the darkness? Snakes?

"Listen," Ray squatted beside him already out of his bed roll.

"What is it?" Something clattered in the distance but he could only see the shapes of shrubs against the night sky.

"We'd better hide." Ray gathered up his belongings, crouched behind a bush, and told Buddy to do the same. "Hurry up, it's getting closer. It could be bandits."

Or murderers. Buddy slid in beside Ray.

A horse and wagon came into view, rattling and clattering like a marching band.

"Listen," Buddy whispered. The sound of someone singing came out of the jungle of noise.

"Come on," Ray said. "Maybe we can get some food." Before Buddy could convince him not to, Ray ran out from behind the shrub and stood in the middle of the road waving both arms in the air.

"Whoa." The wagon clattered to a standstill and a short fat man sitting on the bench like a pumpkin on a ledge, leered down at Ray. "By the jumping jolly jingles, there's an apparition in the road!"

"Mister, please, where you headed? Don't mean to scare you, but my brother and me," Ray pointed to Buddy cowering behind the bushes, "we're wondering if we could hitch a ride. Maybe get a scrap to eat."

"Oh, I see," he rubbed his chin with pudgy little hands. "You were wondering where I was headed? Well then, don't that beat all, since, to the best of my recollection, I am just now making your acquaintance. For you to be wondering about me prior to my knowledge of having met you smacks of divine intervention. Am I correct in that assumption?" The little man swung down from the wagon, his short body encased in a tight-fitting vest not quite covering his belly. His woolen pants, held up by suspender straps and wrinkled at the crotch, stunk of sweat and wood smoke.

Ray looked at him, his face screwed up on one side, confounded by his gibberish.

Buddy slipped out from behind the bushes and walked to the wagon to try to read what was written on the tarpaulin cover. He couldn't make it out in the pale moonlight. Pots, pans, boots, brooms, shovels—no end of paraphernalia dangled from the wagon's frame. More junk than it seemed possible for a small wagon to haul. The little man stepped up to him, a big smile on his round face, his upper lip etched by a dark moustache.

"Sandy MacPhee, boys, making your acquaintance." He gave them a tip of his hat then set it back on his round bald head. "I bring the store to you. This here," he motioned to the wagon, "this here is Sandy's Travelling Mercantile. I specialize in pots and pans, brooms, dust mops, clothes, shoes, ointments, and medications—should you be distracted by an uncomfortable itch or other ailment. What'll it be, boys? See something there you fancy?"

"We can't buy anything." Buddy admired a handsome pair of plain boots; the kind that wouldn't pinch and rub and cause blisters the way his cowboy boots did. No one in New York City would wear smashed up cowboy boots.

"Mister," Buddy said, "you're a stranger to us, but we're starving. Haven't eaten for three days." If he told him they wolfed down the last of their hobo jungle food this morning they might not get so much as a scrap of sympathy.

Sandy MacPhee paced, his stomach sticking out in front of him like he had a melon tucked up under his vest. "So you boys are looking for a handout, is that it?"

"We're willing to work," Ray fired back at him. He took a

dim view of freeloading.

At the front of the wagon, a corner of the tarpaulin lifted and a woman with hair foaming around her face like a waterfall poked her head out.

"What's the hold up?" She crawled out onto the bench then climbed down, stepping up to Ray and Buddy to give them a thorough going over. She wore a nightgown, the kind that went way down in the front and showed off what Ray called the great divide.

"Boys, may I present to you, Mrs. MacPhee. The finest fortune teller and healer between here and Missouri." They mumbled their greetings, then Sandy continued. "The boys here are in need of nourishment, Annabelle. Think we could manage something for them?"

Something about the way he said it, with a little twitch in his lips, made Buddy suspicious.

She examined Buddy, then Ray, and smiled. "I imagine we could rustle up a meal in exchange for services. They're skinny enough; they'll come in handy. Especially this one." She poked Buddy. "We'll get them something to eat now, but tomorrow, after they've helped us, we'll fatten them up proper. Sound fair to you Sandy?" Wrinkles set in her face deep as cracks in dried-up prairie, visible even in the pale moonlight. But her hair looked like a young girl's, the colour of straw. Mother used to talk about fancy ladies who got their hair colour out of a bottle.

Sandy spat tobacco out onto the road and wiped his chin with a dirty white cuff. "Oh that's my girl. She's got the business sense. She's the thinker in this here organization, boys."

Buddy smiled and nodded his head in agreement without a clue what he found so agreeable, only caring about the eating business and wishing they'd get on with it. He'd promise anything, do anything, for even a crust of bread.

"Scrawny as they are," Annabelle pinched Ray's bare arm, "they'll come in handy for part of the act. Providence stuck you out in the middle of the road, boys. Just today I was thinking how the liniments are getting rank in the heat, might even explode. Someone was taking care of us, Sandy, when this sickly pair appeared like ghosts before us."

"That is the truth, Annabelle, just as surely as you spoke it."

Sandy hooked his thumbs in his vest pockets and eyed the boys with satisfaction.

"Yes," Annabelle MacPhee said, "I think this could work pretty good. Okay, boys," she brought her hands together and rubbed them, "how about some bread and pork hocks? Think you could make short work of them?"

"Oh yes," they answered straight away.

"In exchange for services, you understand?"

Yes, yes, they understood.

"Nothing's free in these times, boys." She climbed back into the wagon and in a while reappeared with a plate stacked with bread and pig ankles. They plunked themselves down on the side of the road and ate so fast Buddy thought for sure his belly would ache. Annabelle MacPhee disappeared inside the wagon. When they finished eating they climbed up onto the wagon and seated themselves next to Sandy. They rode along in silence until Ray asked Sandy where they were. Sandy laughed and said he thought that was the funniest question he'd ever heard, then he repeated it and laughed some more. "You boys are some kind of curious travellers that don't know where you are. You're in the state of Kansas."

"Oh," Buddy said. He'd heard of it.

"Is it close to New York City?" Ray asked.

Now Sandy roared, and from inside the wagon Annabelle shouted for him to shut up if she was going to get any sleep at all, though Buddy wondered how anyone could sleep through the constant clatter and rattle of the wagon. "I need all my rest for tomorrow." Annabelle grumbled.

"Which direction is New York City in?" Ray didn't seem to mind that Sandy found him so humorous.

Sandy pointed back over his shoulder. "Back the other way boys. We're headed west."

Buddy and Ray both straightened. What if they were headed straight back to Uncle Wes?

"How far's Wyoming from here?" Ray must have been thinking the same as Buddy.

"Oh, it's a long ways off. A long ways," Sandy said.

"You sure?" Ray asked.

"I said so, didn't I?" Sandy raised the reins and smacked them down over the horse's rump.

The tip and toss of the wagon had Buddy's head dropping to his chest, had him dozing, and once he woke up leaning on Ray's shoulder with Ray's head leaned against his.

Early in the morning, a small town surrounded by hills arose in the distance out of the mist. Sandy rode up the main street and stopped close to the town square. The few people out on the streets took little notice. Buddy heard Annabelle rummaging around inside the wagon. "Boys, get in here!" she called out.

The inside of the wagon, dim in the morning light, seemed a combination bedroom and store room. A mattress took up a small patch of floor surrounded by mounds of stuff.

"Take a seat boys, if you can find a spot." She shoved clutter aside with her foot to make room.

Buddy found it hard to concentrate on what she wanted from them that afternoon—something about food and a percentage—due to the absence of her long, curly blond hair, no longer tumbling down around her face, but sitting over in the corner on the end of a broom handle. Replacing it, her own hair—short, brown, straight, thin, and patchy. She looked thirty years older.

As she explained the work, Buddy watched a large black spot bob up and down on her wagging chin and saw that it was drawn there. She leaned into a mirror balanced on a pile of blankets and dabbed her face with powder until she looked white as a ghost, then smudged red puddles on her cheeks. She painted blue over her eyes, circled them with black rings very close to the eyelashes, then smeared on bright red lipstick and rolled her lips together. She smiled into the mirror and ran her finger over her teeth, which appeared yellow in contrast to her white face. She reached out for the broomstick and removed the wig, fitted it over her head, and shoved her scraggly hair up under it. She picked up a pencil and paused her instructions as she enlarged the dot on her chin.

She leaned back from the hand mirror, and pleased by what she saw, set it down. She picked up a little bottle with a hose and knob, squeezed the knob, and the wagon filled with a scent so strong Buddy's eyes watered.

She handed them each a packet of food tied up with twine. "I hope you're both clear on the instructions. You do exactly as I say. The crowd can turn; I've seen it happen." Her blue eyes scrutinized them as if sizing them up. "Believe me, you don't want that. So, you go on your separate ways today. Neither of you has seen the other ever before—you understand that? You don't so much as look at each other sideways. You got that?"

"Yes." They nodded; they understood.

She pulled the canvas aside a crack to peek outside. "It's quiet out there now. Not too many people around. Ray, you go first and go that way. Buddy, you go the other way, but wait until Ray is out of sight. Make yourselves invisible and come back to the wagon when you hear the bell ringing, early this afternoon. But remember, you don't know us. We never seen neither of you before. And you don't know each other, neither. And don't forget, you're both in an awful state. Make sure you act like it, but not too much. Don't overdo it, or people won't believe you then, neither." She studied them for a few moments. "Folks ought to believe the two of you, since you both look like something that's washed ashore. Okay, Ray, you git."

Ray slipped down from the wagon and headed across the big open square.

In a few minutes Annabelle told Buddy it was his turn. "Mind you go in the opposite direction. And don't be obvious—you slither out of here slick as a snake, so folks don't connect you with this wagon."

Buddy headed across the square then towards the outskirts of town, until he came to a river. He stayed there for the morning, stretched out in the thick grass on the river bank, dozing until a piercing sun pried at his eyelids. He didn't mind this time alone. He was always with Ray, always sifting and sorting his thoughts through the screen of Ray's opinions. Some day that would change.

He tossed pebbles into the muddy river and watched little splashes interrupt the surface. The water surged by and he followed it to a bend, up a ways. Where did the water go, he wondered? Did it empty into a big ocean or dwindle out into nothing? The river itself gave no clues about where it might be headed; no clues about its depth. Like him and Ray, rushing to New York with no idea about what lay beyond the next bend or what to expect when they arrived. Just going along taking handouts as they went. After today, after they did what they had to do for Sandy and Annabelle in exchange for food and money, they would take charge of their own affairs.

He leaned back and closed his eyes. The gush of water sweeping his dreams along in a somersault world filled with rattling, clattering wagons, angry preachers, violent sinners, hands that reached out from dark corners and grabbed him. Dark eyes sunk into unshaved faces, open mouths filled with broken black teeth, the zig-zag of a snake from out of nowhere, and a parade of family members popping up, unable to see him or hear him calling out to them.

The sound of a bell ringing woke him up. In his dream it was heaven's bell, but when he opened his eyes to the glare of afternoon sun, he came back to the river and Annabelle and Sandy's plan.

He joined the crowd at the town square that gathered beside the wagon. Sandy spoke from on top of the wagon's seat, his little arms gesturing around his round belly like loaded springs. A young man emerged from out of the back of the wagon and lowered himself to the ground.

"Who's it going to be next?" Sandy shouted to the crowd of farm folk, shopkeepers, mothers with children, and people who'd come to town for supplies. A young fellow shot up his hand and Sandy shouted. "Up you go then. Don't keep Persephone, Voice of the Future, Goddess of Healing, waiting.

Annabelle a goddess? That fake old crow? Buddy edged deeper into the growing crowd and listened to Sandy's spirited preaching accompanied by the jingle of the bell he rang. Buddy would credit Annabelle, an ample woman with fake hair, a painted face, and a bossy disposition, with making one hell of a good pork sandwich. She didn't scrimp on the meat, but she sure as hell was no goddess. He figured the pair of them, Sandy and Annabelle, for swindlers.

While the young man stayed inside the wagon with Persephone, the Voice of the Future and the Goddess of Healing, Sandy kept up a continuous stream of banter and rang his bell. The boots would stop chilblains; the pants would keep you warm in winter, cool in the summer; the pots, pans, and fry pans would turn out gourmet cooking; the shovel dug the deepest hole in the least amount of time; and the Navajo Indian rugs had the woven-in promise of keeping evil from your house. One and all should feel free to browse the merchandise while they waited for Persephone.

"Stay right here, folks. Witness her healing powers first hand! Experience the miracles!" Sandy pulled his rumpled handkerchief from his pocket, raised his black gentleman's hat, and mopped his brow.

The crowd watched the little man with their mouths open as if they expected him to disappear in a puff of smoke. They craned their necks to see the necklace of magical shells he held before them, plucked from the healing waters of the Mediterranean Sea, worth hundreds of dollars. He would sell it at a steal for good, honest, hardworking people. Why shouldn't they too have an opportunity to experience the healing and protective powers of the Mediterranean Sea?

Buddy's part in the swindle was coming up and his stomach soured in anticipation. He hoped his parents in heaven were looking the other way and that the whole Scott Constellation was on the dark side of the moon.

A man came out of the wagon, grinning and shaking his head. At least he looked happy.

Sandy announced to the crowd that the Vision of the Future portion of the show had now ended—unfortunate for folks who had missed the opportunity to hear what lay ahead for them—but they shouldn't go; the Goddess of Healing would soon emerge and demonstrate the power of her medicine and her touch.

Buddy's palms sprouted sweat and his legs turned to willow whips. He spotted Ray on the opposite side of the crowd towards the back. Ray saw him too, then, as agreed, they made no further acknowledgements.

Sandy asked the crowd if they had medical problems. Ailments such as rheumatism, blocked bowels—which could lead to madness—poor vision, foul breath, scabby skin, open lesions that resisted healing, limbs that refused to work, shaky hands, cloudy vision, dizzy spells, or crepitus?

"Folks, we avoid the topic of physical weakness, human frailty, but I guarantee, once you acknowledge it and put your faith in the healing powers of Persephone, Goddess of Healing, you will be rewarded with good health and rejoice at your humble admission."

Annabelle emerged from inside the wagon, her blond hair

wound in a fancy gold cloth, sparkling in the sun. Her eyes appeared huge outlined in black, topped off with blue, and her cheeks blossomed like two red roses. She towered over Sandy like a statue, her sweeping red and gold gown shimmering in the afternoon light.

"Ladies and gentlemen," Sandy shouted, "I present to you the amazing Persephone, gifted with the power to heal."

The crowd shouted, whistled, and clapped. A dog barked and children, once engaged in a running game at the edge of the crowd, jumped up and down, screamed, and giggled.

Sandy rang the bell. "I must request quiet and stillness or Persephone's powers will not work."

Persephone stretched her arms out wide and raised them up, palms open to the sky. She closed her eyes and tipped her head back. She stood like that for a while, the crowd silent; then she spoke, her voice raspy and hushed.

"I feel the presence of something. Is it good? Or is it evil? Quiet! All must remain quiet!"

Buddy sensed something too, the worst kind of deceit he'd ever been partner to.

"There is illness amongst you. Serious illness. But you are afraid. Cast aside your fear. Approach the Goddess of Healing. The Goddess knows that you must come forward, and if you don't some of you will experience certain death."

The crowd sucked in its breath then fell silent again, casting about among themselves for the sickly.

"Excuse me there, Madam Healer," someone shouted from the back. Buddy knew it was Ray. "I am ill and I am not afraid to say. All but the last drop of hope has drained out of my well."

Buddy thought some terrible curse had come over him to talk in such a way.

"Step forward young man. Come to me so that I may better see you."

Ray started toward the wagon dragging his left leg, a leg that worked fine until now and was so badly busted up with some horrible disease he could barely make it through the crowd.

Sandy went to him and assisted him up onto the wagon next to Annabelle. The Goddess of Healing placed her hand on his head, closed her eyes and said, "Be still my child. I am getting something." She moaned, went silent, then suddenly she looked at the crowd, her eyes wide open, but the pupils seemed to have disappeared.

Someone screamed; it was truly a hideous sight. Buddy could turn his eyelids inside out to scare his younger brothers and sisters but he couldn't do the trick that turned Annabelle's eyes white.

"I am in communication with a medium. I need complete silence or the spell will be broken." She stroked Ray's hair, yanked his ear, and felt his forehead. "You are fevered, my son."

Buddy spotted saliva at the corners of Ray's mouth as he made a loud gurgling noise. Several women gasped and clasped their hands over their mouths.

"Hush," Annabelle shouted, then in a low raspy voice said, "Tell me my son," she lowered her face close to Ray's. "Have you ever been bitten by a snake?"

"Yes," Ray said, a bank of saliva foaming on his lips. He looked for all the world like a rabid coyote.

"Rattler?"

"Yes."

"You carry the poison in your leg. Is that where it bit you?"

"Uh-huh." With effort he raised his pant leg to show a scar where a rattler actually had bitten him—a long time ago—and Grandpa had been there to suck out the venom. Grandpa, an expert at healing snake bites, knew exactly where to apply the tourniquet, how far to cut with the knife, and when to stop sucking out the poison.

The crowd rose up on their toes to view this poor half-crazed victim, this unfortunate who might topple at any second as the poison entered his heart.

Persephone the Healer picked up a small jar and raised it up for all to see. "This," she displayed it for the audience to see, "is the elixir of health. This will cure this poor unfortunate." She stopped and inquired of him what his name might be. Ray spoke quietly into her ear. "This poor Aylmer, will be rid of his terrible suffering, and the constant fear he lives in. His fever will be gone."

Again she put her hand to his forehead. "I must work quickly, I don't have much time. He's burning up. The body cannot endure temperatures such as this for long."

Ray's entire body gyrated as if someone gave him a real good shaking. He moaned, long and loud, sounding like a dog left alone, his head rolling about on his shoulders.

The audience mumbled and whispered. Persephone grabbed his arm and assisted him to lie down on the wagon seat. She dipped her hand into the jar and held her hand high for all to see the jellied substance heaped on her palm. "This is the cure," she shouted. "This, Persephone's Healing Liniment, will strike the poison from his body, put up a barrier around his heart. This will purify Alymer's blood."

She crouched beside Ray, pulled his pant leg up, and smeared the jelly over his leg. Then she opened his shirt and wiped the jelly over his chest, letting her hand meander over his heart.

"Oh, oh, oh," Ray yelped, loud at first then dwindling to a sigh.

"Can you feel the pain?" Persephone placed her hand on his head.

"No," he whispered loud enough for the crowd to hear. The tremors had left his body; he lay motionless.

Persephone looked up at the crowd. "His fever is gone. Persephone's Healing Liniment sucked it out through the skin." Ray had propped himself up on the seat and appeared to be awakening from sleep.

"Rise," Persephone ordered. "Rise up and walk. Walk without pain. Walk without the fear of poison striking your heart."

Ray rose slowly and pressed his foot down gingerly on the wagon floor. He took several timid steps until he stood confidently on both legs; a triumphant grin spread across his face.

"You see," Persephone spoke to the crowd. "Witness the poison banished from his body."

Ray gave a little hop on both legs, then one leg, then the other. He looked down at his feet, his arms extended wide as if to say, I'm amazed. He twirled around.

The crowd clapped; some whooped, some whistled.

This whole business stirred up Buddy's stomach like he might be sick. How terrible to cheat these folks. Some looked to be poorer than his own family, and there they were, lining up to part with their hard-earned money on jars of worthless goop.

Sandy passed around his hat for people to drop their coins into as he dispersed jars of ointment. Persephone the Healer helped Ray the actor down from the wagon and once he hit the ground he demonstrated how he could move without the least agitation—without the slightest limp. Several people reached out and patted him on the back. "Good for you son, good for you. Believe in the Lord and thou shalt be cured!" an old man shouted.

"Is there anyone else out there who is ailing?" Persephone shaded her eyes with her hand and scanned the crowd, first in the direction away from Buddy, then back his way. "Anyone suffering from sickness or another malady that needs the curing hands of Persephone the Healer?" Again a sweep the other way then back to Buddy.

She'd warned him and Ray if they didn't comply, she and Sandy would find them and whip their scrawny little asses from there to kingdom come. If both he and Ray did as agreed they would receive their payment, but not until nightfall at the river's first bend beyond the edge of town. Buddy wasn't sure he wanted anything to do with this filthy money, but it would get them out of here and set them on the road again.

"Well then, this is certainly a healthy crowd," Persephone continued to address the assembled. "I am very happy for you. There must be something in the soil in these parts to keep you all so free of disease." A few laughed as she looked directly at Buddy, her eyes intent on him.

Here goes, he thought, and collapsed to the ground. He began to squirm and shake and moan and sputter and spit; his mouth wide open and his tongue hanging out. Soon Sandy knelt at his side.

"He's having a fit!" he shouted to Persephone, then leaned close to his ear and whispered, "Stop your kicking so I can pick you up, you little bastard."

Buddy squirmed harder and moaned louder. If he was going to cheat people out of their money he'd put on a good show and make Sandy and Persephone work a little harder for it. "Ahhhh, ahhhh," he twisted and squirmed, remembering a story his father told about witnessing someone having a fit. He made his arms and legs go rigid and produced the worst kind of moaning and grunting. A cross between a wolf's howl, a jay's screech, and the moos of a calving cow.

"Stand back, give us space." Sandy slipped his arms under

his stiff body. "Make way. I need to deliver this poor wretch into the healing hands of Persephone."

Buddy twisted about again then went stiff as a board. He started to spit gobs of foamy phlegm right up into Sandy's face. Sandy glowered and pinched him as hard as he could on the ass. Buddy howled. Sandy hissed out a few swear words under his breath as he struggled to the wagon. He hoisted Buddy up and stretched him out on the wagon seat.

"The devil has invaded his body." Persephone addressed the crowd but it was meant for his ears—a warning not to overdo it. "These tremors can be strong, but when they are extraordinary like this, they are part of a sick mind."

She was the one taking money from these poor innocent people. Wasn't she a fine one to talk about a sick mind! Buddy moaned louder and convulsed harder.

"I will apply the ointment and be forewarned. I must use some strong words to penetrate the brain. This treatment is not for the weak. Avert your eyes, if you must." Persephone knelt beside him; his body flipped about like a fish out of water. She whispered in his ear, "You stop this right now! Settle these agitations right this instant or you'll not receive so much as a penny."

"I'll show the people I'm faking if you don't pay me," he hissed back.

"Stop right now! Settle down so I can apply this ointment."

"Cure me, cure me!" Buddy shouted. It came out sounding like "hur me, hur me."

"You asked for it you lousy little bugger." She slapped a liberal amount of salve on his forehead. It burned through his skin and made him yelp louder. There was something more in it than ordinary bee's wax, that was certain. Lye maybe. She ripped open his shirt and slapped a handful on his chest.

"Brain and heart," she explained to the crowd. He kept up his twisting, delighting at the sight of the sweat on her brow, and the sound of her huffing and puffing as she slapped on the salve. The sun beamed behind her, set her headdress glittering. Her costume would be unbearably hot.

"The next handful goes on your nuts if you don't settle down and get cured. Once I get this ointment on them, you'll be dancing all right, and running to the river."

Okay, maybe it was time to stop; he let his body go still.

"The ointment has taken hold; the devil is gone." She raised her hands to the audience's cheers in a gesture of triumph.

Her gold turban had shifted and covered one eyebrow, and blue from over her eyes bled with sweat down her face. Her entire headdress sat cock-eyed like a tipped nest. Sweat stained her robe under the arms and streaked down her back.

"Rise my son." She extended her arms out straight, palms down over Buddy. "The seizures have been cast out, the devil is gone, the ointment has burned them both away."

She was right on that account. Right now it burned his skin and he wouldn't be at all surprised if it left a hole.

"Rise," she ordered. "Rise up without fear. The fits have gone."

He rose and stood before the crowd as if in bleary-eyed wonderment, pretending to notice them for the first time. They stared back.

"You see," Persephone said. "A normal boy again. He can leave here without the fear of another seizure ever again in his life."

Leave here; he'd go along with that.

Persephone placed her hand on his shoulder. "What do you think?" she asked him, wanting him to express something beyond the meek smile he gave her. "Do you feel better, my son?" She opened her eyes wider to encourage him to participate with her next bit of acting.

He'd done what they agreed on; he'd give her nothing more.

"Uh-huh," he mumbled in a voice as flat as a Johnny cake. He let his mouth hang open to give the appearance of slowness and stupidity. Maybe folks would think twice before buying the rancid liniment.

"Once again Persephone's Healing Liniment has cured a wretched brother," Sandy shouted and waved his empty hat in the air. "Folks, step right up and buy some. Maybe you're fine now, but who knows what the future brings? Many of our neighbours have died from the measles, pox, mumps, typhoid. Prepare yourself for a pestilence."

The crowd stared at him as Buddy passed through, stepping back out of the way for fear of catching whatever had possessed his brain. He couldn't get to the river fast enough, would jump in without bothering to strip off his clothes, and rid himself of this ointment and the whole stinking business of conning people. He may be a lot of things, but as his mother and father in Heaven knew, he was no cheater.

He jumped into the fast-flowing river, the water cooling the awful burning caused by the ointment. He dove under to rid his forehead and hair of the sticky goop and felt the relief of cold water against his face.

As he lay drying in the sun, Ray came along, stripped off his clothes, and jumped in. "Jesus Lord Almighty, that stuff she rubbed on me hurt like hell." Ray stuck a leg up out of the water to have a look at the affected area, all blistered and blotchy red. "They sold a lot. I think we earned ourselves a fair chunk of money."

"There was nothing fair about it!" Buddy said. "I don't want to talk about it, either. I can hardly wait to meet up with those scoundrels, get our money, and get the hell out of here."

Nothing to do but wait for the night, and as they did, they reviewed their afternoon performances. Ray told Buddy he found his stiffness very convincing. "If you're a corpse."

Buddy complimented Ray on foaming at the mouth. "Just like the old mare whenever she had to trot. You slobbered up just like her."

They waited, and well after dark ate the lunch Persephone had prepared for them, once again crediting her with making a fine sandwich with thick slabs of meat. Despite their best efforts to stay awake, they fell asleep to the soothing trill of the crickets and the sound of rushing water.

They were awakened in the early morning by the sound of voices. Buddy lifted his head to see a small group of men rushing toward them.

"There they are, the little buggers! Grab them by their scrawny little necks!" the lead man shouted.

Buddy and Ray jumped up and ran. The voices stayed close behind for a long time until Buddy thought he could no longer hear them. He looked behind him and they were close enough for him to see their red sweaty faces. "There they are! Let's catch the little bastards!

They ran harder until the voices had gone and they knew none of them would catch them. They'd outrun them; they had youthfulness on their side. They kept on running with their pockets empty.

Chapter 13

The Statue of Liberty — October 1927

Months of wandering turned into years, going from farm to farm looking for work and sleeping outdoors. They hitched rides to keep moving, like Duke and Squire had taught them, and often ended up dumped in the middle of nowhere. They were grateful when they found places willing to trade work for home-cooked meals and a decent cot to sleep on. They saved some money, but never enough to take to the bank.

They spent a long stretch with a family who treated them well, fed them good food, and spoke to them in a manner kindlier than most. They let Buddy tell his stories and the children were captivated by them, their mouths hanging open with wonder. Buddy couldn't help but remember his own brothers and sisters who also listened with rapt attention and who he hadn't seen for so long. For months the kindness of the family was enough, but then it was time to be on the move again—headed to New York City to find work. Paying work. As they'd done so many times before, they slipped off in the early hours of the morning while it was still dark and there was no one to witness their leaving. This time they left a thank you note.

One morning, after sleeping curled up in a ditch, they stood at the roadside with their thumbs dangling and watched a vehicle approach. Ray made it clear he wasn't spending another night sleeping in a god damn ditch freezing his balls off, and flagged it down.

"You boys headed to the city?" The trucker peered down at

them from his window.

"Sure are," Ray called back.

"Get in then. It's a long ride." The trucker motioned towards the back and flicked his cigarette butt out onto the gravel road. "Help yourselves to the fruit and vegetables I'm haulin'. Make it look like nothing's missing or the buyers will notice. I only stop for gas. I'll take you right downtown."

They hoisted themselves up over the tailgate and fell into a storeroom of stacked crates and bulging burlap bags. The truck coughed to life, the exhaust so loud and explosive they had to shout. "Here," Ray tossed Buddy a pile of empty bags to make a bed. They pulled sacks of flour from a stack, leaned back on them, and settled in for the long haul to New York City.

Buddy eyed the wall of boxes across from him, swaying with the motion of the truck, and eventually fell asleep. Food entered his dreams: restaurants with chandeliers, grocery stores stuffed to the ceiling with meat, fruit, vegetables, and bakeries with row after row of fruit pies and cakes.

Buddy and Ray dozed and lapsed in and out of conversation. They pissed into a bucket and stretched to pull cramps out of their legs, settled back into long sessions of silence, jostled about on their burlap sacks, and fell back to sleep. Once the driver came back to see how they were holding up. "Another eight to ten hours, boys, and we'll be there. I told you it'd be a long one."

A tug on Buddy's boot jarred him awake. The truck had finally stopped.

"Okay fellas. Get your things and let's go. I've got work to do. Grab some fruit to take with you." The driver lowered the tailgate and they stuffed their pockets with apples before tumbling out. They stood in the street and took in the activity surrounding them.

Finally, New York City, the three words chiselled into Ray's brain ever since they left home. The city of Ray's dreams, a dream Buddy willingly followed.

Buddy was surrounded by more buildings then he'd ever seen in one place. They'd steered clear of big cities. They lived and worked on farms or in small towns while they saved up their money. Ray said the rural life was what they knew and if they went to a big city like Chicago they'd be robbed, cheated, swindled, and swallowed up whole before they even got a glimpse of New York.

The driver waved, they shouted thanks, and the truck disappeared down the street and around the corner. Ray turned in all directions, open mouthed, taking in the shops up and down the street—some with their wares displayed outside their doors as if spilled out onto the sidewalk. The street, crowded with cars and sidewalks teeming with people, smelled of souring vegetables. Here they were, finally.

Now what? It didn't look as if prosperity resided in the homes of some of the people who passed by. Did laziness stop the people from grabbing what was practically handed to them? Father always spoke of laziness like it was some kind of disease.

They talked for so long about this moment they'd never thought beyond arriving. So willingly he'd been scooped up and carried off in Ray's dream of the Promised Land, pushing reason so far away he could no longer see it. Ray had never been to New York City—it was his idea of hope, a story he invented to keep them going. Buddy knew better. If he learned one thing in all his seventeen years it was that nothing came easily. What made him think this place would be any different?

As he looked down the streets, he saw no gold. No one rushed up to them to welcome them with open arms. The people passing on sidewalks went about their business the way they did in all towns—eyes straight ahead, minds set on chores, without seeing what the vegetable truck hauled in from the country. A pair of drifters with nowhere to go and only a few coins between them, cowboy boots squashed flat by hundreds of miles of walking. He and Ray must look pathetic and that was how he felt.

Ray said a goddess, the Statue of Liberty, would welcome them. She was a mother to all newcomers. Visible from everywhere in the city in the daytime and at night she held a great torch to lead people to her. The statue made everyone feel welcome and safe even if they didn't know anyone. Ray spoke often about her magical powers and how, once you laid eyes on her, you could feel your spirits lift.

"I don't see the Statue of Liberty," Buddy said, desperately in need of having his spirits lifted.

"Must be in a different direction than the one we're facing."

A car horn blasted, sounding like the squawk of geese angling overhead on a fall day. They moved onto the sidewalk.

"Let's ask someone where we can find the Statue of Liberty," Buddy said. "Maybe if we could see it, we'd know what to do from there."

They picked along sidewalks snarled with shoppers, merchandise, people hauling wagons, dogs, children threading through adults, and the squalor of voices—an explosion of life. Around them the crowd moved with purpose as if everyone had some place to go.

Well, by God, Buddy had a purpose too.

"Excuse me, Ma'am." He stepped up to a woman towing a child in hand. He thought he might have startled her, the way she jumped back a bit, as if he'd jumped out at her. "Could you tell me which way to the Statue of Liberty?"

She made a sour face and walked away. Perhaps she hadn't heard him. Maybe she was deaf. Or rude—the uppity sort. Or from another country and she didn't understand English. Ray said people came to this city in boats from all over the world, and they were made to take a bath as soon as they got off the boat so everyone who arrived in the city would be clean. Everyone but them. Buddy looked down at his tattered pants worn too thin to patch, a shirt with holes for elbows, and a sweater that every day became smaller as the hole in the front got bigger.

He stopped a man, more determined now than ever to find the Liberty lady. When they found her she'd give them a place to start from. Ray knew for an absolute fact she was by the ocean, and they wouldn't feel so…so lost.

"Sir, could you tell me where we can find the Statue of Liberty?"

The man studied him and took his pipe out of his mouth. "Is this a joke?" He stuck the pipe back in and chewed on the stem.

"No," Ray said.

"New York City." A cloud of smoke escaped his lips and drifted in the air.

"We know, but which direction?" Buddy asked.

"South," he said.

"Which way's south?"

The man removed his pipe, scanned the street, then pointed. "That way, but it's quite a way. Good luck." He stuck his pipe back in and walked away.

After a few blocks Ray said they should find out the exact distance. "If it's too far, we'll hitch a ride."

Ray stepped up to a black man, his arms moving back and forth faster than a flywheel as he bent over a man's shoes, rubbing them vigorously with a white cloth.

"Excuse me please," Ray said.

The shoeshine man stared at them, his arms never breaking rhythm as they tugged the cloth back and forth over the shiny black shoes. Beads of sweat bubbled at his grey hairline. "You want a shine, boy? You best wait in line." He looked down at their cowboy boots. "You could do with more than a shine. Can't make a silk purse out of a sow's ear. No sir, uh-uh, can't do it."

The man in the chair lowered his newspaper and examined Ray and Buddy's boots. "They'd fall apart if you tried to give them a buff," he said.

"I'd like to ask you a question," Ray said.

"Well ask away, boy. Won't cost you nothing. Make her snappy. I'm a workin' man," the shoeshine man said.

"How far is the Statue of Liberty?"

"Didn't I just tell you I'm a busy man? I've no time for foolish questions."

"It's not a game. I'm not from here. I don't know how far away it is."

"We're from Wyoming," Buddy added. "We just got here a few minutes ago." The shiner wouldn't notice if he got polish on his hands, he thought, and it struck him as kind of funny.

"Oh, so you be a pair of country boys, then." The shoeshiner's hands continued the fast sweep over the shoes.

"That's right," Ray said. "We lived on a ranch."

"Where's your horses?" he asked, then exchanged glances with the seated man.

"Let's go," Buddy grabbed Ray's arm to pull him along. All these fellows wanted to do was make fun of them and they weren't in any kind of mood for it.

"Did you forget your horses, leave them at home, boys? It's quite a walk all the way from Wyoming." The shiner flicked out his cloth, snapped it back, then refolded it without looking at his hands like a magician doing a trick.

"How far to the statue?" Buddy asked again.

"What would you say, Boss? Any idea?" the shoeshine man asked the man in the chair.

The man in the chair tipped his head back and looked up at the grey sky. "Five hundred miles. Give or take."

Ray scowled and started to walk away. All they sought was a little straight-forward instruction. Buddy followed him up the sidewalk.

"Hey!" the shoeshiner called out. "Where you going?"

"We told you, the Statue of Liberty," Ray stopped and called back, his voice so tired it sounded as if it couldn't hold up the words.

"How do you imagine you're going to get there?" the shiner shouted.

"Same way we get everywhere," Buddy said. "We'll walk." He raised his bundle and clutched it close to his chest.

The shoeshiner whistled. "That's some walk."

What of it? They were used to it. On the prairie folks walked twenty miles, sometimes every day, and never even thought of complaining. City people were soft, maybe even lazy, and maybe it was no wonder judging by all the cars passing in the street—more cars than Buddy had ever seen in one place.

"Well at the rate you're going now," the man in the chair called out, "you'll be there by Christmas."

Ray stopped, turned around, then strutted right back and positioned himself in front of the two men. He stood with his legs apart, a way of standing he had and showed he meant business. "I'd really appreciate it if you dropped all the hogwash and just told us how far."

Buddy stood next to Ray. He'd hurry him along; he wanted no part of a temper outburst from Ray.

"You pipe down, son, and mind your manners." The shoeshiner's face went serious.

"Like I said before," the man in the chair said, "about five hundred miles, give or take some."

"How can it be so far away?" Buddy asked before Ray could say anything. He knew New York City might be a lot bigger than he expected, but surely it couldn't be that big, could it?

"Just where do you suppose the Statue of Liberty is?" The man in the chair leaned forward, his forehead crunching into wrinkles, his deep-set eyes hard on them, and the hint of a smile on his lips.

"New York City," Ray said.

"Yes, you're right there." The man seemed to mull that over. "And where do you suppose you are?"

"New York City," Buddy said.

The two men looked at each other. "Don't that beat all?" the shiner said and pointed across the street. "See there," he said. "Read that sign over the store. What's it say?"

"Debt — trott Dry Goods," Buddy stumbled on the first word.

"Okay, now search a little farther down the street," the man in the chair said. "What does the blue sign say?"

"Detroit City Ladies Wear," Ray had no trouble pronouncing it.

"That tell you anything?" the shiner asked.

The shoeshiner gave Boss a quick glance and shrugged. "Do you think that if those stores was in New York City, they'd call them Detroit this and that? You're in Detroit City boys, that's what them signs is telling you. Dee-troit, not New York. Um, hm, no siree. Dee-troit. Just as sure as I'm looking at you, you be here."

"You've blown a fair ways off course," the Boss said. "You're north and west of where you thought you were. Somewhere along the line you took a wrong turn." He seemed serious now he knew their confusion was genuine.

Buddy threw his bundle down on the sidewalk. His chin quivered but he wouldn't cry in front of these two strangers, and he wouldn't break down in front of Ray, either. They'd see from their reaction this was a terrible setback.

The man in the raised chair removed his feet from the shoeshine stirrups and climbed down to the sidewalk. He rummaged in his pocket, pulled out a wallet, and handed the shiner a bill, his newspaper folded up and tucked under his arm. "Do you boys have a place to go here in Detroit?"

"Not really." Ray's voice possessed not an ounce of energy. "We were headed to the Statue of Liberty. That's where our new life was going to start. From there, we'd find a place to live and a job."

"Anyway, it doesn't matter if we don't have a place to go. We're used to making do." Buddy could barely hide the disappointment in his voice but he didn't want pity either. He and Ray were made of tough stuff and just watch if someone didn't believe it. They could manage on their own. "We haven't had a place to stay in a long time. Suits us fine. We like it that way." Buddy loaded up his voice with defiance in case this man in the fancy suit and shoes didn't get it the first time, with Ray all the time saying, "That's right."

"That so?" the man said. He nodded and scrutinized the two of them. Buddy saw how his shirt collar looked as white as white against his neck and stiff as a board. "Tell you what, and I don't mean any offense by it, boys. Since I can see you are a pair with a great deal of pride, why don't you come back to my place? My wife can arrange an excellent meal; there's nothing she likes more than someone who appreciates good food. Maybe we could sit down and work out a way for you to get to New York City, since you're hell-bent on getting there. I can guarantee you whatever we come up with is going to be a lot faster than the way you're going at it."

"We'll work for the meal," Buddy said to let him know they weren't a pair of freeloaders. What kind of work could they do for this man with the shiny shoes, a fancy suit of clothes, a white shirt, and striped tie? He seemed like he had money, the kind of person who might peer down his nose at the likes of Buddy and Ray and take a dim view of their way of surviving.

"One step at a time. That's all we need to take." He tipped his head to the side, grinned, and nodded his head. "I'm sure we can find something." He reached his hand out to shake the shoeshiner's hand. "Thanks, Delmont. I'll see you in a couple of days and in the meantime, you take good care."

"Okay, boys, follow me." He started up the sidewalk. A sharpness in his step had them trailing along smartly to keep up. They turned the first corner toward the most beautiful car Buddy had ever seen. It shone like the man's shoes and reflected clouds off its white hood. Buddy and Ray stopped to admire it. The car had brown leather seats and a man sat in the driver's seat. Ray whistled out loud and said, "This here's a beaut." He reached out about to touch the car's gleaming paint, but their escort said, "No touching."

Was it his car? He didn't seem to be moving away from it. Right then the driver noticed them and jumped out, rushing around behind the car to the back passenger door, and opening it. "Good shine, Boss?"

"As usual."

The man in the suit turned to Buddy and Ray. "In you go boys."

Ray slid across the spacious back seat and Buddy followed. The man in the fancy suit got in and the driver closed the door, then took his place behind the steering wheel and started the car. They'd ridden Model-T's and rundown farm trucks but never had their hides been hauled in anything so fancy. It even smelled fancy, like the best horse tack you could imagine. They pulled out into the street and Buddy thought he might be floating.

The man in the suit leaned forward to talk to his driver. "We'll not bother with those other stops, Ned. Just take us home. I've got a hunch these boys are in need of a good meal."

"Okay, Boss," the driver looked into the rear-view mirror to see the pair of drifters seated in the back.

The Boss settled back in his seat and folded his hands in his lap. He had smooth skin and even, clean fingernails. The kind of hands unfamiliar with manual work. "Now then, I guess if you're going to be guests at my house you should know who I am and I should know who you are. What do you say? Sound like a good idea?"

They nodded, yes, but shyly, still adjusting to the excitement of the car. "My name is Mr. Ford." He held out a hand for Ray to shake, then Buddy. "I make cars such as this. Not many like this, but I make a lot of other cars."

"Mr. Henry Ford?" Ray asked.

"The very one."

"I heard about you in school," Ray blurted, his excitement plainly on display.

Mr. Ford must have thought that was funny; he laughed out loud. "Hear that Ned, I'm a fossil already. They're already taking me in school."

Mr. Ford turned to Buddy and Ray and asked them who might they be, and after hearing, told them to settle back and enjoy the ride since Fair Lane—the place where he lived—was several miles from the city in a little place called Dearborn.

Book Three

Under the Tree — June 1973

Buddy couldn't help laughing, though it hurt in every bone and used up so much of his breath he wished he wouldn't. But what a pair of jackasses thinking that in all of the United States there was only one city—New York City. No matter how many times he remembered the story he couldn't help but laugh. Though Ray eventually confessed to stringing Buddy along.

Something woke him if he'd even been sleeping. No way to tell, no one to ask. He seemed to be slipping in and out of time. Or was he slipping in and out of his mind? His memories seemed so real he half expected to see Linda sitting there beside him. *Keep on. I'm listening. You're so fuckin cool, man.*

Must have been Spirit's whinny that brought him around. He can hear the horse now, huffing and snorting, worked up by the storm.

High overhead the tree's outer branches scraped back and forth against the black sky. Was this night or had the storm turned daylight to darkness? How long had he been lying here? Minutes? Hours? Days? His loose thoughts roamed every-which-way following a trail of disorder, the way they do in dreams, dreams that went on forever but might take only seconds.

His left arm tingled, felt tight, and his neck ached from being lodged between a tree root and a rock. He had to piss something terrible. He didn't need another problem to solve.

Spirit whinnied again. Some horses would take right off to the barn if they sensed a storm coming. Spirit would be gone soon, he felt certain.

"That what you waiting for old buddy? For the storm to pass? Me too."

The stable owner would appear any minute now. He could

picture her sliding down the steep ravine in her massive rubber boots, puffing on a smoke. The first thing she'd say to him would be a reminder about how he'd signed a waiver which said she was in no way responsible for the accident. Speaking of smokes, he hadn't had one since this morning. Even then he only took half. Dr. Grant would be pleased since he'd been bugging him to quit for so long. He had cut way back but couldn't seem to leave it alone completely, especially when he drank. *With those lungs, Buddy. You're playing with fire. It could kill you.* He told Grant that something would eventually, same was true for everyone, and Grant gave him a dirty look. What if this turned out to be the event to end his life? He could almost hear his boys, David, Doug, and Donnie saying what the hell did he think he was doing?

The sky lit with lightning then turned black and the world rumbled with the aftermath. Buddy used to tell Donnie that thunder was a giant burping after a big meal, and Donnie, wide-eyed and gullible, asked if the wind was his fart. It hurt Buddy to laugh.

He searched for Spirit, the white diamond standing out even brighter now, a tiny yield sign in the dark. Still keeping his distance, agitated by the weather in the same way Misty, Bishop, Breeze, and the other horses would be. Not a storm went by when he didn't think about those horses. Peat and Mary, too.

Something struck the back of Buddy's hand, then the sound of dirt pelting something. But who would be throwing chunks of dirt? No, he was wrong. Not dirt. Raindrops. Huge raindrops. The kind that precede a torrential downpour. Their touch upon his hand felt like heat, as if he was being touched by hot matchsticks.

As the rain came down harder, he opened his mouth to take in the water. A drink served to him by the heavens, it cooled his parched mouth. He kept his mouth open until it pooled at the back of his throat then swallowed. He did this over and over, his eyes closed tight against the driving rain.

The rain would solve his bladder problem. As soon as it came down harder he would let it go and let nature wash the piss away. That gave him something to look forward to; not having a full and painful bladder to remind him of his helplessness.

How far did he get with his stories with Linda? Just to Detroit, wasn't it? Because when he finally finished it was 4 o'clock in the morning and his little granddaughter, Jenny, was an early riser and then everyone else would get up. If Meg caught him up all night with Linda, Lady would have company in her doghouse. He told her they would continue the stories the next night, but maybe he should be glad she never got to hear the rest.

In Detroit he stood on his own two feet only to get knocked down again and again. *Always keep up your guard.* That's what Father and Duke said, and then Hadley. That's what he was learning to do in Detroit. But he wasn't a fast learner.

The rain beat down harder, driven by sudden gusts of wind. Around him trees shifted in a restless dance. His stories would protect him—take him away from the hard ground, the tree roots jabbing up into his back, the jolts of pain crossing his chest.

Chapter 14

Detroit — 1927

The food. Brought by an army of women in grey dresses and white aprons. Etta, the one Mr. Ford spoke to, the one in charge, the one that spoke to them. "Have them wash their hands and faces and get them started on a good meal. There'll be ample time for clean up later."

"What should I feed them, Sir?"

"The evening's selection, the full treatment. Won't hurt for a couple of the bankers to have their portions cut back. Might even be doing them a favour." Mr. Ford pulled a pocket watch out of his vest. "I'd better get going or my name will be Mud with the Mrs. Enjoy your meal, lads." He left through a swinging door with a round window.

Etta led them to a nearby washroom and supervised as they soaped their hands, face, and neck. They scrubbed until their skin reddened, dried off, and took their seats at a long kitchen table.

An arsenal of cutlery, glasses, and napkins, was spread before them. Then came the food: artichokes and rich butter sauce, chanterelle mushrooms and goose liver, fiddleheads, shrimp, lobster, filet mignon, potatoes, a salad, then sorbet to clear the palate. Etta explained everything, as they'd never seen the likes of many of the dishes set before them, especially the lobster; Ray thought it was a large insect. Finally the last course—strawberry flan and crème brûlée. Buddy could never remember being so full and certainly never on anything so splendid. When they were done, the kitchen staff gathered round. "My word," one said, and made a tisking noise the way Mother would. "It's hard to believe two young fellows could make so much food disappear."

The kitchen door swung open and the little crowd dispersed

like cats in a barn. A woman with a poker-straight spine crossed the room to speak with Etta. Her feet struck the tile floor with clipped authority. Buddy thought it must be Mrs. Ford.

He wanted to lie down to take pressure off his belly pushing tight against his waistband. With his gut full and aching, his pinched smile seemed more the distress of someone holding back a fart than the expression of gratitude for such a feast.

They rose as Mrs. Ford approached the table. She offered her hand to Ray, then to Buddy, and introduced herself.

"Have a seat, please."

She looked more like a school teacher than a fancy lady, practically the queen of the United States. Her short brown hair pinched into tiny waves with streaks of grey, hugged her round face and gave her a no-nonsense appearance. She had a gentle voice. "Now who might you be?" she asked Ray. "And does Ray possess only one name?"

Ray stammered out his last name.

"And you are?" She turned to Buddy and nodded as he told her. "Well it's nice to meet you both. I hope you enjoyed your meal." They said yes, they'd never tasted anything like it. "Good then," she said. "William will be here shortly to take you to your room at the Powerhouse. Henry mentioned you might be lacking in food and sleep. William will show you to the shower, then a good sleep is in order. I know about boys your age. I've got a son, he's a fair stretch older than you two, but I do recall he could consume a near inexhaustible amount of food and boundless sleep when he was a young man."

Buddy would go along with anything Mr. and Mrs. Ford and Etta said.

"Enjoy your stay lads." She left them to carry out an inspection of the food being prepared, sampling every simmering pot and every platter on the counter. After she'd spoken with Etta she disappeared through the swinging door.

Etta sent one of the women in the kitchen to fetch the William fellow, a slim, severe looking man in a black suit, white shirt, and black bow tie.

"I understand you've got a catch of the day," he said to Etta as he looked at the two of them, one eyebrow cocked.

"Yes, I do. They're not so lively now they're weighed down with food. I've got this to say about hunger, it keeps us alert. They're stuffed full like sausage casings. Look at them," Etta said. "Dopey-eyed, if ever I saw."

William strode to the table, leaned closer to them, and made a hmmm sound as if someone had just asked him a question and he was trying to come up with an answer. He clutched his hands and Buddy saw how smooth they looked. Not the hands of a labourer. "Okay then boys. I've got my orders. Where's your luggage and I'll carry it."

Buddy held up his little sack, which, in the brightness of the kitchen looked terribly grimy. He realized he'd been hauling rags clear across the country.

"Oh dear," William said. "That's a nasty looking clutch of something-or-other, isn't it?" He shook his head. "You carry it. Follow me; I'll take you to the Powerhouse."

They thanked the kitchen staff for the best meal they'd ever had in the whole of their entire lives, which made the ladies smile, and proceeded with William out the back door and into a car.

"Fair Lane is magnificent, boys. Nothing short of magnificent. Consider yourselves lucky to be brought here. Some kind of angel watched over you and put you in the company of Mr. Ford, I can tell you that."

Buddy twisted in his seat to get a glimpse of the main house as they drove away. They'd gone in through an entrance covered in ivy and surrounded by trees, and didn't get much of an impression. It was a grand home, the largest he'd ever seen, with so many chimneys he couldn't even count them and a back wall that curved like a castle. The house didn't resemble the fair of its name and was bigger than many of the buildings he'd seen earlier in downtown Detroit. How could one family live in such a large house?

"How many rooms are in Mr. Ford's house?" Buddy asked.

"Fifty-six." William pulled the car up close to a stone building standing on the banks of a river. "Do you know the name of the river?" he asked. They both said no. "I don't imagine either of you were any too promising in your geography studies," he said.

"We're not from around here." Ray never liked anyone implying he might be thickheaded.

"I guess we'll let you off the hook then." William faced the river as he spoke. "That is the Rouge River boys. We pump part of it right into the building where you are going to be staying."

The building appeared small but when they went around to the back they saw that it had a wing with big doors all across the front.

"How come it's called the Powerhouse?" Buddy asked.

"Well, that's exactly what it is," William said. "If your history is better than your sense of geography, you'll already know that Mr. Ford is a great inventor."

"We know that!" Ray said.

"Good for you!" William sounded like he might be playing around with Ray. "In this building, water is converted to electricity. There are two generators inside and they produce hydroelectric power to run Mr. Ford's estate. Isn't that a good idea, boys? Mr. Ford is full of good ideas. You'll figure it out if you stay around here long enough. But first, I'll take you to the garage side. You can meet some of the fellows you'll be lodging with, and you can have a look at some of our cars." They followed along a path to another part of the building and stepped into a hall with the most beautiful motor vehicles Buddy ever saw. William led the way around a large airy room. "This is a Lincoln, and this is Mr. Ford's personal Model-A. He's got some nice things inside it." They stopped to peer through the rider's window. "He drinks Poland Mineral Water, and the contraption on the right, the thing that looks like a hole, holds it for him."

A grinding noise came across the room. Was Buddy seeing right? Had he eaten so much he'd given himself a dizzy spell, or was that car turning all by itself? He jabbed Ray, "Look," and pointed. No, the car was definitely turning.

William laughed as he noticed their surprise. "It's a turntable. The mechanics use it." He waved to a couple of men working on a motor. "Come along. That over there is a vehicle that got Mr. Ford a lot of his wealth, so he calls it Sweepstakes. He won an important race with it and after that people wanted to buy his cars. That's a Fordson, a tractor, and over there, Mrs. Ford's Detroit Electric Model 47 Brougham. She uses it to drive around the estate. Did you happen to notice all the electrical outlets here?" He pointed to a few places on the wall. "It's to keep her car charged with electricity. The estate's very big. A car is necessary to get around. Over there is a truck Mr. Ford uses as a kitchen when he goes camping with his gentleman friends."

As William strolled along the row of cars, he called out greetings to the mechanics. "We call them the M-boys," he explained. "They're your dorm mates."A few mechanics sprawled underneath vehicles with only their feet showing, others leaned over motors, their heads tucked under raised hoods, and two fellows polished a car with fluffy white cloths. The garage smelled of oil, gas, grease, and polish, but not strong and not at all unpleasant.

"In the evening we open the garage doors to air it out. We like to keep the vehicles smelling sweet. And, as you probably noticed, very shiny."

As shiny as Mr. Ford's shoes, Buddy thought.

"Okay, let's get you to the dorm." They followed William down a long hall to a narrow staircase and climbed to the second floor. William's black hair, flattened to his head with tonic, glistened under the overhead light.

"This is where you'll bunk. Until you get yourselves sorted out." He led them into a room with a row of beds and dresser bureaus lining one wall. "We'll have some chores for you while you're here, to earn your keep. I understand you've requested that. But not today. You've had too much to eat. We wouldn't get a minute's work out of you."

He told them to take the last two beds at the far end of the room. "Go to it boys. Put your sacks on the floor. Don't get them anywhere near the beds or we'll all be lousy. The shower is over there," he indicated a door, "and there's plenty of towels in there, too. Then, bunk down for the night. Here," he pulled something out of a dresser drawer and tossed them on their beds. "Nightshirts. Put them on after you shower. Leave your clothes on the floor by the bathroom door. I'll have someone tend to them." His face curled up as if he'd whiffed something most foul. "You're bunking in with the mechanics who work in the garage. They're a good bunch. They'll be up later, once they've finished for the night."

They waited for him to leave then stripped and went into the shower room. A spout came from the ceiling inside a cubicle. "I guess we stand inside there." They stepped inside and waited but nothing happened. He saw a tap and turned it.

"For Christ sakes!" Ray screamed. "It's bloody freezing."

They jumped out of the shower and stood with their hands

clutched to their chests, shivering as water streamed down. Buddy reached in and turned another tap and the cold water got warmer.

Buddy fiddled with the taps until Ray declared the temperature right. They both got in and lathered their bodies and hair with soap. Buddy relished the feel of warmth streaming over him and wanted to stay under that steady stream long enough to take the ache from his muscles and soften his calloused feet.

Ray toweled dry then reached in and turned the water off. "Don't want to drain the Rouge, do we?"

Buddy wrapped himself in a towel big enough to dry two of him, slipped the nightshirt on over his head, and flopped down on his bed. Across from him the faint light of a day's ending came through the drapes. He struggled to stay awake but sleep came long before night fell, held him fast when all the other men came in from work and through the next morning when the same men left for work.

Mr. Ford offered them permanent jobs, food, shelter, and a paycheck on one condition.

"Everyone here drives, lads. It's mandatory. And no driving until you learn about the automobile's internal combustion engine," Mr. Ford explained on a shopping trip into Detroit to buy them new boots.

They worked alongside the mechanics as helpers. Then one day, a day Buddy looked forward to for a long time, a mechanic gave him his first driving lesson and he experienced movement unlike the kind he felt as he raced Bishop or Breeze across the plains. He would do just about anything to feel a horse under him again; but this, the speed of an automobile, was something different. A power that wrapped around him and took its direction from his arms—a precise power that relied on him. He practiced turning the car around in a space the size of a small room, guided it around the sharpest corner without causing sway to the backseat passengers, and kept his speed even, not erratic. Power, motion, speed, grace, elegance; a formula for driving built into his body. "You're right at home with this" the mechanic said.

Not so with Ray. He bumped into curbs, ploughed into lamp standards and trees, and drove with an erratic stop and go motion that churned up the calmest stomach. Ray didn't care either; he said cars were unpredictable—not for him.

"You're an old lady," Buddy told him when Ray grumbled about having to take more driving lessons.

"I prefer horses. I don't mind riding in cars, but someone else can do the driving." He claimed to be confounded by motors, never did catch on. "A tangled up mess. Something from outer space."

"No aptitude whatsoever," one of the mechanics explained to Mr. Ford on one of his visits to the garage. Mr. Ford asked Ray if he might be happier as a groundskeeper and away from cars altogether.

"That would be right up my alley."

"Just so long as everyone's happy." Mr. Ford shook Ray's hand, then clamped a hand on Buddy's shoulder and gave it a light squeeze. "I hear Buddy here has a real aptitude for driving. I'm going to get him to do a little driving for me and Mrs. Ford."

Ned, the Ford's private chauffeur, started calling on Buddy to take Mrs. Ford out if she was going somewhere without Mr. Ford. "She's fond of young people and she likes a steady driver, one that's not all stop and go or too fast. She took a shine to you boys the first night you came," Ned said. "I need a second stringer."

Occasionally Buddy drove Mr. Ford late at night, after Ned brought the couple home from evening events. Mr. Ford proceeded on to other engagements, while Mrs. Ford preferred to call it an evening and stay home. Ned wanted someone younger, someone who could stay up until the wee small hours of the morning. He feared falling asleep at the wheel.

He covered Ned's days off and drove Mr. Ford to his car factories, around the city, and many times to city hall. Mr. Ford bragged to the business associates they picked up about Buddy, his youngest driver; he told them how he knew to handle speed and be safe.

"He understands real horsepower. But his brother! Just the opposite." Mr. Ford took great satisfaction from converting Buddy to the automobile, though the slightest nudge was all it took.

Once he was satisfied Buddy was right for the job, Ned handed over more night runs, claiming to need his beauty sleep.

Sometimes Buddy arrived back at the dorm at two or three in the morning, but it didn't matter. He'd still get up early with the rest of the M-boys to work on the cars in the garage and yank apart their motors. Or he'd spend hours shining them to a brilliant luster, the way Mr. Ford liked to see. Just like grooming the horses in the early morning, brushing their coats to a shine, back in the West.

"Ray, I've got a little announcement to make," Buddy said from the side of his bed as they sat facing each other, the only two in the dorm since the rest of them had gone to Auto's Speakeasy in the city and wouldn't be back until all hours.

"Well, say it and never mind the pussyfooting."

"I want my own place in the city. It's time for me to move out of here."

Ray hunched over, his head bowed to the floor, and shuffled his feet as if he'd just figured out he had a pair of them, then raised his soft brown eyes to Buddy. He looked so much like their father just then, traces of their mother too. "Before you get going, I've got something to tell you. I'm going back home; I'm going back West."

The news knocked the words right out of Buddy; he couldn't think what to say. He hadn't expected this; hadn't seen it coming at all.

"My life's back there; the West is in my blood. We've been treated very well at Fair Lane and my leaving has nothing to do with being here. It took me a while to figure it out, but I'm homesick. I'm going back to Wyoming. Then I plan to move to California."

"When are you leaving?"

"In four days. I was just working up the nerve to tell you."

"Not one for long goodbyes, are you?" If Buddy hadn't started the conversation, would Ray have told him at all, or would he just take off and leave a note? He was good at disappearing, practiced as they both were with slipping away in the night. "That's some kind of news. What the hell, Ray?"

Not once had he thought of them being apart. He hadn't thought of himself as the one being left. What had he expected? They'd be together forever?

Why would Ray want to bust up the only family they had? Why go clear across the country? Here he'd been feeling bad about moving out of the dorm to find a place in the city and all along Ray was cooking up something much bigger.

"I've saved enough money for a train ticket. And to get me settled somewhere." Ray lowered his voice almost in apology. "I thought about staying. I can't. I need to get going with my life, get myself established, get a job I like. I don't mind the yard work here, but it's not what I want to do for the rest of my life. Hell, who knows, maybe someday some woman will tolerate someone like me enough to want to settle down and have kids."

Somewhere along the line, and without Buddy noticing, Ray had grown into a man. "What about New York City? What about your dream?"

Ray laughed. "Most of what I was telling you was a bunch of hogwash. I even managed to convince myself. You've got to have dreams, a good story to latch onto. But at some point, you've got to start living in the real world. I belong in the West. You, too."

"I don't feel like I belong anywhere." Buddy thought about the two days that tore apart his life forever. The terrible storm; first his father; then his mother. He wasn't sure he could go back to a land that had cruelly taken so much from him.

"You can bet your bottom dollar I'll be steering clear of Uncle Wes's, if that's what's got you worried." Ray must have seen the crease in Buddy's brow as his news settled in. "I will try to find our brothers and sisters and find out what's become of them."

Ned let Buddy drive Ray to the train station in Ray's favourite car, the red roadster. Buddy wore his chauffeur's hat and Ray sat in the back with both arms extended across the back of the seat, soaking up the attention, pretending to be a movie star or visiting dignitary. People watched as they pulled into the station, taking peeks at the special person in the back important enough to have a chauffeur, to see if it might be someone they recognized—someone who had their picture in the newspapers.

They walked together along the crowded platform barely knowing what to say to each other. "Not only am I not anyone important, but not all that long ago I was nothing more than a tramp," Ray said.

A tramp? Buddy had never seen it that way but now that Ray said it, now that he had decent clothes and money in the bank, he supposed that's who they'd been. On the outside. Not much had changed on the inside.

The train tracks gleamed in the sunlight, two silver ribbons headed west.

"It doesn't seem natural waiting on the platform with a ticket already paid for. We should be lying down in the ditch waiting for a train to stop at a siding," Ray said, looking down the track, watching for the train.

In a while, a whistle blasted. An engine lurched into the station and ground to a full stop down the platform. All along the train conductors flipped down steps and passengers spilled out, some into waiting arms, while others appeared befuddled as if they'd unexpectedly fallen to earth. Like the two of them when they arrived in Detroit.

They took it in, the ordinary events of coming and going, without saying anything.

In truth, Buddy had no idea what to say and he knew Ray would be no better. What could be said after all this time? They'd been together all of his life.

"Well," Ray said when the train had unloaded. "I see they're starting to board. I guess this is it; I'd better get going. Don't want to be left here on the platform staring at the train as it pulls out of the station." The huge crowd with suitcases and sacks milling on the platform pressed towards the stairs at the doorways of the railcars.

Buddy clasped Ray's hand. Ray's smile was forced as he patted his shoulder. "You take good care of yourself, little brother. You don't have me watching over you anymore. I'll write to you in care of the Fords at Fair Lane and let you know my address once I've managed to get settled. You'll be hearing from me." He let go of Buddy's hand and bent down to pick up his bags without looking into Buddy's eyes. Buddy knew why. Except for his temper, Ray played it close to the chest. "Don't go breaking any speed limits," he said, and strode off disappearing into the crowd.

Buddy watched as Ray waited in line to board the train. Mingled with the others, his shoulders broad in the new tweed overcoat he bought for the trip, he could pass for a stranger. Now he was at the front of the line. He passed his ticket to the conductor, had it punched, stepped up into the train, and disappeared without one glance back at Buddy.

The platform emptied of all but a few people. Buddy waited until the train disappeared before leaving, his hands shoved deep into his pockets, and his collar up against a fresh, cold wind. Emptiness punched a hole right out of his centre. No one to answer to now, no one else to account for, and no one to confide in. Though he never wanted to admit it, he always knew the day would come when he'd be alone. And he knew he'd never be ready for it.

It would be a long time before he would see Ray again.

Chapter 15

Spring — 1930

A warm breeze fluttered the curtains and drew Buddy outside into the sweet scent of evening to walk the streets of grand houses, their yards filled with chestnut, elm, walnut, oak, and maple. Houses abandoned by their owners—people who'd lost their businesses on account of the crash. Yards, once tended with care, now overtaken by weeds and tall grass, sloping porches, and blistered paint; neglect moved in quickly and made itself at home. With so many out of work, few had money to buy. Business owners walked away: left everything behind but what they could carry.

Mrs. Gordon, the landlady at his rooming house, found a solution for hanging on. She would have preferred not to have strangers living in her house and made it obvious with her look of disgust, her thin lips pinched downward whenever she came upon a boarder. She still gave Buddy that face even after all he'd done for her. All year he'd worked on his room, plastering, painting, and fixing the windows. Down in the basement, he scraped away old varnish, sanded, and restored wood furniture to nearly new. Enjoyable work; peaceful work, as he listened to the radio—Amos 'n' Andy, blues, jazz, and country music. At least he got to listen to what he wanted when he wanted. Back at the dorm the mechanics, the M-boys, ruled the radio and Buddy and Ray had to go along with it.

He might see the M-boys tonight if he liked what he saw at Auto's Speakeasy—if he didn't, he wasn't sticking around. So many times they tried to coax Buddy and Ray into going there, called them a pair of pussies, momma's boys, when they said no. The M-boys made them nervous the way they carried on when they got drunk. But he'd at least go and have a look since his social schedule had dried to a trickle. The occasional nod and hello from another boarder and not much else.

Across the street from Auto's he watched people arrive in groups, all chatter and laughter, dolled up like they might be headed off to a wedding. He waited until there was no one around, crossed the street, opened a door to a steep flight of stairs, and picked his way up, moving towards a muffled din growing louder as he climbed. He opened a door onto an explosion of noise, laughter, music, heat, and swarming bodies. From out of the smoke and dim light someone called his name.

On the far side of the jammed room a man waved both his arms. "Buddy boy! Over here!"

It was Billy, one of the M-boys from the dorm. Buddy angled through the crowded room, squeezing between chairs, brushing by men and women dressed up in their fine city clothes, and tables loaded with jugs, glasses, and overflowing ashtrays. A man hammered at a piano, his shirt sleeves raised by silver bands, and belted out a song as if his life depended on it. He didn't seem to mind or take notice of the noise competing against his singing. By the way folks behaved, it was hard to believe hard times lurked right outside the door and something called a depression was going on.

Buddy thought about beating it—going back to his room. Even though the speakeasy was rowdy and packed, he felt like he stuck out like a sore thumb. Billy had his arm slung across the shoulders of a lady, their heads together. They seemed to be sharing a joke.

"Park it right here, Buddy." Billy pulled out an empty chair and motioned for Buddy to sit. The two young women seated with him wiggled in their seats, their mouths stretched into brilliant red smiles as they waited for introductions. "Buddy, these two beautiful ladies are Barb and Georgette."

Barb, the one in a purple dress, whispered something in Billy's ear. Georgette moved her chair to make room for Buddy.

Billy poured each of them a glass of something amber. "Raise a glass, my friends. We'll drink a toast to Buddy's appearance here tonight." They raised and clinked their glasses. "After your brother left, we thought you were a goner, wouldn't come out with the boys for fun. I almost took you for a Bible thumper or one of them funny boys."

Buddy took a big sip of the liquid and choked as the fluid burned a path all the way down his throat.

"What the hell is this? It tastes like kerosene."

"That's the best rye money can buy. All the way from Canada. Rye whiskey. Here," Billy reached across the table and topped up Buddy's glass. "We're just getting warmed up. Let's have another toast." He raised his glass high once again. "Here's to all of us. Here's to prohibition. Long may it stay."

For the rest of the night everything that could be toasted got toasted, or so it seemed. Dizziness overcame Buddy, but in a pleasant way. Warmth ran through his blood and he felt close to Billy, the girls, and the strangers who stopped at the table to talk.

Georgette leaned over close to Buddy; her breath upon his ear sent a shudder through him.

"Is it true," she whispered, "you are all by yourself?" Her hand touched his thigh leaving a hot imprint.

"My brother left some time back. He was the only family I had here."

Georgette squeezed his leg again. "You poor baby. You're all by your lonesome. You got to promise me you'll call on me whenever you get lonely. Nobody should be lonesome, wouldn't you agree?"

"I couldn't agree more. Especially at night, that's the worst, when the boogeymen come out." He sounded foolish, even silly, but he didn't care and she didn't seem to either. Now she stroked his arm and a couple of times laid her head on his shoulder, her hair grazing his chin as she nuzzled into his side.

Drinks and stories and the piano player hammering out one tune after another. Buddy knew every word to "The Reckless Hobo" and bellowed it out along with the others. The room full of singers sang sad and pretty, sounded for all the world like a choir of angels.

Talk, laughter, stories, touch, singing, the most fun he'd had… since, he couldn't remember when. In a long, long time.

Buddy opened his eyes, gazed at the ceiling—uncertain if the knock came from inside his head or at the door—turned to the window, the blind up. Sunlight flooded in, stabbed his eyes and made them ache and water.

"Hello? Are you all right in there?" He recognized Mrs. Gordon's voice. Couldn't she just go away and leave him alone?

Somehow, he'd made it to his room. Vaguely he remembered slipping on the stairs coming out of Auto's, Georgette's body draped around his, or was it the other way around? But the rest of it? Maybe it would come to him.

"Are you all right? Answer me!" Mrs. Gordon shouted again.

"Yes," he squeaked and passed his hand over his forehead. It felt like someone hit him with a two-by-four. He swore his head weighed fifty pounds. Fifty pounds of throbbing flesh.

"Well, that's something. I'll ask you to drop by to see me once you're decent, Mr. Scott. We need to discuss a few matters." Mrs. Gordon's quick footsteps descended the stairs.

He stared at the wall beyond the foot of his bed. The pale green the most putrid of colours —pond scum during a dry summer—Mother's pea soup—maybe he'd paint it again. Thank God he had today off. He pulled the pillow over his head. What happened to Billy and the girls?

He pushed the pillow aside and saw a scratch from the elbow to the wrist. How did that happen? Obviously he'd taken a tumble. He swore he'd never get drunk again.

He flipped over onto his back. Too much activity for his stomach. He got out of bed, staggered out into the hall, crossed to the bathroom, and heaved into the toilet. His head thundered and his stomach hurt. Jesus. Never, never again. He stumbled back to bed.

"Don't forget, Mr. Scott," Mrs. Gordon heard him moving around and called up the stairs. "Once you're up and decent, I'll have a word with you."

No doubt the meeting would be about last night. He'd probably violated a number of the rules she posted everywhere in the house: Turn Off When Not Using; Quiet Please: At all Times; No Smoking in Parlour; No Feet On Furniture; Remove Shoes Before Entering House; No Disturbances after Ten P.M; Quiet on the Stairs; Kitchen Privileges During Specific Times Only; Do Not Remove Dishes From Kitchen; Clean out the Basin After Use; Restrict Bathroom Activity After Quiet

Time. On and on and on.

By four, he was finally up and decent enough to face Mrs. Gordon in her parlour. He bounced his cap off his knee as she lectured him on his demeanour, as she put it, of the previous night. "Entirely unacceptable, Mr. Scott."

"Call me Buddy."

"You're from the country aren't you?" she asked once she finished refreshing his memory about the house rules, her black-button eyes drilling through him.

"Yes."

"I thought so." She gave him a thorough going over from top to bottom. "You dress the part."

Probably true. Why shouldn't he wear his dungarees and flannel shirt when he wasn't wearing his chauffeur's uniform? He had no one to impress, might as well be comfortable.

"I'd like to explain something to you, Mr. Scott."

"Buddy."

"Yes, well," she leaned forward in her straight-back chair. She reminded him of a crane, spindly, and long-legged. "Here in the city we do things differently. We don't come in at all hours of the night, in deplorable drunken condition, and make such a racket we wake up the entire house. Perhaps that's fine for you country people. You have wide open spaces. You can make all the noise you wish. You can go out in the field and howl like animals if you like and it won't disturb anyone, but not here. The people here in civilization are in close quarters. They are mindful of their neighbours and respect the privacy of others. Country people don't have businesses to run or obligations to meet. They have to tend to animals. Here we deal with other human beings."

Country people, according to her, seemed little better than animals themselves. Country people had nothing to do, their work completely insignificant. How many times did he see Mother and Father fight their way through a blizzard to get to the barn to feed and water the horses in the early morning hours when day had not yet bled into the night sky?

"One warning, Mr. Scott, that's all you get. Make sure it doesn't happen again."

He behaved badly, he knew it, and he deserved some kind of

dressing down, but she had no business belittling him and his family or the kind of life he came from. "Mrs. Gordon, could I ask you something?"

She sat back in her chair, surprised that he would have anything to add. "I'm listening." She drummed her spidery fingers on the armrests.

"I want to ask you a question about something you said. You seem to imply that country people are not quite up to city standards." He chose his words carefully to give the impression he was a man of reason and education—a stickler for accuracy. "The way you speak leads me to believe you see country folk as inferior to city folk. Did I understand you properly?"

"I said nothing of the sort. I merely said country manners have no place here in the city." Her voice sounded nervous and tight. "I imagine there are some nice people in the country," she added grudgingly.

"Yes, there are. Now let me tell you something, Mrs. Gordon." He rose from the settee, and crossed the room to stand before her, his hands sunk in his pockets, not wanting to appear too menacing.

She stared up at him, her eyes widening.

"I've never met any people finer than country people." He thought of his parents' genteel manners, and the farmers who picked up him and Ray as they made their way east, some who offered food when they barely had any to spare. "How much of this country have you seen, Mrs. Gordon?"

"Parts of Michigan, mostly the Detroit area."

"Well then, I guess I've seen a lot more than you. There's a lot of space between here and Wyoming, and it just so happens it's full of country people. And do you know why?"

"No I do not." It was obvious she did not like having to answer to anyone.

"Because it's full of country. Not cities. Miles of land, lots of it rugged, some uninhabited and some farmed. And I can easily say that the people who work the land, who make their scrap of a living working unforgiving soil are the finest people I've ever met. They've got a reputation for their hospitality, unlike city folk. As for your warning about my condition last night, I'll take it under advisement."

He exited the parlour and took the stairs two at a time back up to his room. He sat down on his bed and stifled his laughter into a pillow. The expression on the old bird's face, her little gasp of shock once he finished with his speech. Few would have the nerve to speak such plain English to her. Where did he get that word from? He picked it up somewhere. Under advisement? He barely knew what it meant!

The next day, Mrs. Gordon's judgment still in his ears, he thought he'd poke his nose into some clothing stores. He had free time and some money saved up. And what if he met Georgette again? Wouldn't he impress her if he came across as a little more downtown in new duds? Oh, the feel of her hand upon his thigh. Maybe Mrs. Gordon was right. Maybe he did stick out like a Scotch thistle in a field of clover.

He spent a few hours in Cooper's Haberdashery. He bought two casual shirts, two neckties, two pairs of trousers, one pair of shoes, three pairs of underwear, two suits—cotton linen for summer, a wool suit for winter—and a cream-colored silk scarf, two fedoras, and a light straw hat to go with the summer suit, the other a heavy felt for winter. Mr. Cooper barely noticed him when he'd entered the shop but couldn't thank him enough by the time he left, escorting him to the door, holding it open for him, bidding him good-bye, and following him right out onto the sidewalk to shake his hand once again. Folks weren't buying these days, never mind a whole new wardrobe.

He spread his clothes across the bed, tried on each garment, then checked himself in the mirror, front, back, and side view. A stranger stared back. How could he live for so long inside his skin and know so little about his own appearance? Most of the time he and Ray never had a mirror. Uncle Wes said the act of admiring yourself in the mirror was an act of vanity, a mortal sin, though it never stopped Wes from admiring himself in front of the vestibule mirror—the one over the table on which the Bible sat. It was plain to see how much he enjoyed the scenery.

Buddy leaned in closer, parted his hair with his fingers, and saw how dark it had become. It held no traces of blonde and was not as thick as it used to be. He smiled at his reflection, the crinkles at the corners of his eyes webbing out a little into his face, and held his mouth rigid as if he might be deep in thought, his eyes narrowing. This made him look serious and gave him an air of authority with a dash of wisdom—and sophisticated. What would Mrs. Gordon think about him now?

He sat on the edge of the bed and thought about Ray. Ray shielded him from the world and, in a way, from himself. But now there was no Ray, no one to talk to—no one to hide behind. The mirror showed a man sitting on the edge of a bed in a room with a few sticks of furniture. A man who barely recognized himself.

He arranged the clothes on the bed and smoothed out the wrinkles.

He vowed no matter what kind of clothes he wore, no matter the get-up he rigged himself in, he would stay loyal and never forget where he came from—would never forget his roots—Mrs. Gordon's snootiness drove the notion home. But he had to keep up with the world as a matter of survival. Her rudeness left a sour taste in his mouth but maybe she'd also done him a favour.

He picked up a part-time job driving as a public chauffeur—an agency one of the M-boys tipped him off to as a way to bring in some extra cash. It left him little time for going out on the town. Towards the end of the summer a break came, and he wore the cream-colour linen suit for the first time. He swept his hands over the crisp fabric, adjusted his tie, topped his head with the straw fedora, stopped at the mirror for a full-on view then two side views, and left his room, taking the stairs lightly, two at a time on the balls of his feet.

Mrs. Gordon spied on him from her usual place. He passed by the parlour door slowly, his hat tipped to conceal his face. Out on the street the curtains moved a little as she tried to identify the stranger who slipped unnoticed into her house, a problem she'd agonize over for the rest of the day. Tonight there'd be a new note for the tenants. She'd turn her frustration into a rule: All guests must be registered.

His new leather shoes glided easily on the sidewalk, put a spring in his step he felt through his entire body, and gave him the sensation of being taller. Though five ten was not tall by any stretch. He brought his shoulders back, opened his chest, raised his head, and settled on treating himself to dinner out.

Traffic thickened towards the centre of the city. Couples walked, the women with their hands crooked inside the men's elbows. He envied their closeness, their conversations. His dapper suit made no difference to the feeling of being alone.

He turned down one residential street after another, lined by maples with massive canopies. In the West, slim poplars stood thin as pencils against the sky and willows hunched along the recessed creek beds, their roots sunk deep in search of precious water which would dry up by late summer. But here the trees, large and majestic, brooded in the breeze.

He looked up into an ancient oak tree, loaded up with starlings like so many black apples, and crashed into a large wood box obstructing the sidewalk and pushed up against an iron fence. A head popped out of an opening in the box.

"You blind or something?" a young girl asked.

"I beg your pardon?" He might not have heard her correctly.

"Are you deaf, too? I asked you if you were blind. What's the matter? You can't see something as plain as the nose on your face without bashing into it?"

She couldn't be any more than seven or eight years old but what a tongue she had on her!

"You shouldn't play here," he said. "Since you're taking up half the sidewalk, you might expect folks to crash into you."

"Well then, folks should watch where they put their feet, shouldn't they? You can't walk straight ahead while looking up in the air and not expect to crash into something. Any damn fool knows that. I saw you coming. And I thought to myself, that jackass is going to walk right into me. It don't make no sense not to watch where you put your damn feet."

"What kind of talk is that for a little girl?" If Pearl, Maudy, or Hazel had talked in such a manner in front of Mother she would have paddled their backsides and washed their mouths out with soap.

"You can ask me, can you? On whose authority?" She glared at him with eyes so fiery blue they made him uneasy. She made an odd noise, a hissing sound, as she nodded her head which shook her mop of tight red curls. No brush had passed through that tangle in a while and even if one did he doubted it would make a difference.

Why did this sidewalk urchin smile and stare at him? Why did she nod as if she knew something he didn't? "What in blue blazes are you doing in the box?" Buddy asked.

"We live here." An impish smile accentuated her chubby cheeks. A galaxy of large sandy freckles sprayed the bridge of her nose, her skin so fair it wouldn't tolerate sun—the kind of skin Mother would insist stay covered.

"Who else is in there with you?"

She shoved a rag doll out of the opening of the box and let it dangle. "Me and Jack."

"Jack? That's a boy's name. That's a girl doll. How come you call it Jack?"

"Jack needs to be tough. Like a boy. It's short for Jacqueline."

"Oh, I see. And how come Jack needs to be tough? Aren't you a good mother?"

"I am not Jack's goddamn mother. Jack and I are friends, that's all." Her smile vanished and her red eyebrows pinched over her burning blue eyes. "We're roommates. We live together."

"Where?"

"In the box!"

She receded back into the box and called out that it was time for Jack to sleep. Buddy bent down to peer inside, to see what this child, this wild cat, played in. He could see how she would find such a large box a wonderful playhouse. Blankets, pillows, clothes, plates, cutlery, a mug, shoes, crammed every inch of the inside and in the centre, like a hen sitting on a nest, sat the little girl with Jack in her lap.

"Did you haul all this stuff out here this morning?"

"No."

"When?"

"When I moved out here."

"When was that?"

"In the spring. I don't know. You know, Mister, you're a snoopy bastard." She held Jack up to her face. "When Jack? When did we move here?" She turned her head and pressed her ear into the doll's mouth, then nodded and said, "Uh huh." She stuck her head out the door. "Jack says we got chased out eleven days ago."

"Chased out of where?"

"The big house."

"Is that where your parents live?" A once grand house stood on the other side of the iron gate, at the end of a long sidewalk.

"I don't have a dad. It don't bother me."

"Of course you have a dad. You can't get born without a dad."

"I don't have one! And I sure as hell don't need one! One parent is enough. My mother lives in the big house. Are you going to see her?"

"Why would I want to see her?"

"She'll make you happy."

"Oh. Does she make you happy?"

"No, silly. Only men. She doesn't make women or girls happy."

"Does she make you stay out here?"

"This is my job. I stop the men on the sidewalk and send them in. Except you. I didn't need to stop you. You walked right into me." She stuck her head out of the hole like a turtle sticking its head out of the shell. "Where you going in them fancy clothes, anyway? Are you rich?"

"Nowhere. For a walk. I just bought these. Do you like them?"

"Hmm," she cast her eyes up and down. "They're nice. But they don't seem to belong to you."

Wasn't she quite the little observer? And sassy; they didn't come much sassier. Smart, too. Still sitting cross-legged, she wiggled up closer to the door and once again raised Jack to her ear.

"What, Jack?" She listened to what Jack had to say and nodded her head up and down. "Uh, huh. I think so too."

A smile dimpled her chin, a deceptive smile, one which seemed to say she might know something he didn't. As if she played a game with him. She was not to be trusted, that much he knew.

Her eyes steady on him she kept up with her silly grin and made her hissing noise. It wouldn't take long before the noise bugged him, and if an adult stared at him in such a manner, he'd say he was being sized up, probably for reasons of no good. He started to walk away.

"Where you going?"

He turned around to look at the urchin in the box and felt foolish that such a young child had such a command over him—put the chase on him, then stopped him in his tracks.

"Downtown." He took a few steps ahead.

"Do you want a friend?" she called out.

He'd thought in terms of seeking company but not in his wildest imaginings did he come up with the idea of a young child. Wasn't it illegal? "How old are you?"

"Fourteen."

"You are not. How old are you?"

"Thirteen."

"Tell me another one."

"Jesus Christ, Mister, I'm telling the truth. I don't give a damn if you don't believe me." She made her hissing sound. "And anyways, what's my age got to do with it? I asked you, Mister, do you want to make a friend or don't you? Yes or no?"

He should have known what her temperament might be with hair the colour of fire. What a hell cat she'd grow up to be! Well, he'd like company and apparently she would too. What harm would it do to have her walk downtown with him? He'd take her for a soda pop or an ice cream and bring her back before dark. And he hadn't had the company of a child, especially a young girl, since he said good-bye to his sisters. "Okay, you can come along if you like, but shouldn't you tell your mother?"

"What the hell you talking about, Mister? I ain't asking for me. I'm asking for my mother. She and her ladies can be your friend. Now, is it yes or is it no? I haven't got all day. There's lots of folks passing by I could be stopping. So move along if you're a chicken. I got to make money. Don't I, Jack?" She held the tattered doll up to ear to listen to what Jack had to say, and shook her head in agreement. "Jack says beat it, Mister."

He'd misunderstood the business about friendship. "How much to see your Mom?"

"Ten dollars." Her hand went out and a palm turned up, ready to collect.

"Ten dollars? What the hell's so special about your Mom?"

"You pay your money, you find out. That's how it works. You're not from around here, are you?"

"No. I'm from the West. Out there, little girls don't live in boxes on the sidewalk."

"Well lah-dee-dah. Ain't you something special, Mr. Fancy-pants? Ten bucks or you and your fancy suit can git your scrawny ass down the sidewalk." Jack nodded her head in vigorous agreement.

Her hiss reminded him of a snake winding through prairie grass. He dug into his pocket, took out his billfold, leafed through the bills, and counted out ten dollars. The girl's eyes bulged at the sight of so much money.

"Away you go then, Mister. Have fun. No man ever comes out of there the same." She counted the money he gave her, just to make sure.

"And why not?" This mother of hers, what was she; a magician, a fortune teller, or a witch? He didn't care what she was. He paid the urchin for the privilege of giving her mother a piece of his mind. He saw some pretty pathetic situations, but this, kicking a child out onto the street while you lived in the lap of luxury, this was just about the worst he saw. Some people had to be told.

Chapter 16

The Big House

Buddy raised a lion's head door knocker and let it slam against the door. He repeated smashing the knocker until he heard, "Coming, coming."

The door opened, a hand snaked out, grabbed him by the wrist, and pulled him into a dark vestibule. A woman barely five feet tall emerged from the shadows. Behind her, candles flickered in a candelabra on a table. They splashed light onto the red walls, dark wood, and the red carpet on a broad staircase. Melting paraffin and perfume hung heavy in the air.

"Come here," the woman drew him deeper into the vestibule.

Off to the side he glimpsed a room filled with ornate furniture, heavy drawn curtains, and more candelabras. The woman's hair, almost white, twisted and piled on top of her head in an elaborate stack. Sparkly things stuck in it, caught the candlelight when she shifted and glittered like snow in moonlight.

"Well? I don't have all day. Which girl do you want?" she asked. Her dark eyebrows appeared painted on, her skin so white she might have been dusted in flour. The low, scooped neckline of her long gown showed a deep valley between her breasts. "Are you going to stand there gaping at my cleavage or are you going to speak?"

Hands swept over his shoulders, rubbed his back, slid up and down his torso, came from behind and toured his body.

The woman in front of him laughed. "Never mind, I know why you're here. You've got his attention girls. I'll see you after, Mr. ...what is your name?"

"Buddy." He could barely talk as his tie unloosened and his suit jacket slipped off. A young woman with long auburn hair flowing to her shoulder blades, dressed in a blue gown, stepped in front of him, and slipped her hand in his—so warm and soft. She put her other hand on his chest and whispered, "Follow me."

A woman with short coal-black hair rubbed his back and pushed him along to the staircase while the other drew him up the steps. The staircase bent at mid-point and carried them to a wide hall with shiny wood floors, tables loaded with flowers and candles, and many closed doors. A man came out of a room and placed his hat over his face and said good day from behind it.

The women led Buddy to the end of the hall. He was pulled into a room and pushed from behind. The door closed and he was alone with the long-haired woman. He stared at the largest bed he'd ever seen, a boat adrift at sea, loaded with a cargo of cushions and a tent overhead. The woman drew him to the bed then pushed him down on it.

Her hands seemed to have a life of their own, took over his body with peculiar authority, unhesitating, implicit in their business of unbuttoning his shirt and then his pants.

"One rule." She loomed over him, her face inches from his, her hair brushing and tickling his face. "No kissing."

He lay back against the heap of pillows as she took over his body like a storm with nothing he could do to stop it. A storm so fierce his body tossed about on high waves powerless on this great heaving vessel which carried him to places unknown, sailing him in and out of prairie landscapes (howling winds and blinding snow), his voice drowned by its forces. Then he was drifting on blue still water, the sunlight pouring down on his nakedness, every pore of his skin open to receive its warmth.

The woman's face inside the frame of her hair loomed into view over him. She seemed plainer now that he studied her more closely.

"First time?"

"Yes." He told the M-boys in the dorm he got it regularly any old time he wanted. Either lie or be teased. They probably knew anyway, the way they nodded and smirked and said, "Oh yeah? That right?"

Why now think of Wes's rants in the barn as the boys lay on their cots? "The fire that burns in your loins is a sign of weakness:

a sin. God condones it only under the sanctity of marriage. God will strike you, punish you, if you indulge in wickedness other than the Godly union between man and wife. Those who are weak and act upon their lusting will be visited by disease that will chew their organs and devour their brains."

His mother put it differently. "Wait for the right girl, Buddy. Share it with her. Honour yourself and your future wife. Save yourself for her. Not everyone does. That's human. But try. Don't hate yourself too much if you can't hold out. No matter what, always be respectful." What would she say if she knew what he'd just done?

With his father out in the barn. "Some have greater drive than others, Buddy. You are the only one who will know how to deal with it. But if you're going with the ladies of the night, make sure they're clean. You don't want to end up with the clap."

Uncle Wes's words overpowered the voices of his parents and he tumbled from glorious physical release to shame.

Beside him, sitting on the edge of the bed, the woman slipped on her robe and rose. He would dress and go downstairs to meet the woman who answered the door, the mother of the sidewalk creature, he imagined, since she carried herself as if she was in charge. The woman ran her hands through her long hair and flipped it back off her shoulders. "What's your name again?"

"Buddy."

"Well, Buddy, aren't you even going to thank me? I just gave you the memory of a lifetime."

He'd no idea what he was paying for out on the sidewalk. She'd taken advantage of him; they all had.

She tied the ribbons at the neck of her gown, one eyebrow arched, a sly smirk on her lips as she examined him on the bed. She was older than he thought— somewhere in her early forties.

"Oh I see," she said when he remained silent. "It's like that is it?" She placed her hands on her small hips. "You're one of those. You're better than me. You see yourself above all this, do you? That's what lots of them like to think. Doesn't stop them from coming back once a week, sometimes more. I've heard it all, trust me. But still they come back and bring their silly excuses. The flesh is weak. You'll find fresh water and towels over there." She pointed to a wash stand on the far side of the room. “Clean yourself up and go.”

He was different from the other Tom cats that came prowling around here. He’d never come back. Lured here in the first place, swept in right off the sidewalk, unwillingly. He hadn’t resisted, but why would he when he didn’t know what would happen once he got inside?

Downstairs in the parlour, surrounded by heavy furniture smelling of polish and oil paintings with broad gold frames, he waited for the mother of the little girl to appear. She drifted silently into the room: the effect of her long, flowing gown that covered her feet.

“What did you say your name was?” she asked, a pinched smile on her red lips.

“Buddy.”

“My name’s Goldie, for obvious reasons.” She gestured at her hair. “What can I do for you? Book an appointment, perhaps?”

He’d never set foot here again. What happened upstairs felt as wonderful as anything had felt before, but it was a mistake. “It’s about the kid in the box out front.”

“Marion.”

“Is that her name? Well, Marion then, I want to talk to you about her.” Buddy spun his fedora in his hands. “What you’re doing is not right. Having her out there collecting money, sending people in to you. There’s a hell of a lot about life I don’t know, but what you’re doing to that child is just plain wrong, that much I do know. Making her live on the street—that’s cruel.”

She ran her hand over the back of a velvet chair and laughed. “Now see here, Mr. Buddy. I don’t make her do any such thing. She’s out there because she wants to be. I could drum up business without her but I have to say I get more on account of her; she’s good at what she does. The box is her idea. She likes it. If she told you that I forced her out on the sidewalk, she’s lying. She’s a natural born liar, to put it mildly, or a natural actress, whichever way you want to interpret it. Marion’s a she-devil and I dare say she comes by it honestly. She’s been taught by the best, raised as she’s been by the women here. Raised to survive, I might add, and on her own terms.

“One more thing, Mr. Buddy. Your fancy clothes, they don’t cover up who you really are. I can tell by your hands. You work with them, I can see that, and you’re no high society man. Anyway, it’s time for you to march yourself and your superior airs right on out of here. I've got business to do." She sounded as composed as if she talked about the weather. He couldn't remember when he'd been so quietly and completely scolded.

"I'm the last person to put on airs!" he blurted. She wouldn't say something so false if she knew what he came from.

She walked towards a door at the back of the room and stopped. "Let me give you some valuable advice. If you're going to wear the clothes, act the part. Act like a gentleman. Especially now you're all grown up. Acting the part, Mr. Buddy. That's what we all do."

It was true his fingers were thick and calloused from tinkering with motors and from shining cars. "My clothes and hands don't matter a damn. What does matter is the way you're treating your daughter. You live in here, surrounded by all this, and she lives out on the sidewalk like a common beggar."

"Why don't I show you her room?"

"No thanks."

"It's the largest room in the house, her bed's bigger than mine, and she has every toy a child could ever wish for. Would you like to see it?"

"No."

"Well, I've spent as much time as I care to explaining my private matters to you. I can see she's tricked you, line, hook, and sinker. And another thing: in this house it's the women who have the say and any man who dares to defy the house rule is dealt with immediately." She clapped her hands. "Girls," she called out. Two young women entered the room with a large black dog pulling on its leash. "Show Mr. Buddy to the door please and wish him good day. Youth," she said as she opened the door at the back of the room, "I suppose he'll get over it."

"You see this dog, Mr. Buddy?" One of the women placed her hand lightly on his elbow. "He is very well trained. I hope I won't have to give you a demonstration."

The other woman opened the front door and pushed him outside. "Thanks for calling." The door closed abruptly behind him.

At the end of the gate he rapped on the top of the box. The red-haired girl stuck her head out. "Who's there?"

"I talked to your mother."

"Did you now. Let me guess." She put her finger to her chin and rolled her eyes back. "She told you that I am a terrible liar and that she doesn't make me stay out here in this box. Did she offer to show you my room? Well, guess what? I don't have one. Okay, so now who's lying?" She stared, all the time grinning and making her hissing noise. "That's something, isn't it? Just when you figure you understand, someone comes along and messes it all up. You don't know do you?" She laughed and withdrew back into the box calling out to him. "Now go away. Jack and I need to get some sleep. See you soon."

No she wouldn't see him soon and neither would her mother or the ladies inside the house. He had seen as much as he ever wanted to see of all of them.

He stretched out on his bed still wearing his new suit. Somehow, despite her smart tongue, the little girl had worked her way under his skin. As he lay considering Marion, he knew something about her was not childlike. Which one of the two lied? Which one played him for the fool—the mother, the daughter? Both?

Too restless to sleep, he rose, stood before the mirror, swept the wrinkles from his linen suit, and crept downstairs. The clock in the hall said 11:40, well into quiet time at the boarding house, the time Mrs. Gordon thought residents should be tucked in their beds. He didn't care. He couldn't stay in his room tonight.

He inched open the front door and eased out onto the porch. Behind him a door squeaked on its hinges. Did the woman ever sleep?

Autos was as packed as before. He spotted Georgette, Babs, and Billy on the far side of the room hunched around a small table. Billy spotted him.

"Hey Buddy, over here!"

Georgette looked him over, pleased by what she saw. "Aren't you dashing! Quite a change from the last time I saw you."

Billy poured a glass of rye whiskey and shoved it across the table in front of Buddy. "Have some hooch."

It burned all the way down and curled in his stomach like a cat in a patch of sunlight.

Billy poured Buddy another glass, put his arm around Babs,

and announced to all of them he had a surprise.

"I love surprises," Babs said. "What is it?"

He topped up their drinks and motioned for them to lean in closer. "A friend lent me his yacht for a week. I say we take our party down to the boat."

Buddy didn't have to work for another few days, but even so he should take it easy—based on the memory of the first night he came here. "Another time, Billy." He licked the heat of rye off his lips.

Billy poured him another shot. "Buddy's a party pooper, isn't he Georgette?"

"Yes, he is." Georgette curled her lower lip into a pout and put her hand on Buddy's leg. "What's the matter?" she asked. "Not old enough to stay out late?" Without waiting for an answer she rubbed the fabric of his pants between her fingers. "Hmm, very nice." Her perfume smelled like lilacs.

Lights from the yacht club ribboned the water and illuminated patches of fog. The boat was much bigger than Buddy had imagined it would be. They followed Billy down into a large salon. Billy flicked on some lights and Buddy took in the cabin with banks of blue velvet seats and rich wood trim, probably mahogany, a dining room, and kitchen galley.

"There are more decks above us," Billy said. "There's a bedroom down there," he pointed to a door at the end of a narrow hall, "and a bathroom," he pointed to another door.

Billy found the liquor cabinet and arranged glasses on the table.

"Who owns this?" Buddy sank down on one of the benches. Georgette kicked off her shoes and stretched out beside him while Billy poured drinks.

"A friend," Billy said.

"What friend?" Babs asked.

"Never mind. A friend." Billy served the drinks and sat down beside Babs. "If I had a boat like this I'd take it all over the world."

Buddy had never heard of most of the places Billy said he'd take such a boat.

After another drink, Billy asked Babs if she wanted a tour and they disappeared outside. Buddy heard them climbing to another deck.

Georgette and Buddy stayed behind and sipped their drinks.

"I'm comfy right here," Georgette said. "It's chilly." She pulled her shawl more tightly around her.

Buddy figured Billy had gone to be with Babs in the way he'd been with a woman earlier today and he had no inclination to be with Georgette in the same way. He felt tired and was beginning to think coming here was a mistake. Georgette liked to have fun—he couldn't blame her, but her eagerness was getting on his nerves. And she talked too much. He couldn't even say what all she'd been going on about since Billy and Babs left the room mostly because he plain didn't care about how exciting it was to be on such an expensive boat. He wasn't going to get all worked up about other people's wealth. He didn't criticize folks for having it, but the effect of their possessions didn't amount to a hill of beans.

Georgette was saying something about a canoe ride she took when she was young when she went to a friend's cottage in Canada, and how the canoe tipped and she fell out. "I thought I was going to drown."

Buddy's head pounded. He wanted to be in bed at the boarding house. He wanted to be alone.

Georgette poured herself another drink and topped his up. The booze didn't seem to slow her down any. She was talking about a fellow she knew who could play the saxophone very well, extremely well, better than anyone she'd ever heard before—good enough to get on the radio, she imagined, if he set his mind to it.

Well good for him, but at two-thirty in the morning he didn't much care. She was babbling. She'd had enough to drink.

"Let's go up top," he said. "Get some air."

"No, it's too cold." Georgette was catching on he wasn't paying any attention to her and must have noticed something had soured between the two of them.

"Fine then, stay inside if you like." He owed her an explanation for his lack of interest; it must have seemed obvious to her, and rude. After all, he'd agreed to come here. "I'm sorry. It's been a long day. I'm tired I guess."

"I guess I've got no choice but go outside with you since I don't want to sit here by myself." She followed him up the stairs and onto the deck, then around to the stern, kept up a steady chatter about how cold it was, and kept making a brrr noise in case he didn't quite get it.

"Why don't you go down below?"

"Not by myself!"

He took off his jacket and slid it over her shoulders.

Down the shoreline, Detroit sparkled like a prairie night sky pressed down close to the horizon. All those lights, all those people. He wrapped his hands around the rail and steadied himself; too many drinks and the slight movement of the boat made his legs spongy.

Georgette's hand landed at his waist, her head rested on his arm. He didn't want to be held. He didn't shrug her off but he didn't return her touch either.

"Let's go to the other side," he said.

The other side of the boat faced the open water and a black foreground stretching all the way to Canada. Sporadic lights twinkled from the far shore. Over there, the great wilderness he and Ray talked about.

"You seem deep in thought," Georgette said.

"Canada's over there."

"Yeah. So?"

"Between us, somewhere out there in the blackness, is an invisible line."

"Oh. Okay, well, I'm freezing. I'm going inside." She went back to the stern and he heard the cabin door close. So much for his geography lesson.

He stared across the black water and thought of Marion's bright eyes and how they gleamed when he said he was going to see her mother. It must have been a game to her. He imagined himself going back to the little girl, the sidewalk urchin who would give him her goading stare, making fun of him. Perhaps that's what mother and daughter intended, the two of them knowing far more than they let on.

The brisk air sobered him until his hands, wrapped around the rail, ached from the cold and he went back inside. Georgette was asleep on one of the long, upholstered benches. He found a blanket and draped it over her, slipped off her shoes, then sat on the bench opposite, and poured himself another drink.

Chapter 17

Overboard

The violent sway of the boat shook Buddy awake almost pitching him off the bench. Georgette raised herself up on an elbow and shoved aside a strand of tangled hair. A motor droned. He pulled on his shoes and started towards the stairs, leaving unanswered Georgette's question about what was going on.

He heard a woman scream.

Out on the deck, Babs leaned over the rails and cried out into the night.

"What's happened?" Buddy shouted, seeing right away she was drunk. "What is it? Calm down!" Cool air mixed with flecks of water hammered at his face as the boat tore into darkness. What the hell was Billy doing going at such a speed?

Babs sobbed and tried to tell him something, but between the blast of the wind, the motor's roar, and her drunkenness, he couldn't make it out. "What's happened?"

She pointed to the water, at the ribbon of white foam churned up by the boat. "Billy fell in," she stammered.

That couldn't be true. Billy would be driving the boat. He grabbed her arm and guided her. "Come on, we're going inside." They zig-zagged their way across the deck to the stairs leading up to the bridge.

She tried to wrench free of his grasp. "He fell overboard! she screamed. "Back there. Listen to me. Why don't you listen to me?"

Buddy grabbed her arm again and pulled her up the stairs one at time. She was too drunk for him to even know what she was saying and he didn't expect Billy to be any better. Once he got her to Billy in the steering station, she'd be his problem. What was he thinking leaving her to wander around alone? He might have passed out. Whatever had happened, this was bloody dangerous.

On the stairs they pitched from side to side as waves hit the boat broadside. Babs' dress, plastered against her body by wind as if it had been poured on, left her shoulders bare, nothing to keep her warm, and only thin little straps no wider than shoelaces.

Buddy pushed the door open and looked around the room. "Billy!" he shouted.

"He's in the water! I'm telling you, you idiot! What's the matter with you?"

The helm spun one way, then the other, as if steered by a ghost.

Buddy grabbed the wheel, its play loose and indirect, piloted the boat out of a large, circular course, and pointed the bow directly into the waves to ease the pitch. He'd no idea where to steer; he couldn't see anything ahead, only the darkness they rushed into. He found the gas lever and slowed the boat, then fumbled for a key on the steering column and turned it. Silence. The boat swayed gently. Babs slumped into a chair and sobbed.

Outside, waves splashed against the hull and something clattered.

"Where did he fall?"

Babs shook with cold and gave him a disgusted look, didn't bother with an answer.

Buddy draped a blanket over her shoulders.

"I'll tell you once more, he fell over the rails at the back. He was up here steering, then he wanted to show me something outside, and how the boat could steer itself. He was drunk and staggering, we hit a big swell and he flew over."

Her pink lipstick smeared around her mouth like a pink rash.

"How long ago?" If he had some idea about time they could backtrack and go to the spot."

"I don't know, I don't know," she sobbed. "It seems like hours, but it could have been five, ten minutes."

Georgette appeared in the doorway, her face pinched with worry and confusion, her hair tangled around her face. She was still drunk. "What's going on? Where are we?" She looked around the cabin. "Where's Billy?"

"He fell overboard," Buddy said.

"You're lying."

"No we're not, you stupid bitch!" Babs screamed. "Why would we joke about such a thing? Do you see him somewhere?"

"Jesus. What's the matter with her?" Georgette looked consumed by Buddy's suit jacket, as if her body was hung on hinges. "Someone can't hold their booze," she said.

"Look, we're trying to get things sorted out. Just sit down and keep out of it." Buddy put his hand on Babs's shoulder. "Where do you think he fell?" As soon as he asked her he knew the impossibility of it. Blackness surrounded them and far off in the distance, the lights of Detroit. Billy would be out there somewhere—where would he begin to look? Buddy couldn't see anything on the water. The boat would have running lights, but he had no idea which switches they were in the jumble of controls. Billy was a fool. A damn stupid fool.

"Both of you stay here. I'm going out on the deck. Maybe I'll hear something." They didn't need another accident tonight, which was what would happen if either one of the girls went out to stagger around in their high-heeled shoes and tight dresses.

Wind ripped at his shirt and whistled through the rigging. Water slapped the sides of the boat, but out across the water nothing sounded like a human cry for help. City lights didn't extend this far out and towards Canada it was even darker. They'd never find him. He leaned against the rail, cupped his hands around his mouth, and shouted. His voice wouldn't carry, not in this wind. He had to do something and shouting was a little better than doing nothing.

"Billy!" Going back inside would make matters worse and the wait would seem longer. He felt bad for Babs and Georgette, but what good would all their crying do?

Somewhere across the water a horn blasted; a light crossed the darkness and disappeared. Buddy kept up his calls. He roamed the decks, going from one side to the other, from bow to stern, gave up, and went back inside to join the other two.

At dawn, the three of them, wrapped in blankets, went out on the deck to search the water, but daylight revealed no more clues than night had.

A tugboat captain spotted them adrift, pulled up alongside, and fastened on. He and another boatman climbed on board, their eyes scanning the water as they listened to the story. Buddy could have told them there was nothing to see; he'd been staring at it ever since morning's first light hoping to see an arm rise up out of the water.

The tug crew hooked the yacht up to their boat and they limped back to shore, straight into a brisk early morning wind.

Georgette and Babs sat in the salon, mouths downcast, faces ashen in the grey morning light, and their blank eyes heavy with lack of sleep. Buddy would be glad to be separated from the smell of their cheap perfume, their simpering voices, and their accusing eyes.

He went out to the second deck and made his way to the bow, facing Detroit. The drowning would be in the paper and his name would be linked to it. Not because of Billy drowning, since Billy wasn't famous, but because of the boat. Its rich owner a figure of some importance, though Buddy didn't know who he was. How had things become so screwed up?

The morning sun shone brighter and burned away the last of the mist, the day on its way to shaping into something fine, which struck him as callous and harsh. The crew on board the tug stared at him as if he were a murderer and whispered among themselves in a foreign language.

His suit seemed out of place. Who was he trying to kid? Goldie was right; it was all a big act, had nothing to do with who he was. Yesterday he thought he looked impressive, thought he'd made the change from country hick to a downtown man, suave and worldly. Now he felt foolish, like a fraud, pretending to be something he wasn't, the suit nothing more than a costume. Look at the luck it brought him.

What he wouldn't do to talk to Ray right now. He looked up at the sky. Not even the Scott Constellation to talk to. Last night's incident would earn Buddy a reputation—it was unavoidable.

After they heard the story, the police gave the boat a thorough investigation while Buddy, Georgette, and Babs waited in the club house at the dock.

At the station, they drank mugs of strong coffee and went over the circumstances of the night before. Everyone who came into the station sized them up in their rumpled party clothes.

The girls were taken away to be questioned again separately. Buddy reported his side of the story to an officer, who, after hearing it, disappeared then came back and asked Buddy to repeat it again starting from when Buddy fell asleep, then again from when he found Babs on deck screaming. Several times he was asked how inebriated Babs appeared to be and about his own level of drunkenness.

"Not at all," Buddy said. "I had a couple. I'd fallen asleep."

Buddy gave the details four times and the cop said, "It sounds like an accident."

"That's what I've been telling you all morning."

"Take it easy." The cop gave him a weary look, his droopy eyes red-rimmed. "You realize there'll be an investigation."

"No."

"Well there will be. Not to mention all the searching that will go on until the body washes up. If it does. Be prepared, is what I'm saying. It'll be in all the papers, too. You're about to become infamous." He must have noticed the look on Buddy's face. "Famous," he said, "for the wrong reasons."

The police took the girls home first and dropped Buddy off a couple of blocks from his boarding house. Mrs. Gordon was talking to someone in the kitchen. He tiptoed up the stairs and stayed in his room for the rest of the day and out of trouble.

First thing the next morning Mrs. Gordon called him down to the parlour.

"Scandal." She tossed the paper on a footstool. "There's nothing I despise more. Bad enough, Mr. Scott," she sniffed indignantly, "you come in at all hours and in who-knows-what condition, but now this. This article seems to imply the boat was stolen. This is completely unacceptable! And then a drowning, of all things!" She put on a grand performance of being offended but it was obvious she enjoyed the drama.

"It was an accident," Buddy said. He didn't care if she believed him or not. She'd made up her mind about him from the start, the way she looked him up and down with her critical eyes: a country bumpkin, ignorant, unworldly, stupid.

"The police will determine that. By week's end I want you moved out of my boarding house. No later. You should be out of here today, but I'll go easy on you."

"Oh well, aren't you kind."

That put fire in her eye. One brow shot up into an alert, incensed arch.

He'd be out of there as soon as he could, before week's end, to act on his own interests, he explained. The suggestion he might want to leave made her shift in her seat. He'd had enough of being spied on and preached to about his behaviour. "Mrs. Gordon, you're going to miss me. What will you do when I'm gone? I've given you a certain amount of entertainment, haven't I?"

She muttered something under her breath.

Someone knocked on the front door. Mrs. Gordon rose to answer, her heels striking the vestibule floor in short clips. "My word," she said. "What now?"

Buddy followed along behind her. Two police officers stood in the doorway. "Come inside." Mrs. Gordon ushered them in away from the prying eyes of the neighbours. Buddy had seen the two officers at the station, one an older cop, probably close to retirement, the other a rookie, a young fellow.

"We've got some news for you," the older cop said. "The body has turned up. Drifted up near the docks. A kid found it when he was out there playing. Mistook it for a fish at first. Until he got a closer look."

Mrs. Gordon raised her hand to her mouth and gasped. "I must sit down."

"The next of kin are being notified," the other cop said. "We don't require anything more from you right now, but don't go anywhere. Stay close. There'll be an autopsy, and once they confirm an accidental drowning your name will be cleared."

Clear his name? Did they mean they thought this was murder?

“I’m moving soon. As of Friday, I won’t be living here anymore. I got the boot.” Buddy motioned towards the parlour where Mrs. Gordon would be straining her ears to hear their conversation. “My landlady doesn’t like tenants who get their names in the paper.”

The older one screwed up his mouth and seemed to think something over. “Don’t you worry about her, son. You’re not the first tenant from this house to end up in the papers. She runs a boarding house, not a convent. Some unusual folks drift through these doors. I don’t imagine you have a place to live yet. That right?” He said this loud enough for her to hear.

“I’ll find something.”

“Tell you what,” the young cop eyed Buddy and pushed his cap back off his forehead, which left a smooth shiny imprint across it. “A few of the fellows room together, and someone just left. I think we can squeeze you in.”

Mrs. Gordon came into the vestibule, stared for a moment as if expecting them to include her, then disappeared into the kitchen. The old cop nodded, smiled, and tipped his hat to her. When she was out of hearing distance he said, “I swear to God if her ears were any better she’d know what the ants were saying to each other out in the yard.” He raised his voice once again for her benefit. “We’ll be on our way, now. Come on Buddy, we’re taking you in.” The old cop winked at Buddy and whispered, “That’ll give her something to think about. How long will it take to get your belongings together?”

“Not long. Fifteen minutes, maybe.”

On his way up the stairs he overheard them talking to Mrs. Gordon in the kitchen, explaining how they’d take Buddy in and give him a place to stay. “Don’t you worry. We’ll keep an eye on him.”

An idea she seemed to support wholeheartedly. “That’s what young people need. A little time locked up at the station might keep him out of trouble.”

“No, no Ma’am,” the old cop said, that’s not what we mean. “He’s such a nice lad we’re going to give him a place to live. He can room with some of the cops. What did you think? You’re not a religious person, are you Mrs. Gordon? A person of faith wouldn’t have such dark views of their fellow humanity, would they now? They wouldn’t think the worst of folks. No sir, not if they had faith.”

Buddy packed his bags, left them at the bottom of stairs, and joined the others in the kitchen. "My money's on the dresser. I'm paid up until Friday," he told Mrs. Gordon.

Some of the fellows who hung around the boarding house made him nervous. Odd looking characters, sewer rats up to no good, slinking around. They drifted with some of the cops. How was it cops attracted such shady people, people from the wrong side of the law?

Buddy refused to give his roommate, Rip, one ounce of information about the Fords—even though he was always poking around for it. Rip busted people with booze, took their bribes to avoid a charge, and confiscated the booze which he either sold or drank.

"Yup," he laughed. "I've got my hands in the cookie jar right up to my elbows." He stretched out on his bed. "I don't get paid enough to live on straight wages. I don't get paid close to what I'm worth dealing with the earth's scum. My life's worth more than my pay, that's for sure. You've got to be creative to make it worthwhile."

Buddy slept with his money under his pillow and woke up often. He went along with whatever Rip said, laughed at his stories and pretended to approve in order to stay on his good side. Rip was God and the Law at six feet four, weighing in at two hundred and eighty pounds if he weighed an ounce. Sometimes he threw an arm around Buddy and hugged him, ran his hands through his hair to rough it up, called him Kid, and dropped big hints he'd let him in on some of the action. Rip's muscles seemed to be all in his arms—not too much upstairs. Buddy wanted no part of the action Rip was talking about. He was lying low, staying out of trouble.

Some of the boys in the house belonged to a ball team and invited Buddy to join them after they saw him throw a baseball. And not bad at batting either. He slipped out to the ball park whenever he could to get out of the boarding house, tossed the ball around, and batted a few with anyone who showed up. Another way of avoiding trouble while waiting for chauffeuring work.

On the way home from the ball park he always visited Marion in her box. Sometimes he paid his money and went inside The Big House for a romp with one of the girls, vowing each time would be the last. Always after, through the physical relief and the calm that came with it, shame came over him. A sense that no matter what, he could not fully enjoy the pleasures God had given him. Haunted by thoughts of his mother's disappointment of the type of woman he chose and Wes's searing condemnation.

"How was your girl, today, Buddy?" Marion asked, her grin showing how much she enjoyed making him uncomfortable.

"It's getting cold," Buddy looked down at the dead leaves piled against the fence, then up into bare branches, evading her question.

Marion held her doll up to her face. "Jack, do you care about the weather?" She pressed the doll's head to her ear and nodded as she listened. "Jack doesn't give a damn," she grinned.

"That's not a nice way for a little girl to talk."

"I told you. I'm not a little girl. Anyway, it doesn't matter about the weather. I'm leaving soon. Jack, too."

"Where are you going?" She was teasing him again, no doubt.

"We're saving money to go to Canada. My grandmother has a farm there. I go every winter. She has animals; I like them. Better than people. I don't like staying in The Big House. So, I won't." She tipped her head back in defiance. "My grandma says my mother is unfit. She says she's always been a load of trouble. Anyway, Goldie don't give a damn where I go, as long as I'm out of her hair. This time, I'm not coming back."

She looked at Jack, holding the doll inches from her face. "What you saying Jack?" She held Jack up to her ear again and listened, nodded, then raised her eyes to Buddy. A curl dangled in the centre of her forehead and reminded him of a rusty bed spring.

"Jack told me to shut up, not to tell you about leaving, since it's none of your damn business." As an afterthought she added, "Jack can be plain spoken. She likes to have me all to herself. Jack would rather listen to the wind in the trees than talk to folks, since most people talk nothing but a load of rubbish anyways. Maybe you already figured me and Jack don't much care for people."

One cold night, Buddy headed out to avoid the boys gathered around the kitchen table at the boarding house. He'd turned down their offer to sit in on an all-night poker game. Too much money was crossing the table. He had a few nights off and nothing scheduled with the Fords. He'd pay Marion a visit, see if he could bring her anything, food or blankets, though she'd never ask.

He walked to Marion's box and tapped on the top.

"Beat it," she said from inside.

"It's Buddy."

She poked her head out and gave him her impish grin. It wasn't as cold as it would be soon, what with winter coming. The air had some bite and there'd already been a hard frost. How could it happen in this world a child had to live like that? But if anyone tried to talk her into going inside he knew the kind of reception they'd get.

"I want to show you something." She raised her face to him. "You've got to stick your head inside." Buddy sank to his knees in front of the box. She pulled back a blanket on top of a mound of clothing and underneath it lay a ginger cat with tiny kittens lined up at its belly, suckling.

"These are my babies." Marion balanced on her haunches, looking at the kittens with the sweetest smile he'd ever seen on her face. She ran her hand along the mother's side. The cat opened her squinty eyes and purred.

"The mama's an old stray. I found her in the bushes, all ragged and wet and half starving. I made her better, made her healthy. Now she's got six babies." She stroked the cat's side.

"Put your head down, Mama. You need your rest," Marion said. "There's a good mama, taking care of your babies, aren't you?"

She'd forgotten about him; how happy she looked as she stroked the cat and talked to it. The cat purred louder.

The heat of the cats warmed the inside of the box. It smelled of birth, a scent he remembered from the barn on the ranch—a sweet, musky smell. Marion saved the cats, but the cats, on a night as cold as tonight, were also saving her.

"You're a good mama, yes you are. You've got beautiful babies," Marion said softly.

Buddy stayed, admiring the cats without talking until it was time to go. He'd have a talk with Goldie, tell her that even out on the prairies their animals got better treatment than what she gave her child. He said goodnight to Marion and let himself through the gate without making a noise; he didn't want her to know his plans.

In the front parlour the warmth of the fire spread over his chest as he took in the plush red furniture. When Goldie finally appeared and he complained of the treatment she gave her daughter, she laughed, and the big black dot near her lip moved like a spider darting across her face.

"If memory serves, I think we've already had this discussion, haven't we Buddy? Didn't I offer to show you her room? The offer still stands. She chooses to live the way she does. She loves to tell stories, to be the queen at the centre of the drama. She's a lot older than what she looks and she plays it for all it's worth. Haven't you figured it out?"

Here's what he'd figured out for sure; he couldn't trust either of them.

"I've got clients to tend to, Buddy. You can appreciate they don't like to be kept waiting." With that, she turned on her golden slippers and left the parlour. A couple of the girls lounging nearby and listening came to him now, touched his elbow lightly, and led him to the door. They knew him well enough they didn't bring out the dog.

The thermometer continued its plummet. He couldn't get the idea of Marion sleeping out in the cold out of his mind. He'd go check in on her.

Her box was gone, the sidewalk as bare as a sidewalk should be, yet it looked strange not to see it shoved up against the fence.

He ran up the sidewalk to the porch, knocked at the door, and asked to see Goldie. Goldie laughed when she saw him; his presence seemed to amuse her. "Yes Mr. Buddy. Are you paying us a visit today?"

"I want to know what happened to Marion."

"Marion? Marion who?"

"Your daughter, the little girl on the street."

"Oh, her," she tossed her head back and laughed. "She's not my daughter. But it made a good story. You can't imagine the number of people who came to me to reprimand me for my cruel behaviour. But like you, Mr. Buddy, they got taken in. She was good for business. And don't you worry, she got a share of the earnings."

"Who was she?"

"I don't know. Just a beggar. She's gone now. Vanished, like she never came." Goldie gave her hair a little pat, as if some of it had fallen out of place, which it hadn't—it was so stiff it looked like a carving. "Enough of the chatter Mr. Buddy. Who can I get for you today?"

He could practically hear what Marion would say after he told her what Goldie said. *Oh, so I'm not her child—that's what she said. I'm a complete stranger to her, am I? And, did you believe her? That woman is such a liar.*

She must have gone to Canada to be with her grandmother on her farm, took the mother cat and the six kittens along with her. He didn't know what to believe so he would believe that.

After Marion disappeared he kept himself even busier. He boxed at the gym, hung out at the ball park, and he never went back to Goldie's house again. Not once.

Chapter 18

Crouch

Buddy picked up extra jobs chauffeuring and banked as much money as he could. His public clients couldn't hold a candle to the Fords, couldn't even come close, though some liked to think they could. The Fords asked him about his life, how was it going, listened to him, and asked him about his plans—he held their attentiveness in high regard. Edsel, Henry's son, enjoyed his stories about boxing and baseball and told stories of his own.

Rip hooked him up with some of the people he knew who used a public chauffeur, but Buddy wished he'd leave him alone to drum up his own business. Especially when it came to the likes of Kelvin Crouch, a real lowlife, who carried his wealth with offensive vulgarity. Crouch insisted Buddy drive for him because he knew Buddy was a second-string driver for the Fords. He even tried to pump Buddy for information about his famous clients: Buddy would have none of it.

Kel Crouch treated his wife, Madam, Buddy was told to call her, like a stray dog he had no use for. Buddy despised him from the first time he drove for them. Once, Crouch told her to shut her mouth, told her if he wanted another fucking opinion he'd ask for it. Someone else rode with them, someone Buddy picked up on a street corner. He looked mean with a ragged growth of beard and stinking clothes. Buddy looked in the rear-view and saw money change hands.

"I share my driver with Henry and Edsel Ford," Kel Crouch said to the low-life. Nothing could be further from the truth. *His driver?*—bull shit. *Share?*—like hell. He'd love to shake Crouch, dump him on someone else, but he hadn't been with his new employers long enough to have that kind of pull. He took his spot near the end of the seniority line.

Friday night he picked up Crouch and Madam at their home, a large place with cheap appointments meant to impress, not the kind real money bought. The maid met him at the door with a curt greeting, instructed him they'd be along shortly, and for him to wait at the car. Madam came out first, a large woman wearing a glittery pink gown, like a little girl playing dress-up, highlighting her generous proportions. The volume of her dress dwarfed Crouch's size more than usual. He was about as tall as she was wide and her dress would swallow him whole out on the dance floor.

The Fords always spoke to him. "Nice evening, Buddy. Hope you didn't mind waiting." Or, "Thank you for waiting." After what they did for him and Ray, they could do just about anything and he wouldn't complain. He could never repay them.

The Crouches bickered all the way to the car without so much as a hello as Buddy held the door open for Crouch, first to reach the car and slide in before Madam. "We wouldn't be late if it hadn't been for all the time it took for you to fix your hair."

"And you'd like me to look like a clown, would you?" Madam gathered armfuls of her dress, raised it above her dimpled knees, and turned sideways to stuff herself into the car.

"I don't care how you look, just so long as we get there on time for the reception. There are people, I'll remind you, I need to see."

"Oh yes, remind me again. It's slipped my mind from five minutes ago when you last screamed it at me."

Buddy closed the door on their jabber, got into the driver's seat, and drove down rain-streaked streets to the Grande Ballroom without exchanging a word with them. They stopped their nattering only to take the occasional swig from Crouch's mickey.

The Ford car was parked close to the entrance, a privilege few had, along with the mayor and other dignitaries. On his way around the car to let the Crouches out, he waved to Ned, the Ford's regular driver, busy polishing headlights. Couples streamed inside, passing a hedge of flashing bulbs as reporters snapped pictures for the morning paper.

Madam barged ahead and Crouch shouted at Buddy, "Be right here at the end of the night."

Where the hell did he expect him to be? Home in bed while they hitched a ride home?

Crouch motioned with his arms toward a row of chauffeurs across the street. "Mingle with them. Make a good impression." Meaning Buddy was supposed to hobnob on their behalf. Now that was a good joke. Every private and public chauffeur in the city knew about Crouch. Say Crouch's name to anyone in the business and he knew what kind of reaction to expect.

He parked in the closest spot, several blocks away, and came back to talk to some of the drivers having a smoke at the side of the theatre. "How'd you manage to be scheduled with those boors?" a driver asked.

"Just lucky, I guess."

Crouch and Madam tumbled out of the ballroom, almost the last to leave the party. Buddy brought the car around to the front—easy to do with everyone gone. They'd had plenty to drink, more than they should have—Crouch would have smuggled it in—and they were still bickering.

"I saw you looking at that cheap little hussy."

"Why don't you get off my back, woman?"

They carried the argument into the car and all the way back to their house. If the Fords had any differences they kept them behind closed doors. He opened the door for Madam and Crouch, and looked forward to watching their back ends disappear inside their house.

"Wait here," Crouch said, and tromped on a cigarette he threw down on the driveway. "I need another drive."

At two in the morning where else could he be going? In his condition he should be going to bed.

Madam slammed the door in Crouch's face. He staggered back to the car and shouted at Buddy to take him to an address Buddy knew well.

He waited until Crouch came out with a girl he'd never seen at The Big House. She could be new since he kept his word and hadn't been there since Marion left. Crouch told him to drive to the Point Park on the edge of town.

Droplets of rain speckled the windshield as they drove across town. The car bobbed and swayed as they bounced over the potholes on Point Park road. Buddy pulled into a parking lot overlooking the water and turned the car off.

"Okay, now you vamoose," Crouch told him. "Stay lost until I honk the horn."

Buddy stepped out of the car and pulled up his collar against the wind, strong here by the water.

It was all he could do to bite his tongue, stop himself from saying, *now look here you goddamn little weasel. I get paid to drive, not walk around in the middle of the night, in the rain.* He'd talk to the dispatcher tomorrow and he'd never drive for this idiot again; he didn't care how much they offered to pay him or how many trips he missed. Some things were not worth this kind of degradation, including freezing his ass off so some low-life could get laid.

Rain flecked his cheek. He gazed across the water to the lights of Windsor and gave his collar a tug to lift it higher. Damp sank into his bones. It was late and he was tired. He lit a smoke and started down the road he came in on. He hadn't brought a heavy coat, only his light chauffeur's jacket; he'd no idea he'd be going for a nature walk tonight. Only the lowest would make an employee, and not even a permanent employee, stand out here in the rain, wind, and cold.

He walked farther, lit another smoke, and shivered against the night's chill. When he'd gone a long way from the car he turned around and started back again. It occurred to him he might be too far away to hear the horn. He launched his cigarette off his fingertips and watched its trail of sparks sizzle as it hit the puddle.

Dandy. Just dandy. He'd been out here the better part of an hour. Was that son-of-a-bitch going to have him standing out here all night? Oh, you bet he would bring this us up with the dispatcher. He came with the best references. He deserved better than being assigned to some two-bit hustler who probably couldn't get a hard-on. That's what was taking so long. The little son-of-a-bitch couldn't get it up.

Buddy heard something. Was it the horn? Or was it voices?

He walked further, stopped, and listened. Just his imagination. No, he did hear something. Not leaves rustling, not the water. Screaming. He ran towards the car and the noise got louder. He saw nothing through the steamed windows but he heard plenty. The sounds of a woman's muffled screams as if a hand covered her mouth, then a man shouting.

"You bitch. You fucking well bit me!" Then the sound of something; flesh connecting with flesh—a slap. Another scream.

Buddy grabbed at the handle and flung the car door open. He reached into the back seat and grabbed Crouch by the shirt, pulled him out of the car, and shoved him to the ground.

Crouch squealed like a baby pig then shouted at him, "How dare you touch me you good-for-nothing imbecile!" He sprawled on the ground wearing only a shirt, his stupid little shriveled up prick a worm in a black thicket.

Hitting a woman! What a cowardly little shit! He'd give him a lesson he'd never forget. What did he think? Because he'd paid her he was free to beat her?

Buddy grabbed his shirt and hauled him to his feet, then hissed in his face. "I'm going to knock a little sense into you!" Buddy punched him with a hard left hook, caught him up under the jaw so hard he heard it crack. Then he punched him again and jabbed one off the end of his nose. Crouch drooped, still in Buddy's grasp. He gave him another sharp punch in the gut to finish him off. Blood streamed down Crouch's white shirt. From now on Crouch would wear another nose. Let that remind him in case he ever tried to pull this kind of stunt again.

Buddy shoved him back onto the ground. Fire ignited his blood, took possession of his body, and roared in his ears. Every inch of him burst with a crude energy he'd never felt before. What kind of person would do that to a woman? He could kill him with his own two hands.

Behind him, the girl whimpered, her clothes bundled and pressed into her stomach. Her nose bled and blood dribbled down her chest.

Headlights burned up the road, grew stronger, and swept over the three of them—Crouch sprawled on the ground, Buddy standing with clenched fists, and the girl inside the car now pulling on her clothes. The oncoming car lights caught the oblique streaks of rain and two cops emerged out of a cruiser, night sticks in hand, and approached them.

"Well, well, what do we have here?"

Crouch's bare ass sprouted luminously in the dark.

The young woman, fully clothed now, slipped out of the car and stood in the rain.

"Can anyone here talk?" One of the cops bounced his nightstick in his palm.

Buddy thought he'd seen him around but he didn't know him. One of the fellows he lived with at the boarding house would know him for sure.

"I think you'd better get your scrawny ass back to the car," the other cop said to Crouch, "before that puny thing makes me sick."

Buddy snickered.

"I don't think much that's going on here is particularly funny." The cop flashed his light in Buddy's eyes.

Crouch scurried back to the car, his lily-white backside and stick legs glowing in the night, grabbed his clothes and went behind the car to dress.

"Okay," one of the cops said, "what's the rumble?"

"I'll tell you what the story is..." Buddy began.

Crouch rejoined the group, stuffing his shirt inside his pants. He pulled on his tux jacket and interrupted Buddy.

"He tried to kill me." He pointed at Buddy and shook his finger. "Do you have any idea who I am? I'm Kelvin Crouch."

"I'll tell you exactly who you are, you're a goddamn coward. Anyone who tries to beat up a woman is the worst kind of scum there is." Anger clenched Buddy's jaw so tight he could hardly speak. It was all he could do to stop himself from tossing off another punch.

"Do you hear?" Crouch said to the police. "This man is out of control. I was out with my lady friend and he attacked me. I want him taken in, I want him charged."

"You lying bastard!" Buddy shouted. "Ask her, ask the woman!" Buddy pointed to the young woman standing by the car, her hair flattened to her head dangling in long, dripping strands and her dress plastered against her body. "She'll tell you what happened."

He'd called her a woman, but huddled in her soaking wet dress she appeared to be no more than a girl. She buried her face in her hands and sobbed.

One of the cops went to her. "Well?"

"I don't know, I don't know," she whimpered, her voice as small as a child's. "I don't know what happened."

"Get in out of the rain," the cop said, and opened the car door. "No point catching your death."

"I'll tell you what happened," Crouch pointed at Buddy. "This idiot went berserk. He attacked us. I'm pressing charges! He assaulted me." Crouch pointed to the blood that dripped from his nose. He looked a sorry sight all right.

"That's a goddamn lie."

"Shut up all of you. We're going to the station to get this sorted out."

"Can you drive this car back yourself?" one of the cops asked Crouch.

"Yes, of course I can. I don't want him near me."

"Okay then, we're taking you in." The cop snared Buddy's arm and led him to the police car. He told Crouch to come directly to the station to make a formal statement and press charges.

"Damn right I will," Crouch said.

The young woman spoke up. "Can I get a ride back with you?" she asked the cops.

"Don't see why not," one of them said.

"You sure you can get back all right?" One cop said out the window of the cruiser as Crouch stood in the rain in front of the big car Buddy chauffeured.

Buddy hoped he drove it into a tree. Hoped he split his goddamn head open.

On the way downtown, the girl leaned close to Buddy and whispered, "I'm sorry. Goldie would be so angry with me if I said anything. I can't lose my job. He's a regular client. Goldie can get very nasty. She can lay on a real beating."

The pair of them, drenched to the bone, shivered in the back seat. Here he was in the back of a cop car with a lady of the night, a victim of a scumbag's beating. All that was bad enough, but to come out on the wrong side of blame with the possibility of being charged… just his luck. He looked at the miserable wretch beside him.

"Forget about it," he said. "You've got to take care of yourself. I know that. But you tell Goldie that guy's nasty. You hear? If you don't, I will."

She nodded and sniffed.

"What's your name?"

"Sally."

"Well Sally, you ever thought about another occupation? One that isn't so dangerous?"

"Yeah. But at least at Goldie's I have a place to live. That's way better than what I had."

"Cut the chit-chat, you two," one of the cops turned to face them. "This isn't a social."

Sally smiled weakly at Buddy and drew her shoulders up into a shrug.

After more questioning at the station, the cops drove Sally to The Big House and threw Buddy in a cell with a couple of drunks who shared flasks they smuggled in. They were well beyond the point of needing anything more to drink. One of them retched in the corner then washed his mouth out with whiskey, the other so drunk he pissed himself. Buddy sat on the edge of a cot but dared not lie down, fearing what either of them would do if he fell into unguarded sleep. But he accepted their booze, the whiskey burning down his throat and into his stomach, warming his insides. A balance for the chills, his clothes still wet and unlikely to dry in the dank cell.

Whenever one of the young cops passed outside the bars, they looked inside. "You getting to know each other, scum?" "Look lively, maggots." "There's a fine group of lice." Buddy told them he played baseball with some cops in a league.

"Yeah, sure you do, buddy. And my mother is the Queen of England."

Buddy named names, his roommates, even Rip, but they ignored him. Nothing would get him out of here.

In the morning he stopped by the desk to gather his personal items, his watch and wallet, and asked what charges Crouch had pressed. The desk clerk raised his huge head, his sad-dog eyes taking him in as if he'd seen too many of Buddy's kind and far too much of life.

"None."

"Well, what did he say when he showed up last night?"

"He never showed."

"Why the hell did I have to stay in the lockup with those two worms pissing and shitting and puking?"

"For your own good," the desk cop said.

"How was that for my good? I was doing a job. Chauffeuring for that slime Crouch."

"Well, maybe there are some folks you should avoid," the tired cop said. He looked up from the book he wrote in. "Look son, doing a night in the drunk tank is not the worst thing that could happen to you. Laying a beating on him, or worse, killing him would be. Lots would love to kill that slime, I grant you that. From now on, you look over your shoulder. He's got a lot of connections in this town. So you thank your lucky stars you had a peaceful time of it. I see a lot here and I can tell you're a good chap. Stay away from Crouch. Use more caution when choosing your employers."

"He chose me."

"Like I said, be careful. That's not the first time we've rescued someone from Crouch. As for the girl, folks need to watch out for themselves. You're not here to save the world, not unless you're Jesus Christ himself. She calls her own shots, too. She's been in these scrapes before. And with Crouch, too." He drummed his pencil on a stack of papers. "And one more thing there, Buddy. I hear you're a hell of a ball player. Keep it up. Now get the hell out of here. You seem like a decent sort, I don't want to see you back."

Buddy stepped out onto the sidewalk and squinted into the early morning sun. The sidewalks, still wet with rain, glistened in the light. The cement smelled earthy and the morning air still held the chill of night. It was a long walk home and he hoped Rip wasn't there.

Hands shoved deep into his overcoat pockets, collar up against the cold, the wool scratching at the back of his neck, Buddy walked along the sidewalk headed for downtown. He'd been doing a lot of that lately, walking, putting in time, checking in at the office. Word spread as fast as a grass fire stroked by wind about his tussle with Crouch and his night in the slammer.

"Hey, Buddy, I hear you busted both his arms," one of the drivers hanging around at the public chauffeurs' office said.

"I heard you split his head open. Don't imagine any brain came out," another driver said.

The rumours shortened Buddy's assignment list. Ever since the incident with Crouch he could count his drives on one hand. He couldn't have picked a worse time to lose hours, not that he'd picked it either. All around him people were out of work with nowhere to go, nothing to do. So many homeless folks on the street.

"Hey mister," a young boy ran up alongside him, his hand open, and lines of dirt etched into his upturned palms. "Change, mister?"

Buddy pulled the lining out of his overcoat pockets and let them dangle. "See? Sorry, kid." The boy's jacket was so thin Buddy thought he could rub the cloth and put a hole in it.

Cold brushed his cheeks and shot a twinge up his nose. Another day without any driving assignments. He hadn't driven once, not once, for the Fords since word leaked out about the Crouch incident. And who knew what they heard, rumours being what they mostly were, a pack of lies. They'd cut themselves free of scandal. He'd seen them with another driver, a fill-in, at a time when Mrs. Ford would be meeting with her horticultural group. He couldn't blame the Fords for dropping him, but it sickened him to think he'd been tumbled by the likes of Crouch.

And right now was the worst time to be out of work in Detroit—anywhere in the whole country, for that matter. Out on the edge of town, where the trains slowed on their way to the heart of the city, migrants—black, white, yellow, all colours, shapes, and sizes—leapt out of boxcars. Men, women, and children sank low in the grass and weeds. Stealing into town, pretending they weren't drifters, trying to shake off the disgrace of homelessness and appear established, trustworthy, and employable. They weren't fooling anyone, not in these times. Whole families, their possessions carried in sacks or battered suitcases, with youngsters clustered around them. Heartbreaking, it was. Every day more and more homeless people filled the streets trying to find a better deal, a factory job building cars, giving up on country life. The country gave up on them. The ground so hard, Buddy heard say, you couldn't pierce it with a pitchfork; the winds carrying so much dust around you couldn't see your hand in front of you. He could spot those folks from a distance, pain on their grim faces, as if they faced a prairie wind full of grit.

Along Brush Street makeshift shelters made Marion's box seem like a palace. On street corners, men peddled apples brought in from Washington State which put a few coins to rattle inside their pockets, their wives squirreling away the rotten ones to boil into mush and feed to the children.

No sir, this was no time to lose a job.

Buddy headed to the ball park, an oasis of stillness and quiet in the late fall night. This place, it's empty bleachers and the ground spotty with puddles, brought him peace and calm. Here was the possibility of order; unfairness did not have the upper hand. Scraps of paper, candy bar wrappers mostly, scuttled over the ground like crabs. He hunched deeper into his coat and lit a cigarette. On warm summer evenings there'd be a few people in the stands, the smell of cut grass, and bugs swarming in the light of a lowering sun.

Across the field the backdrop of downtown buildings made it look like everyone was making out just fine and prosperous—walls contained a lot of secrets. One thing for sure, if he was going to be underemployed this was the last place he wanted to be—this or any other city where misery was in plain evidence everywhere.

Chapter 19

City Gym — 1934

Never let down your guard, one of Hadley's favourite sayings, Father's, too. Hadley seemed like a father for a while.

The City Gym smelled of leather soaked and cured in sweat, like horse tack—one of the reasons he liked being there. Curly, the owner, hired Buddy to keep the spit buckets and garbage empty, sweep the place, clean the toilets and the locker room, and be there when some of the boys wanted to stay late. Boxing was forbidden when Curly wasn't there, in case of injury and bad tempers, and Buddy made sure the "no-women-in-the-gym" rule was never broken.

"These guys go at it over a broad and they'll kill each other," Curly said, running his hand over his head, as bald as a billiard ball. "Keep the alley cats out of here." Buddy set up a cot in the mop room where he napped, often not bothering to go home at night.

He watched Curly's special trainer, Hadley—he stood no taller than Buddy, no more than five ten, and probably weighed less than him—work with the real fighters, the ones making money. Hadley put him in mind of a deer; timid, shy, always watching, and nervous-like. At first it seemed a strange quality to find in an ex-boxer until he saw how Hadley knew the game in a way others didn't, seemed to breathe it, and understood it from the inside out. Hadley could predict when a fight would end, call the sequence of punches that would take it there, and could pinpoint a fighter's strengths and weaknesses minutes into the first round.

Hadley worked with Delroy, a boxer gone pro. They circled the bag as if tied together by a short invisible rope, Hadley half-crouched, shouting at Del, and tucking in close enough behind him to be his shadow. "Jab, jab, jab, right cross, left hook! Watch your feet, keep them moving, get them in position. Jab, jab, jab, right cross, left hook!" Over and over, until Buddy wondered how it was Del didn't turn around and take a poke at Hadley.

Buddy worked out right along with them, but on the sly from across the gym, following their moves and learning as much as he could about technique as he swung at a bag. Until one day Hadley noticed him.

"Come on over here and throw a few punches." Hadley waved him into the ring while Del rested on a stool, wiping sweat from his forehead with a towel.

Hadley positioned himself close to Buddy and had him swinging at the bag. Buddy's punches wouldn't go where he wanted them to go.

"There's something else you can do, Buddy, that's going to make a big difference." Hadley motioned over to Delroy. "Delroy there's done it; he'll tell you about it, what it did for him. You want to know what it is?"

Of course he did.

"Go down to the Golden Ballroom and see The Widow. Take a few dancing lessons and you'll find a big improvement. And the ladies will love you, too."

He convinced himself it wouldn't hurt to snoop around the Golden Ballroom. He stood inside the door and watched a roomful of couples sweep around the vast room; arms pumping, legs striding, skirts flaring. When the music changed their steps changed too, faster or slower. Buddy's feet wouldn't stay still, tapping with the music.

"You interested in lessons?" A slim woman with wavy black hair tumbling to her shoulders placed her hand on his arm, eyes strikingly blue against milky-white skin.

"I'm from The City Gym. The trainer Hadley told me about this place. I'm just watching."

"That's what they all say. Do you have money?"

"Yes."

"On you?"

"Yes."

"Okay, we're in business. Take your shoes off and come with me."

"I'm going to pass on…"

"Do you want to box good or don't you?"

"Well, yes, I…"

"Then do as I say. I won't hurt you."

Her hands on her hips, her flowing turquoise dress cascading down from the waist to just above her ankles, she watched as he untied his shoes and slipped them off then led him by the hand onto the dance floor.

"This here's the Suzie Q. You watch and follow what I do. You've got to think with your feet." She smiled at him as she moved her body. "By the way, my name's The Widow," she said as she demonstrated the steps.

"How come you're called that?" He tried to follow her moves.

"Unlock your knees; keep your eyes up and off your feet. Look at me. In the eyes."

She guided him around the room with surprising strength in her arms.

"Ever since my husband died I've been called The Widow. I've stuck with the name in case I get carried away and have thoughts of marrying again. My name suits me fine; it puts me in memory of my husband, the worst bastard to ever walk." She stopped abruptly. "Loosen up! You're moving like you're made of wood. Come on, let go." She shook her entire body, wiggling her shoulders and hips and arms, and invited him to do the same. "You're getting there," she said, and pulled him out across the floor.

They danced for two hours. To watch her, you'd never think there was any kind of Depression going on. All of life seemed gay. He'd known so little about dancing but by the end of the night he'd done the jitterbug, the Charleston, the foxtrot, the waltz, and the Suzie Q.

Later, at her house, she showed him more moves for which he required no teaching.

One day Buddy asked Hadley about his history. An overhead bulb shone down on Hadley's short silver brush cut and raised flecks of red in his whiskers.

"Not much to tell," Hadley said. "Your run-of-the-mill story, really. I was married. Had three kids. They're grown, have families of their own, the works of them scattered clear across the country. Nobody stays put these days. Especially since work is always someplace else. My wife died eight years ago and I'm putting in time. That's it, really. I worked on cars—worked on motors. I used to box, was pretty decent at it. I've always been involved in boxing. Mostly training now. Anyway, these days, it's me and the four walls at home." Hadley seemed embarrassed he'd talked for so long. "It's pretty unremarkable." He made it sound like an apology. "You Buddy? How about you?"

"Ah, I don't know," Buddy said. "I spent a few years floating around here and there. Ended up here. By accident, really."

"You got family here?"

"No, no family. Got a few friends, that's all."

"Where you from?"

"The West." He wouldn't explain the tragedy that started his journey so long ago. He remembered the stories so many times he wondered if they were even true.

"That's it?"

"That's it."

Hadley didn't push any further.

One afternoon Hadley invited Buddy into the ring for a few rounds, just for fun. Hadley landed a punch off Buddy's nose that cracked right up into his ears. Buddy grabbed his face and felt an awful tenderness which made his eyes sting and water. Blood gushed and dripped over his gloves to the floor.

"You moved it east," he said. Touching it darn near drove him around the bend. His eyes wouldn't stop watering.

"Sit down, sit down." Hadley guided him from the ring, his face so bloodied he couldn't see where he was going. "I'm going for ice." He headed off to the supply they kept in the back room.

Buddy pressed the ice lightly against his nose and winced at the sting running up it like a zipper.

Hadley paid Buddy a lot of attention after he smashed up his nose. He invited him back into the ring to play around, "Bob and weave, Buddy, bob and weave," but Buddy lost confidence he knew he'd never get back, despite all the coaching.

"It's like falling off a horse. You need to get right back on to get over your fear. And don't ever let down your guard," Hadley said.

Those were Father's words. "Don't tell me about horses. I know all about horses," he said from behind his raised gloves.

One night while Buddy was cleaning out spit buckets, Hadley asked him if he was doing anything on the weekend. "I've got friends up in Canada I'm going to visit. Thought you might appreciate a change of scene."

The idea of going to a whole new country seemed unlikely and strange, but he wasn't working and he had nothing planned. Why not?

Hadley had one foot on the bench, head down as he tied his shoes. "You'll like it. We're going to a little village in southern Ontario. Farnwell. Don't bother looking for it on a map—it's too small to get a mention. I'll pick you up early Friday morning. Be ready at seven."

Thursday night, as he packed up his bags for his trip with Hadley, he heard some of the cops he boarded with talking about a body that washed up in the river: blown up like a big ugly fish and blue-grey, the color of a dolphin.

"It was one of those girls from The Big Whorehouse," someone said.

"It took a while to identify her, she was pretty messed up from being beaten and in the water. Her Madam, Goldie, came down to identify the body. Now there was one heartless bitch. She took one look and said it was Sally. She said she'd recognize those hips anywhere, too big for such a tiny girl. Doesn't that beat all? Can you imagine that? Goldie's one tough customer."

Buddy slammed the lid on the suitcase. He knew who'd done it. Couldn't prove it, but he knew it in a place more reliable than any other—in his heart. The thought of the body tossed into the river like a piece of garbage sickened him, filled his night with feverish dreams. He swam below the surface of wakefulness with pictures of blue, bloated fish-women floating in the river, hair spread across the water's surface like a weed.

Early in the morning he sat on the front steps, his small suitcase beside him, and watched his breath drift around his mouth. He was glad for this break, glad to be leaving, if only for a short time. Glad to be going to a whole new country. Hadley would be here soon.

Across the street a cat came out from under a bush, a mouse dangling from its mouth, and dropped it close to his feet. It sat watching with disinterest as the maimed mouse tried to crawl away. The cat batted it a couple of times, picked it up again, shook it hard, and tossed it in the air. The mouse lay on the ground and breathed its last. The cat stood, strutted over to a bush, raised its tail, and sprayed, marking an end to its night of back-alley fighting and mice killing. A final statement to the cat world.

Book Four

Canada

Under the Tree — June 1973

Lightning crackled overhead followed by a long roll of distant thunder. The storm had passed, missed him.

He couldn't move the fingers of his left hand—they'd swollen up like sausages and now his whole hand was as big as a ball glove. Cold seeped through to his bones from being completely soaked. He didn't have to piss anymore; that was something to be happy about. He should be thankful for the rain. The tomatoes could do with a good dousing. If it hadn't rained, and he'd actually made it home, he'd be out in the garden watering them. He'd watered them this morning; that's when he got his big ideas about today to go riding and take Carolyn with him. Such a glorious morning, filled with sunshine and birdsong and a warm breeze—the sky clear then, blue and promising. Was it any wonder he wanted to do something different; to celebrate, to shake loose his restlessness?

Another roll of thunder sounded like a bowling ball racing along an alley.

Carolyn would have been home ages ago and told Meg about his disappearance and they would have called the police. They'd be looking for him by now. It was only a matter of time— of waiting. Unless Meg thought he was pulling some kind of prank. It was true he'd put her through enough, but he wasn't one for disappearing; she knew that. Carolyn would tell her about the circumstances leading up to his disappearance. His hard ride with Spirit which took her by surprise and shouldn't have. He told her about riding Breeze and Bishop and she loved his story about Whitey's horse, Peat, and the day he *Busted out Peat* story. Had she forgotten that? When she was little that was one of her favourites, along with *The Wild Creature Story*. She used to ask him if he was cowboy. Cute. No, just a farmhand who could ride.

Today he busted out Spirit. Or had Spirit busted out him? Carried him out of his present life and sent him back in time. He gave him one hell of a ride and now here he was, not so much busted out as busted up.

"Spirit," Buddy shouted as loud as the pain in his chest would allow. "You still there boy?" The thunder rumbled off in the distance as the storm lost strength, though that could change. There could be another one brewing out over the lake. They came in clusters.

He raised his head, gasping against the pull in his chest. He saw a faint flicker: the white diamond between the horse's eyes. The horse was still there, still watching him, and still fearing the storm. Some horses cowered, others went berserk, running in circles or making a beeline, and stopping only when exhaustion overtook them—running until the fear left them. You couldn't always predict how a horse would react. Maybe he was hanging around to watch over him. Maybe the horse was sorry for what he'd done.

He must be losing his grip to think that. As soon as the thunder stopped Spirit would go back to the stable and the woman who ran the place would put two and two together. Or the police would come. Someone would find him. They would be out looking for him now. Soon they would find him.

He must not fall asleep; he had to watch for the searchers and for this he had to be awake, but the stories washed over him in powerful waves more real than ordinary recollection.

Would someone, anyone, turn off this goddamn rain? The fingers on his right hand trailed in the dirt. Mud. No use getting mad—that would only stretch every second even longer and make matters worse.

He'd put Meg through so much. Did she think he might be staying out on purpose; had deliberately ridden away? It was true he'd done a lot of stupid things.

So many times he wanted to stop, tried to stop, then he'd start up again because it made him feel better about himself—less like a failure. Until the next day when the demons got into his head and he felt nothing but shame.

In the early days when he wore his Detroit suits, when he

first appeared in Farnwell and he and Meg turned heads out on the dance floor at the Odd Fellows' Hall, he didn't feel like a failure then. Dancing the Suzy Q like no others, with Meg on his arm. And everyone loved his stories. Meg's brothers, Archie and Thomas, and her sister Betty asked to hear them. Even her parents, Norma and Patrick, sat still to listen. At first Meg did too, then she'd busy herself with something else.

Buddy met Meg the same weekend he left the United States for the very first time, when Hadley took him to Farnwell to visit with friends. A good fellow that Hadley. Already in his late sixties when they met, he took to Buddy as if he was his own kid—rescued him. Worked with him at the Detroit City Gym and taught him how to be a better boxer. But that wasn't all he was teaching him. He knew what he was doing when he took him to Grace and Whitey's farm. He knew it would do him some good and keep him from falling in with a bad crowd in Detroit. He never said it; he didn't need to. Hadley wasn't one to launch into much explanation.

That weekend up in Canada the music at the Odd Fellows' Hall—the piano, the accordion, the two fiddles, the guitar, and the motion out on the dance floor—everyone from the village and the farmers from the area were there to let off steam and have a good time. Meg, just twenty-two years old, so sweet and pretty, a glint in her eyes; so full of fun and a touch of mischief.

Grace and Whitey were as close as he ever got to having parents again. Whitey always said he was the best damn milker he'd ever seen. Just remembering that made him laugh out loud, which stirred up the pain anew and sent his nerves swarming in a tangle of electricity. If he was a good milker didn't he have Uncle Wes to thank? He couldn't think of one damn thing he could thank Wes for.

Chapter 20

Whitey and Grace, Peat and Mary

Farnwell-1937

They arrived in mid-afternoon at Whitey's small dairy farm a few miles from the tiny village of Farnwell. Hadley had friends he wanted to see in the village and left Buddy with Grace and Whitey at the kitchen table in front of the large kitchen window, looking over their fields, drinking tea, and eating butter tarts.

Whitey was telling Buddy about his farm operation—the few head of milking cows and the horses. "Not much now. I'm winding down."

"Horses?" Buddy asked.

"Maybe in name only. Mary used to pull the wagon and sled. She's long since retired and she earned it. And Peat, well..."

"He's of no use," Grace said, pouring herself another cup of tea then offering some to Buddy. "I keep telling Whitey to get rid of the horses, but we've still got them." Grace's hair was pulled back into a twist at the nape of her neck. Up top it was thin and wispy, and reminded Buddy of a weed gone to seed. She looked as fragile as the teacup she cradled in her hands.

As soon as they'd finished tea Buddy asked Whitey if he could go out to the barn and have a look at the horses.

"Okay with me," Whitey said. "But just so you know, Peat's not cuddly, if you had thoughts about riding him. And also, in case you're wondering, it's Peat as in bog. He got stuck in one when he was a young horse and the whole incident spooked him. He's high-strung and hard to manage. He almost killed someone once. You can try and cozy up to him all you like, but I don't recommend riding him."

Buddy headed out to the barn ahead of Whitey, stepping around Queenie the old farm mutt stretched across the back door. He opened the barn door and the dank smell of dung and straw drifted out. He thought of the barn back home.

Buddy found the horses' stalls and then Peat. The horse, wary at first, settled with his voice until he was able to stroke his nose and between the eyes. He opened the stall door and moved inside and in minutes Peat relaxed enough for Buddy to stroke his sides.

"What do you say we go for a ride, Peat?"

Whitey came into the barn, leaned against the stall, and tamped his pipe on his open palm. "You've made headway with him, I can see that. Riding him is still not a good idea." He puffed on his pipe though it wasn't lit, his eyes narrowing as he stared at Buddy.

"I've ridden lots. And probably worse." Buddy moved around Peat like he meant business, without making eye contact, talking to him, and settling him enough to slip the bridle over his head. He led him outside into the paddock, a small enclosure beside the barn, and after several attempts, slipped a saddle on. All the time under Whitey's blue-eyed scrutiny beneath a cloud of long white hair.

He led the horse around the enclosure and after a couple of attempts mounted him. Whitey wore the same worried look for so long—his eyes pinched so hard his whole forehead looked dented—Buddy wondered if it might be permanent.

He coaxed Peat around the paddock, working him up to a trot then down to a walk. Maybe that was enough for one day. Peat must have sensed he was headed back to the barn; Buddy felt him hold back. He leaned down into Peat's neck. "Okay, old boy, you win. Let's see what you've got." He pulled hard on the reins, turning the horse around sharply, and jabbed his heels into his sides. Whitey, leaning against the fence to watch, puffing on his lit pipe, disappeared as the horse exploded into motion. Peat heaved himself up over the corral fence, and headed out into the open fields, Buddy shouting at him to go harder.

Wind blasted past Buddy's ears, his skin burned with speed, his legs ached as they pinched in tight around the horse, his spine grinding with movement as if his whole body was shaken awake from the inside out. He rode around the field several times. On one of the rounds he saw Pearl standing at the kitchen window.

Finally, Peat wore himself down into a canter, then a trot, and they rode back into the barnyard. Whitey held the gate open and

Buddy took Peat into the barn.

At first, Buddy couldn't figure the expression on Whitey's face as he stood with his pipe in his mouth, shaking his head.

"He's far from being done riding," Buddy told him. "He's got lots left in him."

"What the hell do you think you were doing? For all I knew, that horse was taking you for a ride. I already told you that horse almost killed someone, and that someone thought they knew horses too." Whitey's voice sounded gruff and not at all like the soft-spoken man at tea.

Buddy thought Whitey might have been a little impressed but too stubborn to say so.

"Did I appear to not know what I was doing?" He ran his hand over Peat's shoulder then along his flank.

Whitey studied the ground and rubbed his stubbled chin, then looked Buddy straight in the eye.

"Not from where I stood," Whitey said. "If I'm being honest."

"Well there you go," Buddy said. "That's your answer."

Buddy knew what he'd done was wrong. Whitey and Grace didn't know him; he was a stranger to them. He probably shook up the old man when Peat took the fence, but it was right for the horse and he knew it. Whitey let the matter drop, didn't bring it up again, and Buddy made up his mind about something right then.

Buddy and Hadley slipped in through the back door of the Odd Fellows' Hall. They wove their way through the crowd to the end of the stage and looked out onto the spin and swirl of dancers. Around them people stomped their feet and clapped in time with the band and gave the odd hoot. Hadley warned Buddy the dance hall could get hot, no matter how cold outside, so he wore his light summer suit. Others wore suits too, but none so fancy as his.

Someone spotted Hadley straight off and hauled him away to a group off to the side seated around a table. Buddy joined a line of men strung along the wall to watch the action on the floor.

At break time the hall emptied in a stream out the back door.

Buddy hadn't done one turn on the floor, but the sweat poured off him as if he'd been out in the rain. In the parking lot, illuminated by a single lamp, groups huddled together. Hadley leaned up against a tree, its top limbs combed by wind which had picked up even since they arrived, and the snow fell harder.

"How you doing, Buddy?" Hadley passed him a mickey. Buddy took a swig and passed it along.

"I haven't seen you out on the floor. Dancing's the idea here, you know." Hadley took another swig. "And don't tell me you're not up to it; I know otherwise."

Buddy could count on one hand the number of times he'd seen Hadley drink, and never at the gym.

A young woman approached them, her arms folded across her slight middle, her head down, and when she reached them Buddy recognized her as the girl he couldn't take his eyes away from out on the dance floor. Not that she was the best dancer, not the worst either, but definitely the prettiest girl. Something about her captivated him. The way she tossed her wavy red-blond hair as she threw her head back and laughed. As if she didn't have a care in the world and the self-confidence that came with it.

"Hadley, I heard you were up for a visit." She shook Hadley's hand, eyed Buddy, and gave him a quick smile.

"Meg, this is Buddy. He's a friend of mine from Detroit." Buddy shook her hand and passed her the mickey. "Care for a drink? It'll warm you up."

She took a swig and made a face as if she'd bit into a lemon. "I don't know how you can say you enjoy that. I'm going back inside. It's freezing out here. Nice to meet you," she shouted back to Buddy as she ran across the parking lot, her body huddled against the cold night, and disappeared inside.

They passed the flask a few more times and the sound of music drifted out, weaving in and out of the whoosh of trees. "I'm going in, too." Buddy's cheeks burned with the cold.

He spotted Meg on the dance floor with a skinny fellow who wore his trousers hiked up high and his plaid shirt patched at the elbows. He watched them dance two more dances then he picked his way across the floor and tapped the fellow on the shoulder. "Mind if I cut in?" which brought a blush to Meg's cheeks.

Partway into the song, she stepped away from his arms to look down at his feet. "Aren't you the fancy stepper? Where did you learn?"

"I took lessons in Detroit while training for boxing. I'll teach you if you like," he offered, when the song finished.

He showed her the jitterbug, Charleston, foxtrot, waltz, and she picked up the Suzie Q as if the dance was made for her.

"You're a natural." His compliment seemed to please her and she looked away, her cheeks rosy, a smile on her lips.

During the slow dances she felt light in his arms, as if she belonged there. At the end of the third set they slipped outside to cool down. Buddy slipped his jacket over her shoulders, let his hands linger there to give her a squeeze, then Hadley offered his mickey. Meg took a drink, puckering up again in a way that made him laugh.

"It's not poison."

"Tastes like it."

The band played a shorter set due to worsening weather, the wail of wind audible now between songs. Meg told him how one stormy night after a dance someone almost didn't make it home, ended up in a snowbank and nearly froze to death. It caused a scandal in the village and the IODE tried to have the dances shut down. From then on the Odd Fellows' had to promise the dance would end early if there was a storm.

"What's that IO business?" Buddy raised his voice over the music.

"The Independent Order of the Daughters of the Empire. They were part of the temperance movement. The fellow who almost froze had been drinking and passed out. He lost a couple of fingers."

The last song of the night was a slow dance. Buddy held Meg closer than he'd ever held The Widow. Her hair felt soft against his face and smelled of fresh lemons. When the song ended he told her to wait right there while he got his coat—he'd walk her home—but when he came back she was already gone.

Outside, snow rippled in waves beneath the lamplight. Up the road, above the roar of the storm, came the jubilant voices of people on their way back to the village.

At the farm—Whitey and Pearl long since in bed—Buddy told

Hadley he was headed out to the barn. The storm wailed around the house and out buildings and snow painted a triangle into a corner of the kitchen window.

"At this hour? What for? You going to read the animals a bedtime story?" Hadley asked as he unwound his scarf and draped it over a chair.

"To check the horses. Not all horses like storms. They can get awful worked up." He grabbed a barn coat from a hook, and a blanket from the summer kitchen, careful to step around the old mutt, Queenie, asleep by the door.

In the barn, he led Peat and Mary from their stalls out into the open area, tethered them near a pile of hay, stroked them and told them stories. They reared their heads when the wind rose, and he rubbed their necks until their uneasiness subsided. He gathered the blanket around him and leaned back in the hay, and remembered a ranch far away, in another country.

The barn door creaked and he opened his eyes to a view of Peat's underbelly. The horse's mouth wriggled over Buddy's pants as he took little nips. Buddy rose, stiff from sleeping in straw and in the cold, and brushed off his clothes.

Whitey settled his long lean frame on a milking stool beside a cow and started to milk, the flow from the teats drilling the bottom of the bucket. His hair stuck out every-which-way, as if combed by a wind storm; he'd been shunning a cut for some time.

"Well now, aren't you a sight?" He gave a light laugh, his knees almost drawn up to this chin as he hunched down on the milk stool.

Buddy planted a milking stool one cow over from Whitey.

Whitey peered under his cow, all the while his big, broad hands stroking rhythmically. "I expect that cow is going to give you sweeter milk this morning."

"Why's that?"

"I imagine she's flattered by the way you dressed up for her." Then he laughed. "Not many milkers wear suits for the job."

As they worked their way along the small herd, Whitey told him how his hired hand Bert ran into some health problems and couldn't do the milking anymore. It was true it wasn't a sizeable herd, but as Whitey said, "You might have noticed I'm no spring chicken."

Buddy fed the animals and mucked the horses' stalls. Whitey leaned against the stall puffing on his pipe which he wouldn't light until he was outside the barn, and seemed to be enjoying watching him.

"You're superior on the end of a pitchfork. It's a relief not to be doing the work myself. The aches go to my bones the way they never did before. And the trouble is they seem to stay there. Has me all but thinking I should give up the farm."

On the way to the house for breakfast, they met Hadley coming up from the woodlot, holding a bunch of squirrels by the tail in one hand, a shotgun in the other.

"Grace'll turn these into pie," he said, hoisting up his catch to admire it. "I'm going to get cleaned up and have some breakfast, then we'd better head back to Detroit. It's mostly dark by five and I want to drive in daylight. You packed up yet?" he asked Buddy.

Buddy examined the sky, overcast and low, then out across the fields covered in a thin sheet of fresh snow, and to the woods beyond.

"The thing is, Hadley, I'm not going back. Whitey can use a hand, I'm pretty sure. I'm staying here."

Whitey didn't say anything, and Buddy knew it was fine with him by the way he stood grinning and Hadley gave him no argument either.

At the kitchen table, after all the breakfast dishes had been cleared away and they sat drinking tea, and after Grace heard about Buddy's plan to stay, she asked Buddy if he had a life in Detroit he could just walk away from. He'd had that life for a long time, but before he could explain to her he had no binding ties in Detroit she said, "It's easier when you're young, I suppose. Your roots aren't sunk too deep." She had her hands curled around the bone china teacup, using the hot liquid to warm them; they looked tiny, like that of a child's. She faced the big window overlooking the pasture where Mary and Peat grazed and said, "We'll pay a fair wage and give you room and board, but there'll come a day, and it won't be long, when all this will be too much for us. And there will be change and there will be nothing we can do to stop it."

On the way to the car Hadley gave Buddy a light punch in the arm.

"Someone's smitten, I'd say." Hadley was all smiles. It looked good to see him less serious after a couple of days in the country. "I'm right, aren't I?" Maybe he wasn't the best judge of romance, but from where he stood last night at the dance he could see that Meg was smitten too. "Meg would be a damn good catch. She's sharp as a whip and pretty. She's the teacher at the schoolhouse. You could do a whole lot worse and not better."

They shook hands and Hadley pulled Buddy into him for a hug. Buddy hated goodbyes. He'd said so many in his life it felt like an old pain opening up, a pain he'd do anything to avoid. Hadley promised to come back for visits. Whitey and Grace stood in the kitchen and waved in unison.

Buddy waved down the long driveway, waved as much to the empty seat beside Hadley as anything, the future he chose to give up, the shadow of another life now disappearing in the distance, a moment he'd return to often. Decisions weren't something he usually got to make. Usually, circumstances forced a direction, with no questions asked, and certainly no choices.

After going out with Meg for a few months Buddy received his first invitation to Sunday dinner from her parents, Norma and Patrick O'Brien. He fussed and preened, lacquering his brown hair down until it gleamed and redoing the part several times to make it run perfectly straight. (It wouldn't be all that long until his part was no longer a problem, judging by the rate he was losing it.) He checked his suit from all angles, giving a tug here and there, then leaned into the mirror to tighten his tie again.

Grace asked him if it was the Queen of England he was off to see when he passed through the kitchen. "Sometimes Norma O'Brien acts like royalty," she said.

He'd met Meg's mother a few times during brief exchanges on the front porch or at the door when he came to pick up Meg before dances. He'd never seen her at the Farnwell General Store, which her husband owned. Buddy often spent evenings at the store after milking or on weekends to help Patrick out and to visit Meg. When she wasn't detained by her teaching, Meg was there most evenings. Norma made a practice of avoiding the store and staying out of the public eye. A heart condition prevented her from standing for long and doing heavy work, but Meg said her mother never wanted the store in the first place. When people rang up the house outside of store hours or came pounding on the door, Norma reminded Patrick of her preference to live in the city. She reminded him again when they asked for their credit to be extended. Meg said Norma thought the store would do much better if it wasn't in the business of giving charity. Patrick had a hard time turning people away when they came to him with their stories of empty shelves and iceboxes, a brood of children clinging to their legs looking sickly and hungry. The Depression had turned his store into a charity.

Meg answered the door wearing a smart looking floral dress she'd made—she was very clever at making things—stepped outside, kissed him on the cheek, and whispered, "Good luck." She took his hand and drew him inside the cool house with dark wood, into the smell of wax and polish and roasting meat.

Patrick sat in the parlour reading a newspaper which he lowered when they entered the room. He nodded and went back to his reading. He knew Buddy well enough from their time in the store that conversation wasn't necessary.

Mrs. O'Brien stepped into the parlour wearing black lace-up shoes with stocky heels, and a navy-blue dress with white polka dots. Her hair fell from the straight part on the right side of her head in stiff ripples like sand on the bottom of a lake.

"Well then," she said, her mouth scarcely moving, sizing up the two of them sitting on the chesterfield. "Usually Meg helps out in the kitchen, but I let her off the hook tonight since she has company."

Buddy rose for the introductions and shook her hand. "It's nice to see you, Mrs. O'Brien."

"Norma will suit fine. Dinner's about ready so you might as well go to the table. Meg, call your brothers and sister. Patrick, time to sharpen the carving knife."

Patrick took his seat at the end of the table behind a large roast beef, his arms flapping as he drew the knife back and forth over a sharpening stone. Buddy, seated next to him, offered to help but Patrick preferred to do it since this was his best knife. Meg sat between Buddy and her younger sister, Betty, who leaned over the table to examine

Buddy. Thomas and Archie, Meg's twenty-year old and eighteen-year-old brothers sat opposite staring at Buddy, averting their eyes whenever they met his.

Buddy could feel the production of sweat inside his suit and worried it would soak through to the outside. The more he thought about it, the more he sweated.

Once everyone was served and the eating began, Norma spoke to Buddy from the end of the table.

"I understand you're quite the dancer."

"Oh, I don't know. I like to dance; I've seen better." Buddy checked his sleeve to see if he'd dragged it in gravy. What kind of impression would that make?

"At the post office I've heard some of the villagers say what a fine dancer you are and how you and Meg make a striking dance couple," Norma said, her tone matter-of-fact. She had a broad square jaw that barely moved and offset her small nose.

"Well thank you," Buddy said. "I'm not all that good—Meg is—but I'll accept the compliment anyway."

"Don't be so sure I was giving one," Norma said, and passed a bowl of string beans to Thomas.

That hit him quite unexpectedly, like a surprise left jab or a hook planted on the chin, the kind he used to take at the gym. "Oh," he said. What else could he say? He sat back in his chair and waited for her to continue.

She chewed her food slowly and chased a piece of carrot around on her gold-rimmed plate. "Where do you suppose all this dancing will get you?"

Mashed potatoes squished up between the tines of his fork. "I'm not sure I understand your question."

"In what way is all this dancing practical?"

"I don't imagine it is, not in the least. Isn't that kind of the point? But one thing's certain, it's a great deal of fun. Isn't it Meg?"

Meg nodded and Betty giggled.

"I like to dance," Betty said. "We do it sometimes at school in the gymnasium, after our regular classes. Next year when I'm in grade ten they'll teach us how to waltz."

"I can teach you that," Buddy said.

"I should think a young man your age living during these times, what with the economy struggling to get back on its feet, would be doing something a little more serious." Three Brussel sprouts tumbled from a serving spoon onto her plate.

Buddy didn't care for sprouts; he found them bitter but when the bowl came around he took two out of politeness. "Well, I think I am doing something more serious, as you put it." Had she asked him here to give him the third degree? "I work at Grace and Whitey's farm and without me that farm couldn't operate, especially now, since Grace's stroke. Let me ask you this, Mrs. O'Brien. Don't you think that a person should have a little fun? Does it have to be all hard work and no play?"

"I should think the play happens after the work's been done. At least, that's how it is in these parts."

These parts. There it was. She meant Canada, and the unmentioned those parts: the United States. Why was it so shameful to come from there? He was proud to be an American. Why shouldn't he be?

"Well, I'll tell you something. Where I come from, very few are strangers to hard work, and that includes me. But along with all that hard work there's hard play. There has to be some fun in life. Without it, we're dull."

"Depends what you mean by fun, I suppose." Norma looked at the boys and spoke sharply, "Archie, get your elbows off the table. You haven't been raised in a barn."

Thomas sat up straighter and Archie put his hands in his lap. They'd barely uttered a word during dinner and now sat with empty plates.

The phone rang. Everyone listened for their ring—one long, two short. Meg jumped up to get it.

"Yes, oh yes," she said into the mouthpiece, "I understand it's an emergency. He'll be right there."

"Why do most emergencies happen Sunday at supper hour?" Patrick ate his last few bites quickly, dabbed his mouth with a white napkin, and pushed away from the table. "Don't hold dessert. I'll have it later."

After the dishes were done, sitting out on the porch, Buddy asked Meg why Norma didn't like him.

"Oh she's like that with everyone. That's the way she is, very direct. Speaks her mind. She liked you."

"She's got a damn funny way of showing it."

Buddy earned a regular spot at Sunday dinners. While doing odd jobs for Norma he coaxed smiles out of her, and sometimes laughter; two things she'd gotten out of the habit of showing during the hard times of the Depression.

Not long after Mary and Peat died, after Buddy had worked with Whitey for years, Whitey told him that he had news. They were sitting at the table having their tea after dinner. Whitey had taken Grace's dinner upstairs to her bed, where she spent all her days since the stroke.

"I've had an offer on the farm," he said.

Buddy nodded. He surely knew it was coming—the horses dead, most of the cows gone, and the land lay fallow.

"It's a fair and decent offer," Whitey said, rising to peer out the window and across the fields. His plaid shirt bunched at the back where his suspender straps crossed, and his big hands clasped behind his back, already idle. He kept nodding his head as if he might be answering someone.

Buddy knew what it meant for him, too. "You and Grace need to take care of yourselves, Whitey. I'm young, I'll find something."

"You've been like a son," Whitey said, his voice full of gratitude. "We could never stay here as long as we have if it weren't for you."

Whitey wasn't just thinking about giving up the farm or even about cutting Buddy loose. He wasn't really looking at the fields either but retracing two lives—two lives about to come to an end. "You're welcome to stay here as long as you need to. Grace would say the same if she had all her faculties. But once the farm's sold, once the deal goes through…," he shrugged his shoulders and shook his head, defeated by trying to see into the future, "I can't say."

Buddy ran his hands over the oilcloth table cover, the floral pattern faded in places, and looked around the kitchen. In the corner, the wood chair with the broken rungs; the saggy daybed where Grace used to lay before she took to her bed for good; the reliable stove which threw out a blanket of heat on cold winter days; the rocking chair by the window with the frayed hand-quilted pad; Queenie stretched in her usual spot across the floor and so seized up with arthritis it wouldn't be long until she went. Even the smell of the place—potato and apple peels souring in the slop bucket by the back door, or Queenie's wet fur when she came in out of the rain. All so familiar—home for the last five years.

Once Buddy had dreams of buying their farm until he gave in and accepted the impossibility of it. He had little in the way of savings. His dreams of owning his own land, with horses, took him back to Mother and Father and the others and to wanting it all back. Just like it had been before. What a dream that was, had always been, and he was too foolish to allow it.

He tried to slam the door on those memories and hold them at bay. Why remember if it just put a terrible ache in him about what he couldn't have?

One Friday night, while helping Patrick at the store, Buddy was listening to a few Farnwell village men gathered around the pot-belly stove talking about politics—berating Prime Minister King for the mess he put the country in.

Patrick wrapped up some sausages in brown paper and string and handed the packet to a stranger in a suit. Buddy overheard him asking if Patrick knew of anyone in the area who might be interested in driving a truck, delivering from Windsor to Toronto and other parts around the Great Lakes.

"I am. I'm interested," Buddy spoke up.

"You got any experience?" The man gave him a thorough looking over, up and down, as if that might tell him something about his driving abilities.

"Driving? I sure do. I used to drive for the Ford family in Detroit. I was one of their chauffeurs."

The group around the stove fell silent and all eyes went to Buddy. Even if they'd known this about him they would have been suspicious; he was an outsider and unless they could verify his story, it was not to be believed. He raised his voice to deliver them an earful as he listed all the different cars he'd driven—the Lincoln, the Edsel, the Hupmobile, the Model T, the Model A, the Deusenburg, the Packard, trucks of course, the speed he could take them up to, lingering on the details, knowing the group around the stove mostly knew the speed of a tractor.

"Report to me on Monday morning and we'll get you started," the man said and stuck out his hand for Buddy to grasp.

"Well then, he's an exotic, isn't he? If what he says is true," someone said from the group at the stove.

An exotic. Now that was funny! He'd been called a lot of things, but never that.

Driving trucks put him on the move for long stretches of time. In Farnwell, he rented a room in a large red-brick boarding house with a landlady and landlord who didn't care when he came or went. He rarely set eyes on the landlady until she tapped on his door one day with news about Whitey and Grace. She'd just got word from someone who had been to St. Thomas where they both went to live in an old folk's home, that they'd slipped away peacefully and almost together, the way it was meant to be.

Grace first, of course, as everyone predicted and because of the stroke, then Whitey not long after.

They'd loved Buddy, these strangers, Whitey and Grace. They loved him not openly or sentimentally or lavishly, but by giving him a place and by being decent and constant and trustful. He'd met their kindness like a son, a good son, by working hard and keeping them in their home and being reliable and caring.

As he drove his truck on his route and looked out over the lake, his eyes set on the fine, tepid horizon and the slight merging of blues, he made up his mind to ask Meg to marry him. He wanted to make something like Grace and Whitey had and something like his parents had too.

Chapter 21

March 1941

"This can't go on." Meg pulled the ties of her housecoat and surveyed the bodies strewn about the living room.

Fists pummeled inside Buddy's forehead—jab, jab, jab, uppercut. He'd overdone it—so had everyone.

Thomas straddled an armchair, head back, mouth open, the rhythm of his breathing rolling in and out. One of his friends lay on the couch, his face to the back. Another lay on the floor curled up around throw cushions as if he hugged a teddy bear.

In the guest room Betty had the covers pulled up over her head; she'd been up half the night puking. Why did girls start out drinking gin; wasn't it like drinking perfume? In another bedroom Archie and two of his buddies were tangled up like tree roots on the double bed.

"It's possible to have fun without all the drinking," Meg said.

"I guess we got carried away."

Archie's last weekend on leave before shipping out to war, along with his snoozing buddies, had been a call for something; he hated to think of it as a party, but maybe that's what it was. A send off, for sure. No more than kids; they acted like it last night, too. How could it be possible they were going off to fight Hitler? With the possibility that some of them wouldn't come back—it made him feel ill even thinking about it. It must have been on everyone's mind. That's why they partied so hard.

"He's leaving, Meg, going off to fight. Maybe you should ease up a little."

Meg used to like to party and have a few drinks. She ripped off his clothes after the Saturday night dances, after the mickey had been passed a few times out behind the Odd Fellows' Hall. Sometimes it was her idea to go to Sam Churley's barn, the local haunt preferred by young villagers. Sam, deaf as a stone, was unaware of how his barn, the handsomest for miles around, provided a useful service.

Sometimes when Norma went off to an afternoon function at the United Church and Buddy returned from his trucking job, before they were married, he and Meg took advantage of the empty house and put a little music into Meg's iron bed frame. They even had a swig or two out of her flask, the one she sometimes smuggled into dances and kept hidden in her room under a pile of sweaters. "To great sex," they toasted. Once they did it on Patrick and Norma's bed, just so they could say they did, though Buddy couldn't stop imagining square-jawed Norma catching them and glowering at his bare backside.

Meg before marriage. The fun they had. Before she changed. Before she became proper.

"They need to go home," Meg said. "Why is our house the party house? Mother and Dad are coming tomorrow and I've got a lot to do."

What was the big deal about them coming to dinner? "It's just your folks. No need to put on the dog." A look he knew well flashed into her eyes. He would say no more. Every time they turned down Meg's invitations she was overcome by disappointment. Somehow her home didn't quite measure up; it wasn't a real home, not compared to theirs. Tomorrow was some kind of milestone to her, a test of legitimacy.

He woke everyone up to their hangovers, listened to their moans and groans and their laughter as they relived last night's antics, recovered from a boozy haze.

Meg was at the sink and didn't join in the conversation or the laughter as she washed glasses, popcorn bowls, and ashtrays.

"Sounds like the works of you weren't even here last night. What does it accomplish?"

"This headache's some kind of an accomplishment." Archie rubbed his forehead and slurped his coffee. "Jesus, Meg, since when did you get so damn serious?"

"Maybe it has to do with this war we're in."

"Well, I'm the one going off to be in it, not you," Archie said.

"Guess I'm not the serious type. I think the whole damn thing's a load of craziness, and maybe acting crazy is the right way to be." He raised his coffee cup. "Let's drink to crazy," then brought it down. "I've got to go. I'm headed to the village to say goodbye to Mother and Dad."

Buddy called out from the front door where he watched Norma and Patrick get out of their car. "Meg, they're here!"

Norma and Patrick made their way along the sidewalk and up the steps, their faces set in such concentration he wondered if they came with bad news. Norma wore a grey coat with a matching hat molded to the curve of her head. She clutched a black purse and black leather gloves. Patrick wore a suit and a tie as if he was on his way to church. He knocked on the door.

"For heaven sakes," Meg called from the kitchen. "Why wouldn't they just walk in?"

"Come in," Buddy said, opening the door and stepping aside. "No need to knock here. You're family."

Lately, Patrick's car had been giving him trouble and he wasn't at all sure about driving it the twenty miles to get here. Once they agreed to come, they made it clear they'd have to leave well before dark in case they had a breakdown on the way home. Meg planned an early meal to give them plenty of time to drive back to the village. Patrick and Norma put considerable planning into leaving.

Buddy trailed along behind Meg as she led them on a tour of the house. "Meg can turn a sow's ear into a silk purse." Just like his mother, she had a natural ability to convert rags to silk, and it made him proud of her.

"That so?" Norma asked.

"I've always said she's got the hands of a magician. She could change crows into doves."

"Buddy, stop, please. You're embarrassing me." Meg sounded stricken; a blush flared in her cheeks.

In the master bedroom Norma asked Meg if she intended for the curtains to match the bedspread. If it was plain to Buddy they didn't match it should be plain enough to her. What was the matter with her?

Why couldn't she say Meg had done a wonderful job decorating? She knew they didn't have any money. She was the one who saved the sugar and flour sacks and sent them along to Meg to convert to pillow cases and tea towels. The war had made fabric almost impossible to find and if you did you couldn't afford it.

Buddy sat with Patrick and Norma in the living room while Meg went to dish up supper. Patrick reminded Buddy they had to leave early. "I remember you saying," Buddy said.

Patrick drummed his fingers on the armrest and Norma sat with her hands folded in her lap. For some reason she still wore her hat, as if she couldn't make up her mind if she was arriving or leaving. Their eyes scaled the walls, went to the ceiling then the window, avoiding contact with Buddy's as if they'd just met—were almost strangers. Buddy started up a conversation about the war, a topic Patrick could latch onto for hours, and as Patrick talked Buddy thought of the countless times Patrick boasted about the details of his house. The bevelled glass in the French doors, the wood trim from the very best cuts of chestnut, the extra-thick walls for superior insulation, and the slate roof which would outlast them both. Patrick built the best house for himself. No one else would ever have a home that measured up.

Several times during dessert, Buddy praised Meg's apple pie, the best he'd ever tasted.

"It isn't the best," Meg said. "The apples are too mushy. And not tart enough."

Patrick said she had an unusual way of accepting a compliment. "It tastes good enough to me."

"Your pastry could be flakier. It's not bad. A little tough. Not too much. Use lard. And make sure your water is ice cold, and that you don't handle it too much. You might have done that here, but it is good." Norma said, eyeing the last bite on her fork.

Meg raised her eyebrows, her eyes opening wide, and gave Buddy a cold stare. He was not to utter one more word about the pie: he'd offended Norma. Not his intention. How could there be so much friction around the dinner table over a pie? He only meant to make Meg feel good. She'd earned it—the dinner was superb.

Meg and Norma joined Patrick and Buddy in the living room as soon as the dishes were done and Patrick said it was time to go.

"We've just sat down for a visit," Meg said. "It's only four o'clock."

Patrick glanced at Norma with the expectation she'd come up with a better reason to leave early.

"Your father's anxious about the car," Norma said. "We need to leave well before dark in case we have trouble on the way home. I believe I mentioned it before."

Buddy and Meg waved goodbye from the front porch. When they went back into the house and sat in the living room, Meg began to cry. "They didn't say one nice thing about our house or my dinner. I spent so much time getting ready."

Buddy tried to convince her they had a great time. Meg, better than anyone, should know they had a funny way of showing appreciation. Finally he said, "They're not the type who give compliments. They don't go overboard. It doesn't mean they didn't like the dinner or the house." He put his arms around her and hugged her. "I know they loved it. I watched Patrick eat his pie. He smiled the whole time."

"Really?" Meg asked, sniffing and dabbing at her eyes with a tissue.

"Absolutely." What would it hurt if his story made her feel better? Meg's folks found it a whole lot easier to find fault than to find good—all lean and no fat—especially when it came to their kids. Sometimes they went out of their way not to indulge their children, and to make them aware they weren't special. Buddy couldn't figure it out. He ran his hand over Meg's hair and felt her warm breath on his neck. She deserved better.

Once Meg became pregnant, Buddy started looking for work closer to home. It meant giving up his trucker's job driving around Lake Erie. He couldn't be gone for days anymore.

One day, while helping Patrick at the store, from the top of the ladder where he was pulling bags of rice from a shelf and carrying them down for Patrick, he overheard one of the potbelly stove regulars say someone had quit the dairy in town. The owners were looking for a replacement.

First thing the next morning, dressed in a suit, tie, white shirt, and polished shoes, Buddy went to the dairy office to inquire about the job. Jobs, like so many things these days, were in short supply.

The man behind the desk, wearing an argyle sweater vest, his sleeves rolled up to his elbows, explained. "I just had someone quit. No notice—now you see him, now you don't. I pegged him as a reliable sort and that just shows you how wrong you can be. But before this goes any further," he looked up at Buddy, "Do you have any experience with horses?"

"Are you joking?"

He placed his pen down on the paper he was writing on and crossed his hands. "Why would I be joking?"

"I was practically raised on a horse," Buddy said.

"Oh," he said. "Well that's convenient. Here's what I could offer you. How do you feel about milk delivery? To houses. I've got a horse-drawn route open. Molly's slow, but she gets the job done. We're phasing out the horses. She's one of the last to go. Do you want to see her? She's still in the yard; she's got today off."

"No sir, it's not necessary. I never met a horse I didn't like. I'm your man, if you'll hire me."

Every day Buddy stuffed his pockets with carrots, apples and pears, and as morning's first light cracked the sky, he slipped Molly treats. Her velvety nose tickled his open palm; her warm breath mixed with the cool air made a cloud of vapour. This time of day brought a sense of calm as the world slept. By seven, after an hour and a half spent bridling Molly, hitching her up to the wagon, and loading it with dairy products—milk, buttermilk, cottage cheese, sour cream, yoghurt and butter—he was on his way making the rounds to his customers, the sound of Molly's hooves echoing down the sleepy streets.

He met everyone on his route and learned their names. Some said hi and let him go; others would bend his ear for the whole day if he let them. That fellow Benson eyed his orders as if Buddy was trying to swindle him.

He and Meg bought a property at a good price from an old friend of Patrick's who wanted to sell off some land: a three-acre parcel close enough to the city that Buddy could to drive to work but far enough away to have the space for a garden and country quiet.

He'd never have a farm or a ranch like the one he dreamed of, but he could call the place home. With a baby on the way he had to be practical and give up on the idea of having acreage with horses. Where would he ever find that kind of money, and who would work the land? His new property would at least give him the best of both worlds, as Meg pointed out. The young contractors were off to war and the older ones couldn't keep up with demand, but after a long search they finally found a builder and work began.

Weekends, Buddy worked alongside the crew, staying on long after they'd gone home. During the week, after he finished his dairy route, he went straight to the new house.

He stayed on until night fell and could barely see the hammer in his hand. He ate thick bologna and mustard sandwiches Meg packed for him and finished with a smoke and a couple drinks of rye from a bottle he stashed there for himself and the others.

The best part of the day was when he was alone, after all the workers had gone. Bats dipped in and out of the framework, skeletal against the darkening sky. Around him poplar and willow leaves slurred in a light breeze. Night owls screeched, crickets trilled, and car wheels rumbled over the gravel road. The air smelled cool and damp, sweetened by sawdust, and earthy from road dust. The sights, sounds, smells, the feel of the place: his land. His home. How strange it sounded. He held a hand up in the air and spread his fingers wide; it covered the frame of the house, the bones supporting it. What peace it brought knowing he touched those bones. Specks of stars brightened in the gathering darkness. He searched for the Scott Constellation.

He sat into the night, losing himself to it, smoking and taking the odd pull off the mickey as he learned the rhythm of his land—how it breathed, how it felt and sounded.

Meg met him at the door after he got home late from working on the new house, her eyes filled with fear and red from crying.

"What's wrong? Is it the baby?"

"The baby's due in weeks and it has no crib. What if it comes early?"

An unfinished cradle waited in the basement; he'd get to it on the weekend. The closer she got to her due date, the more urgent everything became. "There's only so many hours in the day and so far I've got most of them used up with work, and not near enough in sleeping." Should he call Norma and have her come to stay with her? Lately, Norma had complained of spells that left her weak and sent spasms through her chest. Not the best time to call, but Meg wouldn't let up until the job was done.

"Okay, I'll finish it tonight, I promise. Go to bed, get some sleep."

At five in the morning he admired the finished product: a cradle so cute it made him teary. He painted it white with blue and pink trim and took time to paint a string of little yellow ducks around the rim. A whole night's sleep it cost him, but it looked fine. He sat admiring his work and finished off the long night with a couple of drinks. It was pointless going to bed now.

He divided his days into three parts: the milk route, building the new house, and getting ready for the baby. He bought an old green chair in pretty good condition from a customer on his route and stuck it in the basement. At least he could sit comfortably when he took breaks and rested. Many nights, as he admired the progress on something he was making—shelves, a chest of drawers—he fell asleep in the chair.

Meg worked feverishly, too. From the basement he heard the buzz of the sewing machine overhead, roaring sometimes late into the night as she turned out blankets and nightgowns, all decorated with lambs, ducks, bears, kittens, and puppies—all her creations.

One night she held up a new blanket of applique and embroidery for him to see. Several lambs romped on a hillside under a smiling sun.

"You've got real talent. You're a real artist, Meg."

The blanket dropped to her lap and she ran her hand along the satin trim as she spoke of an art scholarship she gave up once. "I was one of two people in the entire province to win," her voice drifting with what might have been.

"You've never told me that before. You should have gone."

"The Depression put an end to a lot of things. I had to stay home and work, help Dad in the store." She raised her head, her thick hair falling back as she looked at him. "It was time for me to grow up."

"You could still go. Your folks have money now, they could repay you. They owe you that."

"They don't owe me anything." She spoke with pride, independence, and an unsettling fierceness. "They gave me a roof over my head; they gave me plenty. It's more than you had."

"I didn't have a choice, and, if I'm not mistaken, neither did my parents." His childhood bore no resemblance to hers.

"I shouldn't have said anything about art school. I don't want it brought up ever again. That's over. It's all water under the bridge."

He wasn't so sure. It didn't feel over.

Late on a Saturday night, a week from Meg's due date, two cars pulled up outside and several young women tumbled out. Buddy went out to investigate. Meg's sister Betty emerged out of the group and threw her arms around him. She reeked of gin.

"My dear brother-in-law, we need a place to party." She motioned towards the girls, giggling and talking. "These are my pals. We need somewhere to have fun."

"You appear to be succeeding quite well on your own." It was obvious they'd all been drinking, this unruly flock staggering up the sidewalk.

Out on the lawn someone shouted, "Hey Betty, aren't you going to introduce us to the hunk? Don't hog him all to yourself."

"Meg's not going to like this, Betty," Buddy said, and lit a cigarette. Betty grabbed it from between his lips and took a couple of puffs.

"She'll get over it. She should have been a nun; she's such a pain in the ass sometimes." Betty wobbled up the steps, grabbing onto the rails. "Come on inside girls and meet my sister. Prepare for cold weather."

"She's gone to bed, Betty. She's due soon. You can come in, but you've got to be very quiet."

They tip-toed into the kitchen, closed the door, and settled around the kitchen table.

Betty poured him a tumbler of rye from a bottle she pulled out of her pocket and pushed the glass across the table. "Take a load off. You've got to tell some *In the West* stories. I promised the girls you would."

Betty sketched in Buddy's early life to the women at the table, describing how his parents died and left twelve orphans alone on a remote ranch in Wyoming. The young women around the table sighed and uttered "how sad, how awful".

"Nine orphans, Betty," Buddy corrected her. "Let's not exaggerate."

He told *The Ray Lost in a Blizzard* story and how he found him, then the *Mother Dying from Childbirth* story.

When he was done two of the girls were weeping and saying how tragic, their reactions enhanced by the booze.

Buddy put his hand over the top of his glass to stop Betty from refilling it again. "Ladies, I must go to bed. You're a lot younger than I am. An old fellow like me needs his sleep. The guest room and the living room is all yours if you decide to stay over, but keep the noise down please. We're expecting a baby any day. Meg needs her rest."

Buddy went down to his chair to admire the shelves he was working on before Betty and her friends came by, draped his legs over the armrest, and fell asleep. Sometime in the night he was awakened by a racket upstairs and smelled cooking. He thought about going up to tell the girls to settle down, but exhaustion overcame him and he slept through until daylight.

In the morning he found a note on the kitchen counter from Meg. "I'll be back in a couple of days, maybe." She would have gone to a friend's or her parent's. He was being punished for last night's party.

As he sipped his coffee and cleared away dishes, the girls started to get up, and one by one wandered into the kitchen looking about as sorry as anyone could.

"Where's Meg?" Betty said, running her hands through her tousled hair, her eyes bloodshot and puffy.

"Gone. For two days, I guess."

"On account of us, I imagine." Betty sat in a chair opposite. "I guess I landed you in the doghouse, didn't I?"

"I imagine you did. And thing is Betty, I can do a pretty good job of getting myself there without any help. She'll get over it. Just give me a hand cleaning up your mess."

When Buddy got home from work on Tuesday, Meg was there to meet him.

"You should have thrown Betty and her friends out," she said. "But what did you do instead? You entertained with your stories. You encouraged them to stay. It's natural I suppose. It's much better having fun with several beautiful young girls than an enormous pregnant wife."

"It wasn't my idea for them to come here; I never invited them. I was working on shelves in the basement."

"You didn't make them leave, either."

"It's your sister. You need to talk to her."

David came into the world on July 12, two weeks late, twelve pounds of raging purple flesh. Poor little bugger had a hard time joining humanity and posed a real challenge to Meg's narrow frame. At least that was how one doctor put it, referring to her uterus like a badly made door.

His head resembled a pear; as if he'd been squeezed out of a tube. A nurse noticed Buddy's anxiousness as he peered through the nursery window at his son and came out into the hall to talk to him.

"A lot of new babies have funny shaped heads until the bones set. Don't let your wife see the face you're making. We don't like our new moms upset. It's hard enough for them to catch onto nursing, never mind having an ugly puss like yours floating around." She shuffled off down the hall on her white shoes as if she was headed to a fire.

When Buddy held David for the first time, the baby looked at him, sized him up, then his face scrunched up like a piece of red paper. His mouth opened so wide Buddy got a clear view down his fleshy throat, and let out a scream like bobcats fighting. Was it the sight of him that made him cry? Was it possible for a newborn to reject his father at first glance?

Patrick and Norma came into Meg's hospital room in time to catch Buddy's first moments with David.

"Fine set of lungs." Patrick peered down into the swaddled

bundle.

Norma leaned over David and spoke quietly to soothe him. "He's badly marked from his trip down the birth canal. It's no wonder, he's quite a size," Norma spoke over the baby's crying. "Must have been all the eating you did, Meg."

Buddy jostled the baby in the hopes he'd stop crying—no use. Nothing seemed to work.

"Hand him to me. Let's see how I do," Norma said.

"For God's sake, make it stop the awful squawking." Patrick pushed the swaddling blanket away from David's face. "Homely little toad, isn't he? No one in our family was homely. Must take after Buddy's side."

Maybe the baby wasn't the handsomest in the nursery, and maybe he did take after Buddy's family, but no one in his family would have said something so nasty. "I was about to say he's the spittin' image of you, Patrick."

"Not at all like me," Patrick said, shaking his head. "No sir, not at all."

Norma couldn't get David to stop crying either. She handed him to Meg and Patrick said it was time to go. He didn't want to overstay his welcome. Buddy followed them out into the hall.

"No turning back now," Patrick said, handing him a cigar. "A wife and now a family. You're in as deep as you can get."

An unusual way to say congratulations but it shouldn't come as a surprise. He watched them head down the corridor towards the exit doors and wondered if they could have made their visit any shorter.

In the hospital room, Buddy stood at the foot of the bed watching as Meg held David to her breast. "He's priming the pump." She smiled down on her new son. "The milk's not in for two days."

He'd never forget the Saturday dance nights, the breaks they took out behind the Odd Fellows' Lodge, the wind whipping through the spruce and the cold air slapping at their cheeks when he'd touched her breasts and felt her warmth, the silky skin. The nights in Sam Churley's barn and her cold hands all over him. Was it possible for him to be jealous of his own son? As Meg's belly swelled it pushed Buddy aside, then right out of bed. And there he was now, the new little man in her life. And right now the sight of the two of them, Meg's head bowed over the baby at her breast, made the most beautiful picture he'd ever seen.

The pediatrician said David's crying had to do with gas and he'd straighten around in a few weeks once the machinery got oiled, all they had to do was be patient. Buddy wondered if he'd ever again wake up without feeling like he'd had the stuffing taken out of him in the boxing ring.

Sometimes riding around in the milk wagon, the rhythmic clip-clopping of Molly's hooves and the crisp outside air, put Buddy in such a restful state he fell asleep. The horse, a more faithful creature there never could be, hauled him along to his next stop, shifted, and whinnied until she woke him up.

One Friday morning he woke up with a start. One of his customers, Paulette Robinson, dressed in a red night robe, had her head through the window staring at him.

"New baby." Buddy said the first thing that came into his head.

"I'm waiting for cream. I don't have any for my coffee," she said. "I hate to wake you up when you seemed to be sleeping so peacefully while you are working, but I need coffee to start my day properly and I can't drink it without cream."

She interrupted his apology. "No need to explain. It's obvious you don't get any sleep."

That night after Buddy arrived home from painting the baby's bedroom at the new house, moving day rapidly approaching, he heard David crying all the way out to where he sat in the car in the driveway. He'd wait for him to settle before going in. He put his head back on the seat, searched the sky for the Scott Constellation, fell asleep, and woke up with a stiff neck just in time to go to work.

Chapter 22

Cream

"You've done it again." Paulette's face appeared in the milk wagon window, black hair gleaming in the sunlight, and her violet eyes lit by laughter. Once again, she woke him up.

"There's something about this street. Maybe it's what you call a sleepy neighbourhood." Another night up late with David then dozing off in the chair after a couple of drinks. Waking up in the morning, his knees locked over the armrest, back hurting, and neck stiff. He barely remembered harnessing Molly in the pre-dawn hours and loading up the wagon.

"Come in and have a coffee. It will wake you up."

"I can't, I'm collecting today."

"What? Your thoughts?"

She crossed the street, a bottle of cream clutched in her hand and disappeared inside her small bungalow. He thought about it: he was already running late, but he had to collect from her too. Coffee would be so good right now.

His hand barely lifted from the door when Paulette opened it and told him to take a seat at the kitchen table. The room smelled of fried bacon. She placed a coffee and a small pitcher of cream in front of him. "It's fresh," she said.

Buddy sipped his coffee and watched as she piled bacon onto a plate.

"How do you like your eggs?" she asked.

"I've only got time to down this and go. Thanks just the same." The coffee tasted wonderful. Strong and hot.

She cracked open two eggs and dropped them into a pan of

sizzling, spitting grease, the room so thick with the smell of cooking he could almost taste it.

"I appreciate the coffee, but it's time I'm off."

"Wait a minute." She dipped a spatula into the frying pan and scooped out the eggs, slid them on a plate, stacked several pieces of bacon on the eggs, edged the plate with toast, and put it before him. "It'll take more time to refuse than to eat it. So eat. I'll just sit here and have my coffee." She seated herself across from him, her dark hair flowing down her red robe, smiling as she watched him eat.

From then on, he started collection day earlier than his regular days to allow time for breakfast at Paulette's. At first he felt guilty, maybe ashamed, about dropping in every Saturday. Meg didn't need to know every part of his work life and he didn't need to know the details of her life at home with David. It was his work, wasn't it? They couldn't share everything.

Paulette was like him; she'd been around the block a couple of times. She liked his *In the West* stories and his tales of roaming across the States with Ray. Buddy gave a sympathetic ear to her stories about a miserable husband who she ditched years ago after he laid another beating on her. Paulette had a leathery, sinewy toughness and not so much as a pinch of fat on her bones, but any man who would hit a woman was nothing more than a coward. She let him have it with a baseball bat. "I clobbered him six ways to Tuesday; I'm pretty sure I knocked him clear out of the park. I'm not sure he'd ever be the same after the wallop I gave him, and I didn't hang around long enough to find out."

One rainy collection-day morning, his eyes gritty with sleeplessness after being up all night with David on account of an earache, he anticipated the plate of eggs and bacon in the hopes it would revive him. He left the house even earlier to give himself time for a second cup of coffee. Today of all days he would need it.

The cold, wet morning air fired a shiver through him—tiredness made him more susceptible to the chills and achy muscles. Paulette's warm kitchen smelled of cooking, the inside lights soft pools of yellow against the dimness outside. Paulette's red robe stretched to just above her ankles; she wore slippers to match. She must have noticed him watching her move around the kitchen.

"You're here early," she said. Sometimes on Saturday she'd be dressed for the day, but not always. "And I slept in. I just couldn't fall asleep last night."

"That makes two of us."

"David keep you up?"

"He had an earache."

"Sounds nasty. Park yourself." She carried a coffee to the table. "Drink this."

"What else would I do with it?" He took a sip; it tasted different. "What have you done with this?"

"It's just a little something my grandmother taught me." She stood with her arms folded, watching him, and grinning. "I bumped it with some brandy. You need it, your skin is grey. It'll warm you up. Lately, you look ten years older."

"Well, I've felt it too." The coffee tasted better than ever.

After he'd eaten, Paulette bent to remove his empty plate and her housecoat fell open. She caught his straying eyes. She put the plate back on the table, picked up his hand, and guided it inside her housecoat to rest upon a breast. Buddy thought to withdraw it but he didn't. Any sense of loyalty he had was consumed by the urge that rose up through his loins. An urge that joined the smell, the warmth, the soft lights, his satisfied belly, the lightheadedness caused by the brandy, and the touch and warmth of her skin.

She unzipped his jacket uniform then started on his shirt buttons, her lips touching his neck, the creases. She pulled him up out of the chair and led him down the hall into a room so dark he barely made out the bed. They fell onto twisted sheets and blankets, and with hungry searching hands she stripped away his uniform and thrust her naked body against his, her skin burning.

After, as they lay together, Buddy watched smoke curl from his cigarette in the dim light. He'd crossed a line, a line so terrible it made him nauseous to think about it. A line which brought the amazing warmth of her skin to his fingertips. Maybe he wasn't the marrying type; maybe he wasn't a family man. Maybe he was never meant to have a home. Who did he think he was having a wife and kid? He butted his cigarette and lay for a minute, intending to get up and leave. He fell asleep.

Beside him, Paulette's black hair cascaded over her back, her face turned away from him. He gathered up his clothes and dressed in the kitchen, his hands trembling as he fumbled with his buttons. How could he have done such a stupid thing? The sex, that was one thing, and then falling asleep, letting his job slip—what would his carelessness have done? He was four hours late.

Outside, Molly shifted as he approached and the rain streamed over her dapple-grey back. Out in the cold rain this whole long time. He rubbed her nose and spoke to her. Her brown eyes, fringed with thick light lashes, told him he failed her, too. He wasn't fit to take care of anything.

At the dairy, he shoved the undelivered milk back inside the cooler and told his foreman he got stuck in the mud. He'd give customers the same story if any complained and finish collecting on Monday.

Meg jostled David on her hip. His crying subsided to sporadic spurts as he tugged on his ear and whimpered. Exhaustion overtook her face, settled into it and aged her too.

"You need to get some rest. I'll take charge of David." He scooped his son from her arms and escorted Meg to bed. "I'll be back in a few minutes."

David sat in his highchair watching Buddy wash the dishes and crack open eggs, his hands stuck in his mouth up to his knuckles, and drooling on his bib.

Buddy stuck flowers he purchased on the way home in a vase and placed them on a tray alongside poached eggs on toast, soup, and applesauce. He picked up David, put him in his playpen in the living room, and shook a rattle in front of his face. He went back to the kitchen for the tray.

"They're lovely." Meg's eyes went to the flowers, her voice touched with surprise. "What are you trying to hide?"

"Oh come on, Meg. Can't a guy buy flowers for his wife for

no reason? Especially when she's having a hard time at home? Doesn't everyone need a lift every now and then?"

"I suppose." She picked away at the food and took a few bites, then pushed the tray aside, slipped down deeper into the bed, gave a deep, appreciative sigh, turned onto her side, and closed her eyes.

Buddy stood beside the bed, watching her drift off to sleep. He thought she was the most beautiful woman in the world. What had he done? How could he have been so stupid? He bent down to remove the tray and kissed her on the forehead. David cried from his playpen. If he fussed in the night, he would tell Meg to stay put and he would tend to him. It didn't matter if he was up all night; he deserved to be. He deserved much worse.

As he cleaned the dishes from Meg's tray, he thought about earlier today. He wasn't in his right mind and Paulette took unfair advantage of him. She'd used the information about his hardships at home, his sleep-deprivation, working all the time to make ends meet, and keep up with the demands of a growing family. He had no strength to resist. The morning with Paulette was an accident. Overwork and tiredness, that's what he blamed it on. It wasn't really his fault.

It would never happen again. He would deliver her milk the same way he did for his other customers but their friendship, if that's what you wanted to call it, was over.

He stood at Paulette's door to collect his money and he told her he wouldn't be staying for breakfast anymore. The smell of cooked bacon came from inside the house.

"Because of what happened?" she asked, her pale skin looking even lighter against the swirls of long hair.

"What else could it be?"

"You're human. Stop punishing yourself. You gave in, we both did. We are two consenting adults. It felt good. Didn't it?" She smiled, her lips full and painted with red lipstick.

"I'm a married man. I have a son. I have a family. It's not the right thing."

She crossed her arms and leaned against the doorframe."You

are the first married man, I imagine, to have sex with someone other than his wife." Her smile, part amusement—part sarcasm, lingered on her lips. "You didn't answer my question. It felt good, didn't it?"

"That's beside the point."

That got a howl out of her. "Is it? Well, I wonder what point it is beside. You'd better get on your way. You're too good for me." She closed the door.

Buddy walked back to Molly and the wagon and moved along to his next customer three doors down from Paulette's, and carried her milk to her door, not expecting Mrs. McKay to be right there to greet him. "You're not held up today at Paulette's?" she asked, thrust money into Buddy's hand and promptly closed the door.

Next collection day he arrived at Paulette's door, hungry, tired, bad weather beating at his back, and smelled bacon, fried potatoes, and fresh brewed coffee. What would it hurt if he just went in and ate? Couldn't they go back to the way it had been before? They could pretend that other thing never happened.

Paulette sipped coffee across the table. When he finished eating she said, "I knew you'd be back. Why wouldn't you come back? What's a little breakfast between friends?" She came around to his side of the table and dropped her housecoat and stood before him naked.

He took her hand, followed her down the hall, and lost himself to the shadowy interior of her bedroom.

He changed his collection route and left Paulette's place until last. He told Meg he had to work longer since his route had expanded. This stretched out his work week, but no customers waited for their milk or commented about the delay. He parked Molly on the next street from Paulette's in front of a vacant lot, away from Mrs. McKay's critical eyes. He saw the curtains at her house shift as he walked up Paulette's driveway carrying bottles of milk in his carrier.

Buddy never charged Paulette for her milk products. "In lieu of favours," she said. Milk, butter, cottage cheese, sour cream, and yoghurt—she ordered more of everything. Where did it all go? He wondered though he never asked or confronted her with the bills. He wrote some of the product off as spoilage, something all the milkmen did. But the part of her outstanding bill he couldn't cover he paid for himself. Meg would notice the dip in cash. He would tell Paulette to cut back, she wanted too much, but he couldn't bring himself to do it. When could he bring up the topic? When he stared into the heaping plate of bacon and eggs, fried potatoes, and toast? Or after their weekly tumble?

As he leaned over to tie his shoelaces, Paulette reached across the table and touched his back.

"You've been good to me, Buddy. I want you to know I appreciate it."

He sat up, saw the little threads of wrinkles around her mouth, her makeup smudged, and her hair messy. He didn't know her age but imagined she was at least ten years older than him. It didn't matter. "It's a two-way street, Paulette." Now, finally, an opportunity to talk about her milk bill while she was expressing gratitude.

"I need more money," she said.

Buddy took a drag from his cigarette. "Who doesn't?"

"I'd like you to help me get some."

He knew of only one way to get money, at least the kind of income you could count on—it meant working. "I can't loan you any money Paulette, if that's what you're getting at. I'm tapped out. I wish I could, but I'm a working stiff and I don't make enough. I've got a kid, another one on the way."

The tips of Paulette's black hair brushed the table top as she leaned closer to him, arms fully extended, hands clasped, and fingers twitching. She examined Buddy, her mouth twisted into a pucker. "Men never fail to amuse me," she said.

"I'm glad you find me so entertaining." Something in her tone sounded odd. This was no time for a conversation. He was due back at the dairy, then home—he was putting in a vegetable garden. He pushed his chair back, about to get up.

"Not so fast." She grabbed his hand and squeezed it until her fingernails gouged his palm. "See, here's what you don't understand. The reason you are amusing, Buddy, is that you expect something for nothing. I need you to give me twenty-five dollars a week, that's what I need. Considering what I give you, I'd say you're getting a good deal."

"Twenty-five dollars a week! I can't do that!"

"Oh, I think you can." She twirled a strand of long black hair around a finger. "You wouldn't want me to call the dairy and tell them I am a customer and I'm tired of seeing your milk truck parked outside while I am waiting for my delivery. I guess you could say I'd be complaining about you delivering the goods while you're delivering the goods, if you understand what I mean." She seemed to enjoy watching him squirm. He felt like a fly caught in a spider's web, struggling to break free. "Or what about a call to Meg? As a concerned citizen. Now, if I do all this, and I will, then you aren't going to have a pay cheque at all, are you? And twenty-five dollars will seem like nothing in comparison with," she lifted her shoulders up into a shrug, "well, nothing. Zero."

"You're blackmailing me? Why the hell wouldn't you go after someone that makes decent money?"

"Well, you actually said it right there. Go after." She leaned with her elbow on the table, chin in palm and smiled, like a sly cat. "I wait for the ones who come to me. The way you did. And the one before you."

So that was why the guy who had the route before him left so quickly and without notice. Buddy liked his job and wanted to hang onto it and his survival depended on it; he wouldn't be so easily pushed away. He reached into his pocket, pulled out two tens, and slapped them down on the table. "This is all I have. You'll have to wait for the rest."

"Oh, that's not a problem. I'll be right here, waiting. I'm good at waiting."

The money was supposed to be deposited into the house fund account. Meg would notice but she'd notice far more if he got fired.

"I hope you don't think this is unfair. You didn't really expect to get something for a few quarts of milk, did you? That's not how the world works. You of all people ought to know that. After all the stories you told me I would have thought you might have caught on a little faster." He let himself out.

Buddy stroked Molly's nose, her muzzle soft as velvet, aware of a twisting in his gut as he was about to throw up. If Paulette was a lowlife, what did it make him? A sewer rat. How could he let himself sink so low? He'd let down his guard. What would Hadley think? Or Mother? Or Father? He was no better than Paulette.

That night, at home, just after he'd put David to bed, Buddy tuned in music on the radio, took Meg by the hand and pulled her up off the couch. "Come on Meg, let's dance. Like old times."

"No, I'm as big as a house and I can hardly reach you."

"Don't be a party poop."

They did a slow shuffle through the living room and dining room then back into the living room. Meg felt warm and familiar. He'd drifted to a dark place and he had to come back. He pressed his cheek into hers and smelled her hair, clean and lemony. He wrapped his arms tighter around her, ran his hands over her back, and pressed his cheek close to hers to kiss her.

She pushed him away. "Not now. I'm tired and I can barely stand up. I'm going to bed."

Buddy stood alone in the centre of the living room, the music still playing. Wind rattled branches against the window pane. The Meg of old times—no more. Buddy too, not who he once was. All he ever wanted for such a long time, he had: a wife, a kid, and another due soon—a family. He owned his land, he had a home, and yet here he stood, feeling terrible. Feeling lost.

He paid Paulette and never stayed for breakfast. He didn't speak to her beyond, "There's your milk." Once he tried to cut back her order, but she caught the difference and reminded him once again her lips were not sealed—she could be a danger to him.

Meg discovered the account balance didn't agree with her records and confronted him about the difference. He made up a story about how he had to lend money to a fellow at work. He was desperate and had kids and Buddy felt sorry for him. He promised to pay him back at such a great interest rate it would have been stupid to pass up the opportunity to make some extra money. "You're always after me to make more money," he told her. How skillful, shifting the blame to her. A true coward. "I thought this was a way to do it. I didn't know he'd do the midnight flip. I was only thinking about you! Okay, so I was wrong, okay so I am an idiot and made a bad mistake." He sounded so convincing, he almost believed himself.

Buddy took some of his pay cheque and gambled on the ponies, and a couple of times came up a winner. The bank account should have been a lot less than it actually was but he managed to top up the account, pay Paulette, and have enough to buy a few bottles of rye.

At night, after he finished working, he sat in the green chair and worried. How would he get out of his situation with Paulette? He could sell his house and move away. He could tell Meg they were moving to the States—he was homesick. He could murder Paulette. Wouldn't the world be a better place to be rid of such scum? Who was he trying to kid? Even if the thought did cross his mind he wasn't capable of it. And who was he calling scum? If she was scum what did that make him?

Sometimes, late at night when he couldn't sleep, he bundled up and went outside into his backyard to search for the Scott Constellation and talked to the stars—his family. Sometimes he heard his mother's soothing voice, consoling, understanding, full of wisdom, and never scolding. "No one said it would be easy." He would never let that voice go.

One collection day he knocked on Paulette's door to leave his money. No one answered. He knocked again and again; still no answer. He walked around to the front of the house and looked inside the front window. The living room was empty. He went around again to the back and tried the door. It was open; he stepped inside. His voice threw back an echo as he walked through the empty rooms. "Hello? Hello?"

Vanished as if she'd never been there. He didn't know why, but he thought to open the fridge. It was stuffed full of milk, butter, yoghurt, sour cream, and cottage cheese.

That night Meg went into labour and Douglas Patrick Scott was born at two AM, a healthy screaming baby with a thick crop of toffee-coloured hair.

Book Five

Under the Tree – June 1973

He had it all. Everything he ever wanted. Everything he ever worked for—a family and a home. A modest income, enough to get by on. He put food on the table and a roof over their heads. He wasn't greedy. Why couldn't he appreciate the life he'd made? He didn't know why he behaved the way he did—so much shame. Only himself to blame. There was no excuse, but a few drinks and his problems went away. Until he sobered up.

His right arm tingled. He opened and closed his fist but his fingers, puffy and swollen, would barely move. *Ginger ale woke me up, Dad.* The kids used to say that when their arms and legs tingled.

Paulette. A name he'd refused to think about and never once uttered since she left. Stories he never wanted to remember. Why dream of her now?

If he'd been sleeping. More like drifting somewhere between awake and asleep, travelling through layers of time. Not unconscious. At least he didn't think so. He could see the trees swaying overhead, hear the rattle of branches, and felt the odd fleck of rain on his face. Surely that meant he was awake. Was he delirious? Like stumbling around talking to people, participating, but not remembering after drinking?

"Spirit. You still with me?" He saw darkness and nothing more. The horse had finally gone. It was about time. The worst of the storm had passed and the horse, no longer skittish, had gone back to the stable. The stable owner couldn't ignore a horse without a rider. That was reassuring.

A whinny came from out of the darkness. Buddy lifted his head as high as he could, the pull against his chest severe like a ribbon of fire. A white diamond glowed in the dark. The horse stood at the end of his feet. Why had he come so close? Spirit raised his head and shook it.

"What you doing, Spirit? You're getting restless aren't you?" he whispered and lowered his head to the ground.

The horse's hooves thumped the ground. He opened his eyes and looked up. Spirit stood beside him and lowered his head to just above Buddy's chest. He could see right into the horse's amber eyes.

"You are one crazy creature." He raised his hand to touch his muzzle but his arm snagged with pain.

Mother Nature had a way of helping the wounded. She brought his stories back, distracted him from his broken body, and sent his thoughts back in time.

More useful than his sessions in the green chair in the basement, though he did a lot of remembering there. In the chair, demons beckoned from the overhead rafters; called out to him. Only a couple of belts, enough to relax—that's what he always told himself. It never turned out that way. How many times had he fallen asleep in the chair and been awakened by ginger ale in his arms or cramps knotting up and down his legs?

He couldn't even feel his legs; they could be cramping or flowing with ginger ale now for all he knew. Buddy closed his eyes and in seconds—or was it minutes?—he felt something on his leg. Spirit was nibbling on his pants, tugging them, bringing him back from wherever he'd been.

"What do you want?" His voice was almost gone, sounded like the squawk of a dying bird.

He had to save whatever he had left in case someone came looking and he heard them off in the distance. He had to be able to shout. It wouldn't be long now. He had to have the strength to call out, *I'm here, over here*. He would take a deep breath and shout as loud as he could. His chest pained and felt dense as a block of wood. He could hear Dr. Grant saying, *Didn't I keep telling you to stop smoking*? Yes he had and he had cut back, but it was too late. Too late for a lot of things.

On the count of three he would shout—pain or no pain. One, two, three.

"Hello. I'm here, over here!" His voice was scratchy and thin, not loud enough to overcome the wind in the trees.

Once he was found and back at home, he could imagine what his kids would say. David would ask him if he was drunk. They'd all think that.

That was just it; he hadn't had a drop all day. Didn't want one. The sun poured down on the newly planted garden, the soft breeze filled with birdsong, the fresh green lushness of the trees, and the blossoms in Meg's flower garden, their scent drifting over the yard—it was enough. More than enough. More than he deserved.

How the kids loved his stories, especially when they were little. Tell us one of your *In the West* stories, Dad. A way to stay up past their bedtime—he wasn't fooled—but he was only too happy to oblige. Wide-eyed, sitting up straight in their beds, he did his best to make the stories real and exciting and filled with danger. Telling the stories made him feel more alive, brought it all back fresh again, uniting him once again with his Wyoming family. When he reached the end the kids would say, *You were a hero, Dad. You were brave.*

They outgrew his stories a long time ago. They went on to make their own. What stories would they tell about their childhoods? The thought filled him with regret.

Donnie never lost his limp, though you'd never notice unless you were looking for it. Does he make himself the hero of that story when he tells it? Would he tell it with pride or anger, pitch it as another day when his older brothers tried to kill him? Or would it be another kind of story? Buddy blamed David and Doug for what happened. They were supposed to be looking out for him—always. He was their kid brother. That's what older brothers were supposed to do. There was a recklessness about them he didn't like. Didn't they understand how precious a little brother was? Donnie was so much like his own little brother, Sammy—it pained him to even think it.

Donnie's head bobbing in the hole. A vision that came in the night, jolted Buddy awake, sometimes gasping. He couldn't settle back to sleep. He went to the basement to sit in the green chair and chase away the nightmare with a few drinks.

After the ice incident his judgment of the two older boys was harsh and unfair. He wasn't proud of that. A father should be impartial with his children, but he couldn't help it. Older brothers challenged younger brothers, dared them, and made them prove themselves, often in dangerous ways. All in the past now—they'd all grown up, and as far as he knew they were friends.

Chapter 23

Donnie and the Ice — 1956

Lady trotted out to meet the car, tail wagging, a slight bounce in her step, and ready for her snout scratch—the one she expected when Buddy came home from work.

He rested his forehead on the steering wheel, the cold plastic searing his skin, leaned back, took another drag from his cigarette, and watched the smoke curl against the car roof and across the top of the windshield.

Lady wriggled and pranced around him when he stepped out of the car and rubbed up against his legs. "How you doing old girl?"

On the way to the house tree branches skinned over with thick ice creaked and rattled. Over the tall hedge at the far edge of his property the sky had gone soft, filled with the swirls of a pink sunset.

In the kitchen Meg had her back to him, her hands in water at the sink. "You're very late. The roads must be bad."

"Slick as hell. There was slush, but it's freezing up again. Nothing like this morning, though. I had one hell of a day. The back alleys were like a skating rink. My muscles are sore from tensing up. I got stuck a couple of times and had to ask for a push. Wouldn't have happened with Molly."

"You and that horse. Move on. She did."

Meg could think what she wanted, but it was true, he and Molly never got stuck. Weather like today's would have slowed them down when he had the residential route, before he switched to restaurant delivery. Buddy warned the dairy foreman not to get rid of the horses and go strictly with trucks. The foreman laughed and told him he had no choice since the entire dairy clear across the country was making the change. "The world's changing, Buddy. You need to change with it."

"The boys went out to play a while ago. They took their skates. I told them to stay in the yard." Meg sighed as if this day had already gone on too long. "I haven't heard them for a while. They never listen to me."

He poured a coffee and looked towards the kitchen window; it was almost dark.

"I'm worried. It's getting late and I couldn't go to find them. How far would I get with two five-year-olds in tow?"

"Two?"

"Sharon's been here all afternoon playing with Carolyn. Her mother had to go to work and her babysitter couldn't get through in this weather. I said it was no problem, I'd take her. Six indoors most the day. Finally I told the boys to go out. Just to get them out of my hair."

Buddy poured more cream into his coffee so he could drink it faster, and studied the pitcher. It was the prize from a box of laundry detergent. The boys fought over the box, spilled the powder out onto the floor, and put a chip in the little jug. Meg was disappointed. She was collecting the dishes and was close to a complete set.

"When did they go out?"

"An hour ago. Maybe longer."

"All three of them?"

"Yes."

Donnie, too, then. He did pretty well for an eight-year-old, but the older boys bullied him and they were a challenge to keep up with. He warned them if they didn't pick on someone their own size they'd have to contend with him. Then see how much they liked it. "And don't forget, I used to box."

"I told Donnie no at first, but he kicked up such a fuss I gave in. The works of them have worn me down. They've been fighting all day. I've just about had it," Meg said, turning to look over her shoulder, her hands still in the water. Her apron ties had come undone and dangled. "I was relieved to get them outside and out of my hair. I couldn't hear my own thoughts."

Buddy carried his cup to the sink. A strand of Meg's hair, the grey intertwined with hints of toffee-colour, covered her left eye but with her hands immersed in dishwater, it dangled there. It might have itched. Buddy swept it aside and hooked it behind her ear.

Poor Meg—done in. She would have tried to do her bookkeeping too, what with month end coming. She'd enough experience handling Patrick's books from the store to take on clients, a job she could do at home while managing the household. But sometimes she wondered if she'd made a mistake and tried to do too much. She felt like she never got anything done, and it was no wonder.

"Okay. I'm gone. Is Carolyn in her room?"

"Yes. With Sharon." Meg scrubbed burned tomato soup off the bottom of a pot with a Brillo pad. "She's having a sleepover at Sharon's. Sharon's mother will pick them up on her way home from work. She's late. I imagine the roads have kept her."

Outside, Buddy looked out across the large yard. The streaks of the pink sunset had vanished. A chill rippled through him, a combination of tiredness and cold, his muscles aching from walking on ice all day.

"Well Lady, let's figure out where they've gone." The dog darted across the snow like a shadow. The cold air, sharp with the smell of frozen mud and water, stung his nostrils. Boot prints fanned out across the yard came together again at a large trampled patch, illuminated by light coming from the kitchen window. The boys stopped there for a tussle, quite a session of it, judging by the snow.

He followed their trail farther out across the yard. They'd stopped around a frozen puddle, cracked and sagged from weight, pocked with holes where they broke through. From there a line of footprints led to the back of the property, David's larger prints in the lead, and to a patch of ice big enough to skate on. Three pairs of boots lay at the edge, the ice's surface scratched with blade marks. In some places the ice hadn't held and was filled with holes.

He had a good idea of where that might be. They had their skates on.

He backed through the hedge at the back of the property, three and four trees deep. Birds rustled and peeped, awakened from their evening's roost. A mingled scent of pine, spruce, and cedar.

Moonlight glowed over the snowy field and wind rattled weed stalks. He listened but heard only Lady's rapid panting and the far-off sounds of cars passing out on the highway.

His weight broke through the crust of snow and caught at his feet, making him stumble as he tried to run. The boys knew not to skate on the pond, didn't they? Hadn't he drilled it into their heads enough times that the temperature had to be below freezing for at least a week before the ice could be tested? They weren't allowed to go there without him. "For the love of Christ," he said and Lady came charging back to him.

Wind seeped through his coat and sweater. He shouted their names and listened. Nothing. He hurried across the field, feet sliding, nearly falling several times. Sleet pellets struck his face and made him squint. Lady ran ahead, nose to the ground, picking up the scent of rabbits and mice.

With luck he'd find no one at the pond. They might have gone to one of David's friends'. Or he'd turn around and go back to the house and find them at the kitchen table eating soup and sandwiches.

He thought he heard something. He strained into the night, heard his own laboured breathing, and the hiss of tall field grass. There. Again. A bird's screech? Lady circled him then bolted ahead and disappeared. He heard it again; it sounded like someone shouting.

Buddy ran, eyes fixed in the distance on the globes of car headlights far off in the distance drifting across blackness.

He stopped to catch his breath and bent with his hands on his knees, the stab of cold air choking him. He heard the voices louder now. It was the boys.

He called out their names and heard a voice shout back.

"It's Dad!" David's voice.

At the pond, he slid down the bank to the dark shapes hunkered along the shoreline. David crouched and held onto Doug by his skate blades. Doug lay sprawled on the ice, a stick in his hand which extended out to a hole. Donnie clung to the stick and whimpered in a small, beaten voice.

It didn't matter how long Donnie had been in the water, he couldn't last long even from now. Whatever Buddy did from here on had to be fast and risky. He spoke in a voice as calm as he could make it, a voice he hoped would soothe and prevent any sudden starts or panic.

"Keep doing what you're doing, all of you. Donnie, don't let go. You're doing fine, just fine. You too, Doug. Hang on, squeeze hard both of you. I'll get you out of there."

"I can't feel my legs. My hands are frozen," Donnie whimpered.

"Just hang on."

"I can't hold on any more."

"Yes you will."

Buddy ran to the shallow end of the pond where the ice would be stronger. He lowered himself to his hands and knees, then to his belly, and slid towards Donnie and Doug. He had to stay as far away from Doug as he could, in case the two of them weighed too much for the ice to hold, but get close enough to take the branch from him.

He inched ahead, the ice cracking beneath him, sprouting out under him like roots and spoke in a slow, steady voice, calm and reassuring to show no fear. "I'll get you out, you're doing great, you're all doing great. I'll have you out of there soon, Donnie."

Donnie's feet in heavy skates would pull his legs down into the frigid water. Colder temperatures would freeze the pond up harder, they had that much going for them, but it would also make Donnie colder. The ice creaked and cracks streaked out under him with alarming snaps. But it held. That was all he could hope for.

He slid as close as he dared to Doug and asked for the stick. "I can't reach you," Doug said.

Buddy squirmed over a little closer and this time managed to grab it. "David, pull Doug in."

Doug's body slid back towards the bank of the pond. Buddy eased over to where Doug had been on the ice.

Donnie's weight strained on the end of the branch.

"Hold onto my pants. Hang on tight!" Buddy told David. "Grab around my ankles!" David tugged on Buddy's pants.

Donnie was silent. "Donnie?" No answer. "Donnie?" Donnie whimpered and sounded sleepy. "Donnie, I'm almost there." Buddy reached out and grabbed him around the wrists hard enough for the boy to say, "Ouch", and pulled him up and forward with all his strength. Donnie rose out of the hole and brought with him a swell of slush as thick as porridge. Then Buddy's strength gave out and Donnie sank back in the water again. The slush and water pooled out and soaked Buddy's coat and gloves. Weighed down with water and ice, Donnie was much heavier than he'd imagined.

Moonlight illuminated Donnie's face and fell upon his half-closed eyes. He appeared to be slipping into unconsciousness. By Christ, no son of his would go this way. Donnie's strength would be waning. Soon he'd let go of the stick, sink beneath the water and out of reach.

Buddy rose up on his hands and knees, risking the ice giving beneath the four-point pressure of his body, then reached out and grabbed Donnie's wrists. He hoisted Donnie straight up as high as he could then pulled him forward and brought him down on the ice. He grabbed him around the scruff of the neck and yanked the rest of him out of the hole. He pulled Donnie in next to him and went down once again on his belly, fearing the cracks he felt ripping under them.

"Pull us by my pant leg," Buddy shouted to David. He felt the tug on one leg, then the other. Doug was helping too.

"Faster boys!" The feel of hard land pressed against the bottom of Buddy's boot. He rose to his knees and dragged Donnie to the bank, gathered him in his arms, carried him up the bank to the field, and stretched him out. He was barely conscious. The other two scrambled up the bank after him and stood watching.

"Is he going to be okay? Is he? Is he?" Doug was almost hysterical. David hung back, frightened and solemn.

Blue under the pale moonlight, Donnie lay silent and still. A few more minutes and… No, Buddy had no time to waste on what might have been. Donnie's coat was freezing up fast in the night air. He unfastened the toggles and pried the stiff coat off him.

"David, give me your scarf." Buddy removed Donnie's sweater and shirt, lifted him so his bare skin would not touch the snow, then wound David's scarf around his upper torso. "Give me your coats," he ordered the other two, slipped them on Donnie, then Buddy wrapped his own coat around him. "Give me your hat," he ordered Doug. He pulled the cap over Donnie's spiked and frozen hair. "Each of you give me one mitten." The mittens, lumped with snow and frozen at the wrists, were warm and dry on the inside. He slipped them over Donnie's hands.

Buddy worked Donnie's skate laces, stiff as uncooked spaghetti, through the holes, then tugged on the ice-encrusted blades. It took a while to wriggle the skates free of his feet. "Give me your sweaters," he told Doug and David. Without protest, though they now wore only shirts, they handed them over. Buddy pulled Donnie's snow pants down his scrawny legs and slipped a sweater over each. As he did this, he told David and Doug that Donnie's life depended on him being warmed up again as fast as possible. He knotted the sweater sleeves to keep Donnie's feet inside.

"Okay boys, we're going to high-tail it back to the house. I'm carrying Donnie, so you'll be faster than me. Run. Stop for nothing. Do you hear me?"

They nodded. Yes, they heard. Buddy bent to gather up Donnie. "They're both fatheads," he whispered.

David and Doug took off running. Buddy shouted after them, "When you get home you tell your mom to shovel lots of coal in the furnace and to turn the oven on high. Tell her what happened. Help her."

"Okay!" they called back. Their running awkward, chopping across the field in their skates, slipping, sliding, arms flailing, sometimes staggering, never quite falling, and Lady barking frantically, thinking they played a game with her. Poor little buggers. They'd be aching with tiredness and damn near frozen themselves. He had to put fear in them to get them back to the house without incident. The events of tonight were enough for one day; hell, enough for a year!

Buddy started across the field, Donnie cradled in his arms. "You okay?"

"Uh, huh."

"Is that your teeth chattering?" Donnie's body trembled like an idling motor.

"Yes."

"Can you feel your feet?"

"No." Donnie started to cry.

"Don't cry, Donnie. Save all your energy for getting warm. You hear? You'll be fine."

"Okay," he sniffed.

Buddy pulled him in closer to his chest and squeezed him tighter to put warmth back in his body. His feet slid. A couple of times he thought he was headed for a tumble but he managed to break the fall and stay upright. Cold air made his breathing shallow but he pushed on as hard as he could, summoning up all his energy—surprised he had any left at all. "We'll be home soon."

He kept up a steady stream of chat to keep Donnie awake, fearing he might be close to unconsciousness. He backed through the hedge and rushed across the yard. Lady charged to meet them.

Buddy turned the knob on the back door and stepped inside onto the landing. Meg appeared at the top of the stairs.

"Oh dear God!" She rushed to gather him in her arms, carried him into the kitchen, and lay him on a pile of blankets on the floor in front of the oven—the door open to let out a blast of heat. It was all Buddy could do to drag himself up the stairs and into the kitchen.

"Where are the other two?" Their skates lay on the basement floor, the ice dripping from the blades.

"They're in a hot bath," Meg stripped off Donnie's clothes, his skin blotchy, red, blue, and white. Though her eyes showed fear, she worked calmly, rubbing him with towels she warmed in the oven. Buddy knelt beside Donnie, slipped his hands under a blanket, and ran them up and down the boy's legs to bring back the circulation. He could lose his legs.

Lady sprawled under the kitchen table, her head resting between her front paws, and her ears flat against her head, eyebrows cocked. If a dog could look worried, she did.

Finally, warmth began to return to Donnie's body and his teeth stopped chattering. Meg took him into her lap and spoon-fed him a mug of cocoa topped with extra marshmallows. Doug and David sat at the table, wrapped in blankets, eating chicken noodle soup and corned beef sandwiches. They didn't say anything. By the time Donnie had taken in all the hot fluids, the cold had mostly gone from him and the blue blotchiness had disappeared from his skin. Time would tell about the damage to his hands, legs, and feet.

Meg told Doug and David to leave the table once they finished eating, and to go and sit in the living room

Buddy took Donnie to his bedroom and sat with him until he fell asleep in his arms. He lowered the sleeping boy onto his bed, cradling his head with his hand as if lowering an infant into a crib. He pulled the edges of the blankets up under his chin and tucked them in around him.

Moonlight streamed in the window. He went to the window to look out and remembered sleeping with his brothers and sisters on cold nights when snow seeped in the cracks around the window panes and spun out across the room. Underneath the heavy quilts mother made from old winter coats, many from strangers, their limbs entwined for warmth. They whispered about who would get up first in the morning to make a fire in the stove and shuddered under the blankets as they anticipated the icy floor, the water frozen in the bucket in the kitchen, and the frozen clothes strung across the hearth.

Ray on Bishop, riding across a snowy windswept plain, his fingers matted and frozen into the horse's mane.

He went to the bed and ran his hand over the boy's forehead. What would Donnie remember? Would his sleep forever be haunted by visions of black water, going under, pulled down by the weight of his skates? Would he ever trust his brothers again, egging him on to test the ice to see if they could skate on it? He'd do anything to save him these fears. Too late. Buddy shuddered but not with cold, though cold had crept into every joint in his body.

Spare the rod and spoil the child. He'd heard Norma say that when she was talking to Meg about some kid in the village who acted up and required some discipline. Patrick and Norma never raised a hand to one of their own but they didn't mind passing out advice to others. What did Meg know about punishment and survival growing up in the lap of gentility the way she did? He hoped she wouldn't ask him to punish the boys.

In the kitchen he stood by the table as David and Doug finished their soup and sandwiches. Faces down, eyes shifting to take quick glimpses at Buddy—they avoided eye contact. He could see they were frightened.

When they were done Meg ordered them into the living room to wait for them. "And try to stay out of trouble."

They sat side by side on the couch, dressed identically in the cowboys and Indians flannel pyjamas Aunt Betty gave them for Christmas, staring at their red-plaid slippers, and lifting their heads to look at Meg when she asked them to.

"What happened today was a very serious matter," Meg said.

"Donnie could have died. And the two of you, told repeatedly to stay in the yard. What on earth were you thinking?"

"I dunno," David said. "I didn't know he'd go through."

"Douglas?" Meg asked. "Do you have an explanation?"

"Guess I wasn't thinking anything."

"That had better not be a smirk on your face," Meg said. "What do you two have to say for yourselves?"

David's fingers fiddled with the tie on his pajama pants. "Sorry, I guess."

"You guess? Look at me when I'm talking to you! Both of you."

"Sorry, I mean."

"You both know the rules about the pond. We've been over and over it. Something terrible could have happened to Donnie." Meg's lip trembled as she held back tears. "Why would you disobey us?"

"I guess we forgot," Doug said.

"Your Dad is going to help you remember. It's not what we want to do, but you've given us no choice."

"Meg, this isn't the time for that. They saved Donnie." Buddy knew what was coming, knew the part he was meant to play. "I was there, at the pond. They'll remember."

"Spare the rod and spoil the child. You didn't come from a normal household. What would you know about proper discipline?"

There it was. He was an orphan; second rate, didn't come from a real family because his parents died, making him ill-suited and inadequate as a parent.

"Come on boys. Follow me." Why couldn't she throw away the rule book on parenting just this once? There were times, sure, when he knew measures had to be taken. The time they disappeared and he and Meg couldn't find them anywhere, were just about to call the police when David and Doug came rolling in long after dark after hitchhiking to town and back—all on a lark. But this was not the time, not after what they'd all been through. David, Doug, and Lady followed him to the basement.

"Are you going to hit us hard?" Doug asked.

"Can I have the strap on my hand instead of my ass?" David held out his open palm.

Lady's tail whipped back and forth as she anticipated dog

biscuits. She sat, extended her paw, stroked the air with it, and whined. Both boys watched as he undid his buckle and pulled his belt through the loops. He pressed his finger to his lips. "I'm not going to strap you," he whispered so his voice wouldn't carry upstairs. "Seeing Donnie in the pond was bad enough. I imagine you feel pretty bad about what happened. Am I right?"

"Yes," they said.

"Here's what we're going to do. I'm going to strike this chair with my belt and one of you will howl," Buddy said. "I'll do it four times; I want four howls. David, you're the oldest, you go first."

David wailed on cue. Doug did a more convincing job of crying than David, with long convoluted sobs and gasps.

"Pipe down," Buddy said. Meg wasn't stupid; she'd know if something wasn't right.

When it was all over they went to the laundry tubs to rub their eyes with water. "Make them red like you've been crying," he told them. They knuckled their eyeballs with water until they looked as beaten as a person could look.

"Come here," he motioned for them to follow. At his tool table he pulled out a grey work sock, trimmed red at the top, pulled out a bottle of rye, and unscrewed the cap. He took a swig, the liquid burning all the way down his throat and on his lips. "That adds fire to the belly." He passed the bottle to David. "Take a little sip. It'll warm you up inside."

David, hesitant at first, eyed the bottle, then tipped it back. He choked and made a face like he'd just swallowed a teaspoon of cod liver oil.

Buddy laughed. "Go on, give it to your brother."

Doug took a drink but didn't choke. A large grin crept over his freckled face.

"Okay off to bed you go. Say goodnight to your mother and go straight to your room."

Upstairs, he listened to their sobs and sniffles, mumbling goodnight as they passed by the living room.

"I'm taking them to their beds," he told Meg.

In a half-hearted voice, a voice filled with sadness and fear and the possibility of what might have been, she called out goodnight. She'd had enough of this day too.

As he tucked them in he told them to keep quiet for fear of waking up Donnie.

"Dad," David whispered. "Is it possible for there to be a real fire in your stomach?"

It would have been the rye. "No. Does it feel like it?

"Yes."

"It'll go away."

Out of the darkness, Doug said, "You stupid ass. Even I know that."

He eased the bedroom door shut and told Meg he'd forgotten to feed Lady. In the basement, he drank the rest of the rye and tried not to think about what could have happened.

After Wes's whipping he swore no one would ever lay a hand on him again. Strapping the boys because Donnie had gone through the ice—he couldn't do it, plain and simple. Donnie's survival was a cause for celebration. Not a cause for punishment.

In the middle of the night Meg shook him awake in his green chair. In all the commotion she'd forgotten to tell him Patrick had called early in the afternoon to say that her mother had taken a turn and he was waiting for the doctor. But the ice storm made it difficult for the doctor to get there quickly, and when he finally did, her condition had progressed too far and she'd been taken to the hospital.

Chapter 24

Ugly Duckling—1957

At the road, Buddy grabbed the mail out of the box before pulling into the driveway. Stuck between the bills was a letter addressed to him, postmarked from the United States, and from a name and address in Des Moines, Iowa. He didn't know anyone in Iowa.

He went to the basement to grab a few minutes of peace before immersing himself in the family uproar. And uproar it would be since Carolyn's school play, *The Ugly Duckling*, was tomorrow night and Meg had committed to making her costume for her part as a pretty duckling. A project that involved several trips to town and a large bag of fluffy yellow feathers. She worked on the duckling headdress last night until two in the morning, and that was after they'd been to Patrick's to clean his house and prepare his week's meals. He was no prize in bachelorhood. It was no wonder after all the years of Norma being in charge of everything domestic. Unfortunately, he'd come to expect Buddy and Meg's help and would have nothing to do with the boys helping him out as he found them too hard to keep track of.

Buddy rose from the chair, reached up into the rafters, pulled out a bottle hidden inside a work sock, unscrewed the cap, and took a couple of swigs. "A little something to calm the nerves before heading into the storm," he told Lady lying at his feet.

M. Jacob, Des Moines Iowa
April 1957

Dear Buddy:

Some time ago Ray, our brother, was in touch with me, after a long and complicated search to find me. We've stayed in touch ever since, though sporadically, despite our promises to do otherwise—we've both been working and raising families—I've two beautiful daughters and a wonderful husband and perhaps you know yourself how challenging it can be to keep up to everyday demands.

He wrote that he thought he'd found your address in Canada, also after a long, hard search, and provided me with the address that appears on this envelope. Since neither he nor I can visit at this time, I thought it best to let you know of our whereabouts in the hopes that we can all reconnect in person. Until such time it must suffice to write in the hopes that this letter falls into the hands of the Buddy Scott to whom I am related. If that is not what has occurred here, kindly put the letter back in the envelope and return it to sender. I apologize for any inconvenience. If, however, this has fallen into the hands of my long-lost-brother Buddy Scott, kindly read on.

It is my dream that one day our family will meet again, and since that cannot happen at this juncture, I would dearly love to begin a mail correspondence with you as I do with Ray. Even though our family was split apart while we were so young, it is still important to keep in touch and perhaps more so because of our tragic childhoods and the loss of our parents at such young ages. Though much time has passed and we all went on to live separate lives, not knowing how each of the others fared, I'd like to at least recapture something. We are still family and nothing will ever change that or the childhood we once shared.

I have some important information to pass on to you about some of our relatives and siblings. I trust that you would want to know. I visited Uncle Wes and Aunt Gabby months after you and Ray ran away. The woman who eventually adopted me, Miss Scoby, Ruth, I called her, insisted I pay them a visit before we moved from those parts.

Wes called you and Ray some awful names and said you were ungrateful and stole money from him. I prayed you'd never return because I thought he would bring you physical harm, as I know he was capable of such despicable behavior, and he managed to convince people you were lawless scoundrels.

As I was leaving (and I must say I was anxious to escape him), Aunt Gabby drew me aside and told me she was ashamed of Wes and the way he treated you and Ray and that she was frightened of him, too. She said there was not a grain of truth to the rumors Wes had started. Eventually I learned that Aunt Gabby left and took Ava and

Nellie with her, and if the story I heard had any degree of authenticity, she left in almost the same manner in which you and Ray left. She disappeared and to my knowledge was never heard from again. I thought you might like to know and it is my intention in the future to see if I can determine where Ava and Nellie live. Aunt Gabby has long since passed, of that I am almost certain.

Perhaps you will recall from so long ago my circumstances after our family was split up. (I used to see you sometimes in town though we never had long for visits.) When I was first orphaned, I was taken in by a family that worked me to the bone and found me to be quite useless as I couldn't keep up with their rowdy brood. I recall just standing still and crying, not having a clue what else to do to govern the unruly children. Word got out that I was more a hindrance than a help, and one day Ruth came by and took me away with her. She was a good and patient woman and she needed to be. It took her considerable time to wean me from my tomboy ways that came so naturally to me on the ranch, and from my stubborn disposition, worse by then after my stay at that horrid farm. I'm certain it must have been like trying to tame a bobcat.

We stayed near Chugwater, Wyoming for a while after she took me in, then we moved, and I had to trade my love of the outdoors and the prairies for city life. We moved to Des Moines, Iowa, and eventually my keen sense of adventure came from books. I was very grateful to her for the college education she provided and for the good home she gave me.

Another one of our siblings, Sammy, was adopted by a family who lived just down the road from me. I would see him occasionally, but the people who adopted him requested I not speak to him in their effort to remove all memory of the family he came from. I can tell you it broke my heart. He was much younger than me and it didn't take long for him to forget me, and all of us, I imagine. This might sound odd, but I was glad when we moved to Des Moines and away from him, as seeing him constantly reminded me of all I'd lost. He and I were very close when we lived on the ranch and I could not stand the heartbreak of seeing him, knowing the truth and having to remain silent, as if we were nothing more than strangers to each other. He grew up to be a fine man, I've been told, but it has also been rumored that he was killed in the war. I am now in the process of trying to verify this.

I've almost determined that Chuck died in a car accident in New Jersey when he was in his late 20s, but I am still in the process of verification. New Baby was adopted and to the best of my knowledge no one knows what became of him, though, again, I've heard rumors. I struck up communication with Pearl after many years, and we managed a visit one year, but sadly she succumbed to cancer. She attained three degrees and taught at a college in Kansas. I don't know if you recall, but she was taken in by Miss Skinner, our old teacher, and she never married.

I've sent letters to Hazel where she resides in California, but she has only replied to one. She doesn't seem interested in renewing an acquaintanceship which leads me to assume that she too would like to erase her history. That is her prerogative, of course, though it seems a shame. We can't change what happened by ignoring it or pretending it didn't happen, though I suppose for some people, going back in memory brings more pain than they can bear, though Hazel did not provide this insight in her correspondence and she is not one for lengthy explanation.

I enjoy the letters I receive from Ray, though, as mentioned, ours is an infrequent correspondence due to the rigors of family life. Ray resides in California, south of Las Angeles, and is also married with children. One day he hopes to track you down, as do I. It would be a dream if we could have a reunion with the survivors of our family. I am certain we would need more than a week to cover all the stories we would have to tell and the memories we share. Please write and let us know about your "new" life, after you and Ray parted ways in Detroit. (And working for Mr. Ford! I still can't get over that!) I'm ashamed I haven't been in touch before now, and a hundred excuses won't make a shred of difference—I've put this off much too long. It would be lovely if we could have a reunion. I will never forget my big brothers Ray and Buddy. I'll never forget the kindness you showed me as a child, though, as the sixth oldest, I was very young at the time and my memories are vague. Perhaps a reunion would revive them.

I have left out so much here, but I hear my daughters, home now from school, and I must tend to the chores of being a wife and mother.

I strongly urge you to acknowledge this correspondence.

Your loving sister,

Maudy

Buddy dropped the letter to his lap. Sixth oldest? No she wasn't. She was fifth oldest—Ray, Buddy, Pearl, Hazel, Maudy, Orwin, Chuck, Sammy, New Baby—the fifth oldest!

Why would she want to distort their ages? Why would she tell him about Wes? He knew. He was there, wasn't he? Did she think telling him about the rumours Wes spread about him and Ray being thieves would make a difference to him now? He knew Wes would have called them terrible names—he did it often enough to their faces. He supposed she meant to make him feel better but who was she to think she could tell him what he'd lived through, come along all these years later as if confirming it really happened. It happened! He knew it! Why couldn't she just leave him in peace?

"Let sleeping dogs lie, eh Lady?" Lady opened her eyes, then closed them again.

And that business about Sammy forgetting about his family and where he came from, as if it never happened, that was not true! Buddy was like a father to him; Sammy would never forget Buddy, and Buddy would never forget the way he called out to Buddy as he rode off in Wes's wagon. It haunted him to this day. *Bubby, Bubby.* How many nights had he awakened from a bad dream hearing Sammy calling him? And now Sammy dead? He couldn't be. She said it was only a rumour. She had no idea what she was talking about. She was making things up. To make herself feel important and powerful, superior because she knew more about his family and what became of them than he did.

He crumpled the letter and threw it in the corner. He would not tell Meg. He'd do his best to forget all that Maudy wrote. She'd found the wrong Buddy Scott. He took another swig.

Meg's scissors slashed through the yellow fabric stretched across the dining room table. "You're up to your eyeballs in it," Buddy said.

"That's an understatement. If I could get the boys to cooperate I'd be in good shape. They've demolished the house." She waved her scissors in the air.

Carolyn ran into the dining room. "Do you know your lines.

Kitten?" Buddy asked.

"Yes."

"What are they?"

"Quack, quack, quack, quack." She spread her fingers to show the number, a big smile on her face. "I say it four times. Then I say, you are a ugly duckling, Ugly Duckling."

"Think you can remember it all?" Carolyn wasn't aware he was teasing her.

"Yes," she giggled and raced down the hall to her room.

In the kitchen Buddy found a sink full of dirty dishes and looked out the window. From the start Meg said the costume should be practical, something Carolyn could wear later if she was going to put a lot of work into it—not to mention money. She didn't have time to throw away, not like other mothers she knew with one or two kids and husbands with good enough paying jobs to hire help. The feathers would go on over a yellow dress Carolyn could wear for Easter, without the feathers, of course. The headdress might get used for Hallowe'en. "Carolyn's outgrown everything. There's only so many times a hem can be turned down. She's filling out everywhere. I can't keep up with her."

In her voice, in the sigh, in the slope of her shoulders, the way her hair sprung from the bobby pin, even in the grey mixed with faded honey-brown; everything pointed to her struggle and told him he wasn't a good provider. She always pushed for him to ask for a raise and told him to be more aggressive and ask his manager for a promotion. His manager wasn't about to come to him, she reminded him. Buddy had to push.

What kind of a damn fool doesn't want to earn more? He didn't tell her he applied for the foreman's job and he didn't tell her when it went to someone else on account of Buddy and another route man getting caught having a nip in the garage. The job had to have some perks, didn't it? Some of the route boys kept a bottle right under the driver's seat. You could mix booze with a lot of things but it should never go on the milk truck. There were some lines he wouldn't cross. Buddy should have the foreman's job and never mind the garage nip. It wasn't a big deal.

Buddy watched from the dining room doorway as Meg's scissors chewed their way across the plain of fabric.

"What about dinner?" Buddy asked.

"I can't stop or I'll never get this done. Then Carolyn won't be in the play." The bag of yellow feathers balanced on the corner of the table. "You'll have to cook dinner."

He didn't mind. He liked cooking as long as he didn't have to follow a recipe. He'd let his imagination go to work and use up the left-overs. Waste ran against his grain. He didn't like the attitude some had that it was okay to be reckless and throw things out.

Downstairs he changed out of his work clothes and took a couple more nips in preparation for the chores. He deserved it after today, after the fight with Mario, the cook at Vito's Pizzeria. Who ate that stuff anyway? Goop on a pie crust. What a guy, Mario; one day nice, the next day as prickly as a hibernating bear with bees up his ass. Accusing Buddy of shorting him on milk then charging him for it. Waving his meat cleaver. Telling Buddy to get his mind on his work or send someone who could do a better job. Bloody goddamn nerve. Just because the little Italian weasel was in some kind of mood, having some kind of bad day, it didn't give him the right to carry on like a lunatic.

And now the damn letter from Maudy and the information about his family flying in on some invisible current of air from straight-out-of-nowhere. It was too much for one day.

He took another pull of rye and tucked the bottle up in the rafters. His legs ached and cramped. He was tired; he admitted it. Tired of slogging it out every day to make ends meet. Tired of getting up at outrageous hours to go to work for miserly wages. Coming home to another shift of work, a wife who didn't think he earned enough, and raucous kids. No one understood better than him Meg was tired too, but where was the fun? Where had it gone? Didn't there have to be some? Shouldn't there be?

In the kitchen he confronted a sink piled high with dishes. "For Christ sakes."

"Try spending a day here and see what it's like for me," Meg called from the dining room. "Maybe then you wouldn't be so quick to criticize."

He hadn't meant for her to hear. "I wasn't criticizing." He pulled pots and pans out of the drying rack and grabbed the counter to steady himself. Lack of sleep. When he finally got to bed last night in the green chair, he couldn't have slept more than two or three hours. Never did, it seemed.

He turned the tap, squeezed soap out of a bottle and watched bubbles burp up on the surface.

What if he told her he got so bogged down by his life he thought he couldn't cope; thought he'd quit trying to dig them out of a hole that kept filling in anyway because it was made of sand. Would any of it make any sense to her? What would she say? Don't be so weak—she said it often enough. Weak? The man who had to sleep with one eye open? Who always had to watch his back in case someone was about to jump him? Who scrounged for meals; wasn't sure if the person he just met was an enemy or friend? Did all that in order to survive—stay alive. He was weak? There was a joke! Her strength hadn't been tested like his. The Depression hit her family hard—sure it had—they didn't get to eat what they wanted, they almost lost their house and their business. But they never experienced hunger and they never had to beg. *I'll weed your garden for a sandwich, Ma'am.* Or steal carrots. What did she know about survival? She'd never been alone. Critical as they could be, her parents were always there; she always had someone to fall back on, someone to support her, someone who gave a damn.

She would say what she usually said. "Stop feeling sorry for yourself. What's done is done. Move on. Stop living in your memories." She wanted no more of his stories about Ray or what he remembered of his family. She wanted them wiped out of his mind. As if they never happened. As if his past didn't exist. His memories were all he had, all he could be sure of.

He dragged the dishrag over a streak of hardened ketchup. Not the Meg he met when he wore fancy suits and shoes when they danced the Suzie Q at the hall. Back when he was a catch—a foreign exotic. After they married she told him not to tell people he came from a poor ranch. Nothing could alter the fact he came from poverty and he wasn't ashamed of it! She wanted him to be someone grand, of position, someone who would turn heads. A man who would have a life that fitted the fancy suits he bought in Detroit and wore when he first met her. And there she would be, hooked on his arm and respected by association. They would be pillars of the community. People who put on airs.

Never ever, ever would he forget what he came from or pretend it didn't happen. He was not ashamed of what he came from. No one, not Meg, not anyone, would take his past from him. And no one would change his memory of it either.

The sewing machine roared in the dining room.

He finished the dishes and started on dinner. The boys were out in the yard playing football; they'd be a muddy mess when they came in. Carolyn was up the road at her friend Sharon's house. He had time to make a casserole. He pulled ground chuck, leftover mashed potatoes and onions out of the fridge and the pressure cooker out of the cupboard.

In the basement on his way to the fruit room for stewed tomatoes, Buddy sat in his green chair for a couple of drinks—the burn down his throat reminding him he was alive.

He woke up early, lit a cigarette, and thought about last night. Shards of shattered memory threw back quick glimpses. And his voice, the sound of it, as if someone else had been shouting.

The top of his head felt tender and damp. His fingers touched a blister. Oh shit, now he remembered. He put all the food in the pressure cooker. Meg shouted at him from the dining room not to use it because it was broken.

An explosion. Food hung from the ceiling. Tomatoes, spinach, onions, potatoes, and ground chuck in a pile of mush on top of his head. The boys couldn't stop laughing. Carolyn stared at her plate. Poor Kitten. Did she get something to eat? Long strings of onions dripped from the ceiling. Stalactites, David called them. Meg shouted at him.

There was something about the dog, wasn't there? The boys laughing and pointing at Lady. Her snout close to the pile of mush in her bowl, tail still, not wagging. She cowered under the kitchen table without so much as a lick.

"Lady won't even eat it," they howled. "How can we eat what the dog won't touch?"

He yelled at them. The last thing he wanted was to make Kitten cry. The boys sat smirking and kicking each other under the table. They were making fun of him. Again.

He made hot dogs for the kids and attempted to clean up the mess. "Why the hell do we have a useless pot around if it doesn't work?"

he said.

"A lot of things around here don't work," Meg said.

His fingertips hurt. What had he done to them? Burned them on the goop that flew around the kitchen. No, it wasn't that. Before he fell asleep in the green chair he took Maudy's crumpled letter and set it on fire. He forgot to let go.

Silent overhead; everyone still sleeping. He would try to slip away to work without waking anyone.

Upstairs he looked at the kitchen clock: five AM. The sky hinted towards day. The sink piled high with dirty dishes. Scraps of yellow material and pattern pieces covered the dining room table. Draped over the back of a chair, a yellow dress covered with fluffy yellow feathers. A costume so beautiful it brought tears to his eyes. How could Meg create something so gorgeous for Kitten in the midst of chaos? How he had let her down.

Lady was under the table, her eyes open, one brow cocked higher than the other, watching him as he shuffled around the kitchen as if she couldn't quite trust him. She was wary of him too. He rubbed her head. "Eh, Lady? Are you a good dog?" She wagged her forgiving tail. If only it could be so easy with people.

Meg must have been up most of the night working on the costume, and she was a light sleeper. He moved slowly and deliberately to avoid rattling pots and cutlery as he tried to clean up his mess before leaving for work.

In the basement he slipped on his milkman's uniform and put his hand up into the rafters. He pulled down the bottle inside the sock and shook it: empty. Shame on him.

When he got home from work, Meg was running around the house in her slip, shouting at the boys, and helping Kitten into her costume as she tried to herd the works of them out the door. The house looked like it might have been plucked off its foundations by a giant, turned upside down and shaken, then set down again. The bag of feathers had fallen from its perch and yellow puddles pooled everywhere.

"Who let the fox out in the chicken coop?" Buddy asked looking at feathers, fabric remnants, thread, and pattern tissue scattered around the kitchen, dining room, and hall.

"I've only just finished." Meg eye's held a familiar wildness.

"The feathers kept coming off and I had to hem the dress. The boys won't do what I ask them. Carolyn has to be there in an hour." She stopped talking and glared at him. "You've been drinking."

"I have not." A couple of medicinal pulls, was all. Not really drinking. Big difference between sipping and drinking.

"I can smell it!"

"I took a short bump. Don't turn it into something it isn't." All day, a headache pinched his brain, his mouth the texture of flannel, and a general fuzziness kept the world at a distance. The rattle of milk bottles jabbed at his head. He tripped going into Arnie's Lunch and broke three bottles of cream, drawing out the kitchen cats to lick at the edges of the white pool.

He tried to drive by the Liquor Control Board of Ontario on the way home, but inside on a shelf glowing warm amber, sat a bottle of rye. Its contents would settle his head, calm his stomach, and turn him into a reasonable human being. Two pulls out of the bottle and he'd be right as rain. Two pulls, no more.

In the liquor store parking lot he took a nip and tucked the bottle under the seat. The rye was only a treatment for last night so he might as well get it started.

David, Doug, and Donnie came into the kitchen and draped their restless bodies over the backs of the chrome chairs.

"You cooking tonight, Dad?" Doug asked. "Cuzz if you are, maybe I'm on a diet."

"Hunger strike, more like," David said.

"I wouldn't call it cooking last night." Doug was enjoying himself at Buddy's expense. "More like entertainment."

"Shut up, the both of you!" It was high time someone around here showed him a little respect. Sure he'd been a fool, but did it mean he should be strung up and ridiculed? He had some pride, didn't he? Leave a guy the hell alone when he knows he's fucked up. That was fair play. Didn't anyone here know the rules?

"You see?" Meg said, her mouth rigid with contempt. "Your boys are treating you like a joke."

What the hell had he even come home from work for? He got better treatment at work delivering milk to Italian, Greek, Chinese, Hungarian, and Polish people: foreign people who barely spoke a word of English. There it was, wasn't it? He was a foreigner, too, wasn't he? An American.

These Canadians, who were they to think they were so much better than him? So smug with their uppity manners, their superiority, their fine china, and their crappy little tea biscuits. Their pleases and thank yous and their how-are-you-todays. Their politeness and meaningless chit chat—usually about their awful weather. Turn your back and what would they say about you then, their tight lips flapping behind their palms, with their tut tuts and their well-I-nevers? Hypocrites. They wouldn't say shite if they had a mouth full of it, pretending they were above it all.

"I'm going to the basement to get ready."

"Make sure that's all you do," Meg said.

He hung up his green uniform jacket—Buddy sewn in yellow letters over the top of the pocket—in the closet he got around to making last year long after his entire wardrobe migrated to the basement. He slipped on a pair of dress pants, a good shirt, and a vest Meg knit him a few years back, then groped in the rafters.

This would be a long night. He took a swig. Just a little bracer, one for the road.

The boys fought and kicked in the back seat, their shenanigans filling the silence between him and Meg. Carolyn sat between them. He told her how ducky she was in her beautiful yellow dress. "You're the prettiest fowl of all, Kitten." He reached over and stroked her head, her blond hair soft against his palm.

"You reek," Meg said then stared out her passenger window. "And don't say a word. I can't bear the lies."

They raced down the street and pulled into the school's parking lot.

"We're going to be late," Carolyn whined.

"They won't start without you, Kitten, not without their pretty duck," Buddy said.

Carolyn's grade one teacher greeted them at the gymnasium door, her nervous fingers fluttering like birds around Carolyn's shoulders as she guided her to the classroom where the other actors gathered. The rest of them found seats in the back of the auditorium.

"She'll never see us. She'll think we didn't get seats." Meg craned her neck to see over the sea of heads in front of them.

The play started immediately with "God Save the Queen" and "O Canada".

The stage swarmed with barnyard creatures milling about, united in their cruelty and ridicule for the ugly duckling. Even though she belonged to this spineless group of creatures, he felt a swell of pride at the sight of his Kitten, his little duck, his Carolyn, all yellow and fluffy, by far the prettiest little girl on stage. She definitely had the best costume even if Meg practically drove him right around the bend making it, and almost made them late with her last-minute insistence on duck feet, which, he admitted were great.

At the edge of his metal stacking chair he stretched his neck to see. He caught threads of the play, heard the word duck often, and then there was his little Kitten walking in a circle and doing the line she had practiced all week.

"Quack, quack, quack, quack. You are a ugly duckling, Ugly Duckling."

His heart tore wide open; he jumped to his feet and shouted, "Bravo, Kitten, bravo!

A few heads turned to see who was making the ruckus. He sat down but clipped the edge of his chair, which must have shifted when he leapt up, fell on the floor and toppled the chair.

The entire audience turned towards the sound of the clatter and whispers flew up around him. He got up from the floor and brushed his pants off, sat the chair upright, sat down, and glared at the people in front of him. Why couldn't they stop gawking at him?

"Don't you have a play to watch?" he asked. The woman bent to whisper into the man's ear. They could say what they wanted—he didn't care.

Meg looked straight ahead, her jaw set. She had pushed him right out of existence. Beside her, David gave him the thumbs up and mouthed the words "Way to go, Dad."

"You were the prettiest and the best," he told Carolyn as they drove home.

The boys laughed in the back seat and one of them, either David or Doug, Buddy wasn't sure which, said, "Yeah, if ugly's pretty."

"I'll pull the car over and give whoever just said it a good throttling," Buddy threatened, not able to bear Carolyn being called ugly. He had no use for bullies.

"Drive." Meg faced the passenger window. "I just want to get home."

"Did you hear a big crash after I did my quack, quack, quack, quack? It was so loud," Carolyn said, her voice light and sing-songy, still excited by all the attention she got after the play. "I heard someone fell off their chair." She giggled.

"Well, duh," one of the boys said from the back seat. "I wonder who it could have been?"

At home Buddy cleared the supper dishes from the kitchen table and started washing up. Meg put the kids to bed, gathered up a basket of laundry, then collected the scattered yellow feathers and stuffed them back into the bag. She wasn't talking to him.

He went downstairs to sit in his chair. Once, he stood and groped for the sock then told himself he'd done enough damage for one night and sat down. "You've got me in enough trouble lately," he said to the bottle lurking overhead.

Lady sat at his feet. "Well, old girl," he rubbed her head. "I made a fool of myself tonight." He hadn't said as much to Meg; he didn't need to. She'd be the first to tell him some time tomorrow.

Chapter 25

Hunting — 1959

Donnie peered down the barrel of the gun, swept it across the yard, and stopped somewhere around the big maple.

"Bam, bam, bam! I got it!" he shouted.

"What did you shoot, Donnie?"

Buddy stood behind him to check his posture, to make sure he didn't hold the 22 too tight up against his shoulder. He touched Donnie's elbows to raise them.

"A bobcat."

"Really? Where was it?"

"Coming at us. Headed straight for you."

"Did you get it?"

"Right between the eyes."

"You've got a mean aim."

Donnie's imagination stretched like vines ever since he was a little guy and old enough to figure out his brothers often excluded him. He invented his own fun. Buddy couldn't always force them to include Donnie. He'd get called a sissy, too weak to stand on his own two feet when Buddy had his back turned.

The bobcat came from *The Wild Creature* story, a favourite of Donnie's. Whenever he told the story Donnie asked him to pull up his pant leg so he could see the scar down the back of his calf. Sometimes he traced the white line with his finger.

Donnie got off a few more rounds of fake shots while they waited for David and Doug. David appeared all ruffled up as if something had chewed on him all night long. He was out with some buddies last night and got home late. Doug followed, dragging his feet so that his boots made a farting sound on the sidewalk. He might have just washed up on shore, though he looked better than David.

They stuffed coats, hats, scarves and gloves, brown paper bags filled with lunches, and thermoses into the trunk. Buddy checked the rifles to make sure the chambers were empty, the way Father taught him.

David drove out into the country passing fields of dead corn, fallow farmland, and scrubland, headed south towards the lake. Down gravel roads, the car rocking over bumps, until they arrived at bushland set back from the road.

"Pull over and park," Buddy said. "Okay boys, this is it. I've hunted rabbits, squirrel, pheasant, and partridge here before."

He used to come here with Meg's brothers, when they were young and foolish, and shot at anything that moved. They built themselves a bonfire and drank rye whiskey out of the bottle until they passed out in their tents.

He patted his coat pocket to make sure his mickey was there for later, after hunting, to fight off November chills.

They crossed fields of dead, flattened grasses, pushed through thickets of shrubs, and headed into the bush. He pointed out deer scat and rabbit turds. Walking along beside them he saw how quickly they were growing up, almost without his noticing, and he thought too about how little time he had with them. Always working—on the house, on the garden, at the dairy, so little time left for fun. Out here in the bush—beneath the belly of the soft grey sky, with threads of mist light upon their faces and spun through the trees, bare but for a few scraggly brown leaves—he finally had time to enjoy them, to do something with them.

They walked for hours and saw not one living creature, not so much as a squirrel, until the boys grew impatient and disinterested. David grumbled he didn't want to go on a nature walk and said there was no point hunting if you couldn't shoot something.

"We'll stop for lunch," Buddy said. He'd wanted to recapture the thrill of hunting with his father, but that was beginning to seem unlikely.

They lined themselves in a row sitting on the ground, leaning against a fallen tree, and ate and drank in silence. The cold and damp of a November afternoon settled in hard and sent shivers through them. They zipped their parkas and pulled their hoods up over their red hunting caps. A thicker mist settled, clung to the bushes, and smudged the outdoors as if the landscape was backing away.

Buddy scrunched up waxed paper into a ball, stuffed it in his pocket, and sank down further to lean his head back against the log. He reached into his pocket for his mickey. The two older boys were talking about one of their buddies who got caught hot-wiring a car, a story that caught Donnie's interest too, and no one noticed him take a couple of swigs—a little warmer-upper.

Buddy closed his eyes and lifted his face to a hint of warmth from a weak sun and pulled his hunting cap down over his face. A shot of shut-eye would give him a boost. He dozed off to the sound of the boys talking. Their voices soothed and comforted him.

When he woke up he saw he was alone.

"Boys!" He listened for them to answer his call. Sparrows rustled in a nearby bush. He looked around and saw the guns were gone. He started into the bush. They were not allowed to hunt by themselves. How many times had they been told? They were not ready. How could they do something so stupid?

"Boys, boys!" he cupped his hands around his mouth. "David, Doug, Donnie!"

He scrambled through rope-like twists of wild grape and hawthorns that grabbed at his parka. The afternoon remained still and silent, giving not so much as a hint of their whereabouts.

A gunshot ripped through the misty silence. He turned in its direction and shouted their names. He heard voices, excited voices. Maybe they caught something. They'd catch something else today, he'd guarantee them that. "David, Doug, Donnie."

"We're coming," David shouted back, and Buddy felt immediate relief.

He heard them coming through the dense underbrush, their voices low.

"Where the Sam hell did you go off to?" David appeared first, then Doug, who seemed to be leading Donnie. Donnie had his face buried in his hands. Blood ran in a steady stream between his fingers.

"For the love of Christ!" Buddy ran towards them.

"It was an accident," David said, close to tears.

Buddy put his hands on Donnie's, tried to pry them from the wound.

"No," Donnie whimpered. "It hurts."

"Where? Where've you been hit?"

"My eyes. I can't see. I can't open them," he said, his voice thin with fear.

Not an eye. Please dear God, not an eye, Buddy thought.

"It was an accident, Dad," Doug said, sticking up for David the way he always did, conspirators to the end.

"Later. We've got to get Donnie to a hospital." All the rest—the reasons, the excuses, the we-didn't-mean-tos—that could all wait.

Buddy felt Donnie's hands tremble. "Can you open your eyes?"

"No."

"Can you see me?"

"No." Blood streamed over Donnie's hands and dripped like syrup onto dead leaves.

Buddy hated the sight of blood with anything he shot, but this, the blood of one of his own—he felt as if he might be sick. But that couldn't happen. If an ounce of the fear bottled up inside him spilled out, he'd fail Donnie, fail all of them.

"David, you and Doug go ahead to the car and bring it back across the field. Take the shortcut through the mud on the way to the car but steer clear of it on the way back. Do you understand?"

"Yes." David was still on the verge of tears.

"Pay attention so you can find your way back. For Christ sakes don't get lost! Donnie and I will follow. Do you know where you're going?"

"I think so," David said, but he wasn't convincing.

"Here." Buddy held out his hand. "Give me your gun. Yours too, Doug." He took the shells out of the barrels and handed the guns back. "You got any shells on you?" They nodded, yes. "Hand them over."

"The two of you get moving as fast as you can. Take the guns but leave the barrels open." No argument from them now, not a peep, even though they all knew the barrels were empty.

He guided Donnie by the shoulders through the bush, pulling

branches away from his face.

"It's okay, Donnie, you're doing great."

As they made their way out, Donnie whimpered, and Buddy kept up a soothing banter and hoped he covered the fear in his voice.

At the hospital, heads raised to watch them enter the crowded emergency room. A nurse whisked Donnie instantly away.

"You'll have to stay here," she called back to the rest of them as she and Donnie disappeared behind two doors marked, Hospital Staff Only.

Buddy stared at the doors and fought every impulse to burst through them and yell to hell with their hospital rules, his boy was hurt and he needed his dad, *needed* him.

A few heads went up in the waiting room. One woman whispered to another seated beside her and they stared at him. Let them stare. What did he care? Go on, have a real good look.

He followed his own muddy footprints across the gleaming beige linoleum, tracking himself like an animal to the sitting area with David and Doug. The reception nurse was on the phone requesting a mud clean-up on account of a bunch of hunters, her eyes fixed on Buddy. What should he have done? Gone home and had a shower first, taken his time, prettied himself up? Wait until it was her turn with one of her kids in emergency with a cut or a break. She'd change her tune then.

Doug and David waited in the sitting area, their bloodied hands spread over their knees, their boots so caked with mud they were the size of tree trunks. They watched him approach, their faces full of the unmistakable look of fear.

"So," Buddy said, once settled into a seat, "who wants to tell me?"

"We're in for it, aren't we?" Doug said, his voice trembling.

Buddy blinked hard to hold back tears and wondered how any of this could be corrected with punishment? Was this about teaching them a lesson? Hadn't they taught him one? He was in charge. There were guns. What business did he have falling asleep or having a couple of drinks?

"What if he loses his eye, Dad?" David said, his voice choking. "What will happen? I'll have to leave home, won't I?"

He shook his head. No. He had a feeling, maybe even call it a superstition. Any talk of Donnie losing an eye, any thoughts of the possibility, any conversation, would increase the chances of it happening. Unreasonable, he knew.

"You don't have to leave home, David. I just want to know what happened. How did this happen?"

They both shrugged. They said they didn't really know. As far as they knew, the safeties were on the guns.

"Maybe he shot himself, Dad," David said.

They were covering for each other. He should have known that's what they'd do.

"We're sorry, Dad," Doug said.

An hour passed—still no word. During a shift change, Buddy overheard nurses discussing the patients and heard Donnie's name a couple of times. The word "filthy" rose above their confidential whispers. Buddy kept an eye on them from across the room.

Finally, a nurse came out of the restricted area and called, "Mr. Scott."

Buddy hurried to her at the Emergency Room doors.

"Come with me, please," the nurse said, her shoes squeaking down a long corridor as she led him to a tiny room.

Donnie sat on the edge of a high examination bed, sipping ginger ale from a straw. A huge patch covered his right eye and most of his forehead just above it.

"Hi, Dad."

"The doctor will be with you shortly," the nurse said.

The sound of Donnie's voice, so cheerful, made Buddy choke up. He couldn't bring himself to ask about his wound. He couldn't bear to hear the unwanted words come out of the child's mouth.

A doctor appeared and consulted the clipboard he carried.

"You're lucky," he said. "His eyes are fine. His forehead was grazed, not even deeply. We put six stitches in it and patched him up. He'll have a scar. Over time it may almost disappear, but probably not altogether. So, he's a fortunate lad—it came pretty close to the eye. I imagine he gave you quite a scare?" He put his hand on Donnie's shoulder. "Once he gets older, I guarantee that scar will attract the girls. He'll be able to tell them a pretty good story." He winked at Buddy. "I imagine you'll want to review a few safety measures when you get home."

"Yes," Buddy said, accepting the doctor's extended hand, and squeezed it hard. "Thank you."

"Don't thank me," the doctor said. "Thank whoever it was who did that for being a lousy shot. In a couple of days, remove the dressing and swab the site to keep it clean and free of infection. Bring him back in two weeks and we'll pull the stitches. Sometimes folks do it at home. I don't recommend it." He asked if there were any questions, then he left.

Buddy looked at his hands, still muddy and bloody, refusing to wash them until he heard about Donnie's eye.

"It's okay, Dad. It's okay," Donnie said, as if he knew what Buddy was going through and understood his torment and how he blamed himself for the accident.

All he wanted was to take his son out on a hunting expedition the way his father had done for him, give him some excitement, a story he could tell to his kids one day.

"What do you say we go home?"

"We'll tell Mom I walked into a branch and scraped my forehead. Almost poked out my eye. We won't tell her I got shot." Donnie sipped his drink and put his full concentration into sucking every drop of ginger ale out of the bottom of the glass. He set his empty glass down and said, "I've got a scar just like you, Dad."

Chapter 26

Scary Monster—1961

Footsteps thumped down harder overhead. From his green chair he tracked his family, their steps a criss-cross of intricate patterns. So much commotion. It seemed almost impossible to believe that twelve years ago they brought home a little pink bundle, his little Kitten.

Something was going on; he could tell. He could guess his family's state of mind, their moods, by the sound of their footsteps. Right now Kitten hurried up and down the hall from her bedroom to the kitchen, excited about tonight's sleepover camping party. Donnie's footsteps went fast then stopped altogether, inclined towards easy distraction and daydreaming. David had a heavy, slow gait—typical for a methodical thinker, and Doug's steps were fast since he was always on the move. Right now the weave of noise overhead belonged to Carolyn, Meg, and Donnie. The other two only came home weekends and not regularly, not anymore.

The party would start with the opening of gifts, then cake, followed by a bonfire after dark. He was assigned fire duty; he had to build and light the bonfire for a weenie roast. Meg would take care of games. Carolyn wanted a game of hide and seek in the yard after dark but Meg said no; it would be too scary, and the last thing she wanted was a bunch of hysterical twelve-year-olds on her hands.

Every day he felt so tired, more than ordinary physical tiredness. Something deeper, more profound, a permanent state of exhaustion he couldn't seem to shake. The sound of the kids arriving woke him up. One by one Carolyn's friends arrived.

He'd blow the air mattresses up with the bike pump later after it cooled down, and after dark he'd light the bonfire. He wanted to put the sprinkler on in the garden, too, but not until dark so the water would soak into the ground instead of evaporating.

He had a wee nip while he waited. He could tell events were getting underway upstairs. The excitement was mounting. Lady lay at his feet.

"Won't do any harm to have a little snort, will it Lady? As long as I stay here and keep out of the way. And behave myself." The dog raised an eyelid revealing mostly the white of her eye, her devil eye, he called it.

He leaned back listening to the party unfold and took another drink. They were opening presents; he could tell by all the squeals.

"Dad, wake up." Donnie appeared before him, the light from the ceiling bulb highlighting the smooth glaze of his gunshot scar—a knocked-over exclamation mark. He wondered sometimes how deliberate Donnie was about parting his hair to reveal the scar, as if he wanted him to be constantly reminded of just how close he'd come to losing an eye or worse. Buddy heard him telling his buddies about how he got shot in the head and he wanted to tell him to quit telling the story. *Don't you know how much it hurts to hear it?* But he knew the pleasure of telling such stories, he knew their value. Meg still thought it was a branch scrape.

"Dad! Are you coming upstairs for cake? Mom wants to know."

"No, I'm not hungry. Tell them to go ahead. I'll just get in the way."

Donnie scowled at him. "You're acting like a troll hanging out down here by yourself. Don't drink anymore."

"I'm taking it easy."

"Yeah, right."

He wanted Donnie to sit down and talk a while, like father and son, offer him a couple of drinks, maybe have an *In the West* story. But Donnie was on his way back upstairs before he could say anything and he'd soon go off to his job at the gas station.

After dark Buddy headed outside, spread the air mattresses over the lawn, and began to pump. Meg called out from the kitchen window. "Come in and get something to eat."

He told her no, he didn't feel like anything. "Too hot," he shouted. The air seemed moist, woolly almost, and hard to breathe. If David or Doug still lived here, he'd have one of them do this, and spare the old man. Who was he trying to kid? He had a fight on his hands to get them to do anything.

He tossed the inflated air mattresses inside the tent. That's as far as he was going with this project—the girls could take it from there. Soon it would be time to light the fire.

He crossed the yard, went beyond the apron of light from the back door and the open windows, passed behind the privet hedge that separated the lawn from the garden, and pulled the hose out into the garden between the tomato rows. He hooked the sprinkler to the hose and put it down on the hard soil. The earth smelled of baked clay and dust. He went back to the house and turned the water on—the pipes screamed as if the whole house had a belly ache—then followed the gleaming snake of hose across the yard and out to the garden. In the darkness the sprinkler hissed and water splattered over leaves. The sound of water brought relief from the stifling night.

Random droplets fell at the fringe of the sprinkler's reach and alighted on his shoes. He sank to the ground, touched the soil, still warm from the heat of the day, and stretched out. He felt clumps of hard dirt poke beneath his thin undershirt; the odd droplet struck his bare legs and chest. The sprinkler purred in the background, a slow, easy, dreamy rhythm. Beyond the hedge he could hear the girls in the house, shrieking, playing, and having fun. The idea of Carolyn enjoying herself on her birthday made him smile.

He found the Scott constellation. There was his mother and father, both of them always watching, always, always surrounded by his brothers and sisters. Right up there just where he'd left them, watching over him. "How are you folks doing?" He blinked as water struck his face.

How long had he been asleep? He pushed himself up and sank into mud up to his wrists. He was soaking wet and cold. He rolled onto his side, then stomach, and struggled to his feet. Mud squished around his shoes and made it hard for him to walk; he was covered from head to toe. He'd sneak into the basement and get cleaned up.

He put his hand to his forehead and rubbed the front of his cranium where a stunner of a headache took up residence. All that cold water hitting him, a frigid mechanical rain—*pppffftttt-pppffftttt-pppffftttt*—had given him a case of the chills. He'd be damn lucky if he didn't get pneumonia.

He started across the yard and stopped. A leg cramp seized his right calf like a dog bite. He stooped to stretch his muscles and flex his foot to pull out the twist. He sucked in the air. He smelled smoke. He'd slept through the bonfire, too. The white canvas tent shone large and luminous in the back door light, and inside a hubbub of giggles and squeals.

He retreated back into darkness to stay out of the light's range. Close to the small apple tree, his right leg twisted up again into a long, hard knot. He doubled over and his face screwed up in pain.

A blood curdling chorus of screams, like banshees on the loose, ripped through the night. Three girls, dressed in pajamas, stood beside him clutching each other and kept up their hideous racket.

"Oh, hello." His smile, fake to be sure, composed mostly of bared teeth—a grimace really. The pain of the charley horse twisted his muscles like a dishrag. The girls gave another raise-the-dead scream and raced towards the house. "Monster, monster, monster!" they shouted. The rest of the girls spilled out of the tent, saw him doubled over, frozen in position by the fist trying to be born out of his calf, and ran after the others towards the house.

Sure, he was a sight, but they were overdoing it. Thriving on each other's hysteria, infecting each other with their loud screams, they stampeded to the back door, pushed their way inside, slammed the door closed, and locked it. The curtains moved and their faces plastered the window. Hands went up over mouths. More screaming.

Finally, the spasm passed and he hobbled across the yard towards the house to a whole new round of screams at a higher volume.

"The monster's coming to get us! He's going to kill us, then eat us!"

So much for sneaking into the basement to wash up, getting cleaned up on the sly without Meg catching him. Why didn't they wake up the whole neighbourhood? Girls this age could be such a pain in the ass.

The lights went on in the kitchen. Meg would be up now; who could sleep through this racket?

He knocked on the back door. "Carolyn, open this door right now. Let me in. It's me, your Dad."

From the other side of the door one of the girls said, "No don't let it in. It's a monster. I saw it. It had brown scaly skin, white eyes, and long teeth. It's a werewolf."

"For the love of Christ, Carolyn, let me in."

More screams. "He'll eat us. He'll shred our flesh. He'll suck our blood."

"That's a vampire, you idiot," someone said.

"Girls, settle down right now. There's no such thing as a monster." Meg's voice. The curtain shifted and her face appeared in the window. She stared straight at him, drew the curtains closed, and unlatched the door.

"There's a strange man out there," one of the girls whimpered. "And he's all brown and scaly. And we're all going to die."

"He's strange, that's true," Meg said, "but he lives here. All of you go up into the kitchen and close the door."

Inside, Meg's eyes met his, but neither of them spoke as he descended to the basement to get cleaned up. Lady's hackles went up and she started to growl at the sight of him. "It's okay, it's only me." His voice settled her. She stretched out again on her mat, sighed, then rested her snout on her paws and gave him the devil eye.

By the time he washed, changed his clothes, and went upstairs, one of the girls had called her mother and three others sobbed intermittently, starting up again as soon as someone noticed they stopped crying. "I was terrified. I thought it was going to eat me," one sputtered through a faucet of mucus dripping from her nose.

He should start shrieking the way she had—*snotty monster, snotty monster*—see how she liked it. Two other girls stroked her long brown hair to comfort her. The sobbing, dripping girl milked the sympathy for all it was worth. The other two girls lived up to their part of the bargain by slathering it on thick with a trowel. Oh, they were all in grave danger. Oh, their suffering. No one had suffered like them. "Nothing like that would ever happen at my house. My Dad would never do that," the Snot Monster said.

"Oh, your Dad never falls asleep?" Buddy asked. He guessed she'd feel better once everyone else shared her misery.

"My dad doesn't sleep in mud," her sobs subsiding long enough to make a clear statement.

"You'll be fine," Meg's reassuring tone also conveyed some impatience. A sign she too had enough of Snot Monster's performance. "You're all tired. Things seem worse when you're tired. You'll see once you get some sleep."

"Oh no, I won't be able to sleep. Not after that, not after seeing the monster."

"Mary Beth," Meg sounded annoyed. "That was not a monster, it was Carolyn's dad. He fell into a mud puddle. Haven't you ever fallen into a mud puddle?"

"No," she sobbed, her mouth turned down in defiance. "Especially not in the middle of the night."

Carolyn sat in the corner, arms across her chest, chin down, eyes up, staring at everyone, wearing a pout as if it had been painted on. Buddy's weak smile was meant to say *we'll make it through this little setback* and she met it with an if-looks-could-kill glare.

Meg, still in her housecoat, went to answer the knock at the door. She was talking to someone, then appeared back in the kitchen with another woman. Meg explained how the girls got themselves all worked up, how it was mostly due to tiredness, and how Mary Beth and the other two insisted on leaving.

"Everything's perfectly fine," Meg said. "But they seem to have their minds made up."

"I must tell you it was most distressing to get a call at this hour," Mary Beth's mother said. "I thought the girls would have been asleep hours ago. At my house they would have been, I can tell you that."

Mary Beth's mother didn't appear to have been called from her bed, with her hair flipped up at the ends, her bangs curled under, and her body encased in a cloud of perfume. "Come on, Mary Beth. Let's get you home safe and sound. Who else is coming with me? You can sleep at my house. Inside," she said with emphasis.

Mary Beth's two sympathizers said they were going, too.

"In my opinion, they're too young to be sleeping out in a tent, anyway," Mary Beth's mother said. "If I'd known the circumstances beforehand, I wouldn't have allowed her to come."

Apparently, she knew how to live, and how everyone else should, too. "Come again." Buddy closed the door after them but not before the woman gave him a dirty look. She should have come earlier, before he got cleaned off; then he could have given her a dirty look back.

"Guess we'll go back out to the tent," Carolyn said.

"Yeah, it was fun," a plump girl with red hair said. "I knew there wasn't a monster, but it was fun pretending. Mary Beth was sore Carolyn was getting all the attention because it was her birthday. She knew you weren't a real monster, Mr. Scott. She's spoiled." She paused then, as if she might have gone over the line and looked at him uncertainly, her curls twisting around her freckled face. "You made a really good monster, though."

"Thank you," he said. "And I wasn't even trying." He liked this girl, liked her instantly, and he could see how her kind, wise words perked up Carolyn's mood. And that's what was important; this was Kitten's day.

He wanted to tell her there were reasons he kept messing up, though he couldn't really explain it. Something to do with when he was a kid. He wished he could turn the clock back, reset time, and erase the stupid part he played tonight on her twelfth birthday. But he couldn't and it was pointless thinking that way. And anyway, it was her idea to pitch the tent in the yard and have the girls sleep outside. Because of his *Hobo Jungle* story, the story she asked for when she was a little girl. Her green eyes glued to him, prompting him when he paused because she'd heard it enough to know what happened next. She always wanted to hear it again.

Or her very favourite story of all, *The Wild Creature*. The look in Kitten's eyes, same for the boys; amazement and fear. They sized him up in a whole new way after that story. They thought of him as a hero, someone they could be proud of. Sometimes he heard them telling their friends, "Guess what my dad did? You don't believe me? Well he's got scars on his leg to prove it." He stood back where they couldn't see him and listened.

Kitten would sit on his lap when she was little, and Donnie close by leaning into him. By the end of the story he'd be holding her so tight, his arms encircling her waist, she'd say, "Dad, you're squishing me." Then she'd turn and look up at him with her beautiful eyes full of wonder and say, "Let's see the scar." Donnie liked to trace it with his finger.

Carolyn and her friends had found an umbrella and were going back outside to the tent. Buddy stopped them.

"Carolyn," he said. "How would you and your friends like me to tell you *The Wild Creature* story? Out in the tent. It would be a kind of birthday present."

He thought she was about to say no, but her red-headed friend piped up and said, "I want to hear it, Mr. Scott. And it will be so much better to hear it in the tent. Spookier."

He really did like Carolyn's friend.

Book Six

The Wild Creature — 1923

Spring thaw, continuing its slow creep across the land, was quickly chased away by winter's weakening gasps. Father called March, April, and May ragged months, not able to make up their minds—cold, then a thaw, cold and a thaw—and they seemed to have a similar effect on the children. One night after barn chores, a hint of warmth still in the air, Buddy and Ray arrived inside the house into a scene of uproar.

Sammy and Chuck fought on the floor, a single body of kicking, screaming, hair pulling, and teary outbursts. Pearl stood in the centre of the room wringing her hands, her slight shoulders sagging with the weight of her worry, and cried out how she didn't know what to do or where to turn. Hazel grabbed at Sammy and Chuck and tried to pry them apart. Useless. She nudged them with her high-laced shoe. "Stop it," she pleaded; they screamed even louder.

Buddy wrestled the two apart and held them by their shirt-sleeves as they twisted and squirmed, then Ray clamped his hands over Chuck's shoulders and steered him to the table. Buddy plunked Sammy into a chair as far away from Chuck as possible.

"You sit there. Don't move. Don't look at each other." The table was set for supper in a slap-dash manner, the cutlery every-which-way, and some of it had fallen to the floor.

Smoke curled from a pot on the stove. Pearl rushed to it and stirred, the wooden spoon striking the side of the pot, then slammed the whole works down on the counter. "I give up! I can't do this! I burned the beans."

"You can too do it. You have to." Ray's attempt to sound like Father failed and was met by Pearl's sideways leer. Maudy passed out bowls and Hazel followed, dishing out a grey-green substance. Long stringy strands draped over the ladle and the broth's odour wrinkled Buddy's nose. He went to say something about the colour but thought better of it.

"The works of you settle down. Stop the roughhouse and squabbling," Ray said, a harshness in his voice warning them he wasn't pretending.

Silence, broken only by slurps as everyone huddled over their bowls and settled into the business of eating the thin broth of onion, cabbage and carrot, flecked with grey rabbit meat one of the neighbouring ranchers dropped off yesterday, and plates of burned beans.

Buddy looked up from his soup, let his eyes drift around the table, and experienced a sudden surge of tenderness and bewilderment and impossibility. Wretches. Miserable wretches. Mother's description for others she thought were in a bad way, often no worse than hers. They'd tried to keep the ranch going the same way Mother and Father had, but some days just slopped up around them the way water splashed out of the Saturday night bath when too many bodies tried to squeeze into the tub. They felt lost not knowing what came next, not knowing what it was their parents—always busy—would be doing, and at the same time drowning in work and worry. Somehow their parents saw far down the road to what lay ahead, knew what turns to take and what had to be done. But none of them seemed to possess their vision or sense of direction, always coming to a dead end.

They withered with work and worry. Hazel would stop in her tracks and sob, her arms limp at her sides dangling in utter defeat, her mouth curved hideously. Chuck would lie on the floor, a remnant of Mother's dress pressed to his nose, clinging to her scent. Orwin wandered, his legs moving, and his thoughts somewhere else. Ray inclined to do the same but on a horse and thinned his sadness out over the flat land. Sorrow took hold, possessing them like a strong medicine.

Someone screamed.

"Oh for Pete's sake!" Hazel jumped up and clutched at her skirt blotched with a large dark blossom. A curtain of milk from Sammy's tipped glass streamed over the edge of the table.

The suddenness of motion and unexpected shriek set everyone off, as if the familiar act of eating had been the glue holding everything together and now the entire fragile structure shattered. Another glass spilled and a frenzy of motion tipped bowls, slopped their contents, and sent spoons clattering to the floor. Chairs pushed away from the table, fell over, and bodies slipped under the table to hide.

Hazel clutched her dress. "Look! Look what you've done. It's all I've got to wear."

Sammy and Chuck cried, "Momma, Momma!"

"There is no Momma!" Hazel shouted. "She can't come back!"

"Everyone. Back to your seats and finish eating," Ray spoke from where he stood at the end of the table. "If you don't quiet down right now, everyone's going to bed as soon as the dishes are done."

Pearl raised her head, chin held high. She didn't like being bossed. "You didn't wash up before coming to the table," she challenged. "Mother wouldn't let you come to the table until you washed up."

"Well, she isn't exactly here, is she?" Ray seated himself, picked up his bowl, and drank directly from it.

Pearl struck the table with her clenched fist. "Just because she isn't doesn't mean you get to act like a pig. Use your spoon!"

Ray glowered at her and picked up his spoon. Buddy went to the basin to wash his hands and worked up a good lather with the bar of soap. He'd let Mother down, too.

Pearl looked under where Sammy and Chuck had joined Maudy and Hazel and told them all to come out and sit properly at the table. "And not another peep out of anyone."

The little ones settled in to eating, the sound of sniffles all that was left of the outburst triggered by spilled milk.

"Where's Orwin?" Maudy said, looking around the table.

Buddy looked under the table expecting to see him pressed against someone's shins. Then it hit him. Orwin hadn't come to the table. "He wasn't even here."

"He was going out to meet you and Ray in the barn before dinner. Did you leave him there?" Pearl asked.

"I never saw him," Buddy said.

"Me neither," Ray said. "He sure didn't give us any help, if that's what you mean."

"I'll go out and look for him," Buddy said.

Buddy slipped on his cap and jacket and stepped out into the brisk night, the sun about to set, the sting of cold air squeezing his nostrils. In the barn he struck a match, lit the lantern, and held it high as he passed from stall to stall calling out Orwin's name. He climbed up into the mow and cast about in the shadows for the sight of a small boy huddled in the darkness, kicked through hay in search of what may be hidden beneath, and sneezed from the swirling dust.

He passed through the barn again calling out Orwin's name, hearing only the shift and snorts of the horses. In the yard, he looked out over the prairie. He knew what had to be done. Orwin the wanderer. "You keep an eye on him," Mother always said, aware of his tendency to let his legs carry on as if without him, his mind somewhere else, the plains ready to swallow up a young boy.

Inside, the children faced him, their eyes wide and anxious as they waited for news. The flames from the fire leaping behind them, the little ones already dressed for bed.

"Where is he?" Ray asked.

Buddy shook his head.

"Oh dear." Pearl raised her hand to her lips as if holding something back. "I should have seen that he went to the barn." Her lips trembled. "I was cooking and trying to clean and the children were crying and I...I...Everyone was in such a state, how could I, how could I do it all..."

"No one's saying anything here about any of that," Ray said, his face dark with worry. "I'll go look for him."

"No, I'm going," Buddy said. "I know the spots he likes. He wanders out back and heads to the creek. He won't be far. You stay here and help get the kids to bed." Having Ray stay with them would bring greater comfort as he was the oldest. No one argued with him.

"Take Misty. Dress good. It's a cold night," Ray said.

Buddy knew it, knew what it meant too, but he shoved his thoughts up against a wall and held them there so they wouldn't stray and cause him to panic.

Buddy wrapped a scarf around his neck and headed back to the barn. He saddled Misty and led her out into the barnyard.

"We've got a job to do." He rubbed her nose and met her solemn eyes. In the saddle, he steered her out across the open plain towards the ruffle of shrubs trimming the creek banks. Orwin liked to stand on the banks tossing pebbles until Mother sent someone to go after him. He liked to watch the water carry the pebbles then sink. In the light of the setting sun, Buddy expected to see his squat figure in the distance making his way towards the creek.

The kids would be having stories now and the younger ones would soon fall to sleep.

Orwin could not have gone far. It wasn't that long since Buddy and Ray came in from the barn. If Orwin hadn't gone to the barn when they were doing chores, if he'd headed for the creek or for a wander over the plains, he would have gone only a mile or two. Mother said she'd never seen such a pair of dawdlers and dreamers as Buddy and Orwin. "So easily given over to distraction."

Buddy's breath smoked out in front of his face. He rubbed Misty's neck. "You're a good old girl."

There was another place Orwin might have gone. Farther down the creek to a dense thicket where he liked to play—a place he used as his imaginary boxing ring.

Something off in the distance drew Buddy's attention. He squinted into the dim light, not sure if his eyes tricked him as he tried to distinguish the approaching figure. Not Orwin, he could now make out. Someone on a horse. Buddy rode towards the figure.

"What you doing out here, son, this time of night? You lost?" The rider looked to be about Father's age, maybe younger. Hard to say in the fading light.

"Looking for my brother. You see him? He's on foot."

"You're the first person I've come across in twenty mile. Maybe more. What would your brother be out here in this godforsaken place for anyway? Bit chilly for an evening stroll." His eyes followed the gob of spittle he shot off to the side. He looked like he thought Buddy might have had something come loose in his noggin, the way he scrunched up his face and angled his head.

"We don't live too far from here. My brother likes to be by himself, goes wandering, loses track."

The rider twisted in his saddle and glanced back over his shoulder as if checking to see if he might have overlooked something, then faced Buddy. "Guess I would have noticed if there was someone out there roaming around on this flat old griddle cake. He would have stuck up like a thistle in a petunia patch." He tipped his hat to Buddy and clucked at his horse. "Good luck, son. It'll be pitch black soon. Doubt you'll find anyone then. And the temperature—she's dropping.

Best you head on home." He rode off in the opposite direction of the creek.

No point going in the direction the stranger came from since he claimed he didn't see anyone. Buddy tugged on the reins, turned Misty around in the opposite direction, and followed alongside the creek. In some places the ice had melted completely and he heard the sound of flowing water.

An hour passed. In the distance the vague humps of faraway hills hunkered against the sky. His fingers had stiffened around the reins. He blew into each glove, his warm breath offering some relief until cold set in again. He slipped his feet out of the stirrups, shook his leg, and flexed his foot to bring back circulation and fight off numbness.

Sensations came over him and awakened certain feelings he wished he'd never have again: alone and small. But he had to find Orwin, it had to be him, and if it didn't happen soon Ray would come looking for him. He didn't want that.

Maybe Orwin had gone back to the house and was leaning towards the fire right now, rubbing his hands together to warm them. He could picture him taking anxious glimpses over his shoulder to look at the door. Hoping at any minute it would swing open and Buddy would appear, near frozen but grateful to see Orwin had made his way home. Buddy should go back then and spare himself the agony of the cold setting deeper into his bones. But no; this didn't stand to reason. He would have seen Orwin making his way home. If Orwin hadn't gone back to the house, Buddy would turn around and go right back out to look for him. He wouldn't give up until he'd found him. And if he felt the drowsiness overtaking him, the kind Father told them to beware of, he would lean down into Misty's coarse mane and whisper, home girl. You take me home.

Buddy followed along the creek until he could see off in the distance, the thicket Orwin used as a fort. It seemed unlikely he'd gone this far from the house, but Buddy wouldn't stop looking until he found him. And that meant searching all his usual spots. Orwin pretend boxed here, knocking every opponent out and prancing around inside the circle of trees, arms held high in victory as the crowd roared. Father showed Orwin the swings. Buddy too, but Orwin, Father said was a natural. Buddy and Ray teased him when they found him fighting his imaginary opponent. "Look at him dance, bob, and weave. Look at him swing at the air. He knocked him out! He's down!"

"Leave me alone," Orwin narrowed his dark eyes and scowled. They knew they shouldn't gang up on him, but somehow they couldn't resist trying to get his goat, riling him to the point he'd take a swing at them. He could never win such a match. They were older, bigger, and sometimes meaner too. Buddy wasn't proud of it.

Buddy leaned forward in the saddle. He thought he heard a sound. Misty's hooves crunching over a small patch of snow.

There it was again, no question this time. Some kind of scary wailing. Something he couldn't identify.

"Heyah," he kicked at Misty's sides, got her into a gallop, and headed towards the thicket—towards the sound. It would be Orwin pretending to be the crowd who had just witnessed his knockout round and who now cheered for him, the champion. As Buddy rode closer to the cluster of bushes the cheering changed to hissing and spits and the occasional screeching howl. It sounded like the devil himself and it sent a shiver through him.

Misty stopped. Buddy knew the horse sensed another animal, a distressed animal, judging by the sounds. When Misty sensed danger she wouldn't budge no matter how many times he dug her with his heels. The screeches switched to low, constant growls then rose again back to screeches. A raw, threatening cry—an unearthly noise like nothing he'd heard before. He jabbed at Misty again, but it was no use. What kind of animal could this be? A cougar? A badger? Wolverine? None of these guesses seemed to fit. Too early for bear cubs. And anyway, they didn't usually come down this far on the plain, staying up in the bush in the hills where there were berries. Though he shouldn't rule it out completely. Every so often Father came upon one or two, along with the sow. "Keep your distance. There're few things more dangerous than a grizzly sow with a cub."

The creature hissed, a long, throaty, agonized sound. At the end of the hiss, a growl, high-pitched and ear piercing. Whatever was making this noise felt threatened and might be cornered by something that would kill it; might be fighting for its life. A noise so raw and harsh it made Buddy cringe. Common sense told him he ought to turn and ride away but he couldn't. He had to know.

A higher pitched screech shattered the air and seemed to linger there. Then another sound, a human voice, small and frail and full of fear, came out of the darkness.

"I'm not going to hurt you."

"Orwin!" Buddy shouted. "Is that you?"

"It's me. Who's that?" Orwin sounded like he was crying.

"It's Buddy. What's going on?"

"I'm pinned by a bobcat. There's something wrong with it. It won't go away. It's got the entrance to the thicket blocked. I can't get out of here. It's going to attack me."

"Orwin, they're more afraid of us than we are of them. Shoo it away. I can't even see it." Even as he said this he knew it wasn't right. Orwin knew it too. For the cat to have him pinned without running from Orwin at first sight meant there was something wrong. The sounds the cat made were nowhere close to how a bobcat sounded and he had a hunch he knew why.

"What's it doing?" He still couldn't see it as it somewhere inside the thicket.

"It's staggering back and forth, and falling down," Orwin called back, his voice trembling. "It tries to come after me then falls over."

"Anything else?"

"It's got white stuff coming out of its mouth. Long strands of it. Right to the ground."

Rabies. If Father encountered such an animal out riding he would shoot it with the rifle he always carried. They'd seen their share of animals around here with the disease. Father had shot and buried more than Buddy could count. If you saw it once you could expect to see more and the last thing you wanted was to get it around the horses. The cat could lunge at Orwin, bite him, shred him with his claws and infect him. And if that happened there'd be nothing anyone could do but watch him die, and there was nothing worse than dying from rabies. So he'd heard.

Buddy slipped down from Misty. He had to go in and get Orwin and somehow avoid the creature, see if he could scare it off. He stroked Misty's mane. "You stay here, girl, we're coming back. Don't you move." He knew she wouldn't.

Buddy inched forward. "Orwin I'm coming for you."

"No. The cat will attack you!"

"It might be too sick."

"It looks really scary. Don't come near it."

"Shut up, Orwin. There's no choice."

He took small steady steps towards the thicket, still unable to make out the animal which kept up its gruesome noise. As he inched forward the animal's screech got louder and more vicious, its hiss and howl becoming one continuous sound as Buddy approached.

Now he saw it. Its head turned to Buddy, its eyes glowing in the dark—the eyes of the devil. Buddy spoke to it low and soft so as not to threaten the animal and further alarm it. Lines of foamy white saliva dripped from its mouth, its lips pulled back over sharp white teeth as it snarled and hissed. It was in the last stages of the disease. A male cat, larger than a female, it staggered and swayed having lost most of the control of its back end. It started towards him then toppled over. Buddy jumped back and then as the cat struggled to get on its feet, it toppled over again. He made a dash, the creature's ghostly hiss and piercing screech so close it hurt his ears. He looked around the inside of the thicket but couldn't see Orwin.

"Where are you?"

"Right here. I'm here." Buddy felt something tug his coat. He looked down. Orwin's hand. He was pressed back as far as he could into the bushes, his eyes full of terror. Buddy clutched Orwin's arm and told him to hang on to him tight and not to let go, no matter what.

"We're making a dash for it! Run as fast as you can until we are well clear of it!"

Buddy blocked the cat right out of his vision as he rushed towards the thicket opening. From the corner of his eyes he saw it staggering to its feet and coming after them. Buddy kicked it as hard as he could and knocked it to the ground. They raced towards Misty who stood just as Buddy had left her. He hoisted Orwin up into the saddle and felt the cat leap onto his back and hang there by its claws. It screeched into his ears, the most hideous sound he'd ever heard, its breath hot against his neck, the stench of its diseased breath filling his nostrils. Buddy reached around behind him and grabbed the cat's leg, its mouth trying to bite his arm. Its teeth exposed, brilliant white in the moonlight, the white foam dripped onto his glove. He grabbed with all his might, felt wild muscular strength in its frantic squirming, tore it off his body, and threw it down onto the ground with all his force. He kicked at it repeatedly and hard until it stopped its struggle and went still. He slid his foot into the stirrup and lifted his other leg up and over the saddle, Misty shifting with the commotion around her, and, as he slapped the reins down over her back, he felt claws scrape into his flesh just above the boot line. The cat lost its hold and fell once again to the ground. They rode away as fast as Misty could go.

"You're safe." He spoke to the back of Orwin's head, his hair soft upon his lips. Blood dribbled down his leg and into his boot. He would not tell anyone about his wound. With one hand he took his scarf from around his neck, spit on the corner, and dabbed at the cut down the back of his leg. All he could do was wait; time would tell.

Orwin shuddered into Buddy, sobbing over and over how sorry he was.

Buddy pulled Orwin in close to him and wrapped his arm tight around his waist. All Buddy could think of was how Orwin got away on them and it wasn't going to happen again. He would deliver him home safe and sound and see the look of relief on the faces of the others, see their fear melt away. They would be so grateful to Buddy for rescuing him.

His lips pressed into the back of Orwin's head, he breathed in his smell mingled with the sharp night air and whispered, "I am not letting go of you."

Chapter 27

Tomatoes — Summer 1963

Buddy stirred his coffee and Meg cut the tips off a batch of yellow beans he picked last night, the garden so muddy from the last few days of rain he could barely get around in it.

Outside, Lady's bark grew more persistent.

"What's got her all worked up?" Buddy stabbed his cigarette into the ashtray. "Better go see." From the sounds of the dog's bark there was a stranger on the property.

A man inched his way up the sidewalk skirting around Lady, her hackles standing straight up as she showed him some teeth. In the driveway a Cadillac convertible glittered in the fall sun like a great white shark, its top down. Who could this be? A bill collector? A salesman?

Buddy hoisted up his khaki shorts and tucked his undershirt in at the waist as the well-dressed stranger approached.

"Yes sir, what can I do for you today?" The man's face was shadowed by the brim of his hat.

The stranger pushed his straw fedora back off his tanned forehead. His white short-sleeve shirt showed off his dark arms. "Are you Buddy Scott?" He squinted into the sun.

"Last time I checked. What can I do for you? What haven't I paid on time?" He had an idea what might be coming.

"Well," the man removed his hat and exposed his bald head fringed with salt and pepper hair, same as Buddy's. "I'm Ray, your brother."

"No!"

"I wouldn't make up such a thing." He held out his hand for Buddy. "It's been a long, long time."

"Ray? No. I can't believe it! Ray, you say?" He searched the man's face for the young man he last saw, ignoring the hand extended out to him, before finally taking it and pulling him into an awkward embrace. A kind of dizziness overtook him as if on the verge of a fainting spell. "Ray? Ray?"

The possibility this could be Ray standing there directly in front of him with a crooked smile on his face, ran off him and wouldn't stick. He turned his eyes to the big maple, unable to comprehend. The tree; the yard—nothing was familiar. "You're really here? Standing in front of me?"

"It's me all right. You're a hard person to track down."

"Where you coming from?" Buddy motioned towards the car.

"California," Ray said. "That's where I live."

"You're Ray?" He just said he was, hadn't he? After all this time he could hardly believe it. Ray standing here in flesh and blood—it would take some getting used to.

"Yes, it's me." This time Ray laughed.

Buddy started to tremble; his knees loose as if they might buckle at any minute. "I think I'm in shock."

"I can see. I know it's quite a surprise. I've caught you unexpectedly."

"Jesus, it's really you?"

"It really is."

Buddy stuck his hand out to shake Ray's and remembered they'd already done this—already hugged. Even so, he hung on longer, primed his arm like a pump, felt the warmth of his flesh, looked directly in his brown eyes, and saw Father's. Somewhere there too was a hint of the old Ray of long ago.

Meg came outside then, drying her hands on a tea towel. She shoved a curl of hair back off her forehead and seemed not quite to believe what she was seeing as she looked from one to the other. The tea towel dangled in her hand.

"What's going on?"

"This man's my brother Ray."

Her eyes continued to travel back and forth between the two. "It's obvious you're related." A tomato stain from all the canning circled the front of her apron as big as a stop sign.

"We're related all right," Ray said. "Like it or not." His smile even looked like Buddy's.

Buddy made a proper introduction between Meg and Ray, finding it hard to concentrate through his mind's uproar. The three of them stood dumbstruck, silent, and awkward. Finally Meg suggested they go inside the house.

Nervous excitement and a feeling of dislocation ran through Buddy, as if a sudden electrical jolt threw him off course. At the back door, he glanced at the willow tree and saw a cardinal, blood-red against the blue sky.

"Do you see the cardinal?" Buddy pointed. "We get a lot of birds." Seeing the bird restored his sense of reality, but mentioning it sounded awkward. Inside, they would sit down and sort things out. But what kind of things?

Meg served coffee and homemade applesauce cake, which Buddy declined due to a nervous stomach. Ray began the long story of how, for many years, he tried to track Buddy down and all but gave up.

"I've been meaning to pay you a visit for a long time, but with a family and everything, it wasn't possible."

Buddy could hardly take his eyes away from Ray—he looked so much like their father, so much like Buddy, and yet he still looked like a stranger.

All the years he'd thought about his family, he saw them as they'd once been. Ray had stopped changing from the time he left Detroit. This man sitting here at the table didn't look anything like the man Buddy imagined.

Meg kept Ray talking—asking him a lot of questions—while Buddy couldn't help staring, still not quite believing it was him. Ray was telling her that he'd written from one contact to another in Detroit to track Buddy down, and his best lead came from the City Gym. Someone working there remembered he'd gone up into Canada with a fellow, Hadley, Ray believed his name was, long since gone from the gym. Then he managed to come up with the name of a town. Once he'd made contact with the store owner in Farnwell, it was easy to track him down.

"I understand Maudy wrote to you at this address but you never answered her. She didn't think she'd found the right Buddy Scott so she never tried again. But how many Buddy Scotts could there be? And once I followed the trail from Detroit, I knew Maudy's address for you had a pretty good chance of being right. Then the guy in Farnwell confirmed it."

"You got a letter from a relative?" Meg asked. "That's the first I've heard of it."

"No. I never received it," Buddy said and sipped his coffee. "Maybe it got lost in the mail."

"I thought I'd come looking for you since I was going to be in Detroit anyway." He'd left his wife there to visit her aunt, a trip they'd been planning for years.

"You sure as hell succeeded in finding me." Buddy fingered granules of spilled sugar on the table top.

"When you didn't get back to Maudy, I thought I'd come and find you myself. If it was really you, I wanted to give you a surprise"

"You sure as hell succeeded."

Meg wanted to know all about his family. He talked about his boys, gave their ages and described what they looked like, and described their personalities and the colleges they attended. His daughter, the youngest, was still in high school. "The two boys never gave me so much as a speck of trouble. I've been lucky there." His daughter was following right along in her brothers' footsteps. "She's the top of her class, always has been." His eyes slid away from Buddy and Meg and seemed to scale the kitchen, taking inventory of the worn linoleum floor and the kitchen cupboards, handmade by Buddy, in need of a fresh coat of paint.

Could he detect in the room's furnishings, in the nicked paint, their struggle to maintain the house and keep up with the kids? Would he guess they just managed on his meagre wages and the small income Meg brought in from keeping books?

Meg and Ray talked about Ray's wife Shelley. She wouldn't be crossing the border to meet them, a disappointment to Meg.

"Next time, I promise," Ray told her.

Ray would think Buddy's house was modest and showed the signs of years of hard living, but Buddy wasn't about to apologize for it. Why bother having a home if you weren't going to live in it? Ray's expensive clothes, his fancy gold watch which his fingers couldn't stop adoring by constantly twisting it on his wrist, were hard to ignore. Along with the Cadillac convertible sitting in the driveway. The imagination didn't have to wander far to know how life was treating him.

"Shelley had an excellent job with a good salary. She chucked it when the third baby came along," Ray said. "Doesn't matter. Her folks have money and she's an only child. I've been fortunate with my job, too. It pays well. I'm in insurance and insurance is a good thing. No one knows better than me. You never know what's going to happen. Isn't that right, Buddy?"

Donnie came into the kitchen, started to ask Meg something about rubber boots, and stopped when he noticed Ray sitting at the table.

"Hey!" examining first Ray then Buddy, then back again, "What's going on?"

"This is your father's brother, your Uncle Ray," Meg said.

Donnie stood with his mouth open, staring from one to the other, then fixed on Ray. His shirt was worn through at the elbow and the other sleeve was patched. The scar above his eye stood out stronger today.

"You look a lot like my dad," Donnie said.

"Well, isn't your dad lucky," Ray said.

Carolyn appeared at the kitchen door and again Meg made the introductions.

Ray studied them and smiled, pleased apparently by what he saw. "You are a handsome pair," he said, and Meg told him about the other two who were away at their summer jobs.

"You're the one who got lost in the storm," Carolyn said, making more of a statement than a question.

"Oh, I got lost in more than one storm," Ray said.

"But there was one that was really, really bad one, wasn't there?" Carolyn balanced on the rims of her saddle shoes. "You almost died."

"You seem to know a lot about it," Ray said. "One storm in particular was more memorable than others." He looked over at Buddy. "I imagine you know the one I'm talking about?"

"It's a good thing my dad found you," Carolyn said before Buddy had a chance to say anything. She was more outspoken than usual, due to her fondness for *In the West* stories. One of the characters from the stories had come alive and sat right here at the kitchen table drinking coffee.

Ray nodded, clasped his hands together, and looked at Buddy, then Carolyn. "I suppose it was a good thing he found me."

Buddy looked at the clutter on the counter and a huge pile of tomato peels. Meg was in full swing with canning. Routine chores had been shoved aside.

Ray asked Donnie and Carolyn what grades they were in, and what sports they liked to play, and what they planned to do once they finished school. Carolyn wanted to know if he had kids.

"Three. They're older than you. They're your cousins."

"Why haven't we met them?" she asked.

She would think if someone was part of the family she'd know them, the way it was with Meg's family. "They live a long ways away, Kitten," Buddy said.

Ray reached into his pocket and pulled out a billfold. "Here," he held out a picture for Donnie. "This is my crew." Carolyn leaned over Donnie to see as Ray told them where they lived and went to school, and pointed out the family resemblance between his kids and Buddy's.

Donnie and Carolyn hung around for a while, listening in on the adult conversation, then drifted from the room, headed out to be with their friends. Meg cleared the table and wiped it off. She suggested they move into the living room. "We'll be more comfortable there."

Buddy kept thinking about the garden, his work interrupted by Ray's unexpected visit. This time of year, with tomatoes ripening on the vine, it was hard to stay ahead of it.

In the living room, Ray sat in the recliner by the window and looked outside. The odd red maple leaf twirled down.

"You've got a beautiful yard," he said. "It's huge."

"Meg does the flower gardens. I'm the vegetable grower," Buddy said.

Ray nodded and threaded his fingers together as if in contemplation. "It's impressive. I don't know how you find the time. I live in a suburban neighbourhood. I don't have a lot of yard to keep up, but even so, I hire someone to cut the grass and tend the garden. Most of my backyard is taken up with a swimming pool."

What Buddy's kids wouldn't do for a pool. "I've always thought a pool would be a lot of work."

"It gets hot where we are in southern California. And my boys belong to competitive swim teams at college, so they got a lot of use out of it. My daughter's a real good swimmer too, but her strength is her diving. She's won first prize in competitions at high school level."

"Your children sound very athletic," Meg said. The idea of Ray's pool seemed to refresh her. "You must be proud of them."

Ray asked Buddy if he remembered much about Wyoming. Buddy waited for Meg to roll her eyes back in her here-we-go-again way, but she didn't. If anything, she seemed more attentive than ever as Ray started talking about the ranch, then about Uncle Wes's, running away, the hobo jungle, *The One Big Thing*, Sandy's Mercantile, arriving in Detroit on the back of a vegetable truck, and meeting Mr. Ford. Buddy and Ray exchanged details back and forth but Ray seemed to want to do most of the telling to Meg, and Buddy let him.

Carolyn came into the living room and curled up beside Buddy on the couch.

"Thought you were going out."

"I did. My friend isn't home," she said, staring at Ray.

Buddy fidgeted as Ray started talking about their parents. Hearing Ray speak of them made him feel as if they were somehow less his parents, or more Ray's, or someone else's entirely. He had them all to himself for so long. Ray talked about the songs their father sang, his joking and his stern nature, their mother's gentleness, and the horses, Bishop, Misty, Breeze, Soldier.

"Do you remember the day we all went to the church and the family got split up?" Ray asked, his voice suddenly somber.

"How could I forget that day? It was one of the worst days of my life." How could he even ask that question; he was after all, only two years younger than him and unlikely to ever forget.

"Worst day of my life, too." Ray repositioned his watch on his wrist. "I'll never, as long as I live, forget the sound of Sammy crying." He shook his head and turned towards the window, overcome.

"Neither will I," Buddy said.

"You can't know how many times his screams come back to haunt me. Every time I think of him calling out my name, I relive the whole awful business."

"What are you talking about?" Buddy could not have heard him correctly. "Are you talking about Sammy, when we went off with Wes in the wagon and those people, those strangers, were getting ready to take Sammy away and he kept crying?"

"Yes."

"He didn't call out your name; it was me he called out for!"

"Buddy, keep your voice down," Meg said. "You've struck a nerve, apparently," she said to Ray.

"So it appears."

Suddenly, Carolyn sat straight up. "My Dad says Sammy called and called him, Bubby, Bubby, and he sometimes hears his little brother's voice in the night. In nightmares. He feels really bad he had to be taken away. So I tell him he saved your life and that makes him feel better. He saved Orwin's life, too, from the terrible wild creature. He's got scars from it."

"Is that right? I'll bet he does." Ray leaned forward in the chair, as if drawn by Carolyn's story. "I'll have to get him to tell me that story and refresh my memory. I seem to have forgotten it."

"That's enough, Kitten," Buddy said. "You go and play and leave us to talk about when we were kids." She'd come to his defense. He was touched by it, but she was too eager.

"I'd like to hear more from you Carolyn," Ray said.

Carolyn seemed happy to oblige, singled out as she was by the special guest who had travelled so far to meet them. "My dad was a hero. If he hadn't found you on the horse, when you went to get the doctor, you would have died. He sent the horse off in the right direction and then went to get the lady who helped babies be born. The midwife."

"Mrs. Rankin," Ray said. "Yes, she did that all right."

"You would have died without my dad. And Orwin too, if my dad hadn't kicked that cat to make it go away." Carolyn settled back into the couch, satisfied by her declaration about her father's heroics, pleased by her boast.

"Well, well, that is one way to look at it, I suppose," Ray said, threading his fingers.

"Carolyn," Buddy said. "It's time for you to leave us. I haven't seen my brother for many years and we have a lot of catching up to do. Why not go down the street and see if your friend is back." Carolyn must have had enough of being with the adults too. She slipped off the couch and headed for the door.

"Let's get one thing straight," Buddy said, after Carolyn had gone. Buddy's memory of the day the family was split up at the church pushed through his mind, and he could barely connect with his tongue to make sense about what he had to say. These were his memories—all he had of his past. His and his alone for so long. "Sammy and I were close," Buddy said. "Sammy was closest to me especially after Mother and Father died. It was me he called out to. And it damn near broke my heart. And it still does!"

"You've got it wrong, that and a few other things it seems," Ray said. "I know you and Sammy were close, but he was close to both of us. On the last day we were all together he called out my name. I heard it. I still hear it, clear as a bell."

"Well there's something wrong with your hearing and your memory, too," Buddy said.

"My memory? You rescued me, did you? Rescued Orwin? Without your help I would have died? Same with Orwin? You've got a lot of nerve accusing me of having a poor memory."

"Oh for heaven's sakes, it doesn't matter, does it?" Meg said. "It doesn't change anything. What's done is done. Sammy's gone, your parents died. It's over!" Colour flushed Meg's cheeks as she spoke to Buddy.

Yes, it mattered, Buddy thought. It mattered a lot. He wasn't going to sit back and let someone come into his life after all this time and take what little he had from his childhood away from him by distorting it. Why should he? Ray was doing the same thing Maudy did with that letter, lying about her age! And she even claimed Sammy too. How dare she! How dare both of them! And there sat Meg nodding her head in agreement with Ray, knowing full well how *The Day the Family Split Up* story went.

"Your memory is playing tricks on you," Buddy said, trying hard to conceal his anger.

"I could say the same for yours, couldn't I?" Ray said.

Same old Ray. Stubborn and pig-headed, always was. Nothing had changed. All the years they were together he let Ray tell the stories about their childhood; he was the oldest. But after he left to go back west Buddy learned to speak for himself.

"Would you like more coffee, Ray?" Meg asked and glared at Buddy. "You?" she asked tightly. She would tell him later this was no way to treat a long-lost brother.

Meg went to get Ray another coffee and the two of them sat without saying a word, the atmosphere in the room gone brittle. When she returned she asked if he knew anything about what had become of the rest of the family and he told the same details that Maudy had given in her letter.

"What about Orwin?" Meg asked. "Do you know what became of him?"

Buddy spoke up then. "Let's move away from this topic. It makes me sad to listen to it all again. It doesn't seem right that all those lives should be summed up in a few measly details." He preferred to think of them as children, the way they'd been, with hopeful lives still ahead of them.

Ray and Meg appeared startled by the sudden welling up of emotion in his voice.

"Some topics are better avoided," Ray said, and turned once again to the window.

After dinner Carolyn and Donnie hounded Ray with questions about California as if they had a Hollywood movie star sitting with them at the table. Meg invited Ray to stay the night.

"Why would you spend money on a motel room when we've got plenty of space?"

Ray said he appreciated the offer but preferred his own sleeping quarters.

"Don't know why, but there it is. I suppose I'm a privacy nut." He had to be back on the road by five in the morning and planned to be in Detroit around eight to pick up Shelley. Then they'd start their trip back across the country. "I've got work early next week, and it's a long way."

Ray wrote down his address, Maudy and Hazel's, and gave them to Meg. He told them if she wrote to Hazel not to expect a response. He said his goodbyes to Meg and gave her a kiss on the cheek.

Outside, Buddy told him he'd give him a tour of the property and show him the garden before he headed out.

They cut across the lawn towards the garden beyond the big maple and the privet hedge. As they strolled through the lush grass, tall after recent rain, an uneasy silence fell between them.

The golden light of the evening from a sun slung low in the sky made them stop, and around them the poplars spoke a watery hiss in the breeze. Neither spoke as if they had an agreement not to. They surveyed the property, taking in the fine evening, the trees alive, swaying in the wind, and the grass thick and green. In Ray's presence, Buddy saw his home in a new way, despite the overwhelming sensation he often had of getting nowhere. Ray's sudden appearance had disoriented him, but as he looked at his land it was familiar and solid—something he and Meg had achieved together. In the radiant light of an early fall evening the beauty of their achievement was even more obvious.

Ray appeared lost in thought, a slight smile upon his lips, as if he too enjoyed the autumn night.

Without warning, Ray jumped back and shouted.

"What the hell?" Had he been stung? Had a bird shit on his head? Buddy stared down at motion in the grass and caught the quick zig-zag of a garter snake. "It's nothing but a garter."

"I don't care what kind of a snake it is." Ray edged back further, his eyes on the ground. "I've seen as many snakes in my life as I ever want to see."

Buddy felt the same way but he wouldn't waste his breath on such a statement. Ray had gone soft. He figured it out earlier when he saw his hands, the smoothness of the skin and the clean, white fingernails. All the rough and tumble they were raised on and experienced together, gone from him, possibly even forgotten as if he was never born into it.

"Come on, I'll show you my garden. This year's tomato crop is the best I've ever had. I'll give you some to take back."

"I can't take them back. Something to do with disease crossing the border."

They moved beyond the high privet hedge and approached the vegetable patch. Buddy explained the rows of vegetables—beans, potatoes, squash, corn, carrots—pointed the various plants out to Ray who seemed not to recognize them, or wasn't interested. "Beans didn't do as well as they should have," Buddy said. "Too wet."

He stopped at the tomatoes not quite believing what he saw. Rows of brown withered plants, every single one, as if he hadn't bothered to water them so much as a teaspoonful all summer. Green and pale red fruit dangled from brown-yellow vines. Tomato blight.

"That's the bumper crop?" Ray exclaimed as if he thought this whole droopy tomato patch might be some kind of joke.

"Was." Buddy scanned the rows for a single healthy plant and shook his head. Not one, not a single untouched plant. "Too much rain."

"Can't you pick the tomatoes anyway, and eat them?"

"Once they've got the blight, they rot fast. They're not much use for anything. I'll pick tonight and tomorrow, salvage what I can. But they won't be any good much longer. Without leaves, the fruit gets scorched in the sun."

"I guess it's obvious how much I know about gardening. I can hardly tell a tomato from a pumpkin."

A feeling of sickness rose in Buddy's stomach. With most of the crop still waiting to be picked, he thought of all his useless work and all the money gone down the drain. All in a matter of a few hours the blight crept along the vines while he sat in the house talking to Ray.

"Despite the tomatoes, I see you've got a real flair for gardening. You take after Father and Mother."

A compliment, probably to make Buddy feel better. But there was such lightness in his tone it was obvious he didn't grasp the importance of the loss, as if it meant practically nothing, just a few wasted tomatoes. What would he know with his whole back yard practically taken up with a swimming pool. No room for a vegetable patch there.

"I often wish Mother and Father had chosen another kind of life, not homesteading. They should have gone to California instead of trying to make a living out of the dust. They were smart enough; they could have made a go of it, had an easier life." Ray jangled coins in his pocket.

Only people without financial worries got to talk this way and pretend their parents could actually make choices. Not people like Buddy though, who every step of the way had to figure out how to survive. Luck had a lot to do with it, but Ray shouldn't go fooling himself. He said his wife's family had money; he should consider himself lucky to have married into it and luckier still his marriage lasted. He dropped by out of the blue to shake up Buddy. To criticize their parents for wrong choices. He could go now, go right back to where he came from.

Buddy's jaw ached from clenching. He scanned the rows of defeated tomatoes looking for some evidence his eyes betrayed him. He found none.

"I've got to work and pick these tomatoes or they'll be too damaged to use. They won't be good for canning. I don't have time to hear your story about how our parents went wrong."

Ray, still with his hands in his pockets, still jangling coins, set his gaze hard on the garden then on Buddy. He cocked his head to one side.

"You've got to be kidding. My stories? You don't like my stories? It doesn't much matter if you don't like my stories because you'll just change things to suit your purposes. Isn't that so? Mother used to say that you were a storyteller. She used to compliment you on your overripe imagination. Guess you haven't lost your ability to make things up."

Buddy glowered at him. Why had he come? To disturb his life? Cause trouble? Make him feel bad? So he could flaunt his wealth?

"I'd love to hear Carolyn's whole take on the night of the storm but I doubt I am going to have the opportunity. Do you think you might have got some details mixed up?"

Buddy's breath tightened and his mouth felt dry from anger. "I've got my own life now." It was all he could think to say; all he could come up with. He had to protect himself.

"Judging by what Carolyn says, I see you've portrayed yourself as quite the hero to your kids."

He could stop anytime. Better yet, he could leave. He'd come snooping and found what he was after. Found that Buddy and Meg struggled to survive, worked hard, tried their best, and didn't come near to his level of achievement in the movie star state. He wasn't Buddy's older brother who was in charge anymore.

"Our parents," Buddy said, once he'd recovered his voice, "worked hard just to survive and to give us a life. The least you could do is show them some respect."

Ray pursed his lips and shook his head. "All I'm saying is it would be nice if we had them longer, and I suspect we would have if they didn't have such damn hard lives."

Bats darted about their heads and swooped down low. A screech owl called from a distance; the sounds coming from Buddy's property seemed to fill their silence.

"What would you do with all those tomatoes anyway?" Ray finally said.

Maybe he meant the question to make Buddy feel better, or maybe he was just curious, but why add "anyway"? As if having so many tomatoes would be a burden, an excess, something that would cause hardship. The word implied he was better off not to have them, better off with the blight. He would have it his way just like old times.

"If you really want to know, we would have stewed them. Turned them into chili sauce, ketchup, preserves, spaghetti sauce, jam, soup. Pretty much any damn thing you can think of to do to a tomato. And we'd eat them with every meal and in between meals, too. Until we turned red. Until our children started to get round and fat and took on the appearance of tomatoes. Hell, we might even take a bath in them. So we could save money. Wait—correction there. To say "save" gives the wrong impression. We'd spend less. Does that answer your question?"

"Jesus, Buddy. It was an innocent enough question. You sure as hell haven't lost your temper and stubbornness, have you? You're as scrappy as ever. We're not on the streets anymore."

"Maybe your question wasn't so innocent. Did you ever think of that?" Buddy started back towards the house, his feet swishing through the grass, and Ray followed behind him. A smudge of sun stained the sky, the yard now mostly engulfed in night's shade.

Meg must have been watching from the kitchen window. As she came outside to say one last goodbye she shouted back into the house, "Kids!" and Carolyn and Donnie came out too.

Buddy and Ray stood with their hands clasped and something passed between them. An understanding of how much time had passed, too much time, and of being too familiar with each other once and yet not knowing each other at all. A shake that took in their differences and a longing to bring something back, something lost and irretrievable, something they could never reclaim—a complete parting. And in their grip, in their hesitancy to release, in the firmness of it, sorrow and understanding of long-established differences. And a recognition of secrets they would never share.

"I'll be in touch," Ray said and Buddy knew the tone well enough to know what he meant. Ray invited them to come to California and to plan on staying with him. "There's endless sunshine." Buddy said he'd think about it. Meg said she'd love to and the kids said, "Yeah! That'd be great!"

They waved at him as he backed out and onto the road, gave the horn a couple of toots, and stuck his arm up high into the air to wave. They watched until the car lights disappeared, then the kids dashed back inside the house.

"We won't be seeing anything so exotic as California license plates around here again for a while," Meg said.

On their way down the sidewalk Buddy told Meg about the tomatoes. She threw her hands up, "Oh for God's sakes. Can anything else go wrong?"

Buddy didn't say anything. She knew what the blight meant; they'd had it before, but never on such a scale and never this fast.

Buddy headed across the yard to the garden shed. He'd have a drink and head out into the tomato patch with a flashlight to salvage what he could. This would be a long night. Ray's visit would pick away at him. He'd go over and over it and he wouldn't be able to leave it alone.

Part way down the sidewalk, almost to the house, Meg called out to him across the darkness of their yard, "Your brother's made a good life for himself."

Chapter 28

The Dinner War

Snowflakes spun, random and frantic. He felt for the mickey under the car seat, pulled it out, and took a pull. One more before Doug arrived then he'd behave himself.

It was 11:30, the bus now a half hour late. He counted four other cars in the parking lot. He banged his numb feet together, turned the car on again, ran the heat full blast, switched the vents to target his feet, and took another swig of rye for warmth. He lit a cigarette, rolled the window down a crack to let smoke curl out the window, and listened to the wind's howl. Any day now he'd quit smoking—Dr. Grant was becoming more insistent. "You're throwing away your health. Your lungs have taken a terrible beating. And what about the drinking?"

It might have been foolish to come early, but back at the house Meg was going at the housework as if Pierre Elliot Trudeau was bringing Queen Elizabeth round for a visit. All day she'd waged war against dirt, heaving around the vacuum cleaner, scrub mop, and scrub pail. Going at it with her usual intensity ever since she learned Doug was bringing home a girlfriend. David and Rhonda were coming from Toronto with baby Jenny on Saturday, and Donnie had Sunday off work. Carolyn kept most of her evening free, otherwise she would have been out all day with Lenny. The whole family would be together for Sunday dinner, something that hadn't happened for a while. Maybe a year.

Buddy spotted the bus up the street, its headlights catching the falling snow. This was going to be a full-fledged storm.

He stepped outside, leaning against the car as he watched passengers emerge and step down to the parking lot, arms encircling their middles and shoulders bunched as they met the sting of weather.

Doug waited for the driver to pull their luggage from the compartment under the bus, his hands shoved deep into the pockets of a short coat with fringe like an old-time movie cowboy. He hadn't had a haircut since Buddy last saw him; it hung all the way to his shoulders. A young woman with long straight hair parted down the middle stood close behind him. She wore a cape affair, though it might even be a blanket, and her skirt ended just above the top of what appeared to be heavy boots—the kind construction workers wore.

Buddy returned Doug's wave and went to help with their baggage.

Linda gave him a full, even-toothed smile after Doug's introduction.

"Oh man, that was some bus ride." Doug threw their knapsacks into the trunk and slammed the lid. "It's a long ride from Winnipeg to here."

"Hop in the front, Linda," Buddy said. "No point being lonely in the back. It's warmer up here."Linda sandwiched herself between him and Doug, and they pulled out onto the street. The wipers attacked the snowflakes and left a smear across the windshield.

"Weather's bad," Doug said. "The snow ploughs and sanders haven't been out on the 401 yet. We made good time until the last leg."

The car fish-tailed and the bottle clattered underneath Buddy's seat.

"You got something under there, Dad?" Doug asked.

"Just a little something. In case of an emergency."

"I've never known you not to have an emergency."

After they passed the city limits Doug asked Buddy for a snort of the emergency stash. "It was a long bus trip."

Buddy reached under the seat for the bottle and handed it to Doug who took a swig then offered it to Linda. She drank and handed the bottle back to Doug. "It's good to see you Doug," Buddy said. "You holding up okay at school?" Doug already had one degree, and now he was studying for another one. Buddy didn't know what all it amounted to.

"Pretty well."

"I see you're not squandering your money on a haircut."

At the house they sat with the headlights shining out across the yard, illuminating bare limbs rocking in the wind surrounded by the blustery night.

"Is this where you live?" Linda asked.

"It's where the bills with my name on them keep getting sent," Buddy said.

She leaned against Doug to get a better view of Buddy and smiled. "It's big, man. I try to avoid having an address," she said. "It ties you down, too much commitment, too much serious shit, man. But this—this is an address."

"Oh." He hoped she kept her notion of no address from Meg, who listened with disdain to stories of students protesting the Vietnam War and the draft. She had strong opinions about long-haired hippies. Buddy told her he wouldn't want his boys going off to war to get killed and Meg said he knew very well that wasn't at all what she meant. "I don't like freeloaders," she said.

"It's a big yard. Lots of trees," Linda said. "I like trees."

"Beyond the hedge there's a garden." Whatever scent Linda wore made him think of freshly tilled soil. Not an unpleasant smell—not sweet like perfume, either. "You'll taste what I grow tomorrow at dinner. Squash, brussel sprouts, beans, corn, tomatoes. We can and freeze everything. If we gave up meat, we could live entirely off the garden."

"Meat's disgusting," Linda said. Her mouth barely moved when she spoke as if she couldn't chew meat even if she wanted to.

"Do you mind if I ask you something?" No one seemed to be making a move to get out of the car, caught up watching the storm move in ghostlike veils across the yard. "What kind of perfume are you wearing?"

"Geez, Dad," Doug said. "That's personal."

"It's not perfume. It's musk oil." Linda told Doug to stay cool. "I don't mind him asking."

They shuffled along the sidewalk to the house, heads down against the storm. "I hope your mother's finished her cleaning," Buddy said, about to push open the back door. "She probably has. It's after midnight."

"That's too bad if she went to that trouble on my account," Linda said. "I'm against housecleaning. I don't see it as my work. It's demeaning work for women."

"She does this for company," Buddy explained. "She likes to make a good impression. There's no stopping her." He hoped Linda wasn't against being clean, too.

"Too bad. It's kind of lost on me," Linda said. "I'm not domestic. Not in the least."

While Buddy held the door open, Doug asked, "Does Mom know we're living together?"

"I don't think so."

"I told David. I hope he didn't spill the beans."

Buddy wouldn't tell Doug that Meg had her suspicions but Doug should have known not to tell David. He knew better than anyone David had a time keeping his trap shut. Last Sunday night, while Buddy lay on the couch watching Pa settle something between Little Joe and Hoss on the Ponderosa ranch, he caught snippets of Meg's telephone conversation. Apparently, as she was explaining to David, the whole generation had no morals. How could she say that? Didn't she remember their trips to Sam Churley's barn after the dances? The stuff they got up to in the hay?

Linda lifted her long skirt and Buddy held the door open for her. Her work boots, scuffed down to the steel toes, were unlaced. Quite the package when he stopped to consider it—the work boots, the long skirt, the cape or blanket or whatever it was, that musky oil, the flowing hair, the gum she worked over, and the strong opinions. She seemed nice enough, and kids these days did manage to get themselves decked out in the strangest getups. But what harm could fashion do? She definitely seemed laid back, as they said, or that other term—mellow, like a colour—but there was no telling how Meg would respond.

At the head of the table Buddy took in the sight of his family, plus Linda. They're all adults, he thought, as if it had happened overnight. But when had it happened? He'd been watching, eyes wide open, yet still not seeing.

It made him teary, melancholy, a direction he was already headed before dinner as he sat in his green chair having a couple of predinner bumps. He considered the space around his feet once occupied by Lady, long departed, listening to footsteps overhead as he often liked to do. He found it comforting.

The light pit-a-pat of his little granddaughter's feet as her parents helped her down the hall—David's slow steps—heavier now with age—then Rhonda's, his daughter-in-law, Linda's thick-socked passage, Doug's urgent gait, and Meg's slower, more determined footsteps. Donnie not yet here, finishing off his shift by now. The musical floor played over his head, the description of his family aching in the wood.

He wanted to reach out and hold them all at once, this family of his. Gather up this unlikely lot and squeeze them hard and ask time to stop, please, just for a minute. Give him a chance to embrace who they were right now, this instant, and give him a chance to catch his breath. David, then Rhonda with baby, Jenny, out of her high chair sitting on Rhonda's lap, tugging on her beads, and babbling. Serious David, a dad—hard to imagine—about to start a new job with the provincial government. Getting ready to move north and farther away from Buddy and Meg—a family man, and tired, too, as most dads are. His hair thinning, on his way to becoming bald just like the old man's. His beautiful daughter had David's eyes. A little preoccupied, maybe even worried about the big move and leaving this part of Ontario. Rhonda, a member of the family for three years now, was the quiet type; a good thing too, since everyone else seemed to feel the need to talk all the time. A sewer and a knitter, she hit it off with Meg from the start, but Buddy could see she held back and stayed aloof.

Doug and Linda. They knocked about all weekend without any unpleasant incidents, though several times he caught Meg staring at Linda, sizing her up. Distracted perhaps by the holes in Linda's mismatched socks and the long skirt with the ragged salt lines along the hem. Buddy liked Linda, plain and simple. Sure, he knew it had something to do with his *In the West* stories which she listened to with full attention, smiling and saying "cool" at the end of every one. "How about another?"

They spent last night in the basement passing rye whiskey and a joint back and forth. He could not resist touching her hair, shining under the bare light. He had wanted to kiss her, came so close, and caught himself. It was the hair, shimmering and fragrant that gave him the urge. He took her from one story to another, which might have got him started on the whole where-had-time-gone kick and put an ache in his heart.

And Kitten—oops, Carolyn, as she wanted to be called. She'd always be his little Kitten, though he'd make this concession towards letting her grow up. Almost done her college courses and would graduate soon. So beautiful, though she didn't need all that stuff around her eyes. She was blessed with Meg's hair; long, blondish red—blonder than Meg's once was (some of the colour might have come out of a box, he didn't know, didn't ask), flowing and curled up at the ends. His little girl, she turned heads that's for sure, caught Lenny's eye. Unfortunate as far as Meg was concerned. The five years difference in age still the topic of many a row, though Meg was becoming less vocal, as if she might be throwing in the towel. Or maybe she was just too tired to argue anymore. Buddy didn't know enough about Lenny to dislike him. Carolyn had to make her own choices, and anyway, what about the five years between him and Meg? Had it made much difference? He was too weary to worry about it. He put most of his concentration on taking his next breath or his next step.

"Quit smoking Buddy," Doctor Grant said. Same message year after year and him too weak to do anything about it. "It's killing you. That's why you can't breathe. You've got emphysema. That's why you feel tired. Quit smoking, then we'll tackle the other issues." Was that the reason for his tiredness, or was it just living? This last visit, Doctor Grant didn't sound as impatient with Buddy as he had before; he sounded resigned. Had he given up on him or was he tired too?

The hint of a moustache outlined Donnie's lip; his scar shone under the light always there as a reminder. Timid and shy by nature, he had grown up in the shadows of his older brothers. They judged, as older brothers do, sometimes harshly, turning him inward to the safe territory of his own thoughts. The tenderness he felt towards his youngest son came from the same tender spot held by his brother Sammy, a place so soft it ached. Donnie had the same kind of sweet, vulnerable character. He had his own life, an apartment, and a job; girlfriends that came and went. He had to fight his own battles. He'd be fine. Before dinner Buddy slipped him fifty dollars to put into his going-out-west fund. Both he and Carolyn had plans to go west. Doug was already most of the way there, living in Winnipeg, and David was moving in that direction too.

Meg asked him if it was any wonder after all the *In the*

West stories he'd brought them up on. She accused him of planting the notion in their heads ever since they were old enough to listen. If all their family went west and left them behind in Ontario, she said it would be Buddy's fault.

Meg, at the far end of the table wearing a dress she just finished making and a hint of makeup. Still pretty after all this time, her hair thick and wavy and fully grey. Plain to see she'd gone to some trouble for tonight's meal. She fidgeted in her chair, her eyes moving about the table loaded with food—most of it from the garden—to see if she'd forgotten anything. Taking stock and striving for perfection with this as with everything, her eyes finally resting on Patrick.

How long had he lived with them? Eight years? No. It must be longer. Ten? Patrick's state of confusion constant these days, his glasses swimming, and his pupils like jelly behind thick lenses. At his last check-up, Dr. Grant said he'd probably had a stroke. Sometimes Patrick stopped at the couch where Buddy stretched out for a snooze and asked, "When did you get here?"

"Not so much when, Patrick, but how?" And Patrick nodded like he knew what he meant and shuffled over to his swivel rocker to watch TV, his dialogue with the tube voices trimmed mostly to, "Bunch of damn idiots." Right now, Patrick seemed perplexed by his spoon and confused by all the people at the table. Meg noticed, too.

"It's okay, Dad," she patted his hand. "It's only the kids." Meg served a small amount of turnips onto her father's plate and passed the bowl to Linda. "Where are you from Linda? Originally?"

"Winnipeg," Linda said. "I haven't strayed too far from home."

"It's very cold there, isn't it?"

"Yes, but I'm used to it."

"I'd never get used to it," Meg said. "I dislike the wind."

"We had a lot of wind in the west." Buddy helped himself to the green beans and passed the bowl to David. "I know all about cold weather. It's true, you do get used to it."

"For once, can we not have the wild west stories?" Meg said. "Let's talk about something else."

"I heard some last night," Linda said, smiling broadly and with a glint in her eyes. "They're cool. I wouldn't mind hearing more."

"Do you have family in Winnipeg?" Meg blocked the drift in

the conversation.

"My parents and two sisters live there."

"Your parents work there, do they?"

"Not my mother. She stays at home. She's a homemaker. But my dad does. My sisters are in high school." Linda passed the platter of roast beef along without taking any.

Buddy fidgeted and cleared his throat, tried to think of a new topic. He had a pretty good notion where this might be headed, and he wished Meg would steer clear of it.

"What's your father's line of work?"

Jesus, why didn't she just come out and ask how much money he made?

"The automobile industry."

"Really?" Buddy said, his eyes watering and blurring Linda's image as the heat of horseradish surged up his nostrils and burst into flames in his frontal lobe.

"Let's not get started on your experience in the automobile industry," Meg said preemptively. "I didn't know there was an automobile industry in Winnipeg," she said to Linda.

"My dad's a part owner of a gas station." Linda set her fork across her plate and faced Meg as if she might be preparing for the next question. "He's going to buy it someday," she added. "Once he's saved enough money."

Meg appeared distressed. Buddy hoped Linda hadn't noticed.

"When he does, my mom will work there, too. She'll do the books. Depending on how good her English is by then. She's studying. My sisters and I try to help her, but she's not the best student."

"What language does she speak?"

"Ukrainian. She was pregnant with me when they came to Canada. I've got two younger sisters, so she was shut in all the time raising kids and never got out much to pick up English. Not very well, anyway, but she's getting better. Sort of. The trouble is, she spends most of her time with other Ukrainian women so that's the language they speak. She's shy, too. Not like me. So that doesn't help. Oh well." Linda heaved her shoulders and nibbled on the end of a green bean. "Mom and her friends make good perogies. Maybe you'll get to try them some time."

A tightness came over Meg's face. "I've got something on the stove. Buddy, I need your help in the kitchen for a minute."

She motioned him to the far end of the kitchen away from the dining room door. "Of all the Canadian girls there are, why couldn't Doug pick one of them instead of someone whose parents are from another country?"

"I'm from another country."

"Don't be contrary; you know what I'm talking about. You speak English. They don't speak English, at least her mother doesn't. I've got nothing against people who speak other languages, but it's not the choice I would make for my son. Can't I be honest about my feelings in my own home?"

"No. Not if it hurts her feelings." End of debate. Buddy went back into the dining room and took his seat at the head of the table again, preparing to defend Linda and her feelings and her eccentric outfit, if need be.

Patrick finished eating while the rest of them were only halfway through their plates. He'd acquired the appetite of a bird. He struggled to his feet and tottered towards the kitchen.

"Where are you going, Dad?" Meg asked.

"My chair," he said, taking tiny shuffles across the dining room.

"It's the other way, Dad."

"What other way? What are you talking about?"

Meg went to Patrick and placed her hands on his shoulders to steer him towards the living room door. "This is the right way, Dad."

"Things get so turned around," he said.

Meg sat down again and asked Carolyn why she was all dolled up.

"I'm going out."

"Who with?"

"Who'd you think? Lenny!"

"Can't you find a nice boy your own age to date?"

"There aren't any," Carolyn said, tipping her head back, her long hair sliding back from her face. She smiled at the ceiling and seemed to enjoy the flippancy of her answer.

"In all of your college there are no nice boys? I find that hard to believe." Meg could keep on all she wanted but she wasn't going to pick Carolyn's boyfriend for her. "Well, I wonder what he's up to. You can't tell me he's not up to something; it's obvious from his hair, all the way down to his shoulders. That's a good indication of when people are on drugs." Meg cut into her slice of roast beef.

Carolyn set her fork down as if preparing for battle and gave Meg a stare—a can opener about to cut a hole right out of her mother. "So, because his hair is long you think he's into drugs? That's a proven social theory, is it?"

Buddy wondered just how long Doug, with his shoulder-length hair, would stay out of the debate. Donnie too, for that matter, since his hair hung below his ears. David was the only one with a sensible haircut. Proven social theory? Since when had Carolyn started talking like that? Is this what she was learning at the college?

"Yes, I do think drugs are involved, as a matter of fact. It speaks of the person's overall attitude, which is that they just don't care."

"You can't judge a person by their hair," Carolyn said.

"Oh yes I can."

"Well then you'd be wrong in your judgment. And anyway, Lenny grew his hair as a way of protesting the Vietnam War."

"Right on," Doug said. "Me too. One thing I'd like to point out, Wilfrid Laurier had long hair. So apparently, according to your deductions, Mom, he was on drugs, too."

"Don't twist things around," Meg said.

Buddy had no idea why a man would want to wear their hair like a woman's. What if he wanted to find a job? No one would hire him.

"You need a haircut," Buddy said. "You too, Donnie."

"What does it matter to you guys if my hair is long; I don't live here anymore. I can grow my hair whatever length I want. Down to my ass, if I like," Doug said.

Linda shifted in her seat and gave Doug a blank stare, making it impossible to tell who she might side with though it was easy to assume.

"No one at my office can wear their hair long or they'll be fired," Rhonda said, absorbed with the baby until now.

"Same with the government," David said. "They won't tolerate freaks."

"Watch who you're calling a freak. I'm growing my hair to make a political statement. Besides," Doug patted the ends of his locks in a mock feminine gesture, "I think it's becoming."

"Sure, for a girl," David said, and Rhonda snickered and held a spoon of potato out for Jenny.

"Well, I support draft dodgers and there's no way the Americans should be in Vietnam. They're just a bunch of imperialists," Doug said.

"So," Buddy thought it was time to jump into the debate. "Now you're an authority on world politics. You can say these things, can you, because you've got a few years of university under your belt?" These kids who knew everything got to him. What about life experience? Didn't it count for something?

"I've got long hair, too," Donnie said. "And I think the war is fucked."

"That's enough of that kind of language." Meg glanced anxiously towards the living room fearing Patrick might have heard. "I've gone to a lot of trouble to make a nice meal and I won't have it ruined by disrespectful language."

"All I'm saying," Doug continued, "is your country is going to get the whole world blown up if they're not careful." Doug scooped another helping of potatoes onto his plate and handed the bowl to Linda, which she placed in front of Meg. "If people see my long hair and think I'm anti-war, anti-Vietnam, then fine with me. I'm making a statement in a quiet, but visual way. The Americans have a lot of nerve."

"What the hell are you talking about?" Buddy took his statement personally. Why wouldn't he? After all, what other American sat at this table?

"Most people in this country are against the war in Vietnam. The Americans are paranoid of a communist threat," Doug said. "It's all a fantasy."

Buddy put his fork down and leaned forward both elbows on the table. "Is that so, Mr. Know-It-All? Then what about the Cuban Missile Crisis? Were we paranoid when the Russians had their missiles pointed this way, or was that a figment of our imagination, too? More paranoid thinking?"

"That was different," Donnie said.

Buddy glared down the table. So, two political authorities was it? Neither Doug nor Donnie had enough experience in life to talk reasonably about such things as war. Wait until they lived like Buddy had to, wait until they'd been homeless, seen a depression, scrounged for their meals, and begged for a place to sleep. What did the two of them know about hardship the way they'd been mollycoddled? Once they had some experience then they could shoot off their mouths. Buddy was about to tell them so but the light caught the scar on Donnie's forehead, the little tunnel the bullet had chiselled, the reminder of what-might-have been.

"How was it different?" He forced his voice somewhere into the range of normal.

"Well for one thing, it was a different government. Two different governments." Donnie didn't sound convincing.

"The Americans think there's a goddamn pinko commie behind every bush." Doug jumped in to rescue his younger brother. "Who wants to live in a country where they shoot their students?"

"I told you to watch your language at the dinner table," Meg said, glancing at the baby.

Linda's eyes shifted from one to another as she followed the argument, a fleck of squash stuck to her lower lip.

"I mean, what the hell. The Americans turned their guns on their own. What about Kent State? What kind of a country turns on its students?" Doug asked.

"Keep your voices down," Meg said. "I'll not have shouting at the table."

"Oh," Buddy said. "So, I'm to blame for that too, am I?"

"Well the American military did it. You're an American. You seem to think they're justified being in Vietnam so, what the hell, how should I know? Maybe you think it was okay for them to shoot the students," Doug said.

"Everyone just shut up," Carolyn said. "Geez, stop yelling."

"So let me guess, Dad. You think that draft dodgers are a bunch of weak-kneed sissies, am I right?" Doug sneered.

"There's something wrong with people who run away from their problems. That's no way to solve anything, by running away and smoking dope."

"Oh, you'd be one to talk. You're an American living in Canada. You ran away. And just exactly what are you doing down there in the basement, you and your Crown Royal, if not running away?" Doug said.

Buddy brought his fist down hard enough to make the dishes and cutlery chatter and rippled the water in the glasses. How dare he! "I had everything taken from me, everything! I never ran away from anything! I never ran away from war! I couldn't go because I was too old and had health problems. Otherwise I would have gone, you bet I would, to stop that maniac Hitler and then the Japs. You don't think they weren't a threat to our country, this one too?" Buddy stabbed the table with his finger his eyes leaping back and forth between Doug and Donnie. "You don't know the half of it. Wait until you've seen what I've seen, what until you've lived the way I had to live. Wait until you don't know where you're going to rest your head, or where your next meal's coming from, or who you can or can not trust! That'll never happen to you because you're spoiled, you've barely had to do a day's work in your precious lives... "

Something came at him through the air and instinctively Buddy's hands reached out to catch it. He stared into the bowl of potatoes Meg had launched like a missile from the other end of the table.

Meg pushed away from the table, her hands on her hips, fighting back tears.

"So, this is the thanks I get for making a lovely meal. All any of you can think to do is sit and scream at each other." Meg turned to address Linda. "Think twice before you get involved with this family." She went around to the high chair and plucked up the baby. "I'm taking my granddaughter. All this bickering is not a suitable environment for a baby." With Jenny in her arms, she stomped off down the hall and shut the bedroom door.

The rest of them sat without eating or speaking. Buddy picked lumps of potatoes off the tablecloth and lined them up along the rim of his plate. "Well, we might as well continue, eating I mean. Meg's right. Enough of the fighting." His chest actually hurt; the flying bowl of potatoes gave him quite a start. Doug sure knew what buttons to press. How could his own flesh and blood turn against him in this way?

"Well, this is a lovely fuckin' meal, anyway," Linda said with a loud sigh.

They ate silently through the rest of the main course, then Buddy offered the pie Meg had made for dessert. No one wanted it.

Carolyn had to split, Lenny would soon be here, and she got up to clear the table. Rhonda and David said they had to start the two-hour drive back to Toronto; they hoped the baby would sleep all the way back. They gathered up all their things from their room, went to Meg's room to collect the baby and to say goodbye, then stopped at the table on the way out.

Donnie said he had to go. "I've got to get up at six for work." He made his goodbye rounds, followed Rhonda and David, and helped them out with their baby paraphernalia.

Doug, Linda, and Buddy sat alone at the table. Linda cleared away the remaining dishes and came back to sit at the empty table sliding her hands over the white linen tablecloth and picking off stray peas and bread crumbs.

"You've been deserted, Dad," Doug said. "And we're going to abandon you, too." Doug patted his stomach. "How about a little walk?" he asked Linda. "After a meal like that, I could use some exercise."

More like a little weed, Buddy thought. It wafted from the corners of the house ever since they'd arrived. They excused themselves from the table and stopped once again with their coats on, on the way out the door. "You just going to sit there?" The fringe on Doug's sleeves swayed like wheat in the wind. "Alone?"

"For a while. I'm thinking about what went on here."

"Families play a lot of fuckin' head games," Linda said. She wanted Buddy to feel better. He wasn't sure it helped, but it was true. He scanned the table before him, the vast smoothness of the white tablecloth stretched out like Gettysburg or the Plains of Abraham. The blotches of spilled gravy, stains to forever remind them of the battle that took place here tonight.

At his very own dinner table, he was the enemy. Why should he take the heat for the United States? Yes, he was an American. Should that make him ashamed? Above all, he was a person, same as them. He should have gone after them for being Canadian. Canadians had some damn irritating habits; hating Americans was one of them.

And here he was, alone at the table with its naked geography. This was home, the one he had been working towards ever since he left Wyoming. And his whole family had abandoned him.

He scraped mashed potato off his shirt button with his fingernail.

Later downstairs, he pulled his footstool up to his chair and covered himself in a sleeping bag used by every one of his kids over the years, the fabric gummy from their bodies. He drew in their scent and wondered how he deserved any of them.

Book Seven

Under the Tree — June 1973

A sharp stabbing pain brought Buddy back from somewhere. Spirit had bitten his arm. With effort he raised his hand, heavy and swollen, and placed it on the horse's mouth. Spirit did not back away and kept his head low over Buddy's chest.

"What the hell are you doing? Do you want me to get up and walk? You crazy old bugger. Can't you see I'm trying my best?" The horse's snout felt soft.

Beyond the horse's head and beyond the treetops, the sky appeared to be lightening. Could this be first light? Had he passed the night under the tree? It might have been more than one night. If this was first light, the birds would be singing. Could be he was seeing things.

So still all around him, not the whiff of a breeze. The silence and stillness in the storm's wake, disturbed only by Spirit's huffing and shifting.

"Ouch!" The horse bit his stomach. What was he doing biting him like that? He'd been talking out loud, telling Spirit his stories, as if the animal understood what he was saying—at least he thought he had. If his coarse, broken mumbling sounded like talking. He couldn't imagine it did. More like sleep talking or drunken talk—he'd done enough of that to know. Telling the horse the whole disgraceful mess about the dinner war, the tomatoes, the *Ugly Duckling* play. A litany of humiliation brought on by his weakness.

So many stupid things, he'd done. Did everyone have such regrets? The night at the table —his family reunion—he should have kept his mouth shut. Let them carry on about politics and hair. What did it matter? Hair was only hair. (Maybe he was jealous because he'd lost most of his.) He should have sat back and listened to their opinions, learned something about them. Instead of being offended.

Spirit bit him again. He caught himself fading to where time was meaningless and images collided like the view inside a kaleidoscope. A jumble of stories. He could barely keep his eyes open, and the deep and penetrating pain in his chest made the slightest breath difficult.

"Okay, okay, I'll try not to sleep. Can't you see I'm struggling?" It wasn't sleep he was struggling with—it was unconsciousness. He'd been slipping in and out of it for a while now. He felt certain. Spirit wanted the sound of his voice for reassurance and to soothe him. If he didn't stay awake, if he slipped away to the other world, the horse would only bite him again.

"You are one smart horse," he whispered, his voice barely audible. He looked up at the blurred outline of the horse hovering over him.

Spirit lowered his head and wriggled his lips over his face as if tickling him, his muzzle soft and warm against his skin. It felt good to feel something alive. To feel warmth. Buddy smiled. "You giving me a kiss? An ugly old fellow like me? You're glad I busted you out of your pen, aren't you? You're thanking me. If I make it out of here alive, Spirit, I promise you won't spend one more day tied up in that disgusting barn. I will get you out of there for good. You busted me out, too, you know."

But not completely—not yet. He had two more stories to tell. Two stories he'd never told anyone, stories he never repeated even in his thoughts. He had to tell them. If he didn't he would never be free.

Buddy looked into Spirit's face, the horse's amber eyes long and steady on him. "I will tell you the truth. I will tell you what I have never allowed myself to remember. What I've never spoken out loud."

There was shame, a terrible shame he'd kept from Ray all these years and he'd never bring himself to tell him. "What happened to me wasn't my fault. Do you hear?" Spirit's head swayed over his chest.

"Something happened when we left the hobo jungle and got on the train, took advantage of *The One Big Thing*—not sure if I told you that story or if I dreamt it, but just so you know, it was a kind of law for the meandering sort—hopping the trains, hitching a free ride. There was a whole set of rules involved with the hobo community you had to mind. They were...a tough bunch. Some of them, the scum of the earth. That is my first story. My other story goes back even further, to *The Terrible Storm* and the night Father died, the night I was sent to go looking for my brother who had gone to get the doctor."

Buddy lifted his hand as high as he could to rub the horse's snout.

Chapter 29

Inside a Boxcar — the American Mid-West—1924

An Untold Story

Buddy stiffened with fear of rustling the straw he lay in. A voice snarled for him to shut up, lie still, and quit his fidgeting. Ray lay close by in the darkness. The trainmen passed by outside, their voices low, keys rattling, their feet grinding over gravel. Inside the boxcar there was absolute stillness as everyone tensed and listened.

Dust tickled Buddy's nose and throat until he thought he could no longer hold back a sneeze. He tried to clear his throat. Someone hissed out of the blackness for him to shut the hell up. The air stuffy with the stench of sweat and piss and dirty clothes and chewing tobacco, the stink of too many bodies crammed into a small space. It turned his stomach and he thought he would throw up. He must steer his thoughts towards pleasantness, something Mother always told him to do when he was sad or sick. Think sweet thoughts. He gathered spit in his mouth and swallowed to take away dryness and to keep from choking. *Let calm reason prevail over a frightened mind.*

He moved his hand slowly across the blackness beside him until he touched Ray's hand. Ray wriggled his finger—I am here, his gesture seemed to say.

A tear ran down the side of his face from the strain of keeping back a cough. Around him the breathing of many men barely loud enough to hear.

The trainmen were stepping closer.

Buddy raised his hand in front of his face but could not see it. This place felt like a coffin and he'd been buried alive in it. His chest heaved with shallow breaths of panic. The pounding of his heart filled his ears. His thoughts must go to pleasant places, must be chased from here: a stifling, hideous place. He'd erase it from his mind as soon as this trip was over.

Squire and Duke never warned them about being inside the boxcar and how it would feel. They never said it was like being locked up deep in the earth and would make him feel as if he'd suffocate. They'd warned them about steering clear of the sewer rats, but how could he and Ray do that when they were everywhere, surrounding them?

He had to clear his throat or have a choking fit.

"I said to shut the hell up," someone whispered.

He told himself again, think pleasant thoughts. He closed his eyes and pictured his whole family gathered around the fire, Father telling stories, the fire drenching them with warmth, while outside the wind howled.

Buddy moved his legs slightly to stretch them and his feet touched something hard. Someone pushed his foot away. He would try to sleep.

Outside the boxcar he could hear the crunch of footsteps, doors sliding open, and the low tones of men talking, their voices coming closer and closer.

Someone snored.

"Shsh," a hoarse whisper. "Wake up whoever it is."

Silence resumed for a long time, and then the trainmen arrived outside their car.

"I checked this one at the last siding. Empty."

"We'll leave it go. We're almost done."

Their footsteps moved on. Duke and Squire said the trainmen could be persuaded to look the other way so long as their palms were adequately greased.

The footsteps continued down the line and until they faded completely. Buddy let out a deep breath and cleared his throat.

"Shut up dimwit!"

They lay silent for what seemed like forever. Fear and the discomfort of having to piss stretched seconds to hours. Something must have happened to the other train, the one that would pass before their train could leave the siding. It was taking longer than it had before when they sprawled in the ditch with Squire and Duke.

He didn't know how long he'd been sleeping but something woke him. He went to speak out loud but once he stared out into absolute blackness he remembered not to make a sound. Something had touched his inner thigh. He reached down but it had gone.

There it was again, on his leg, at his crotch. Rats skittered around in the barn and alarmed the horses—it could be a rat. He reached down, felt a hand, and pushed it away; his body rustled in the straw.

"Goddamn it, still I said!" The same voice that shushed him every time he so much as twitched. "You'll get us all busted. Thrown in jail."

The hand clamped harder on his crotch curved around his penis through the fabric of his pants. He shifted again to escape.

"Shut up, I said. One more move and you're out of here! And you can take the other little shit with you!"

Duke managed to get them spots on the train on account of his position in the hobo community, and he warned them they could get bounced off just as easily. The boys in the boxcar, he said, could get testy. He said they should mind their manners.

Mind their manners? What kind of a stupid joke was that? Buddy's heart raced, the muscles in his chest pinched tighter, and his breathing hurt; he wanted to cry out. The hand trailed over him. He tried to push it away, careful to keep his movements soundless or be threatened by the repulsive hiss that came out of the blackness.

Buddy inched over to Ray to let him know there was something wrong. Ray poked him in the side and softer than a whisper said, "Don't." Buddy had an urge to scream at Ray. You stupid idiot, don't you know what's happening to me! But all he could do was lie still and try to push the hand away as it kept up its dreadful groping. Sweat matted his hair to his forehead and tears spilled down his cheeks—he didn't want to cry, but he couldn't help it—snot dribbled down his upper lip; he couldn't sniff.

Duke and Squire put them inside a nightmare. They'd done it on purpose. He'd heard about men who wanted to touch other men and the idea of it repulsed him, made him want to puke, and here he was inside a cage with a monster pawing at him. The hand worked its way inside his pants and touched his skin. He tried to push it away but it squeezed harder.

Buddy lay as still as he could with the hand going over him, rubbing him. He covered his mouth to hold back his sobs and felt tears dribble over it. He concentrated as best he could not to get hard with the rubbing, but it was useless. Friction made him rigid and friction spent him. He sunk his teeth into his hand to prevent any sound, made certain the pain from his bite was extreme, all the time not uttering so much as a peep.

The hand slithered away into darkness.

Buddy used his sleeve to wipe away snot and tears, then lay tense, waiting for the hideous creature to crawl back.

Out of the trill of crickets and the odd owl's screech came the chug of a train, its long shrill whistle becoming louder. As the train screamed by, Buddy gasped for air, as if he'd been underwater, holding his breath and almost drowning. He sniffed and sobbed, his terror concealed by the racket of the approaching train. The boxcar shook, the two trains so close it seemed they would touch, until the passing train rumbled off into the night and sent out its last shrill whistles.

"Here we go," someone whispered.

The train creaked into motion, the grinding clank of metal as it moved from a standstill, gradually picking up speed until they travelled along at a good clip.

Buddy struggled to stay awake to wait for the thing that attacked him to come back but exhaustion overtook him and finally, long after they began the long rumble down the tracks, unable to fight his heavy eyelids or the train's sway, he curled into a tight ball and slept.

Buddy opened his eyes. A hand covered his mouth. Lips pressed into his ear and whispered, "Make so much as a sound, I'll stab you."

Something pressed into Buddy's side—hard edged, sharp, and pointed. He searched for Ray but saw not so much as a pinpoint of light.

"You haul them overalls down to your ankles. I want to touch your pretty little ass." The lips moved next to his ear. Sour breath filled his nostrils. Hands fidgeted with the fasteners on his overalls until they came loose and pulled his pants down. Then the hands went back over his mouth, crushing his lips into his teeth. "'member what I said, one peep and I'll slit your throat. They'll find you dead in the morning, bled out good like a stuffed pig."

Buddy wanted to scream and cry out; the blade pushed deeper into his side.

Hands yanked at his underpants, the loose underwear given to him by Cowboy Oliver, a man's clothing, slid down easily. "Shift to your stomach. Lie flat, legs apart."

Buddy didn't move. The knife pricked deep into his side and warm blood bubbled on his skin. "I'll slit your throat you little cocksucker." Buddy shifted to his stomach and moved his legs apart. The lips stayed at his ears as the body pressed down on top of him.

A terrible pain ripped through his centre. Over him the body rocked, moved with the sway of the train, the pain deeper and deeper until he felt he was being cut in two. Rocking, rocking, rocking—stabbing, searing pain, hard thrusts, a stake driven into his body, the train's screaming whistle, the screech of the rails, hot rancid breath on his ears, and then the weight shifted away. Buddy's body free of it, the hands over his mouth were the last to fall away. Stickiness between his buttocks dribbled down to his testicles.

Buddy pulled on his underpants and overalls and rolled up into a ball, hating the new soreness, his new shame, crying, and searching for his mother's soothing words. Why hadn't Ray protected him?

The rest of the long night he sat up, his knees pulled in close to his chest for protection.

Finally light ribboned in through slats and as it strengthened he made out the thirty or so men inside the boxcar. Some squatted in the straw, others slept, several stood along the wall holding on against the train's sway, talking and chewing tobacco. Spitting little clots off the tips of their tongues into the straw and stroking their stubbled chins. Buddy looked at each one trying to spot the rat that came after him in the night, but it could have been any one of this mangy lot. Some of the men sneered back at him, curled their lips, and threw their heads back, as if they all knew what happened—taunting him with their slitty eyes. He couldn't know who had done the awful things to him, but he knew they were all dangerous. They'd all done it to him. *Never let down your guard.*

By full daylight all the men were awake and pacing around the car. Men gathered around a hole in the floor to piss down over the flickering railroad ties. Buddy would wait until he was off the train, even though he had to piss a river since last night.

One of the men up against the boxcar wall struck a match, and lowering his face close to the flame lit a cigarette.

"Put that goddamn thing out," a tall man with a long nose and red weathered skin snarled. Buddy recognized the voice from the night, the one that told everyone to shut up. "You chew inside you stupid son-of-a-bitch, you don't smoke. Didn't you hear what happened to the bunch down Massoura way? 'Bout forty fried up crisp as bacon. Cuzza some damn fool idiot. Not here, it ain't happening. Try it again, I'll throw you out myself, and I don't give a good goddamn if the train's movin'. The faster the better. I can not abide stupidity."

The fellow butted his smoke on the bottom of his shoe and slipped the butt into his pocket. He sneered at the skinny man. For a few seconds their eyes locked.

It had to be one hundred degrees inside the car. Last night it was a black pit, a closed coffin, and now it was an oven.

Ray slid over closer to Buddy. "Duke said we take this down four stops and then we wait for another one, headed north. It's got to stop soon. We've been going a long time. At this rate we'll run out of country."

"We're getting off first stop."

"What the hell you talking about?"

"I heard Duke, and now you hear me. I'm getting off next stop and you can go on if you want." Buddy lowered his voice, head down to the floor so no one would hear him. "These are a bunch of thugs. It's not safe here."

"You boys got something to share with us?" A man with a pinched face, eyes encircled with dark rings, spoke from the corner, a growth of thick stubble greying his face. "You making a little conspiracy, are you? Figuring on robbing us?"

"No." The tremors in Ray's voice didn't make him sound convincing.

"I'd hate to tell you what happened to the last fella who tried that. 'Bout your age, too. Poor slob." He stepped over other men sprawled out on the floor. His long underwear, grey and frayed at the cuffs, came down over his boot top until he stood close enough they got a front row look at his stained teeth. Buddy leaned back away from him but dared not take a step and give the appearance of being frightened and guilty.

He circled them, stepping slowly, snorting, and sneering. They sat stock-still until he finished with his menacing strut and went back to where he'd been leaning up against the wall. They didn't move or speak again until the train stopped and they jumped off.

Buddy, in a scramble to get off the train as fast as he could, wasn't watching where he jumped and connected hard with a rock and tumbled down a ditch. A long deep gash ran down the side of his leg and blood dribbled into his boot. It hurt but nothing would ever hurt him as much as what happened on that train.

Buddy and Ray sat low in the ditch waiting for the train to pull away, the way Squire and Duke taught them. Up and down the train men hopped off like fleas jumping on a dog in midsummer and quickly disappeared into high grasses and the woods.

Chapter 30

March 1923 — The Terrible Storm

"Buddy." Mother approached from across the room, her hands pressing the small of her back, the new baby due any day. Her eyes, darkly circled, set even deeper after so many sleepless nights. She'd been with Father these last few days, cooling his fevered skin with snow packs and wet cloths. Her hair had come unfastened and tumbled over her right shoulder as if she'd just risen from bed.

"I need you to go to look for your brother, Buddy. He should be back with Doc by now. I sent him out in plenty of time before the storm hit. He should be..." her voice trailed as her eyes went to the window. "He's knows the route. I can't imagine what's happened."

Buddy and Sammy sat on the floor in front of the fire weaving little horses Father carved in and out of corrals of wooden blocks. Buddy tried to keep the children amused and quiet to let Father rest and recover. Buddy looked up at Mother, her face set with strain and worry.

"Take Misty. She'll bring you back here—she's reliable. Go now while there's time, before the storm hits full force. You can still track him, but in a while it'll be blustery. Mind you keep a watch on the sky and come back on time. Use your head. Don't get daydreaming and lose track."

Buddy threaded his arms through his coat, then went back to Sammy and touched his soft blond hair, the boy's face collapsing as he saw his older brother was about to go. "What about you and the others?"

"Everyone will pitch in with chores and helping with the little ones."

Sammy bashed up the corral, sent wooden blocks flying

with his tiny fists and cried out, "Bubby, Bubby!" He started across the room, arms outstretched, but Buddy had no time to soothe the child—not with the urgency of his task plain enough to see from the look on his mother's face.

"It's okay, Sammy. I'll be back soon." He scooped him up and handed him to Maudy. "Don't let go of him," he said over Sammy's screams.

Outside, with each step the snow squeaked and made him think he wasn't alone. Head down, he gathered his collar up to block the cold around his neck. A small drift had formed at the barn door which he kicked at with his boot and forced the door open. Inside the dim barn the air hung with the musty dankness of manure and hay and the horses huffed in their stalls. They sensed a storm coming long before it hit. Father would sing one of his little ditties in a low voice to settle them and ease their restlessness. *Show me the way to go home. I'm tired and I want to go to bed.* Same as he did for the children when they lay in bed, while outside the wind beat against the house.

He stopped at each stall and spoke to the horses, leaning in to touch and offer a reassuring hand, but the animals backed away. All but Misty. She allowed him to stroke her between the eyes where she loved to be touched. She knew they had to go out looking. She'd done it often enough. Brought Father home through many a blizzard that erased the world, made him blind, and he had no choice but to put all his trust in her to carry him to safety.

"Okay, Misty. We've got a job to do."

At the window the darkening sky pressed down sternly over the white fields, the storm still far away but slowly coming this way. He loved to tell stories about storms to the children and make them sound real, like creatures stalking prey. How they crawled across the plains ripping apart homes, shaking them into little splinters, and sending the people inside flying across the sky and far away. "You're a budding storyteller, but I've enough trouble settling them at bedtime as it is," Mother said.

He visited the stalls again, humming a low tune. He'd stay with the horses for a while—the storm still a ways off— before going out to find his brother. Streams of cold came in through the cracks in the barn walls and sliced the air. He blew into his mittens to warm his hands, crossed his arms, and slipped his hands under his armpits. He'd wait in the corner of the barn behind the pickling barrel where he'd heap straw around himself and try to stay warm. His favourite hiding place when he wanted to get out of doing chores.

He pushed the barrel lid aside and bent over to inhale the contents, his nose twinging with the sharp smell. Still young, his father would say, still pickling. It didn't matter. He picked up the fork which lay on top, it's tines bent, and chipped at the partly frozen cabbage saturated in the vinegar brine. He loved the taste at all stages. Right from when the fresh cabbage strips got dumped in to the later stages when the colour bleached out of the cabbage and it went white and limp and wound easily around the fork, puckered hard into the roof of his mouth.

He ate forkful after forkful. He couldn't make himself stop though he knew he should. He pressed his hand against his stomach. It hurt. He could almost hear Father say, "That's the price you pay for piggishness."

He sank into the hay behind the barrel to wait for his stomach to settle. He moaned and clutched his middle, belched the sour juice up into his mouth. He couldn't ride with such a painful gut. Every step of the horse would jostle it and make it worse. He winced with cramps. He'd have to make a dash to the outhouse but decided not to as he listened to the roar of wind. If his bowels loosened and he couldn't control them he'd squat at the back of a stall and cover his mess with hay.

The barn filled with cold. Behind the barrel he drew in straw until he was buried over his head, sank back, and let warmth soak through. He felt safe in his hiding spot, as safe as when Mother came to say goodnight and pulled the quilt up around his ears and kissed his forehead. *Sweet dreams.*

Wind prowled around the barn, fell silent, and raged again. It spoke to him—jeered at him. *You've left it too late, you stupid fool. Come out now, I dare you, and I will have my way with you. I will lock you in my grip, and slowly, while you struggle and squirm, I will bring you to an icy death.*

He shouldn't think such thoughts; he couldn't help it. He waited for signs the storm might twist in another direction but on it came, its force becoming more and more brutal. His stomach ached even worse and he struggled to keep the brine down. The horses stomped and whinnied, making short, heavy, anxious grunts. When he listened to them he didn't feel alone.

Buddy awakened and it was almost dark inside the barn. He heard someone moving about. That must have been what woke him—the muffle of hay, a voice speaking softly—he couldn't make out who it was. Could be Father, recovered enough after all Mother's care to come to the barn. He'd want to calm the horses the way he always did. Or Orwin. Yes, it would be Orwin! That made more sense. Father was too sick to get up from his bed.

The clatter of reins and a harness, hooves striking the barn floor. He didn't stir, not so much as a finger's twitch. He'd wait in his warm, secret corner safe behind the barrel, wait until Orwin—of that he was now certain—was well away from the barn then he'd go back to the house. What would he tell Mother?

A slight twinge was all that remained of his stomach ache, a reminder of his greed. The storm heaved against the barn and sent shivers through it. On such nights he expected it to be torn apart, thrown out over the prairies, and shattered to a million pieces. A bad one, Father would say, and Buddy would see worry in the narrowing of his eyes. This kind of storm wasted whatever came into its path and made no distinction between weak and strong—took it all.

He'd stay a while longer in his hiding spot before going back to the house. Once again he dozed off.

Buddy rose and went to the barn door, speaking softly to the horses as he passed. No use. They would not be calmed, not until this had blown over. He struggled with the door, pushing against a huge drift much larger than when he came in, and with effort, latched it closed. He threw himself head first into the snowdrift and tumbled around until he was white from head to toe—the way he would be if he'd been out riding—then he trudged to the house, head down against the blast.

Inside all was still. Everyone had gone to bed. He wouldn't have to tell them a story about his terrifying search for his brother out on the plains. No tales of a lame horse and a rescue by a witch.

A fire smouldered in the hearth. Quietly, he added wood he'd brought in earlier and watched embers leap into flames and crackle. He leaned back in Mother's rocking chair and fell to sleep.

Sometime in the night Mother jostled him awake and asked him if had any luck with his search. He shook his head. She put her hand over her mouth and gasped. She bowed her head, tears welling, then placed a hand on his head and rubbed it. "You tried your best, you surely did."

She'd never know he didn't go looking and how much of a coward he was.

By the next morning Father was gone. Died during the storm as if it came for him, to take him away. That's what Mother said. After Buddy saw the body, after he'd said good-bye, Mother told him to go and fetch Mr. Rankin. Special measures had to be taken on account of Father having typhoid.

"On your way to the Rankin's be on the lookout for your brother. We'll be lucky if one's all we lose." Mother's chin quivered but she'd done as much grieving as she'd allow herself to do. The children fussed and cried; the baby she carried was about to be born. She had little time to give over to sadness.

A morning cruel in its beauty, one of the most beautiful he'd ever seen. How could it be that it was also one of the saddest? Dazzling sunshine spilled over pure white snow, the bluest sky, not a whiff of a cloud, a new morning, a new day, not a mark on the snow, and inside he was filled with darkness. As if the storm had entered him.

He rode toward the Rankins' and halfway there he spotted something far off in the distance. He waited and watched as the figure came closer, then he rode over to meet it. He recognized the horse's gait—would recognize it anywhere.

Bishop approached carrying a rider, bent over, his face stuck into the mane. And then what he saw next was an image he would forever try to white out like a blizzard, but it kept coming back, washing over him, drowning him.

Ray on a lead horse, the reins of another grasped in his frozen mitten. Ray's face buried in the horse's mane, his hair entwined and frozen with that of the horse and clotted with snow. Buddy dismounted, touched Ray's leg, and jostled it. Ray slowly turned his face, his lips cracked and swollen, his cheeks a mixture of yellow-purple-red like some kind of strange pulp.

"I imagine I look a sight," he managed through cracked bloody lips. "Baby here?"

"Never mind that now." Buddy looked at the other horse. Breeze.

A body straddled the saddle, a boy's body, facing down into the sparkling snow. There could be no mistaking the broad shoulders, the squat build, and the solid shape of a boxer. He bent down to see the face and under the grotesque mask cast by the storm he saw Orwin.

Buddy turned away and heaved out strings of white worms, the acid burning his throat as his convulsions went on and on even after there was nothing left. When it was over he staggered over to Bishop, smacked his rump, and shouted, "Git" and the two horses rode off to home.

Chapter 31

Under the Tree — 1973

"Orwin, Spirit. It was Orwin and he was dead. Froze to death. Three deaths, not two. Orwin and Father buried together." Words he'd never uttered until now. Tears trickled down his face and the horse licked them away. He would like the taste of the salt. "My story was how Ray went to get the doctor and got lost, and I found him. But it was Orwin who was sent and somehow got lost, and Mother sent me out early to look for him. Early enough for me to find him, long before the storm hit. Ray had been helping her with Father, not Orwin. When I didn't come back, she sent Ray to look for the two of us. She must have been so desperate. There was no ugly witch who rescued me. Misty didn't go lame."

Spirit's head dropped and he brushed his lips over Buddy's face, then turned his immense head and Buddy looked straight into his endless amber eyes.

"I would have rescued him from the wild creature, if only I had the chance. I would have put myself between him and the rabid cat if it had been true." The scar on his leg didn't come from anything so brave as saving Orwin. It came from a rock—when he jumped off the train he landed hard and it tore into his leg and left a jagged gash. He was escaping the hideous thing that came out of the dark, did unspeakable things to him. Every time he told *The Wild Creature* story he saved Orwin again.

With all the strength he could summon, he raised his arm and touched the horse's nose. "You are a splendid creature." The pain of holding up his arm sharpened and he let it drop.

"I was afraid. I've always told myself it just happened, told myself carelessness had me fall to sleep. That is not true. I was afraid, plain and simple, too afraid to go looking for Orwin. When I woke up in the barn and heard someone, it was Ray going out to look for me. I somehow tricked myself into thinking it was Orwin, finally coming home. That was a story I could settle on."

Buddy closed his eyes and saw a young boy curled up in the corner of the barn covered in straw. Curled up the way he'd once been in a place where he felt buried alive, fearing what might come out of the darkness. Come after him. A frightened child. That was all he was. A child. He saw that now. All his life he'd blamed himself for Orwin's death. He always thought he deserved what happened to him in the boxcar, as if he'd invited it somehow. Like he was nothing more than a piece of trash.

If only he could reach across time and touch the small figure cowering in the dark, put a hand lightly on his shoulder, squeeze tenderly; and tell him, *It wasn't your fault.* You had every right to be afraid. You didn't cause Orwin to get lost. You didn't deserve what happened to you on the train. You were a child. No one watched over you. There was no one.

Not the hero, not the great adventurer—child.

When Ray came to visit from California and Carolyn bragged about her dad the hero, he didn't correct her but his eyes shifted to Buddy. That night in Buddy's garden, as he and Ray examined the ruined tomatoes, Ray said, "When I went to look for you, I saw Misty in the barn. I thought you took another horse. But Misty was never lame after that, so that seemed strange. And then, years later, I got to thinking." Buddy knew how to interpret his glare even after all this time. One way or another Ray blamed him, but he should know better. They were both children.

The horse's head bobbed at his chest, the reins dragging over him, then he lifted his head quickly and turned to look back into the bush.

The sun was coming out. Shafts of light, angel shafts Mother used to call them, angled down between the trees. A cardinal sang a mating song; a singular shrill call penetrating the morning air.

Buddy heard voices. Many voices. All talking at once. What if they didn't see him? He tried to shout the way he had before when he anticipated this moment, prayed for it, but he couldn't breathe deeply enough to make a sound. The ground echoed with footsteps pounding the earth.

He looked up at Spirit. The great, faithful horse was calm and unafraid.

"Down there! I can see the horse! I see him, I see my dad!" The sound of Carolyn's voice and then Meg's, "I knew something had happened. Is he alive?" The voices of angels.

"How did he get so far off the path?" Carolyn said, as their footsteps came nearer and he sensed them come into his presence.

He'd been found, saved. Now it was time to let go.

Acknowledgements

To the many people who have supported my writing over the years, friends and family, I give an appreciative and heartfelt thank you.

While telling the story of my father's childhood to Stan Dragland, he said that it sounded like a novel and the idea for the project was planted. David Sobelman taught me a great deal after reading an early draft, and his comments sent me in the right direction. Jocelyn Cullity read portions of the manuscript during its early unruly days and encouraged me to keep going. I am grateful for Melissa Hardy's "inflight" reading and napkin notes, and for pushing me and my manuscript just a bit further.

My editor Maeve Keating gave much appreciated guidance, and her enviable calm rescued me during a category 5 computer technology storm. A very special thanks to publisher D.A. Lockhart for seeing something in the story and for wanting to bring it into the world, and for his dedication and hard work as he brought the book to fruition.

Thanks to Bob Leggett and Barbara Bodnar for their kind and patient reading, and their enthusiasm. Thanks to Sue Hoffman for her "porch reading", and to Jean Ramer for her typo hunts. Thanks to Jim Leggett for his technical historical support. Special thanks to John Leggett for his careful reading and for his notes, helpful comments, and observations.

My son Bryce Jardine read an early version and was very supportive, and my daughter Courtney Burke has always rooted for me. My husband Rick Jardine joined my long musings at the end of his busy days without complaint, and always with interest and relentless encouragement as I navigated the ups and downs of the creative process: he is my reason for "going home".

This novel is inspired by my father, James Frederick Leggett (Fred) 1909 - 1976. He was orphaned at age 12, along with his eight other siblings, when his parents died two days apart. This novel, though fictionalized, had its genesis in the stories he told to my brothers and me when we could sit still and listen. He was a gifted storyteller, and I wish I'd paid more attention. He passed away when I was twenty-four—there are so many questions I've had for him since his voice fell silent, and so many tales I would love to hear again, no matter how often. Writing this book brought his voice back to me.

To the memory of my father, James Frederick Leggett (Fred).

About the Author

Catharine Leggett's short story collection *In Progress* was published in June, 2019 by Sowilo Press (Hidden River Arts) and won the Eludia Award given to women forty years or older who have not yet had a published book. Her stories have appeared in the anthologies *Beyond the Norm, The Reading Place, Slow the Pace, Lose Yourself, The Empty Nest, Law & Disorder, Best New Writing 2014*, as well as in the journals *Room, Event, The New Quarterly, Canadian Author*, and *The Antigonish Review*. Other stories have appeared online in *Wordrunner eChapbooks, paperbytes* (paperplates), *Per Contra*, and a novel excerpt in *Margin: Exploring Modern Magical Realism*, as well as on CBC Radio. She has lived in several cities throughout Canada and the United States, including Vancouver and Chicago, and now resides in her hometown of London, Ontario, Canada.

CPSIA information can be obtained
at www.ICGtesting.com
Printed in the USA
LVHW090754050220
645909LV00001BA/58

9 781988 214276